Here For Us
(Us #1)

By A.M. Arthur

Here For Us

First Print Edition

ISBN: 0-9899188-8-2

Cover art by Lyn Taylor
Interior Formatting by IndiGo Marketing & Design

Dear Reader,

Even though the act of writing is a solitary endeavor, the act of creation doesn't happen in a vacuum. It often happens in the wide world of social media, and an author never knows where s/he will find a flash of inspiration. A reader comment about a character may spark an idea that the author never expected—such a thing happened during the creation of this book. This was initially the story of two men: Jake and Cris. But their story stalled for over a year, until one lovely reader made a comment that blew me away. The unexpected outcome was a March-May-September ménage romance between three extremely different men.

I'm excited to share their story with you, and I hope you enjoy your time spent with these characters.

Special thanks to Annabeth Albert for your keen beta eye and for making this book even better. And also to Lyn Taylor for my gorgeous, spot-on cover.

Finally, many, many thank you's to my Facebook group, A.M.'s Pot O Gold, for their continued support, humor, enthusiasm, and kindness. This book is for you guys.

Chapter One

I need to fucking get laid.

The thought followed Cris Sable through the heavy industrial door that hid the throbbing interior of Big Dick's, the most popular gay nightclub in Harrisburg. The place was hard to find if you didn't know where it was, or if you didn't know the big muscle bear sitting by the entrance was a bouncer. Cris hadn't been to the club in over a year, mostly by choice, but tonight he needed something.

Definitely a drink, although he'd have to limit himself now that he was functioning with one kidney. And, if possible, he wanted to leave with a willing ass to fuck. It had been a long dry spell.

A dry spell of his own making, but still, a guy had needs, and he wasn't looking to get his needs met by a woman tonight. Tonight he needed dick.

He eased his way over to the bar and ordered a margarita on the rocks. Something he could work his way through slowly. The club was in full swing, bodies gyrating on the dance floor, men dry humping their way through the evening. Soon early morning. At the rear of the dance floor, six go-go dancers were on risers, each decked out in one color of the rainbow. Barely-there briefs in a solid color, sparkle body paint all over their chests and legs, and some dancers even had colorful streaks in their hair. Monday was theme night for the go-go dancers, which explained why there were so many. On the other nights of the week that Cris had visited, the club usually only had three dancers.

Cris zeroed in on the dancer in blue. He loved the color blue, and this kid was pretty fucking hot in a royal blue thong, with blue swirls across his pecs and shoulders. Something kind of tribal and arty. He spun around to shake his ass, showing off very taut blue-painted cheeks. Even from the distance, he was cute. The kind of cute Cris liked to wrangle around in bed and fuck through the mattress.

Occasionally, a hand would rise from the crowd with money in it, and the blue dancer squatted low enough for the money to be tucked away in their underwear. Very strip club-esque, but Big Dick's had a strict policy about not touching the dancers for longer than it took to tip them.

He scanned the other dancers' faces and froze solid at the guy at the end. Despite the yellow paint, Cris knew that nearly naked body intimately enough to see past the costume and recognize Colby. Not his real name, and Cris didn't know what it was, but they'd filmed together at Mean Green Boys roughly two years ago. Colby was only with the company for a few months before he quit to be with his boyfriend.

Cris had been intensely jealous at the time. At twenty-eight years old, he'd failed to find and maintain a serious relationship for longer than six months. And even that relationship had imploded when she found out he did gay porn. Okay, so he shouldn't have kept that a secret for so long. He'd been so damned happy to find someone who understood and accepted he was bisexual that he'd been scared to destroy it too soon by admitting to the porn.

But secrets never did a relationship any good, and Lily had dumped his ass hard.

He'd taken a two year hiatus from porn after that, hoping to try and rebuild his flailing love life, before returning to Mean Green. The studio owner, Chet Green, was one of his closest friends—hence the very secret reason for his single remaining kidney.

"Hello, gorgeous." A slinky number in leather pants and a silver mesh shirt slid up to Cris at the bar. Cute, kohl-lined eyes, plump lips that promised they knew how to suck a dick.

Cris grinned. "Who, me?"

"Oh, honey, we both know you're the sexiest thing in the club tonight." A warm arm draped over his shoulders. "Name's Luke."

"Cris."

"Hmm, I think you look more like a Vincent."

Cris tensed. No fucking way could this random guy know who he was. There was no hint of malice in his easy grin, no sign the name was anything other than a really good guess. Cris came from an Italian family from Long Island, and the genes were pretty strong. He'd rid himself of his identifying accent years ago, though, thank Christ.

"Or Vincenzo, or Anthony," the kid said, oblivious to Cris's racing thoughts.

"Well, it's Cris." Rude, fine, but he'd lost any interest in Luke. Cristian Sable was his identity now. "See you around."

Cris pushed away from the bar and eased his way into the crowd occupying the fringes of the dance floor. A few blatant offers came his way, but Cris turned them all down. He didn't realize he'd inched closer to the risers and his blue dancer until the guy was less than ten feet away.

Blue had a face that was both easygoing and sharp. He was enjoying himself without totally letting his guard down. And he was hella cute. Fuckable for sure.

Bodies danced frenetically all around him, allowing Cris to stay close to the wall and shift nearer to Blue. Someone held up a bill between two fingers. Blue wiggled his hips and squatted low so the money could be tucked into his g-string. The triangle of blue material held a very promising package for a smaller guy.

Blue blew a kiss to his patron, then spun in an ass-wiggling circle. His dark gaze roamed the crowd, then paused on Cris. An unexpected thrill shot through him. Some sort of instinctive acknowledgement of the man on the stage, as if they'd been waiting to meet. Blue held eye contact; Cris drew out a long, lazy smile. Blue cocked his head, winked, and then kept dancing. Cris stayed in his spot. Every few minutes, Blue glanced his way. Right into his eyes.

Target acquired.

The dancers came and went from the risers, likely taking breaks in between sets. When Blue winked again and disappeared, Cris had half a mind to try and find him. Except he didn't work at the club, and he had no real excuse to get backstage. Cris sipped his watered-down margarita and watched the eye candy on display. The gorgeous men, the throbbing music, and the heady scents of sweat and sex worked their magic on Cris, and he was half-hard by the time a brown-haired kid with a smear of blue under both eyes sidled up next to him.

Cris studied the familiar face, now scrubbed clean except for those two very appealing smudges. His hair maintained hints of blue glitter. He'd covered that amazing body with jeans and a white sleeveless tee, but this was Cris's dancer. Blue.

"You off the clock?" Cris asked.

"Yup." He grabbed Cris's glass and finished it off with a smirk that did funny things to Cris's balls. "Damn, I think I owe you a drink."

He laughed. "Cris."

"Jake." He snagged Cris's belt and tugged him toward the bar.

The forwardness was a huge fucking turn on, and Cris's cock was at full mast by the time they reached the bar. An older man in a sparkly vest smiled at them.

"Two margaritas on the rocks," Jake said. "My tab."

"On it," the bartender said.

Cris rested one hand on Jake's lower back, and he was surprised by the tiny thrill that vibrated up his arm. Jake pressed into his touch, eyelids fluttering as if he'd felt something similar. Cris leaned in to whisper in his ear, "Blue is my favorite color."

Jake looked up, big brown eyes glimmering with mischief. "Oh yeah?"

"Definitely. It looks good on you."

"Know what else would look good on me?"

Cris saw the flirty line coming, but he played along. "What's that?"

"You."

He nuzzled Jake's ear with his nose. "I agree."

The bartender slid their drinks over. Jake gulped his, while Cris only sipped. And studied his future sex partner. A good six inches shorter than him, and slimmer all over. Dance-honed muscles. Tight jeans that did nothing to hide his erection. A very One Direction boyish hotness about him that made Cris want to fuck him senseless.

"I'd ask if you want to dance," Jake said, "but you didn't bust a move all night."

"Not much of a dancer."

"No good?"

"I'm plenty good." Cris put a little leer into those words. "But I don't like using dancing as foreplay. I'd rather play in private."

Jake pressed his hard dick against Cris's thigh, amusement dancing in his eyes. His voice was crazy sexy in a way that Cris couldn't describe, but he liked it. "So I'm guessing you aren't a fan of the bathroom with the favors?"

Big Dick's had two bathrooms for its patrons, and rumor had it that the bathroom on the left had a bowl of condoms and lube sachets for patrons. Folks interested in a quick—and safe—fuck with a stranger. The bathroom on the right was for regular business.

"Nope." Cris slid his hand from Jake's lower back to grab his ass. "I prefer a nice big bed where I can have my way with someone for a few hours. Upright in a bathroom stall is over too fast."

Jake swallowed hard, his cheeks pinking up. "Sounds like an adventure."

"You up for it?"

"What do you think?" He ground his dick into Cris's thigh. "Think I'm up for it?"

"I might need more convincing."

Jake grabbed at Cris's erection and squeezed, the contact sending happy sparklers down Cris's spine. He really liked Jake touching him. "I'd suck you right here but Richard frowns on public displays of fellatio."

Cris didn't know who Richard was, and he didn't care. Owner or manager, probably. His only priority was getting Jake naked in his bed. He pushed his mostly full glass away. "Then let's get out of here before you get in trouble with your boss."

Jake gulped his margarita, then plunked his glass on the bar. "Lead the way."

He did.

The cool night air did nothing to ease his throbbing dick, nor did the long walk to his car. Jake kept close, their arms brushing, but otherwise not touching. The city was still alive and well all around them, and while Cris was big and imposing enough that few people ever bothered him, Jake walked with purpose. Aware of everyone they passed. He'd danced the exact same way: wary of the world.

Cris silently promised to help Jake forget those shadows that made him walk through life like it would turn against him at any moment. Even if only for a few hours.

The instant they were in his car and Cris had it aimed toward his apartment, Jake reached over and undid his fly. Stunned at the kid's brazenness, Cris didn't protest. He kept three-quarters of his attention on the road, while the rest watched—and felt—Jake tug his dick out of his boxer-briefs. Jake's touch felt like a brand on already sensitive skin.

"Uncut," Jake whispered. "Very nice."

Cris's pulse raced at the compliment. Most of the chicks he'd slept with had been initially turned off by his foreskin. They were used to seeing cut dicks. Dudes were way more appreciative.

Jake played with his dick, sliding the foreskin in a slow, lazy way that barely kept Cris from driving them into a telephone pole. Jake kept hold the entire ten minute drive, a long descent into madness that nearly had Cris demanding Jake suck him off already. His orgasm teetered on the edge without getting close enough to tip him over.

He pulled into the underground parking and into a space between two SUV's. The vehicles would provide great camouflage for a blow job, but Jake proved just how sadistic he was by letting go. He flashed Cris a wicked grin. Wicked and challenging.

This is going to be fun.

Cris tucked himself back in, which was not an easy feat thanks to Jake's teasing. Even in the privacy of the elevator, Jake stayed hands-off. Cris led him down the corridor to his apartment, unlocked it, and let them inside.

The moment he locked the door behind them, Jake spun and yanked his head down. The faint taste of lime and tequila filled Cris's mouth. A very insistent tongue stroked past his lips, teasing and seeking. The spark was immediate and dizzying, electric everywhere they touched.

Cris spun them. He pushed Jake against the door, holding him there with a thigh between his legs. Jake humped his thigh while he devoured his mouth with a very talented tongue that Cris couldn't wait to feel against his dick.

The desperate kiss softened by degrees. Cris dragged his lips along Jake's jaw, tasting sweat and soap, then down to nibble at his earlobe. Jake shoved his hands past Cris's belt to grab both cheeks. The small huffs and groans encouraged Cris to play with Jake's ear some more. Suck the lobe. Lick the delicate shell.

"Fuck," Jake said.

Cris chuckled. "Soon."

"Bed."

That he could do. He untangled them, grabbed Jake's wrist, and led him across the small living room to the single bedroom. Flipped the light on. Jake gazed around. Cris wasn't big on useless objects, so the room had furniture and a mirror. A lamp. A TV and blue-ray player. Little else beyond some dirty clothes he hadn't put in the hamper.

Cris fished a condom and lube out of the nightstand and tossed them up near the pillows. Jake followed their trajectory, then toed off his sneakers. Cris did the same, shucking his clothes as expediently as possible, because hot, cute boy. Near his bed. Also getting naked fast.

This was the fun kind of sex. Chemistry, intent, no cameras or director reminding him not to block the come shot. Cris had every intention of coming inside Jake tonight.

Before Cris could haul Jake in for another kiss, Jake dropped to his knees and licked up the length of Cris's cock. The slick touch spread a wonderful warmth through his belly and chest, that only intensified when Jake nibbled on his foreskin. He bit and played until Cris almost couldn't stand it, before sucking him down onto wet heat.

"Fuck." Cris sifted his fingers through Jake's soft hair, holding on without hurting, because damn. Jake's tongue dragged up and down the underside of Cris's cock, an amazing sensation that made Cris's eyes want to roll back in his head. Except he couldn't stop watching Jake. His stretched lips and hollowed cheeks. The intense way Jake went about blowing him. Cris could watch this all day long and never tire of it.

He'd never been so mesmerized by a sex partner sucking him as he was with Jake, and he didn't ponder the meaning behind that. Only that holy damn, it felt good.

Too much, too fast had Cris's orgasm teetering too close. He nudged Jake off, then ran a thumb over his glistening lips. "Your turn. On the bed."

Jake grinned, licked his thumb, and then did as told. He spread out on his back, hands behind his head, so perfectly wanton that Cris wanted to devour him. To lick every inch of skin, tease every curve and plane of muscle. He also desperately wanted in that taut little ass, and that took priority over exploration tonight.

Maybe Jake would be up for a repeat.

Cris knelt between his spread legs, admiring the boy on his bed. He rubbed his palms up Jake's legs, from calf to thigh, enjoying the perfectly smooth skin. The way muscles jumped beneath his touch. Jake's cock lay flat against his stomach, long and hard with a lovely mushroom head. Fun to play with and play Cris did. Licking around the glans, nibbling up and down the shaft, nosing at the root. Putting Jake's scent and taste everywhere.

Jake's thighs trembled. Hands in Cris's hair kept trying to direct him, get him to suck already, but Cris was stronger. He flattened Jake's hands to the bed on either side of Jake's hips, then returned to his oral assault until Jake started cussing at him.

He looked up into frenzied eyes that dared him to keep teasing. Cris winked, then sucked Jake's length down. Jake hollered, and Cris nearly crowed at the sound. He loved making his partner fall apart, frenzied with need, long before the fucking began. Hard pulls up and down, sometimes scraping with his teeth. Jake pumped his hips, trying to fuck Cris's mouth.

"Fuck, please," Jake said on a gasp.

Cris pulled off. "Not yet."

He released Jake's hands so he could push his legs back, tilting Jake's hips and exposing his hole.

Jake made a desperate noise. "Yes."

"You like getting your asshole licked?"

"Fuck yes."

Cris flicked the tip of his tongue against the puckered muscle, the barest touch.

Jake's hips jerked. "Bastard."

He bit Jake's left cheek, earning a surprised yelp that settled into a long moan. A second flicker of his tongue. Another hip jerk. Cris entertained himself with the tease, alternating long swipes with short flicks, playing Jake's body for all he was worth, because damn, the kid was responsive. Jake never stopped making noise, never stopped thrashing and begging for more, and each little sound made Cris harder. Sent him higher.

Cris snagged the lube without missing a beat. Slicked up a finger while he ate Jake's hole, softening him for the surprise. He lifted his head to watch Jake's face as he pressed that finger inside. Jake's eyes went wide, mouth falling open in a long, desperate gasp. He humped Cris's finger, so Cris fucked him with it, slow at first. A gentle tease, waiting for a sign from Jake.

The moment Jake lifted his head high enough to meet his gaze, brown eyes simmering with lust and need, Cris fucked him harder. Jake's eyes rolled back when he added a second finger, fucking him to the last knuckle, driving Jake higher with only his hand. No sounds beyond Jake's gasps and cries and the slip slap of skin on skin.

Jake raised his head with effort, cheeks stained red, and gasped, "Another one."

Something inside of Cris twisted up tight at the absolute trust shining in Jake's eyes. The need for more, to climb higher, believing Cris could take him there. Three fingers took a little work and a lot of patience. He watched Jake's face for any sign that it was too much, too painful, but Jake panted and gasped and pushed down. Urging him. Precome smeared Jake's belly where his cock dragged on every thrust.

Cris's own cock was painfully tight, desperate to relieve the pressure building deep inside.

"Oh fuck," Jake said. "Oh shit." He grabbed his dick and hadn't pulled three strokes before he clamped down hard on Cris's fingers and shot across his own belly and chest. A blob of white even landed on his chin. Cris stilled his hand while Jake came down from his high, thighs trembling with aftershocks over what looked like a doozy of an orgasm.

Cris gently removed his fingers and wiped them on his thigh, uncertain if he could still—

"Fuck me." Jake held his legs back, keeping position, sleepy-eyed but determined. "You can."

Cris didn't need a second invitation. He gloved up and pushed inside in one smooth stroke that made Jake moan. So good, so loose and ready for him, and it took maybe a dozen hard thrusts for Cris to fall over the edge in a blast of pleasure that lit him up from his toes to his scalp.

He had enough sense to pull out and put Jake's legs down before collapsing on top of the smaller man. Jake draped loose arms around his waist and tucked his head beneath Cris's chin. Warm breath tickled Cris's sweaty chest, cooling the skin. Some guys didn't like to cuddle after sex, but Cris did; especially if he felt an actual connection to his partner. And boy howdy, he felt something with Jake. And judging by the way Jake had burrowed in close, he felt something, too.

"You can stay," Cris whispered, the room too quiet for full volume.

"Okay."

Cris reluctantly left Jake's embrace. In the bathroom, Cris wiped off, then brought a warm washcloth and clean towel into the bedroom. Jake was still boneless, so he let Cris clean off his chest, then roll him over and gently do the same for his ass. Cris kissed each butt cheek. Then Jake's mouth, where he lingered for a long time.

Eventually, they ended up under the covers with the light out.

Jake curled up against him, head resting on Cris's shoulder, one arm slung across Cris's chest. All kinds of compliments rattled around in Cris's head, but the easy silence didn't require them. The sex had been mind-blowing for them both. That much was obvious.

Maybe he could talk Jake into another date over breakfast. He dozed on that happy thought....

....only to wake with morning sunshine streaming in through open curtains. The other side of the bed was empty and cold.

Jake was gone.

And an hour later, Cris realized, so was his wallet.

Chapter Two

Spending half of his day canceling two credit cards, replacing his bank debit card, and getting a new license at the DMV left Cris in a pretty fucking foul mood. No charges had been made to any of his cards, thank Christ, but going through the motions of changing everything sucked. A lot.

And all for a whopping eighty bucks in cash, because the little asshole hadn't used Cris's credit cards.

He should have called the police, and he had no real idea why he didn't. No actual proof, mostly. And he was too curious about why Jake had stolen his wallet. No one did that for shits and giggles, especially after the incredible sex they'd had.

Cris's foul mood followed him into the Galaxy Diner for his once-a-week dinner date with Taro Ichikawa, his best friend for the last six years. They'd met online in a queer chat room, and Cris had instantly been intrigued by the handsome Japanese-American who identified as demisexual—partly because Cris had never heard of that orientation. They became fast friends after realizing they lived in the same city and had similar jobs.

Cris loved having someone in his life who understood complicated sexuality.

Taro was already in their preferred booth in the rear of the diner, farthest from the kitchen. It was the quietest spot in the place, and their usual waitress Gina was chatting with Taro. He had an iPad on the table and wore a guilty smile when Cris slumped into the opposite side of the booth.

They'd agreed no work during dinner.

Must be a big project.

"Hey, Cris," Gina said. "Usual to drink?"

"Can I get a beer, instead?"

"Sure. Sam, Bud or Coors?"

"Surprise me."

"Sure thing."

Both of Taro's slim eyebrows were raised high when she left. "Bad day?"

"Ugh." Cris gave Taro a rundown of his night, and then of his last eight hours. "I'm behind on two projects thanks to that little shit, and I still have to go back to the club tonight to find him."

"Why didn't you call the police and report your wallet as stolen?"

Leave it to a fellow programmer to jump straight to the most logical course of action. "You know that feeling you get when you're with someone you genuinely connect with? Not sexual attraction, obviously, but something deeper?"

Taro shrugged as he sipped his coffee. "Once, maybe."

Cris left the sore subject alone. "I felt that with him, and I'm pretty sure he felt something back. So why do something as asshole-ish as steal a wallet? Especially when he didn't even use my credit cards."

"You've got me, pal." He tapped his fingers on the worn tabletop. "Perhaps he's issuing a challenge."

"A challenge?"

Gina returned with a frosty Samuel Adams. They both ordered their usual choices off the menu, and she wandered away to place them.

"This Jake is a go-go dancer, correct?" Taro said.

"Right."

"So someone in his profession likely gets hit on a lot. Playing on the stereotype, he may also have a lot of casual sex. What if he expected your night to be another one-time fuck, but he felt something and wasn't certain how to proceed?"

Cris couldn't wrap his brain around that one. "He likes me enough to want another date, but instead of saying so, he steals my wallet as a 'come find me' challenge?"

"Convoluted, but you don't know him. Neither do I. Perhaps I'm completely wrong and the kid is simply a kleptomaniac."

Explanation most likely.

Except a watch or an xBox game would take longer to be missed. His wallet was immediate and personal.

"I take it you're going to confront him?" Taro asked.

"Of course I am. I'm sure the little shit will deny it, but if this is a challenge, I'm throwing down the fucking gauntlet. I wasted most of today because of him."

"True story."

Cris pointed at the iPad. "So what's up that you brought that thing in with you?"

"Waiting for a program to update. It's taking forever, and I'm not sure why. I may have miscalculated something."

"Fuck me, dude, I don't think I've ever heard you admit to making a mistake."

Taro flipped him off. "You had a lousy day, but at least you got laid last night. It's been eight months for me."

"Well, it's not as though you spend a lot of time looking."

"Sometimes it's not worth the effort." As a homo-romantic demi, sex for Taro was complicated. Like asexuals, demisexuals don't feel sexual attraction, but with a certain level of emotional and mental attraction, he would potentially be comfortable enough to have sex with a guy—and emotional attraction meant spending time together before the sex, which wasn't easy when so many gay men just wanted to fuck. According to Taro, explaining the intricacies of his sexual identity was too hard to work into a first date, so he stopped dating altogether.

Twice in the past six years, Cris and Taro had had sex—both times because both men really needed the release. They were compatible and both knew it was only sex. No complications or extra emotions. The offer dripped off the tip of Cris's tongue, but he couldn't get the words out.

"Want me to introduce you to one of the boys?" Cris asked instead.

"The boys?" Taro blinked hard. "You mean one of the other models?"

"Sure."

He groaned and slunk deeper into the booth. "Great, and tell them what? Your best friend is having sex withdrawal but he can't go out and pick up a trick like normal people?"

"Well, I wasn't going to phrase it like that, no. Benny's a really nice guy. A little hyper, but you get used to it." Benny was also a recent college graduate who'd spent three years hiding behind the gay-for-pay label. After breaking up with his long-time girlfriend back in February, he'd finally accepted that he was bi.

Honesty was good for the soul. Benny had been happier than ever on-set since coming out. Still pretty hyper, though, but in an endearing way.

"You're serious, aren't you?" Taro glanced around like he was debating the merits of actually sinking under the table. "Am I really that pathetic?"

"Hey, no. Stop it." Cris clasped Taro's hand and squeezed. "I didn't offer to embarrass you, I swear. And I'm not pimping you or Benny, or anyone else out. It's a thought, okay? I worked with great guys. They'll get it, Taro, I promise."

"Worked with."

"What?"

Taro sat straighter. "You used the past tense. You haven't called Chet, have you?"

"Not really."

Gina arrived with their food. Cris dug into his gyro and fries, while Taro precisely cut into his steak salad.

They ate in silence for a few minutes, before Taro asked, "Are you going back?"

"I'm not sure."

Chet owned and operated Mean Green Boys, a small internet porn studio that filmed locally. Cris had been one of Chet's very first models when he opened shop, and Cris had enjoyed it for a few years, until Lily. She had immediately accepted that he was bi, and he'd fallen in love—maybe too fast. After she dumped him for doing porn, he'd quit for about two years. Two long, awful years that he'd spent holed up in his apartment, working from home, and barely socializing. Even with Taro. Cris's self-imposed isolation had led to their weekly dinner dates.

Cris had kept in contact with Chet, though, mostly through emails and texts, and eventually Chet enticed him back into the fold. Cris's home gym had helped him pack on some bulk and muscle, and he'd debuted at Mean Green with a new identity: Dane, Badass Top.

Cris had taken time off from filming this past spring, and even though he was physically able to return to porn, something kept him from making that phone call.

"Getting itchy feet?" Taro asked.

"I don't know. Chet's always been an amazing friend to me, and the guys are great. I just…ever since Dell overdosed last fall, and then that whole thing with Boomer's stalker and Adam getting shot…everything feels different in the house. The vibe is off."

"But Boomer is fine and Adam recovered. And Dell's getting better, thanks to you."

Cris shrugged. "Bobby's mentioned it, too. And Shiloh. They say the scenes don't feel the same. Everything's more somber."

Taro speared a piece of tomato with his fork. "Do you think Chet has lost interest in the studio?"

"Maybe. But it's never been about making money for Chet, and I can't see him leaving so many models without income."

Chet Green was an anomaly in the porn industry. Already wealthy from several other investments, Chet had started Mean Green as a way to help young gay men embrace their sexuality, celebrate sex, and make money doing so. He paid industry-standard flat fees on all shoots, sure, but he also offered long-term models a royalty-based contract, which meant constant income. The majority of the cash earned by the studio went to the models.

Cris had a great nest egg thanks to his films. Money he planned on using to build his dream home, hopefully in the next couple of years. He wanted to wait until he'd found someone to settle down with, but that was proving to be more difficult than he'd imagined. Twenty-eight and still searching, with no prospects in sight.

More and more, he figured he'd build the damn house and get a dog. Or five.

"I don't see Chet flat out shutting down the business," Cris said. "Putting someone else in charge if he's getting burnt out, maybe, but not shutting down."

"Fair enough. But you don't want to go back, do you?"

"We'll see. I mean, going back before was about getting me out of my depression over Lily, right? Becoming a social creature again. I've done that."

"Well, you're more social than you were during the Lily crisis, but you're hardly the poster child for party animals everywhere. Do you regularly hang out with anyone besides me?"

Cris stabbed a fry into a smear of ketchup. "You know why I don't have a lot of friends."

"Yes, I do, and I think you're crazy."

"What?"

Taro pointed his fork at Cris's face. "You had plastic surgery when you were twenty. You've been doing porn for years and no one's come after you, because no one's looking for you."

Despite the good points Taro made every time they had this conversation, Cris didn't acknowledge them. He'd made a clean break from his past eight years ago—changed his face, lost his accent, moved to a new city—but the people his father used to work for were probably still alive, the investigations ongoing. Taro only knew the broadest strokes of Cris's past, not the finer details. Not the horrible things his father had done.

Maybe Cris's fears were irrational. It didn't matter. He liked his small circle of friends.

He didn't like the somber direction their conversation had taken, so Cris reached for something to lighten things up. "You know, if you're so fascinated by my porn career, why don't you give it a shot?"

Taro snarfed his iced tea. Cris laughed at his friend's struggles, then handed over a wad of napkins. "Asshole," Taro said, once he could speak again.

"What? You've got the dick for it."

"Gee, thanks. No. I like sex, but in private. Not for thousands to download and jerk off to."

"Fair enough. And Benny?"

"I'll let you know when I'm desperate enough to have you pimp me out to a fellow porn star."

Cris threw a piece of bread at Taro's head. Taro flicked a leaf of lettuce at him; it landed dressing-side down on Cris's shirt.

Their collective maturity knew no bounds.

Cris called Big Dick's to make sure Jake was on the schedule to dance. The last thing he needed today was to waste a trip to the club. He wasn't in the mood to pick anyone up. He needed a conversation.

The go-go dancers didn't start until ten p.m., so Cris puttered around his apartment, catching up on work, until around eleven. For a Tuesday, the club was hopping. Four dancers writhed around in an assortment of jock straps and other underwear, including Jake. Cris nudged his way toward Jake's platform, close enough to be seen, and then pinned the kid with a hard stare.

It didn't take long for Jake to meet his gaze. The challenge in his dark eyes hit Cris in the balls.

Maybe Taro is right about this.

Jake's gaze returned to his time and again over the next hour, until he left his riser for a break. Cris went to the bar, as much for water as to watch the employee door. Jake never came through it, and after ten minutes, he was shaking his ass onstage again. Cris stayed put this time, out of Jake's sight, until last call.

Once the house lights went up, Cris followed what was left of the crowd outside to the sidewalk. The bouncer had gone inside, so he leaned against the far brick wall and watched the door.

One of the dancers left. Then Jake ejected from the industrial door, a duffel bag slung over one shoulder and a bottled water in his hand.

"If you thought I'd left," Cris said, "you were wrong."

Jake jumped and nearly fell into the opposite wall. His surprise instantly downshifted into anger. "Fuck, dude, give a guy a heart attack, why don't you?"

Cris closed the distance between them in four long strides, getting in Jake's face without crowding the kid. "You stole my wallet."

He raised his chin. "Prove it."

The kid's got balls, I'll give him that.

"Do you know what kind of day I had?" Cris snapped. "Canceling all my cards and getting a new ID?"

"The fuck do I care? It's not my fault you lost your wallet."

"You're lucky I didn't call the police."

Jake's flat lips twitched into something like a smile. "Like I said, prove it."

"Is this how you get off? Get someone to fuck you, then fuck them right back? You like being an asshole that much?"

His smile cracked a little. In the dim streetlight, a pale streak of blue stood out beneath Jake's left eye. Not a smear of leftover makeup like last night. A fading bruise. Cris reached for it without thinking, and Jake flinched back.

Cris's stomach clenched. "Who hit you?"

"Clumsy dancer," Jake said.

Bullshit. "Try again."

Jake's eyes narrowed. "We aren't friends, Cris. Don't worry about it."

"We could have been if you'd stuck around this morning, instead of nipping off with my wallet. Hope the eighty bucks scored you some good dope."

Jake surprised him with a hard shove that knocked Cris back a step. "Fuck you. I'm not an addict."

"Just a thief, right?" He held up a staying hand. "I know, prove it."

This was exactly why Cris stuck to a small circle of friends and worked with computers for a living. Code made sense. It was precise and functional and easy to tweak if something went wrong. People were way too fucking complicated most days, and Jake was everything he hated about human interaction.

But something he couldn't explain kept Cris from giving up and walking away. Some driving urge to solve this particular conundrum.

"Look," Jake said, "sleeping with you was a mistake."

Cris folded his arms. "Really? Because I seem to remember you coming like a hot spring."

That endearing glare returned. "Maybe you were breaking a long blue-ball streak."

"Somehow I doubt that."

Jake shoved him again, and the physical aggression was... kind of turning Cris on. "Fuck you, asshole. I may shake my ass on stage six nights a week, but I'm not a fucking whore. I don't go home with strangers like that."

"What made me special?"

"You aren't."

Ouch.

"Maybe I've seen your porn online and wanted to test drive you for myself," Jake snarled.

Cris blinked. "You have?"

"Duh. My roommate is Jon Buchanan. Boomer? Not that I ever seen him anymore since he shacked up with his boyfriend, but whatever."

Okay, I didn't see that one coming.

Jon/Boomer quit Mean Green last winter after falling in love with a guy named Isaac. Cris had met Isaac once, and besides being flighty and socially awkward, Isaac and Jon seemed like they were genuinely happy together. And while getting recognized occasionally by a Mean Green fan happened, Cris had never had a hookup tell him they'd seen his work.

Instead of skeeving him out, though, it made last night's encounter even hotter.

He pulled out all of the dominance and charm he used in his scenes and channeled it into a feral smile. "So how did I do?"

Jake couldn't hide a flash of lust that brightened his eyes. He even licked his lower lip in a way that demanded Cris lean in for a kiss. "You were okay," Jake replied.

Cris laughed out loud. "You weren't so bad yourself. Especially when you were humping three of my fingers."

Jake glanced around, but they were alone in the alley, the air heavy with the stink of motor oil. Cris was getting hard just thinking about playing with Jake's ass again. He'd been so fucking responsive.

Jake rose up on his tiptoes and curled a hand around the back of Cris's neck. Warm breath puffed into his ear. "Hold onto the memory," Jake whispered, "because it's not happening again." He pulled away, putting a few feet of distance between them. "Goodbye, *Dane*. Thanks for the performance, now fuck off and leave me alone."

The disgusted tone Jake used when saying his porn name kept Cris rooted to the ground while Jake stormed away. Maybe he'd totally read Jake's signals wrong, and it all had been about banging a porn star. Maybe Jake really had gotten elbowed by a fellow dancer, and Cris was reading too much into the shiner.

Maybe.

Maybe not.

Chapter Three

Jake Bowden let himself into the apartment expecting darkness, not the glow of the cheap lamp on the equally cheap table that had come with the apartment. He hadn't left it on, and he paused halfway in the door, his heart galloping away at the notion of a burglar.

Except he had nothing to steal, and he doubted his roommate did, either.

Said roommate, Jon Buchanan, eased that initial panic by offering a tentative smile from his spot on the couch.

Jake stared. He hadn't seen Jon in….well, a while. Their schedules didn't mesh on the best of days, and ever since Jon started dating some dude named Isaac, Jon was hardly ever home. His belongings had disappeared from their shared apartment by degrees, so Jake had no reason to expect the guy tonight.

There he was, though, straight-backed and so concerned Jake kind of wanted to punch him. "What are you doing here?" Jake shut the door and jerked the deadbolt into place. "Boyfriend get tired of taking it up the ass and need a break?"

The acerbic barb dripped off without thought. Jake actually liked Jon, but old habits died hard, or whatever. People were easier to handle if kept at arm's length.

Jon actually fucking flinched. "No. Jake, I am so sorry."

He dropped his bag by the couch and headed for the fridge, thirsty as hell after so many hours dancing. And then there had been Cris, but *not going there.* "Sorry for what?"

"I honestly meant to tell you sooner, but time got away from me, and I didn't want to tell you like this."

Jake paused with the freezer halfway open. Frozen dinners were his go-to after a long night, something to calm the angry gnawing in his belly. Jon used to give him shit about the high-sodium, super-processed food he ate, until Jake bit his head off about paying Jake's grocery bill, and the guy backed off.

He eyeballed Jon, taking in the genuine misery coming off the guy. Despite being roommates for several years, they weren't really friends. But Jon was usually a perky dude. Straightforward and optimistic in a way that made Jake want to scream at him to stop farting rainbows all over the world.

He closed the freezer door. "Tell me what?"

"I didn't re-sign the lease."

Numbness crept over him. "What lease?"

"For this apartment, Jake." For an instant Jake thought the guy was going to cry, but instead, he let loose a gush of word vomit. "I already practically live full-time at Isaac's as it is, and when the renewal paper came over, I sent it back with the not renewing box checked, and I swear I meant to tell you, but then life happened, and we've been so busy planning our trip to scatter Henry's ashes, and I am so sorry."

Jake stared, trying to get some of those things to make sense even as cold terror raked down his spine. Jon was leaving. He was the only name on the lease, because Jon had gotten the apartment before his roommate. Jake had no credit to speak of, so no one was going to let him sign his own lease.

No one will let me sign a lease.

He tried to rein in his terror, keep it off his face. He was very, very good at faking it in all kinds of situations, and he smoothed his initial fear over with a flat, cold glare. "How long?"

"The end of the month."

God fucking damn it!

Two weeks. Two fucking weeks to find somewhere to live or be kicked out to the street.

"I know it's not much time," Jon said. "Do you have someone who can help you out?" The genuine need to know, to make this better for Jake when they were barely friends, made Jake's eyes sting.

Now was a great fucking time to start giving a shit. "I'll be fine," Jake snapped, harder than he'd intended.

"I hate dumping this on you, and I'm a jerk for forgetting until now. And I know we aren't the best of friends, but if you need a place to crash, Isaac has spare rooms—"

"No." No way was Jon telling Jake that he was homeless in two weeks, and then trying to swoop in like some savior and offer Jake a place to stay. No. Way. In. Hell. "I always land on my feet."

Everyone left him eventually, so Jake had a lot of practice at improvising on his own.

It was why he kept his life contained to a single, large duffel bag. Extra shit like memorabilia and sentimentality took up room he needed for his go-go costumes.

Jon stood abruptly and came closer. Flicked on the kitchen light. "Shit, Jake is that another bruise?"

He rolled his eyes and tugged a random frozen meal out. Yanked the tray from the cardboard box. Shoved it into the microwave without reading the instructions for peeling a corner or cutting a slit or what-the-fuck-ever, because he was about to be homeless again.

"Jake?"

Jon touched his arm. Jake's skin prickled, alarm bells came out of nowhere, and he spun, shoving Jon away. Jon stumbled a few steps, his blue eyes going wide. Jake was several inches shorter than him and wiry, where Jon was tall and muscular. But Jake knew how to defend himself and put off unwanted touching. He taught himself after the first incident with a high school bully

"I've been a shitty roommate," Jon said. "And an even shittier friend."

"You said it yourself. We aren't friends. We never were."

"We could have been if we'd both tried harder."

Jake shrugged, shooing away that briefest pang of wistfulness at the idea of having a real friend again. "Can't change it now. So why don't you go back to fucking your perfect boyfriend, while I eat my sodium-filled dinner in peace?"

"I really am—"

"Sorry. Yeah, I got it."

The floor creaked. Jake stared at the rotating microwave plate until the front door opened, then shut with the softest of clicks. He glanced over his shoulder to be sure, but yeah, Jon was gone. Jake's throat tightened. One more person who'd walked out of his life and left him behind.

Fuck him and his stupid apartment.

Jake ate that meal, and then another one, because why the hell not? He couldn't take them with him, and he wasn't giving management the pleasure of kicking him out at the end of the month.

Necessity had taught him how to live with the barest essentials. After he ate, he started packing, stowing away the things he couldn't bear to part with, and leaving behind the shit that was easy to replace. It was after four by the time he fell into his bed for the last time. He slept until almost noon, ate the last two frozen meals, drank the last of his orange juice, and then dropped his key on the coffee table.

He wasn't coming back.

Marla waved to Jake from behind the sign-in desk at Prairie Hills Senior Center. Jake waved back as he scrawled his name on the guestbook. Prairie Hills was a ridiculously stupid name for a nursing home in the middle of a city that had no hills or prairies anywhere close by.

Train bridges didn't count as hills.

"I think he's having a good day," she said. "How's your eye?"

"It's fine." Jake forced a smile he didn't feel, grateful she didn't ask why he was hefting around a duffel bag on his visit. Or why he was back again two days after his last.

The staff at PHSC was pretty chill. No one ever questioned his declaration that yeah, he was Ned Thurmont's great-grandson, there to visit his dementia-riddled Grandpaps. No questions, no need for ID. Apparently, the residents didn't get a lot of visitors—yeah, Jake's eyes sometimes watered at the mixed odors of bleach and old piss—and the décor was really fucking drab. Plus, dementia.

Probably easier on family to forget these poor souls existed.

It also meant old Ned sometimes forgot what year it was, forgot who Jake was, and punched first, asked questions later. Jake had taken home more than one shiner because of the old grump, but it was worth it.

He shuffled down the stuffy corridor, past open rooms and the occasional blaring TV. Basic cable shit. Talk shows and cooking demos. Almost time for evening meals to be delivered, too. After three years of visiting Ned, he knew the routines.

Ned's room was at the end of the first hall, door open. A stream of muttering greeted him when he stepped inside. So did a stronger smell of urine, and *Jesus Christ*.

The front of Ned's pajama pants were wet, only he was too busy lecturing a framed print of the Serenity Prayer to notice. Jake dumped his duffel bag and huffed. "Damn it, Ned, you forget where the can is?"

Ned held up a silencing finger and continued his speech. Jake stepped closer, the words growing louder. Not English. French, maybe?

"Ned? *Je n'ai pas't savoir vous parlent le français.*"

"*Oui.*" Ned turned, bushy white eyebrows high on his wrinkled forehead. His saggy skin was liver-spotted and covered in whiskers, but his bright smile made Jake grin. "*Vous parlez français, mon garçon?*"

"Not for a long time." At least now he had the old goat's attention. "You pissed your pants again."

He looked down. "So I did. So I did."

Jake pulled a clean pair of flannel pants from the wardrobe and handed them to Ned. "Go clean up. I'll hang here."

"You're such a good boy. What's your name again?"

"Jacob."

"That's a fine name. *Merci*, Jacob."

After Ned disappeared into his bathroom, Jake poked around. No puddles on the floor, so the mess had at least been contained. Poor old guy. He was ninety-six, had no family besides his "great-grandson Jacob," and lived more in his own mind than in the real world. He was also the only constant thing in Jake's life right now.

Kind of ironic, considering that a hungry, homeless Jake had first signed himself in as a visitor so he could steal food from some unsuspecting old fart's lunch tray. Jake had picked Ned's room at random, and he'd never imagined he would like his mark. Or that he would continue to visit without the intention of stealing food. Even after Jake got a job and a place to live, he'd continued to visit Ned once a week. Sometimes he brought magazines or word find books.

Today he was there because he had nowhere else to go until the club opened at seven. Jake wasn't performing until ten, but hanging around backstage was better than the street. And he still had no idea where he was sleeping tonight.

Storming out of the apartment like a child pitching a tantrum was a really mature thing to do. Now you're homeless and could have had two weeks to form a plan.

No way was he calling Jon and asking to be let back inside, so he could get his own key back and sleep there. And no fucking way was he paying management twenty-five bucks to open the door.

The apartment was gone. He'd figure something else out.

Water ran in the bathroom sink for a while. Jake stared at the mostly bare walls. Ned didn't leave anything up for long. Not pictures he ripped out of magazines, not the occasional poster Jake brought for him. The only mainstay was that old, yellowed Serenity Prayer.

The water shut off, and a moment later, Ned shuffled out of the bathroom stark naked. Jake rolled his eyes. "Hey, Gramps. Pants."

Ned looked down. "Oh dear. Was it always that wrinkled?"

Jake burst out laughing, unable to stop himself. Ned sounded so sincere, as if he was seeing his dick for the first time in fifty years.

"Don't laugh, Wilson, yours isn't much bigger when it's all flappy like this."

The new name shut Jake up. Ned didn't talk much about his past or his family, and he'd never mentioned a Wilson before. Ned knew what Wilson's dick looked like, which made him what? Brother? Friend?

Boyfriend?

Nah.

Jake wanted to know more, so he played along. "And how would you know what my dick looks like when it's all flappy?"

Ned smiled. "Seen it enough times, haven't I? Always running around the house with no clothes on like a scallywag."

What the fuck is a scallywag? Sounds like an STD.

"You know me," Jake said.

"After all these years, I know you better than you know yourself."

Jake was getting to know Ned way more intimately than he'd ever wanted, because Gramps wasn't showing any signs of covering up Flappy. Ned's mind was still rooted in this particular moment in time, though, and Jake didn't want to let go yet. "Remind me how many years it's been?"

Ned laughed, a raspy sound Jake rarely ever heard. "Too many. Too many and not enough." His expression glazed over, distant. It swung back to the Serenity Prayer. "Fifty-six years we lived together. Nineteen since you left me. Oh, Wilson."

Grief fractured his voice, and then Ned started crying. Panicked by the sudden sobbing of an old man, Jake grabbed the blanket off the bed and wrapped it around Ned's shoulders. He led him to the bed and nudged him down until Ned was on his side, hugging a pillow to his face. Something inside of Jake twisted hard at the sudden, fierce grief that told so much.

They were a couple. Ned is gay and his partner's gone.

Maybe that was why Ned didn't have family that visited. Maybe they all disapproved of his life with Wilson, and they'd written him off. Not bothered to understand.

Just like Jake's father, writing off both wife and son for a younger, freer piece of ass.

Fuck him anyway.

He and his mom had been okay.

Until they weren't.

Ned's grief turned the key that Jake had used to lock down his grief over his mom's sudden death. From happiness to heart attack in less than a minute. Ventilators in ICU for two weeks before they turned the machines off. Jake had watched it happen. Watched the woman who'd raised him, been everything to him, take her last artificial breath and die.

Her new job's insurance hadn't kicked in, so Jake lost everything. The new condo they were about to close on, the furniture they'd ordered, everything. At twenty, he'd been homeless in a city he'd only known for two years.

But he'd survived that, and he would survive this.

Uncertain what to do next, Jake read the Serenity Prayer to Ned. The words seemed to break apart the cloud of grief surrounding him, allowing it to drift away until Ned was sniffling softly, eyes closed.

"Mr. Thurmont?" a grating voice from the door asked.

Jake shushed the food service lady. "He's starting to drift off."

"It's dinnertime." The gray-haired woman looked pissed that anyone as old as Ned dare sleep through dinner.

"Leave his tray. I'll make sure he eats when he wakes up."

She huffed, but did as he asked. She was new these last few months, and he didn't like her much. Feeling was probably mutual. Lady probably went home to a house full of cats and a knitting bag.

Jake poked beneath the tray's hard plastic cover. Something vaguely resembling strip steak in brown gravy, the same gravy over a glop of mashed potatoes, steamed carrots, two packs of crackers, and a cup of Jell-O. Probably sugar free. He tucked the crackers into his duffel bag, but left the rest alone. He'd stuffed himself with those frozen dinners, and he'd get something cheap before hitting up Big Dick's.

Never hurt to keep something stashed, though. Rules of survival.

He usually only visited for an hour or two, but no one commented on him hanging for almost four hours today. Ned slept through most of it, waking long enough to eat his dinner, as promised. Jake watched a lot of mindless television programs. Mostly sitcom reruns and game shows, until visiting hours ended at eight.

Duffel bag slung over his shoulder, he began the twelve-block walk from the nursing home to Big Dick's. Only May and it was already hot as balls outside. He stopped at a deli he liked, because their subs were packed full and fairly cheap. Jon would have picked on him about all of the sodium in the salami and ham, and fuck him anyway for Jake's current situation.

Except Jon isn't the idiot who impulsively walked out of the apartment two weeks early.

He was forever doing stupid, impulsive shit like that when he got upset. Sometimes he was amazed he'd ever made it to twenty-three without a serious accident or injury.

Hah! I probably jinxed myself.

Only time and a lot of extra-good luck would tell if he lived to twenty-four.

Big Dick's opened for business at seven p.m. and closed at three in the morning, seven days a week, and Jake had worked there as a dancer for almost three years. The elevated dancing stages had always been part of the place—at least, according to Richard Brightman, one of the owners—but in the early days of the club, they were for volunteer dancers. After a while, Richard realized that adding hot young go-go boys to the payroll would keep customers coming back night after night for more than just the music and bathroom favors. Jake had a few regulars who liked to tuck five-dollar bills into his g-string for a few extra package swings in their direction, and he fucking loved the attention.

Plus, now that he was dancing six nights a week, he'd been able to quit his day job clerking in an electronics store. Probably a good thing for all, because he didn't have the best brain-to-mouth filter, and stupid people pushed all his buttons in the worst ways. He was probably one more customer complaint away from being fired when he quit.

Bear Henson, the other owner, was on his favorite stool outside the club, ready to bounce anyone with a fake ID. The nickname fit the guy, who was barrel-chested, muscled all over, and had a bushy don't-fuck-with-me beard. But beneath the bruiser exterior was a super-nice guy who treated his employees like family. Even their general manager, Mario Fuentes, was super chill with everyone.

"Hauling around your dirty laundry?" Bear asked.

Jake hefted the duffel bag and winked. "Dead body. Didn't have time to bury it before work."

Bear laughed, a deep, throaty sound. "Need to borrow a shovel?"

"I just might. Later."

The heavy thumpa-thump of the club music settled into Jake's bones the moment he walked inside. Until this past week, the club had been his sanctuary. A place he could come to, shake his ass, and forget all the things that had gone wrong in his life. Find a good fuck whenever he was in the mood. Now, he kept looking over his shoulder, wondering if Cris was going to be there.

Cris Sable, a guy who revved his engine with a smirk and had fucked him like no one else ever had—with urgency, agency, and a big dick. And no one had ever rimmed him like that—*nope*. He needed to stop thinking about Cris's tongue and dick. He needed to stop thinking about Cris, period. No more fucking around until he figured out his new living situation.

He scanned the current crowd on the brief walk to the Employees Only door near the bar. Finding a decent looking guy to go home with (and hopefully crash with) was probably his best bet for the night.

I want to go home with Cris.

No, shut up. He thinks you stole his wallet. He doesn't trust you anymore.

Pissed at himself for being so stupid, he shoved through the swinging door and nearly ran over Shane.

"Dude, what did the door do?" Shane asked.

"Nothing, sorry." He blinked at Shane, confused. Shane only danced on their Monday theme nights. "Why are you here on a Wednesday?"

"Doing Richard a favor. Apparently Pax has food poisoning and Xander has the flu, and he couldn't find anyone else last minute."

"So it's just me and you dancing?"

"I think Felix is on the schedule, too, so the three of us."

Fewer dancers meant more tips, which worked for Jake. Maybe he'd make enough to spring for a motel room, so he didn't have to trick out for a bed. Definitely the better scenario.

"Coming in for an extra night is better than hanging around at home alone while Noel is working," Shane said, then got his moony look on his face. The guy was disgustingly happy with his boyfriend. They even had a house and a dog in a little town outside the city, which made Jake hate them both a little bit.

I wonder if Cris likes dogs.

He bit the inside of his cheek to keep from actually screaming at himself to stop thinking about Cris. "Yeah, I guess so."

The dressing room was tucked in past the kitchen, near the door to the upstairs management office. It was a shoe box, but there were two dressing tables and a small bank of lockers for personal stuff. Too small for his duffel bag, so he shoved that into the corner near one of the tables. He stowed his phone and wallet in a locker, then quickly changed into his black g-string, a pair of black hot pants and a silver mesh shirt.

He had an hour to kill before the show began, so he headed back out to the main club to flirt. Hanging out with the customers, letting them see him on the floor, helped pry those extra bills out of their hands when he started dancing. He chatted with regulars, flirted with new faces, and even got two free drinks out of it. The influx of tequila into his system helped soften some of the sharp edges of his current homeless situation, and he started enjoying himself.

Didn't stop him from wondering if every tall, dark-haired hottie was Cris, though.

By the time he, Shane and Felix took to their elevated platforms and starting shaking their asses for cash, Jake couldn't think about anything besides Cris, and it was driving him nuts. Was Cris going to show up? Would he ever talk to Jake again?

Was he sleeping with some other guy right now? He constantly scanned the crowd for Cris.

His distracted thoughts started fucking with his dance moves, keeping him from staying on beat. He even missed a few outstretched hands flashing cash, and that cash ended up in Shane's thong, instead of his.

God-fucking-dammit.

He fled his stage for a break, gulping down a bottle of water in the locker room. This was fucking ridiculous. He was better than this. Sure, he could get a little obsessive over things. He made dumb, impulsive decisions a lot. But this was a whole new level of distracted, because it was affecting his income. Even when he was depressed and angry at the world, it didn't affect his dancing. He didn't let it.

"Get it together, Bowden." He glared at his reflection in one of the mirrors. He'd applied silver glitter to his eyebrows and below his eyes to match his shirt, and he looked like some sort of pissed-off Stephanie Meyer vampire. Not as sexy as he'd hoped.

Then stop glaring at everyone, you idiot.

After a few deep breaths that did little to calm his racing nerves, he returned to the platform so he could finish out the night. Shane kept tossing concerned looks his way, especially when they put on an impromptu duo performance and faux-grinded on each other—those moves always got monetary appreciation from the crowd. Jake relaxed a bit more after that, and he pocketed more cash than he expected after such a rotten start.

He avoided chatting with Shane or Felix by hiding out in the employee bathroom for as long as possible. The dressing room was empty when he finally returned. He took his time changing into street clothes, wasting every possible minute he could before he'd be on the street. A motel room was financially possible, but too many in a row would chip away at the cash he'd previously saved for next month's rent. It was a bandage on a gushing problem, not a solution.

The dressing room door creaked open. Richard stuck his head in, then jerked in surprise. "Jake? You're still here."

"Yeah, sorry." He shouldered his duffle, resigned to wandering the streets until he found a cheap room to rent. Preferably one that didn't rent by the hour.

"It's not a problem, you're just usually the first person out the door when the show is over." Richard came all the way into the room. The rainbow sequins on his vest caught the light from the dressing table mirrors and sent a scattering of colorful stars across the floor. He was forever wearing those awful vests, but somehow they worked for the guy.

Jake wasn't sure how to respond, so he said, "Sorry," again.

"You okay, son? You don't seem like yourself tonight."

"I had a bad day. I won't screw up tomorrow, I promise."

Richard crossed his arms and gave his duffel bag a hard look. "You in between places?"

How the hell did he do that?

"Yeah, so? I'll land on my feet. I always do."

"Where are you landing tonight?"

"I don't know yet. Look, I've been taking care of myself since I was twenty. I'll figure it out." He tried to get past Richard, but the slightly taller man blocked his path. "Dude, I'm off the clock."

"You think I'm going to let you leave this club so you can trick out for a bed, or worse, sleep on the street?" Richard's tone had shifted from concerned employer to concerned parent. Richard and Bear had a son who was a few years older than Jake, so those paternal instincts to coddle him were probably kicking in.

"I told you—" Jake started.

"Yes, you always land on your feet. Why don't you stop being a stubborn, independent guy for a little while, and stay with me and Bear for a few nights. Until you figure out your next move."

Jake's lips parted. "Huh?"

"Gabriel's room is officially a guest room now that he's living with his boyfriend. I'd rather offer it to you than see it go empty while you're struggling to get your feet under you, which is usually easier to do with a roof over your head."

People aren't generous for nothing. He'll want something.

Except never once, in the almost three years he'd worked for Richard and Bear, seen or heard them solicit any of their employees, despite the fact that they were all attractive gay guys in their twenties.

"I can see your suspicion in your eyes, Jake," Richard said. "This offer is completely string-free, I promise. Bear is more than enough man for me to handle, and we've never once been unfaithful to each other in twenty-five years of being together. I'd never break your trust by demanding sex in return for a room."

Richard's blunt words loosened a band of worry from around Jake's gut. He'd known that, but hearing it helped drive the point home. A free bed for a few days, versus shelling out for a motel room. Comfort and safety, versus trusting a stranger's bed.

I can be a rational adult and make a smart decision. He's your boss. He won't fuck you over.

Trusting people wasn't something Jake did easily. People had a habit of screwing him over, either on purpose (like his father) or by accident (like Jon), so keeping everyone at a distance was easier. Safer. It was why he'd been an asshole to Cris. It was why he couldn't take Richard's offer at face value and simply accept it.

The fact that he was considering it was a pretty big win, though.

"I guess a steady paycheck isn't a good enough reason to trust someone you barely know," Richard said. "That's my fault. You're here and gone so fast most nights that I never get a chance to get to know you. Or vice versa. I'm sorry about that."

"I do it on purpose."

"I kind of figured. Look, Jake, I get that you're guarded, and my money is on your trust being broken repeatedly, until you finally had enough. I've known a lot of guys your age, and I've seen that same distrust in their eyes. But you can't live your life expecting everyone you meet to hurt you, or one day you'll be forty-five years old and alone and wondering what the hell happened to your life."

Jake absorbed Richard's words, hearing their truth, but still unable to commit. So he avoided. "Speaking from experience?"

"Bear's ex-wife held onto old hurt until it nearly imploded her life."

"Ex-wife?"

"Long story, but how do you think we got Gabriel?"

Good point. "Listen, I really appreciate the offer of a room, but the whole reason I'm kind of homeless is because my former roommate fucked me over. And okay, maybe I made things a little worse for myself with an uber-bad decision, but I can't change it now."

"Then make a good decision and take a leap of faith. I promise I won't hurt you or break your trust, Jake. You're a great dancer and a dedicated employee, and I'd never do anything to drive you away from the club. Neither will Bear."

"Neither will Bear what?" Bear asked.

Jake had been so focused on his conversation with Richard that he hadn't heard the door open, or seen the big man come inside the dressing room.

"Do anything to hurt this young man if he stays in the guest room for a few days," Richard replied, then kissed Bear's bearded chin. "He's lost his place and needs somewhere to crash."

Bear blinked at Jake, a surprised, almost hurt expression on his face that made Jake feel like an ass. "Why would he think either one of us—oh. Trust issues?"

"Trust issues."

Jake grunted. "Fine, okay." His pulse raced at the enormity of the decision he'd made. "Okay, I'll stay at your place. Where is it, anyway?"

"Paxtang," Bear said.

Nice neighborhood, and not too far that he couldn't still get a bus into the city.

"And remember, Jake," Bear added, "we're putting a lot of trust in you, too, by inviting you into our home."

Fuck, if they ever heard about pretending to steal Cris's wallet, they'd never let me stay.

Great. He'd managed to go an entire ten minutes without thinking about Cris, and now that record was fucked all to hell.

"I understand," Jake said. "I'm not a thief, and I don't bring tricks home."

"Good to know." Bear smiled. "Then how about we all get out of here? I'm exhausted."

"Sounds like an excellent plan," Richard replied.

Jake could only smile and follow them out, hoping like hell he'd made the right decision.

The easy banter between Bear and Richard during the drive to their house eased Jake's distrust a little more. Their affection for each other was clear, even after being together for a bazillion years. They had so much history, including an ex-wife, and it made him curious about the pair. He stayed quiet, though, drawing as little attention to himself as possible.

Their house was more modest than he expected, surrounded by other middle-class homes. The club was incredibly successful, but they lived in a humble neighborhood and drove a basic Ford sedan.

Huh.

Jake clutched his duffel bag tight on the walk to the front door. The interior of the house was rustic and warm, with lots of wood tones and dark furniture. Richard asked if he was hungry or thirsty, but all Jake wanted to do was face-plant in a bed and not move for ten hours. Bear led him upstairs to a half-open door. Told him where the bathroom was before saying goodnight.

Jake shut the door and leaned against it. The room had a queen bed and dark wood furniture. Smelled faintly of fresh paint. He couldn't help but wonder what it had looked like when Gabriel lived here. Jake wasn't friendly with Gabriel, but he was Jon's best friend, and Jake also knew Gabriel from the club. He bartended when they were understaffed, but Jake had never engaged the gorgeous guy in a conversation deeper than basic greetings. He always seemed sad up until recently, and sad meant complications Jake didn't need in his life.

I wonder if his dads know he did porn.

Jake laughed out loud at the lunacy of his current situation. His ex-roommate, a former gay-porn star, was best friends with Gabriel, also a former porn star and son of Jake's employers. Jake had recently slept with Cris, yet another porn star friend of theirs, and thanks to internet torrents, he'd seen all of them fucking in various combinations.

Now Jake was sleeping in Gabriel's bedroom.

Who says the universe doesn't have a goddamn sense of humor?

Chapter Four

Cris arched his back away from his desk chair, not surprised when several vertebrae cracked in sequence. He'd gotten engrossed in his work and not taken a stretch break like he usually did, and now his neck was stiff—one of the many dangers of being a self-employed programmer, along with drinking too much coffee and forgetting to feed himself on a regular schedule.

Three-thirty. He'd untangled the problem he'd set out to fix at quarter-to-eleven, so it was way past time for a break. Maybe even quit for the day, since he was ahead of schedule on this project. Definitely time for food.

A quick check of his refrigerator reminded him that he'd once again forgotten to go to the grocery store. Microwave meals weren't his favorite, but he kept a few in the freezer for these kinds of emergencies. He'd just pushed the start button on a chicken lo mein meal when his phone rang.

Dell's name on his screen nearly made his heart stop. He hadn't spoken directly to him in almost three months—Cris's last shoot before taking a leave of absence. He liked Dell from the moment he met the shy, soft-spoken kid, and he had an incredible eye with the digital camera he used to film scenes. Chet's nephew had been through hell, nearly died, and—shit, what if Dell's rejecting his kidney?

Dell and Chet don't know you donated your kidney to Dell. The whole thing was anonymous. Stop.

Cris answered the call. "Hey, Dell."

"Hi, Cristian, how are you?" Dell's casual tone didn't suggest an emergency, but he'd used Cris's real name, instead of his porn name, so it wasn't business.

"Doing pretty well. What's going on?" Cris flinched at his own abrupt tone.

"To be honest, I'm a little worried about Uncle Charles."

Cris was one of the few people besides Dell who knew Chet's real name, and the fact that Dell had called him Charles meant this was serious. "What's wrong with him? Is he sick?"

"Not really. You remember how upset he was last year after my overdose?"

"Of course." Chet had found Dell passed out in his room with a needle in his arm, and he'd called Cris for emotional support. Cris had gone to the hospital with fellow model Jon, who'd also worked with Mean Green for years. Chet had been an absolute mess while Dell was in a coma. Even after he woke up, Dell had damaged his kidneys badly enough to need a transplant.

After more than three months on the list and going to dialysis three times a week, Dell had "miraculously" received a donor kidney from an anonymous source. Cris hadn't donated his kidney to be a hero. He hadn't done it for accolades or thanks. He'd done it because his friend Chet was suffering, watching his beloved nephew dying a little bit more each day. Cris had given a bit of himself to save a life worth saving, because everyone deserved a second chance.

"Well, it's hard to explain," Dell said, "but it's like he's gone back to that place. I've been clean since that night. Haven't been sick since the transplant, and I'm taking all my medications. Honestly, I feel better than I have in a long time, but it's like he's getting worse. He's depressed all the time. He never leaves the house anymore. Mostly he sits in the den watching TV. We're barely shooting twice a month, and we used to shoot twice a week."

"That's not like Chet." In the eight years since he'd known Chet, Cris had never seen the man in a depressed state. Sad for all kinds of reasons. Upset for others. But this sounded serious, especially if the studio wasn't producing like it used to.

"No, it's not. I've tried to get him to talk to me, but he says I've got enough on my own plate and brushes me off. The rest of our family cut us off, and Uncle Charles doesn't have any other close friends or even exes that I can ask for help, so I figured...I mean, you've been around since Mean Green opened...could you talk to him? Please?"

"Of course, I'll talk to him." Not even a question about that.

"Oh God, thank you. He's home and no one's filming today."

Cris stared at the microwave. "Right now?"

"He's been like this for months, and it's gotten worse these past few weeks. He's worn the same robe for four days. Please."

He couldn't say no, not the way Dell was begging, the concern in his voice all too clear. "Okay, I can be there in less than an hour."

"Thank you, Cristian, I mean it."

"You're welcome."

He hung up, no longer hungry, but unwilling to waste the food. So he forced it down, then grabbed his keys and left. Chet lived in a suburb of Harrisburg, about ten or fifteen minutes from Cris's apartment, depending on traffic and time of day. Looking at the two-story home from the outside, you'd never suspect he filmed gay porn illegally in his basement. Old-fashioned prostitution laws forbade the filming and sale of porn in Pennsylvania, but Chet used various channels to make sure all of his films were distributed by his parent company, Green Enterprises, out of California.

Mean Green Boys had grown from a handful of single-camera jerk-off videos into some very artsy, high-quality porn movies, thanks to Chet's eye for detail and his genuine affection for his models. The business was a labor of love for Chet, a way to help young men make money and express themselves sexually, not a moneymaker, so if he was neglecting the business…it was serious.

Cris pressed the bell, then used the brass door knocker. Counted to fifteen. Did both again. Pounded on the wood. "Chet? It's Cristian."

The knob rattled. The door pulled back slowly, and an unnervingly disheveled Chet squinted against the streaming sunlight. His normally styled salt-and-pepper hair was unwashed and flat against his head, and he wore a red silk robe instead of clothes. "Cristian? What are you doing here?"

"Dell called me." No reason to beat around the bush. "He's worried about you and the business."

Chet let out a long, slow breath, then stepped back from the door. "You drove out here, you might as well come inside."

Cris followed him into the den. The television was on, muted, playing what looked like an afternoon talk show.

"Can I get you a drink?" Chet asked. "Water? Soda? Scotch?"

"I'm fine."

"Mind if I do?"

"Of course not."

Chet settled into his leather recliner, so Cris took the edge of the sofa closest to him. Watched silently while Chet wandered to a side table, where a tray holding several crystal decanters and glasses rested. He poured himself two fingers of Scotch, then took a small sip. He'd never seen Chet drink during the day before. "You think I'm a hypocrite, I suppose," Chet said.

Okay, that wasn't how Cris saw this conversation starting. "Why would I think that?"

"I got on Dell's case so hard about his drug use, and here I am drinking in my bathrobe before five o'clock."

"I don't think you're a hypocrite, but I do think something's wrong. Is it about Dell?"

"Not at all." Chet glanced at the ceiling, which indicated Dell was upstairs. "He's been doing so well since he received his new kidney. I couldn't be happier for him, or prouder, and I hate that we'll never know who to thank for giving him a second chance. That boy is the best thing in my life right now."

Not Dell. Next usual suspect. "Are you getting bored with the studio? Dell mentioned you aren't filming as regularly as you used to."

"Not bored. I suppose I've depressed myself into such a state that being around my boys makes it worse. They're all still so young, still so full of life and beauty and chances for love."

Oh, I get it. "You're lonely, aren't you, Charles?"

Chet's long, slow blink was as good as a verbal yes. "I'm forty-eight years old and I've never been in a serious, long-term relationship. I've allowed my drive for success to overtake my personal life to the point where I no longer have one. These past few years watching Colby, Tony and Boomer all find lovers and settle down has driven that home more deeply. Yes, Cristian, I am lonely." He sank deeply into his leather recliner, that glass of scotch clutched close to his chest. "So very lonely."

Cris's heart ached for his friend, even as he started to see the man in a new light. When he was cleaned up and dressed, Chet was incredibly handsome. The definition of a silver fox. He had money, manners, and a great body. He was a fantastic businessman, a fair person to work for, and he tried to give everyone the benefit of the doubt. He believed wholeheartedly in second chances.

How on earth is he still single?

Cris blinked hard. Instead of his boss or his friend, he saw Chet as a sexual creature with needs and desires that had gone unfulfilled for too damned long. Suggesting he download Tinder probably wouldn't go over well, and if Chet hadn't dated in twenty years then an app wasn't going to cut it. He needed to get out into the world, not deeper into technology. He already hid behind his cameras and computers.

"You're coming out with me tonight," Cris said.

Chet jackknifed into a sitting position and didn't seem to notice he'd sloshed scotch on his lap. "I'm what?"

"I'm picking you up at nine o'clock and taking you to Big Dick's."

"That's a club, right? I've heard the boys mention it." He blanched. "You want to take an old man into a place full of pretty young things? Are you insane?"

"Clearly. And you are far from old. Hell, you're about the same age as the owners, so knock off the old shit, grandpa."

Chet squared his shoulders and squinted, his inner alpha male reacting to Cris's challenge. "Grandpa?"

Cris grinned. "Come out to a gay club with me tonight. I dare you."

"Fine." He glanced at his damp robe, eyebrows knitting. "Um, what exactly should I wear?"

Charles Greenwood was so busy trying to imagine his impending night out with Cristian that he nearly let his pork chops burn. He rescued them from the cast-iron frying pan he'd cooked them in seconds before their darkly crisp exteriors would have transition into black char and dumped them into a paper towel-covered plate to drain excess grease.

The last time he'd set foot in a gay club was eighteen years ago, before he'd moved from California to Pennsylvania, and he'd sworn never to go back into one. The chaos of the place hadn't appealed to him, nor had the open drug use or obvious sex acts happening in full view of both security and the bar staff. Charles was all for freedom of sexual expression, but even he had limits of what he wanted to see in public.

He'd heard of Big Dick's from his models. Apparently, one bathroom had bowls of condoms and lube sachets, and even encouraged patrons to have sex there, while a second bathroom was sex-free. While he liked the idea of a bathroom meant for actual bathroom uses, he wasn't sure how he felt about the owners encouraging public sex.

Perhaps the club scene had changed since he'd last been involved. Coke and crystal meth had run rampant back then. He despised the idea of Cristian or any of his other models using those kinds of drugs, just as he'd despised his own nephew using them. Charles himself had battled against addiction—removing himself from familiar temptations had been one of his driving forces in leaving California.

He'd desperately needed a do-over.

The parmesan couscous had come together nicely, so he pulled that pot off the heat. He enjoyed cooking. It helped him relax after a long day's work, and he'd neglected it quite a lot these past few weeks, leaving Dell to fend for himself. Tonight's dinner was as much an apology as it was a thank you. Cristian's visit had been exactly what he'd needed to kick his ass back into gear.

His beautiful Cristian.

From the moment he'd first walked into Charles's small rented office to audition for Mean Green Boys, Cristian had entranced him. And he'd only grown more lovely and amazing as he aged, going from a nervous twenty year-old boy to an intense, laser-focused twenty-eight year-old man. Charles had mourned the loss when Cristian first walked away from the studio, retiring his original persona of Cal Strong, and then rejoiced when he returned as bulked-up, bad-ass Dane.

But Cristian was stuck, and Charles was at a loss in helping him move forward. Cristian was a successful programmer who made his own hours, so why keep doing porn? It wasn't for the money. Perhaps to fill a void in his life.

I've wanted to help him fill that void for years.

Charles had never admitted to his feelings for Cristian out loud, not even to himself. He kept those feelings locked away in a little box, deep inside of his heart. He was Cristian's employer, and Charles never, ever wanted to be the creepy boss who came on to one of his employees, or make an employee feel obligated to "be nice" to the boss. Long ago, he'd come to terms with wanting Cristian from a distance.

Except today's visit had been an incredibly personal one, and it had awakened those old feelings with a vengeance. He still wanted Cristian. He always would. And as long as Cristian was still technically an employee, Charles could never act on those feelings. Going to a club with him was already toeing uncomfortably close to the line, despite Cristian issuing the invitation.

He was also embarrassed at having reached for scotch instead of water during Cristian's visit. The scotch was kept for social and business calls, and the only alcohol in the house, thanks both to Dell's addiction and Charles's own past issues with depression. But Cristian's unexpected concern had tripped his nerves, and he'd needed the liquid courage. He'd likely need a bit more of that courage if Cristian truly expected Charles to dance tonight.

With the couscous and pork chops on the table, Charles emptied the microwave steam bag of mixed veggies into a bowl, then added those to the spread. He went to the base of the stairs and hollered, "Dell, dinner!"

Dell appeared almost immediately at the top of the stairs. "Smells great." He didn't descend, though. "Are you mad at me for interfering?"

"No, not at all. Come down, please."

He did, slowly, taking his time, which was common since his surgery. He'd healed from the incision site, but sometimes stairs were troublesome. "I didn't know who else to call, since you weren't talking to me."

Charles took one of Dell's hands and squeezed. "I'm very grateful to you for calling Cristian. He made me see how much I've hurt the people I care about by withdrawing as I have, and I'm very sorry. I've been selfish."

"It's okay."

"Dinner is my attempt at saying I'm sorry for neglecting you. You are the best thing in my life right now. I hope you know how much I love you."

Dell's eyes glistened. "Thanks. I love you too, Uncle Charles. You're the only person who's ever totally accepted me for being me."

"I didn't have all my shit together when I was your age, either." That was the understatement of the century, but he'd yet to tell Dell about his more colorful days of indulgence, before he really set his sights on the future and success.

"Bet you didn't need a kidney transplant when you were only twenty years old."

"No, but I took enough risks that I could have died ten times over."

Dell startled. "Really?"

"Someday I'll tell you about it, but not tonight. Come on, before dinner gets cold."

They both settled at the kitchen table and dug into the food. Dell had told him once that his favorite food was crispy pork chops on the bone, so that's what they ate. He seemed to enjoy the meal, and that warmed Charles's heart. All he wanted for his nephew was a happy future, one kidney or not, and he did seem happy. Definitely healthy.

The one unasked and unanswered question circled around Dell's sexuality. While he'd briefly hung with another model last fall before the overdose, Chet saw no indication they were still friends. And Dell didn't date. At least, not that he'd ever told Charles. Dell had no trouble watching and filming men having sex, but he also never seemed turned on by it. Men or women, he seemed wholly uninterested in dating, which was odd for a man his age.

At least he doesn't seem lonely. Not like I am.

"So Cristian is whisking me away to Big Dick's tonight," Charles said. "It's a gay club in the city."

Dell paused with a bite of pork chop halfway to his mouth. "Yeah? He's helping you get a social life?"

"Seems so. Why don't you come with us? It could be fun, getting out for a while. Dancing."

"I'm not much of a dancer." Dell snapped off the bite of pork and chewed.

"Excellent. You'll look as awkward as me."

"I just...don't think clubs are a good idea right now. Maybe after I'm a year sober, but not yet."

"Of course." Charles could have slapped himself for being so insensitive. "I'm sorry, I shouldn't have mentioned it."

"It's okay. I want you to go out tonight and have fun. You deserve some fun after all the stress I've put you through."

"Nothing you did was intentionally malicious, Dell. You're alive, and you're healthy, and that's what matters most. Just... don't do it again. I have enough gray hair for a man my age."

Dell laughed. "I won't, I swear. No more illegal drugs for me, ever, for the rest of my life. It's not worth dying for."

Charles raised his glass of sparkling water. "Amen." He tapped the rim of his glass against Dell's. "To new adventures and happy futures."

"Cheers."

After dinner, Dell volunteered to do the dishes so Charles left him to it. He spent the next solid hour second-guessing Cristian's suggestion of tight jeans and an even tighter shirt. His tightest jeans still looked good, encasing his ass nicely and showing off his package with precise definition. The tighter shirt thing had him perplexed. The vast majority of his closet consisted of pressed button-down, collared shirts, and he was uncertain if they'd be appealing in today's club scene.

Dell wandered in and surveyed the crime scene—Charles's bed was littered with every single shirt from his closet, and he'd deemed none of them worthy of tonight's outing.

"You're definitely over-thinking this," Dell said.

"Well, what do you suggest?"

"Wait here." He disappeared and was back in under a minute with a t-shirt that he thrust at Charles. "Wear this."

Charles examined the front of the dark gray shirt. "Who is Fading Daze?"

"A rising indie band. And do something with your hair."

"I was planning to once I settled on clothes, thank you."

"Well, hurry up. It's already eight o'clock. Cristian will be here in an hour."

"Fuck me." He clutched the band shirt in one fist. "I'm going to look like an old fart who's trying too hard."

"No, you're not. Showing up with someone as handsome as Cristian is going to give you serious points in your favor. Plus, you know, you're not that bad looking yourself."

Charles laughed. "A compliment from a handsome young man. Too bad you're related to me."

"Some people have a thing for older men. What's that called in romance novels? May-December relationships?"

"December sounds as if I'm an ancient man in a wheelchair. Can I be September, instead?

"Okay, fine, May-September."

"With someone your age, it would be more like a March-September, wouldn't it?"

Dell rolled his eyes. "Hair. Do it. Make it nice."

"I know how to style my hair, thank you very much."

Charles was still fussing with his hair at quarter-to-nine, when Dell swooped in with a tube of gel and a comb and fixed it into a style that he actually quite liked. It was less pretentious than his usual preference. Almost hip, and it hid some of his gray. His nearly wrinkle-free face made him look about ten years younger than his actual forty-eight years.

Maybe this won't be a total disaster after all.

For the second time that day, he jumped out of his skin when the doorbell rang. Unless a shoot was scheduled, visitors rarely came to his door. Dell gave him a thumbs-up, then disappeared into his own room.

Charles forced himself to take the stairs at a steady pace, despite the instinct to hide. He didn't back down from challenges, no matter how badly his palms were sweating or how quickly his heart was now racing. One club outing wouldn't kill him. He needed to get out of this house for a few hours and socialize.

With Cristian. My beautiful Cristian, whom I can't have.

He flung open the front door. Cristian smiled at him from the stoop, his hand outstretched to ring again. Dressed head to toe in black, combined with his dark hair and tan complexion, the man was an Italian god, and he oozed sex. Charles was in real danger of an erection over how amazing the man looked, so he averted his gaze and thought about nearly burned pork chops. Ladybugs. The new camera he wanted to buy for the studio.

"I like the look," Cristian said. "I'm guessing Dell helped."

"He did. Hopefully no one asks about the band on this shirt, because I couldn't name a single one of their songs."

"Ditto."

Cristian kept staring at him, which was somewhat unnerving, so Charles blurted out, "You look amazing." Then he blushed.

"Thanks." Something odd flickered in Cristian's eyes. "Ready to go show off, grandpa?"

"Careful there, this grandpa can still spank your ass." As soon as Charles said the flirty words, he regretted them. He'd been far too forward, bordering on inappropriate.

Except Cristian didn't flinch or frown. His nostrils flared in an appealing way, and he swallowed.

No way. No way in hell. Don't even go there.

"We should, ah, probably go," Charles said.

"Good idea."

A strained silence fell over the car on the drive into the city. Charles kept his attention on the windshield and the front view as Cristian navigated the streets, taking them deep into the heart of Harrisburg. He parked in a public structure.

"It's easier than trying to find a spot on the street," he said when Charles questioned it. "The club is only a few blocks away."

Despite having lived in the Harrisburg suburbs for nearly twenty years, Charles hadn't thoroughly explored the city yet. He recognized major landmarks, of course, and he vaguely knew where they were now. Cristian surprised him by turning off the main avenue into an alley of some sort. Men loitered a dozen or so yards away, most of them smoking. A big bear of a man in a leather vest was perched on a stool near an unmarked industrial door.

"Is this a club, or an underground rave?" Charles whispered.

Cristian chuckled, the smooth sound caressing down Charles's spine. He'd been keenly aware of Cristian's proximity during the entire walk—his body, his heat, his cologne. The man was sex on a stick, and Charles wanted to lick him from top to bottom.

Find someone else to lick. Cristian is off limits while he still works for you.

The bouncer didn't ask either of them for ID, but he did give Charles a lengthy once-over before opening the door. "Enjoy your first visit, guy."

Charles cast a curious look at Cristian.

"He's one of the owners," Cristian said as they entered the throbbing club. "He knows everyone, especially the regulars."

"Are you a regular?" He had to shout now thanks to the level of the music.

"Not compared to some. Shooting scenes at the studio used to be good to scratch an itch, but sometimes you want something that isn't being filmed."

He could understand that need.

The club patrons were an impressive mix of ages, ethnicities and gender expressions, and Charles was surprised that he was not, in fact, the oldest person there. While the average age skewed strongly toward mid-twenties, he spotted several other heads of gray hair among those bobbing on the dance floor.

"Buy you a drink?" Cristian asked, tilting his head in the direction of the bar.

"Sure." Might as well start with that liquid courage before he dared trying to dance.

Cristian squeezed his way up to the bar where two men were working. One was, indeed, close to Charles's age and wore a sparkling purple vest over his hairy, bare chest. The other was probably Dell's age, with spiky blue hair and sharp features. The older man ended up taking their order.

"Sprite for me," Cristian said. "Chet?"

Charles had no idea what was popular nowadays. "Surprise me."

"I don't see many faces in my age bracket," the bartender said with a broad grin. "Richard Brightman. I'm one of the owners."

"Chet Green. It's lovely to meet you."

"Same here. First drink for newbies is on the house."

A few moments later, Richard returned with a bubbling glass of Sprite and a Collins glass with something pink inside. "House special. We named it after the joint. I hope you like white rum."

"I'm an equal opportunity drinker," Charles said. "Cristian, are you sure you don't want anything stronger?"

"I'm the designated driver tonight." Cristian handed over his credit card. "Start a tab, okay, Mr. Brightman?"

"Can do." Richard took the card to the register.

They wandered to the edge of the dance floor so they weren't crowding the bar. Charles sipped his drink. It was strong, with a strawberry flavor and hint of lime that he quite enjoyed. Similar to a strawberry margarita, but without the salt or tequila.

One his second sip, Cristian asked, "So how's the Big Dick taste?"

He sputtered the liquid and nearly gushed some out of his nose. Cristian started laughing so hard he almost dropped his own drink. Some lovely person shoved a handful of napkins at Charles so he could clean himself up.

"You did that on purpose," Charles said, a little embarrassed but not at all angry. Cristian was too damned adorable when he laughed like that, and he didn't laugh nearly enough. In the studio, he was always so serious and focused on the job, living completely within the Dane persona he'd created. Charles wanted to see this playful side of Cristian more often.

"I couldn't resist." Cristian wiped tears from his eyes. "And you know I'm not the first person to get a good spit-take out of a drink called Big Dick."

"Good point. Also? You're evil."

"I've been accused of worse."

The off-hand comment intrigued Charles, but Cristian had already looked away, out toward the sea of gyrating male bodies. Charles did the same while he nursed his drink. A few women were dancing here and there, but the vast majority of the crowd was definitely male. Some were shirtless, showing off six-pack abs and perfectly defined pecs. A lot of sweaty, tan skin to admire.

The beat of the music changed several times, and soon his drink was empty. Cristian dashed off and returned with a second Big Dick for him. "So what's your type, anyway?" Cristian asked.

Charles hadn't taken a sip yet, so he didn't choke on his Big Dick twice in one night. His type was standing right next to him. Even his one ex-lover in California had been from Sicily. While Charles's own heritage was a mix of Polish and Irish, he'd always been attracted to Mediterranean men. He couldn't lie to Cris's face, so Charles gave Cristian a version of the truth. "Oh, you know the old cliché. Tall, dark and handsome."

Cristian's smirk did funny things to Charles's insides. "How about you guzzle that Big Dick, and this tall, dark, and handsome will swing you around on the dance floor. Maybe attract another specimen for you to explore."

Charles was definitely on board with that plan—except for the "another specimen" part. He could very happily spend the rest of the night dancing with Cristian, but this wasn't a date. It was a friendly outing to get Charles into the world again. Ease him back into the idea of dating. Finding someone to love.

Too bad the one he wanted was off limits. "Be gentle with me," Charles said. "It's been a while."

Cristian's smirk only intensified, which made it difficult for Charles to finish his drink with any sort of grace. A bit of the liquid made it past his lips. It dribbled down his chin, and before Charles could fix the problem, Cristian reached out and wiped it away with his thumb. The simple, affectionate touch sent tiny ripples across his skin and warned his dick that something exciting was about to happen.

Charles dared meet Cristian's gaze. His dark, thickly lashed eyes simmered with something Charles didn't dare try to name. Instead, he put his glass on an empty bar rail and then licked his lips. Slowly, with direct intent. Cristian's nostrils flared again. He snagged Charles by the wrist and pulled.

He allowed Cristian to manhandle him out into the pulsing throng, nudging their way past other groping, grinding couples. Hands brushed his arms and hips and ass. Heads turned to look at them, and why not? Cristian was gorgeous, and he was there with Charles—a middle-aged pornographer who had no business lusting after a man twenty years his junior.

Until Cristian stopped, turned around, and draped his arms lightly over Charles's shoulders. They were nearly the same height, but where Charles was slim, Cristian had a finely honed, muscular physique that made him seem taller. More in control. And Charles gratefully handed that control over, trusting Cristian to take care of him. He rested his own hands on Cristian's waist, enjoying the warmth of the skin beneath that thin, black t-shirt.

And then they were dancing. Cristian led, thrusting his hips and moving his feet in a way that kept perfect time to the beat of the song. Charles eased into it with jerky motions that smoothed out as his untrained muscles began to understand. Until a kind of instinct overtook him. It thrummed in his blood, warming him from the inside out. Time seemed to stand still beneath the thrill of the dance. He was hard and aching, dancing in a room full of men, and he'd never been more free.

Cristian pulled him in closer, shifting so one thigh brushed dangerously close to Charles's erection. He tried to put space between them, but Cristian held tight, his motions never stuttering—and then Charles's own thigh pressed against Cristian's hard cock. Dancing around so much beauty and eroticism had given Cristian an erection, too. It didn't surprise him at all.

Except the music slowed a fraction and Cristian engulfed him, fitting their bodies together in the most perfect way, each man riding the other's thigh, and the intense pressure on Charles's cock made him gasp. Cristian's hands curled around his neck, holding him still, keeping their gazes locked while their bodies continued to move.

"Christ, but you're amazing," Charles said, unable to contain the words or the emotions behind them.

Cristian leaned in and nuzzled Charles ear, sending goose bumps across the back of his neck. "You're not so bad yourself, grandpa."

Emboldened by the tease, Charles allowed his hands to slide from Cristian's hips to the top of his finely-toned ass. Cristian responded by rutting harder against his thigh—a very natural response to stimulation. Charles refused to read more deeply into it than that. They were out together, having an amazing time, and their bodies were reacting to adrenaline and to arousal created by friction.

Except everything inside of Charles insisted he kiss Cristian.

A new presence behind Charles snapped him out of it. A man with a full beard and impressive neck tattoos pressed against him, a thick erection riding the crease of Charles's ass. Cristian looked past Charles at the new man and appeared to communicate in some silent way, because they both began to grind against him, moving Charles to the music with their bodies. Turning him into the center of a very sexy sandwich, and he never wanted those feelings to end. The unique, fleeting sense of being exactly where he needed to be, and the powerful sense of being wanted by two men at once.

I forgot how much I used to love this. Oh, Cristian.

A cheer rose up in the crowd, just as the song shifted again. Their dancing trio stuttered a bit as Cristian lost focus. Charles glanced behind him, up toward several elevated stages where four young men dressed in very little were dancing. Charles paid the go-go boys very little mind at first—until he realized Cristian was glaring at one of them.

Charles tapped his chin. "Are you all right?"

"Yeah, sorry." Cristian flashed him a sultry smile. "Where were we?"

"Right...about..." He slid his right hand down to palm Cristian's ass. "Here?"

Cristian's eyelids flickered. "Here is good."

"Are you certain?"

"Never been more—Tony."

Charles blinked. "Excuse me?"

Cristian slowed, almost stopping entirely, and put a good six inches of space between them. A quick glare sent the bearded man at Charles's back away. Charles glanced around, confused by the quick change in Cristian's mood and the use of—oh. He spotted Gabriel Henson heading toward them, led by a grinning blond man who had to be his boyfriend Tristan. Gabriel had filmed for his studio under the name Tony Ryder, and he'd retired last year to pursue a career in hotel and restaurant management.

Charles had heard only great things about the young man who'd stolen Gabriel's heart, but he'd never met Tristan in person—until now, because Charles and Cristian were clearly Tristan's intended destination. And it hurt a little that Cristian had pulled so far away, as it embarrassed to be seen dancing so closely with his boss.

I shouldn't have allowed things to go as far as they did. It's my fault he's embarrassed.

Tristan bounced to a stop next to them, grinning widely, his enthusiasm a living thing that engulfed him and spread to others. Gabriel slung an arm around his waist, more tentative than his partner. "Hey, guys, sorry to interrupt," Gabriel said.

"It's no interruption," Charles said, proud he didn't stumble over the lie. "It's good to see you, Gabriel. You look well."

"I am, thanks. Um, Tristan got excited because he, um, recognized Dane, and he wanted to say hello."

Cristian went perfectly still. While Mean Green was relatively small compared to many other porn companies, they were also local and the models were occasionally recognized in public. Charles couldn't imagine this was the first time "Dane" had been noticed by a fan.

"It's true!" Tristan said as he bounced on his toes. "I mean, mostly I'm excited because you're a person I don't know, but whose face I recognized in a crowd after only seeing you in videos. That doesn't happen very often because of my memory issues."

Tristan's excitement made more sense with the explanation. Charles knew bits and pieces about the boy's memory impairment and the slow, but steady progress he'd made in the past two years, thanks to a clinical drug trial and Gabriel's loving patience.

"You've seen my videos?" Cristian asked.

"Oh yeah, I'm a huge fan of Mean Green." Tristan eyeballed Charles. "We haven't met, though, right? I'm Tristan Lavalle."

"You're correct, we haven't met," Charles replied with a smile. He extended his hand. "Chet Green."

"Seriously? Wow." Tristan shook his hand with that same bubbling enthusiasm he'd shown Cristian. Charles wasn't used to being recognized or fawned over. "You used to be Gabe's boss."

"I was, yes. And while I was sad to see him go, I'm proud of him for the life he's leading now. I wish such happiness for all of my models." He glanced at Cristian, whose attention was elsewhere.

"And we are very happy," Gabriel said. He pressed a kiss to Tristan's temple. "Come on, you said hello. Let's stop hogging their time."

"Okay, okay." Tristan smiled at Gabriel with so much love and affection that it almost hurt to witness it. "Nice to see you guys. Now go back to shaking those asses."

The pair melted into the crowded dance floor. Cristian resumed dancing, but his motions were stiff. Uncertain. Charles couldn't seem to make himself move. He'd thoroughly embarrassed Cristian in front of his peers, and he had no business dancing with the man any longer.

"Chet?"

Charles shook his head. "I'm sorry. I need to use the restroom."

"Okay. There are two, so use the one on the right unless you want a shock."

"Duly noted."

Charles threaded his way to the rear of the club. He needed a few moments to collect himself. To convince himself that tonight hadn't been a colossal mistake.

If I lose his friendship over this, I'll never forgive myself.

Chapter Five

After Chet's abrupt departure, Cris headed to the bar for a bottle of water. He'd worked up a good sweat dancing, because holy fuck, Chet could dance. He was slim, but toned, and he'd instinctively followed Cris's lead the entire time, living inside of the music. Thirty years younger. Happy and free. And Cris had been overjoyed to give him those things, spurred on by a growing attraction to the older man.

An attraction he knew for certain that Chet shared. Sure, most guys got erections dancing like that, but the affection in Chet's eyes had been both humbling and exciting. The desire in his expressions. The hunger that made Cris lose his mind a little, urging him to make a move.

Until the poorly-timed interruption from Tony/Gabriel and his boyfriend. Cris and Gabriel had never been friends outside of shooting, so he hadn't known his actual non-porn name until Chet said it. He was vaguely aware of the boyfriend's issues, and his excitement over recognizing "Dane" was kind of cute, but the pair had royally fucked up the vibe between Cris and Chet. Chet had reacted like he'd been caught fucking Cris, when all they'd been doing was dancing. And then the obvious bathroom excuse.

We were having a fantastic time, so what the hell?

At the bar, he waited his turn to order and passed the time by scoping the crowd. Except every new, cute face got replaced by Chet's. Chet smiling, laughing, dancing his heart out. Waking up an attraction that Cris had—if he was truly honest with himself—felt from the moment he first interviewed for Chet. Chet had always been handsome, and his openness had appealed to a younger Cris, who was still searching for his place in this new life, after leaving his old life behind forever. Chet embodied honesty and stability, and he'd always been kind to Cris, even welcoming him back after a two-year absence, despite the abrupt way he'd quit.

Yes, Cris had been attracted to him, but Chet was his boss, and he'd buried that deep, deep down and tried to forget about it. Until that drunken night early last year when they'd both faced unexpected emotional crises, and they'd found comfort in each other. Chet had just gotten the news about Dell being kicked out by his family, and he was weighing the merit of bringing Dell to live with him, versus the realities of exposing him to the porn business. Cris, on the other hand, had heard through a contact at the local FBI office that his piece of shit father had had a heart attack in prison.

The man hadn't died, but it had shaken Cris, who hadn't given much thought to his biological family in years. He'd blocked the first nineteen years of his life out as completely as possible, but this had brought it all screeching into his present.

So he and Chet tried to drown their sorrows in tequila shots. Cris had admitted to some of his guarded past, but he had no idea how much of it Chet remembered. Cris apparently had a higher tolerance for tequila, because he hadn't forgotten the way Chet had cried over his nephew, whose story was so similar to Chet's. Or the way he'd clung to Cris, his lean body fitting so perfect against Cris's chest. His scent.

The way he'd tasted of tequila and salt when he kissed Cris like he needed him to breathe, and then promptly passed out in Cris's arms. Cris had never forgotten. The next day, Chet seemed fuzzy on their evening. He didn't mention the crying or the kiss, so Cris had kept those memories to himself. Partly because Chet would feel awful if he thought he'd forced himself on an employee; partly because the memory was too precious to share, and it reminded Cris of all the things he loved about Chet. His integrity and strength and desire to see young queer men succeed and get all of the opportunities they deserved.

Cris kept the memories a secret, because if he told Chet about the kiss, he'd have to admit that he'd liked it. He'd wanted more. He'd have to admit that the reason he clung so hard to Mean Green and hadn't moved on yet was fear—fear of facing his attraction to Chet. Fear of rejection. Fear of acceptance.

Fear of creating something good and real, only for his past to show up and try to destroy it.

"Dude, you ordering?" the blue-haired bartender asked, snapping his fingers near Cris's nose.

"Sorry, man," Cris said. "A water." It came fast, and he guzzled it down. With only one functioning kidney, he needed to be careful with his hydration. He left the bottle on the bar, then turned, searching the crowd for Chet.

His gaze, naturally, drifted to Jake, writhing on his platform dressed in sparkling black boy-shorts and nothing else. A few bills were tucked into his shorts, and he was shaking his ass for more.

A bolt of jealousy shot through Cris, which he stomped on hard. Jake wasn't his. Jake was an asshole who'd stolen his wallet, and then gone out of his way to taunt Cris about it.

But that *ass*. He wanted Jake again, and not only because the sex had been amazing. Something about Jake drew him in, made him want to protect the guy from the bad things in his life. But Jake had made his feelings for Cris crystal clear, so there was no point in pursuing the idea.

Cris blinked, surprised to find Jake's platform suddenly empty.

His phone vibrated.

Text from Chet: **Gabriel and I have engaged in a business discussion while Tristan dances. Enjoy yourself for a bit.**

He nearly typed back that he had been enjoying himself, you idiot, but refrained. Instead, he sent a winking emoji, frustrated that Chet now seemed to be actively avoiding him. And who the hell was Gabriel—oh, wait. Tony. Chet was hiding with another ex-model, rather than talking to Cris.

Fuck my life.

Jake appeared in front of him like a rosy-cheeked mirage. His dark eyes were outlined in kohl, giving them a more dramatic effect that made him incredibly kissable. "Out with your dad, tonight?" he asked.

Cris quirked an eyebrow. "Jealous?"

"Hardly. But you two looked like you were going to start fucking on the dance floor. Over me already?"

"I was never *under* you, Jake." He enjoyed the way Jake flinched. "Besides, I'm not into thieves, as a general rule."

"Hey, Jake," the blue-haired bartender said. He leaned over the bar, a bottle of water in one hand. Jake took it. "This the guy you've been hung up on all week?"

Jake glared at the guy. "Go away, Pax."

Cris stared at Jake, utterly confused by Pax's statement. "You've been hung up on me?" That made no sense, especially after the wallet thing. Unless Taro had been right, and Jake was challenging him somehow. Not that he'd admit Taro was right, because Taro would hold that over his head forever. "Jake?"

Instead of answering, Jake grabbed his wrist and pulled him away from the bar, toward the far wall where fewer people lingered. "Yes, okay?" Jake snapped, his face flushing bright red. "I like you, and I feel really bad about Monday."

"You mean stealing my wallet? Because that's not something you do to people you like. I spent half the next day running around cancelling my credit cards, and let's not even talk about the driver's license shit."

Jake rocked on his heels, head down. "I'm sorry."

Cris stared, shaken by the apology, considering how proud Jake had been about getting away with the theft. "Okay, that's a start. Why'd you do it, though?"

"I didn't."

"Really? Because when I woke up on Tuesday, my wallet wasn't in my jeans, my apartment, or my car, and I know I had it when we left here the night before. So if you didn't steal it—"

"I hid it, okay?" Jake finally met his eyes, as miserable as Cris had ever seen him. "I stuffed it under your kitchen sink, behind cleaning supplies that looked like they hadn't been touched since the first Bush was in office, so I knew you wouldn't look there."

"But why?"

"Because I liked you, okay?"

Cris wanted to reach out and shake Jake until full answers came out, because none of this made any sense. "You liked me, so you made sure I'd hate you by pretending to steal my wallet? Are you high?"

Jake straightened and level a glare at Cris. "I don't do drugs, asshole. Look, I'm sorry. I was really into you that night, and we had such a great time, and I got scared. I don't trust people very easily, and bad things always seem to happen to people I do trust and care about, so it seemed easier to end things before they started. I know I could have left and never spoken to you again, but sometimes I...I do stupid, crazy, impulsive things, and they always backfire. I push people away first so they don't hurt me. Hiding your wallet was mean and stupid, and that's not who I am."

The explanation made a strange kind of sense, but part of it still stung. "So you assumed I'd hurt you, and you pushed me away?"

"It's not that simple, Cris."

"Isn't it? I'm not the asshole in this situation, okay? I invited you, a stranger, into my home, and we had what I thought was a great connection and amazing sex. And then you stole from me. Wait, pretended to steal from me, so you could avoid getting hurt, but you don't know me."

"I know." For an instant, Jake looked ready to burst into tears. He blinked hard several times, then cleared his throat. "I fucked up, and I'm sorry. I guess there's no way you'll ever give me another chance, huh?"

A mental image of Jake beneath him, writhing on three of Cris's fingers, panting for his dick, flashed through Cris's mind. "Broken trust is hard to fix, Jake."

Jake's face fell. "Okay."

"That wasn't a no. I need to see if my wallet really is where you say it is before this goes any further."

"I get it, and it is. I'll give you my number. When you go home and find it, text me. You'll see. I'm not lying, I swear."

His earnestness nearly convinced Cris, but Jake had already burned him once. He couldn't let his guard down again for puppy dog eyes and a bubble butt. If he gave Jake a second chance, he would do it at his own pace. Make Jake earn it.

That could be kind of fun, actually.

He put Jake's number in his cell. Jake stared at him as if he expected Cris to go look for the wallet right away. "What?"

"Surprised you're still here," Jake said with a cocky grin. "I mean, I know you want another go at this ass." He tilted said ass in Cris's direction.

Cris absolutely wanted another chance to eat that ass and drive Jake insane with pleasure. "Even if I do, I'm here with a friend. I can't exactly run off and leave him just to prove you're not lying again."

Jake crossed his arms. "I'm not lying. If you find that wallet exactly where I say it is, then you owe me a blow job."

"I do, do I? Seeing as how I'm the one who had go through the hassle of cancelling—"

"Okay fine, I'll owe you a blow job."

Cris's skin prickled with interest. "How about you owe me a date? No sex required."

"I guess that's okay." Jake tilted his head, that shy smile back. "Thank you for hearing me out, and for maybe giving me another chance."

"You're welcome. And stop pushing people away before you get to know them. You're too young to be so damn cynical."

"You're too cute to be so single. I guess we both have problems." Jake winked, then melted into the crowd, his break probably long over.

Buoyed by the fact that Jake might not be a jerk and a thief after all, Cris began circling the dance floor, scanning the perimeter for Chet. He said he was talking to Tony/Gabriel, but the pair didn't seem to be anywhere in the back of the club. Curious, he turned to the dance floor in time to spot a head of familiar silver-streaked hair bobbing around.

Chet was dancing with Gabriel and Tristan, as well as an extended circle of other guys. He had a drink in his hand and looked so happy that Cris's heart swelled. Chet was always so serious lately. Watching him loosen up and enjoy himself was everything.

He should be enjoying himself with me, not strangers.

Tristan spotted him. He bopped his way over, his joy too much to resist, so Cris let him drag him out to the group. He stayed several people away from Chet, though. Heading straight for him was too pathetic, even for Cris. He danced with less energy than before, until a sharp pain lanced through his left side.

"Fuck." He pressed a hand over the scar and bent his head, drawing in careful breaths.

"Cristian?" Chet was there, pressing a warm hand against his neck. "Are you all right?"

"Got a stitch in my side." Close enough to the truth.

"Then let's go rest."

"No, I've got it. You stay, keep dancing." He didn't want Chet to stop and worry over him. Cris wandered to the rear of the club where there were a few scattered tables and chairs. Found an empty stool that wasn't covered in spilled alcohol. Jake was back on his platform and provided a pleasant distraction from his confusing thoughts about Chet.

Didn't do much for his confused thoughts over Jake, though.

He liked Jake. He wanted to fuck him again. Maybe even try dating him, as long as he kept his crazy in check—and as long as the wallet was under Cris's sink, as promised. But he also liked Chet, and those feelings ran deeper, had existed longer. Chet, who was his boss, therefore unavailable to him.

I could quit Mean Green. Then maybe…

"Bottled water for your thoughts?"

He looked up, startled by Gabriel's voice and the water hovering in front of his face. Gabriel had a second bottle in his other hand. "Um, thanks," Cris said.

Gabriel settled into nearby stool. "Your side okay?"

"Yeah, old injury." *Hah.* "Gets stirred up sometimes when I dance too much."

"Look, man, I know we're not friends, but I'm sorry if we fucked up something earlier. Tristan can be impulsive, but he means well and I feel like we interrupted."

"You did." Cris let out a deep breath, then twisted the cap off his water. "I think you did. I don't know."

"I didn't know you and Chet were a thing."

"We aren't. We've always been close, though. Did you know I was one of his first webcam models when he opened up the studio?"

Gabriel smiled. "No, I didn't."

"I left for a few years. When I came back, I picked a new name, new persona."

"Dane, the Badass Top."

Cris shrugged. "I wanted to start over. Again. Seems to be a theme with me." Gabriel didn't press that subject, which Cris appreciated, so he offered a little bit more. "Chet's been really down since Dell overdosed last year. Dell asked me to try and figure out the problem, so I talked to Chet. He's lonely, having a bit of a mid-life crisis. I thought coming out tonight would help."

"Has it helped?"

"I think it's confused the hell out of both of us." He studied Gabriel, whose patient look seemed to promise someone who'd listen. They'd fucked a few times on-set, but that didn't mean they knew a thing about each other. He'd been insanely jealous when Gabriel quit the studio to be with Tristan and pursue a real career. "How do you and Tristan make it work?"

"It isn't always easy. At the beginning, we spent a lot of time simply talking. Emailing each other about our days. Getting to know each other. It all got easier when his memory began improving because of a clinical drug trial, but we still disagree like all couples do. Sometimes we fight. But we love each other, and we're committed to making it work. One day we want to get married, make it all official."

More jealousy buzzed across Cris's skin again. Gabriel sounded as happy and in love as anyone he'd ever met. "Well, congrats, whenever you pop the question."

Gabriel laughed. "What makes you think Tristan won't beat me to it?" His easy smile flattened out. "Seriously, though, are you interested in Chet?"

"Doesn't matter. Chet swore to himself a long, long time ago that he'd never come on to one of his models, much less openly date one."

"So why don't you quit?"

Because quitting means there could be a chance for me and Chet, but what if he doesn't actually want that? And what about Jake? I can't date both of them.

"It's complicated," Cris replied.

"It always is. One big thing in your favor is Chet knows about the porn, so you don't have to worry about that secret."

Jake knows too, and he threw it in my face.

Except that was the Jake who was scared and wanted to push Cris away, not the Jake who'd practically begged for forgiveness twenty minutes ago.

"Oh, I get it," Gabriel said.

"Huh?" How could he get it when Cris didn't even get it? "Get what?"

"There's a third guy involved, isn't there?"

Cris couldn't stop his head from turning, or his gaze from shifting to Jake's platform. Jake lived within the music he danced to, bringing the sounds alive with each movement of his sexy-as-shit body.

"Damn, man," Gabriel said. "You're caught between a go-go boy and a porn producer?" He let out a low whistle. "I feel like I should buy you a drink or six."

"Water's fine, but I appreciate the sentiment."

"So what are you going to do?"

"Fuck if I know. Take it one day at a time, I guess."

"If you're into Chet, though, won't it make shooting a little weird?"

Cris shook his head. "I'm on a temporary hiatus. Haven't shot in a few months."

"Anything to do with your feelings for Chet?"

I gave up a kidney to save his nephew's life, so yeah, definitely.

"It's not because I'd be embarrassed to fuck in front of him," Cris replied. "I took time off for personal reasons. I told Chet I'd be back when I was ready, but because of Chet's depression, no one's done much filming recently. Hopefully, he'll get his mojo back after tonight, because other models are counting on him for a paycheck."

"Yeah, I remember what that was like."

Cris studied Gabriel. Physically, he didn't look any different than the last time they'd shot together. Still handsome, fit, with an ever-present five o'clock shadow. But something was different. Gabriel had found an inner peace that radiated off him, and it had everything to do with the blond bundle of energy still burning it up on the dance floor.

I want that. Someday.

"You gonna be okay, man?" Gabriel asked.

"Yeah, sure."

"Uh huh. How about you share your digits, so the next time I ask you that, maybe I'll believe you."

Cris had no good reason to give Gabriel his phone number, but he did. He liked the guy, and it wasn't as if he had an overabundance of friends. Gabriel immediately pinged back with a text, so Cris saved his information.

"My name's Cristian Sable," he said. "In case you didn't want to save me under my porn name."

Gabriel chuckled. "Gabe Henson. Nice to officially met you, Cristian."

"Same here."

Cris remained seated long after Gabriel rejoined his boyfriend. His side still hurt a bit, but mostly he was hiding. Hiding until Chet was ready to leave and this confusing, frustrating, ultimately enlightening night could end. Maybe things would make more sense in the morning.

Three hours later, after dropping a very drunk Chet off with Dell, Cris went home to his apartment. As soon as he locked the door behind him, he headed straight for the kitchen sink. Yanked open the cabinets.

Jake hadn't been wrong that he'd rented the place with it still containing a bunch of cleaning the supplies the previous tenant had left behind. Cris wasn't much of a housekeeper, beyond basic dusting and vacuuming, and he had no idea what some of the various bottles did, or if they were even still good. Tonight he didn't care. He began to pull things out and pile them on the kitchen floor so he could root around near the back.

His fingers brushed soft leather. He grabbed the familiar shape and pulled his wallet out of the cabinet. Flipped through it. Every credit card accounted for. All of his cash still there. Exactly as he remembered it. Nothing touched.

Heart hammering, he texted Jake: **Found the wallet. You owe me.**

Jake texted back almost immediately: **Name time and place. Count on it. Night.**

Cris stared at his wallet, happy to have it, but more confused than ever about his feelings for Jake—a cute, fun, sexy guy who'd already caused him so much stress, but whom Cris couldn't seem to resist. And then there was Chet, a man he'd wanted for years and could never have, unless he took the plunge and quit Mean Green.

"Please, God," he said to no one in particular. "A little help here? A sign or a nudge?"

The closest Cris got to divine intervention that night was the incredible orgasm that followed jerking off to the mental image of Jake and Chet taking turns blowing him. As he drifted to sleep, Cris clung tight to the fantasy, because that's all it ever would be.

He could have one or neither, but not both. No one, especially not Cristian Sable, was that fucking lucky.

Chapter Six

Awareness stole in quickly, alerting Charles to three very important things: his entire body ached, his head felt six sizes too large, and he desperately had to piss. In order to achieve the latter —which was very much his most pressing issue—he had to irritate the former two quite badly. It couldn't be helped, though. He was a forty-eight year-old man and far too old to wet the bed.

Getting out of bed took more energy that he possessed, and by the time he'd stumbled into the en suite bathroom, he had to sit in order to manage his business. While he waited for his head to stop trying to explode all over the floor, he took stock of the rest of his body. Sore legs and abs, likely from all of the dancing he'd done the night before. He recalled most of it. Some of the night was incredibly fuzzy, especially after one of his dancing companions started buying him drinks.

He vaguely recalled Cristian delivering home, but not into his bed. Charles was fairly certain that had been Dell.

I wrecked everything with Cristian last night.

His heart ached along with his head and body. It was for the best, though. Cristian had done his duty as a friend and taken Charles out for a fun night of debauchery, and while Charles hadn't met a soul mate, he'd genuinely enjoyed himself for the first time a very long time. Life didn't seem quite so lonely or dire anymore.

He considered a shower, but crawling back into bed was a much better idea, so he took two aspirin and did exactly that. His lovely silk sheets were cool against his hot skin. He covered his head with a pillow to block out streaks of sunlight, craving darkness.

Someone knocked on his bedroom door. As it creaked open, he beat back an irrational hope that Cristian was checking up on him. "Uncle Charles?"

Dell. Naturally. He'd probably heard the floor creaking as Charles moved about. Talking seemed as if it would hurt too much, so he grunted.

"I brought you some ginger ale and a sports drink. Unless you'd rather something else?"

The boy was too nurturing for his own good, and Charles couldn't reward his thoughtfulness with silence. He dug his head out of the sheets and twisted onto his side. Dell stood next to the bed with both bottles in his hands, his expression more curious than concerned. "Thank you, Dell," Charles said.

"You were pretty drunk last night, and I've never seen you hung over before. I wasn't sure what you'd want."

"That's thoughtful. You don't have to worry about me."

Dell put the two drinks on the side table, then eased onto the edge of the bed. "You took me in when I got kicked out. You took care of me last year after the OD and again after I had the transplant. It's way beyond my turn to take care of you."

Charles patted his elbow, which was the nearest, easiest part. "You're a good man."

"Can I get you anything else? Aspirin? Toast?"

"Took aspirin. Need sleep."

"And hydration." Dell unscrewed the cap on the sports drink. "A few sips. Please?"

Resigning himself to being coddled for a bit, Charles sipped the sweet drink, pleased when it didn't seem to further upset his churning stomach. Maybe a slice of dry toast wouldn't be too awful, but he didn't want to put Dell out by asking. He eased onto the pillows to ride out the rest of his hangover. And Dell's inevitable questions.

"I'm going to go out on a limb and assume you had a good time last night?" Dell asked.

"For the most part. I haven't danced like that since I was your age, and it was quite...freeing. Being among so many attractive men, actually being seen by them as a man worth wanting. It's been a long time since I've felt seen."

"I'm glad. But I'm curious about something."

"Oh?"

Dell chewed on his left thumbnail. "Well, I will admit to peeking downstairs when Cristian first picked you up, and you guys looked....I don't know, really into each other. Cristian even seemed kind of nervous, like he was picking you up for a date, not just two friends hanging out. And I know for a fact that your nerves last night were as much over Cristian as going out."

He stared at his nephew. "You do?"

"I notice more than you think. One of the benefits of being the quiet guy behind the camera is the ability to observe. You don't hide your feelings for Cristian very well."

Charles had no reason to deny it, so he asked, "What exactly is it that you're curious about?"

"When Cristian dropped you off, he seemed...sad? I'm not sure. Did something happen at the club?"

Too many things happened. Far too many things.

"I embarrassed Cristian in front of his peers," Charles said, that familiar ache back in his heart. He'd screwed up so badly last night.

Dell frowned. "How did you embarrass him? Bad dancer?"

"Hardly. No, we danced very well together, and that's the problem. We were... very close together, very, ah...intimate? And then a former model and his boyfriend showed up and introduced themselves to Cristian, and he pulled away so quickly. The introductions were awkward. He seemed embarrassed, so I excused myself and gave him space. After that...we didn't really speak the rest of the night."

"Cristian doesn't seem like the kind of guy to be embarrassed about getting noticed. I mean, you guys were dancing in a crowded club, right? Why would running into someone he knows embarrass—wait, because you're his boss? He was dancing with his boss and saw an ex-coworker? So what?"

Dell hadn't been there, so he couldn't possibly comprehend what had happened. He hadn't seen the small visual cues that Charles had seen...and possibly misinterpreted? No, Cristian had actively avoided him for the rest of the night, chatting and dancing with others, but not with Charles.

"Did you ask Cristian if he was embarrassed?" Dell asked. "Or are you projecting, because you're afraid he can't possibly return your feelings, so you're self-sabotaging any chance you might have with him?"

Charles blinked several times, stunned by how perfectly Dell had deconstructed him. "I'm twenty years older than him."

"So what? He's closer to thirty than twenty-five, and that's far above and beyond the age of consent, so what are you actually scared of? Being rejected?"

"Being accepted." He flinched at the self-centeredness of that statement. "My only real relationship was an utter disaster, Dell. We hurt each other over and over, until we finally ended things. Much of it was my own fault. I was so focused on my businesses and being successful that I neglected him. Made him seek comfort elsewhere."

"He cheated on you?"

"Many times, and I forgave each indiscretion because I somehow felt responsible. I loved Stefan, and I couldn't give him the affection he needed. It took many years for me to understand that he loved my money, not me. He got a free house, plenty of spending money, and he could fuck anyone he liked, because he knew I loved him. Knew I liked having him there, even though it made both of us miserable in the end."

Charles hadn't spoken about his four years with Stefan in this great of detail in over a decade, and in some ways it made the burden lighter. Stefan had broken his ability to trust in another partner, to believe they wanted *him* and not his success.

"Do you actually think Cristian wants your money?" Dell asked. "You've known him for ages, and he's never once made a move. Do you really think he's that kind of guy?"

"No." Charles shook his head—a terrible idea that sent a bolt of agony down his spine. "Ugh. No, this is my own issue to deal with."

"You don't have to deal with it alone. Talk to Cristian. Find out what he wants and how he feels, instead of projecting on him and assuming the worst."

"That's excellent advice. How did you get so smart about relationships at such a young age?"

"Four older siblings who liked to vent." Dell's shoulders dropped, and his expression shifted into that same resigned sadness that appeared when he spoke of the life he'd been violently removed from.

Charles didn't know the full extent of Dell's story or why he first began to use illegal drugs, and he hoped one day Dell would tell him. All he knew for certain was that Dell's parents—Charles's brother and sister-in-law—called the police on their own son and had him arrested. The moment Charles heard that through another sibling, he began considering the idea of bringing Dell to Harrisburg to live with him.

When the charges were dropped, Dell's parents refused to allow him to come home, citing the same line that they'd used to cut Charles out of their lives decades ago: he was possessed by the devil. When Dell contacted Charles from a homeless shelter, he'd dropped everything to fly south and get him.

Even after Dell completed rehab, they hadn't talked about it. Not about the reasons for his drug use, not the bruises on his face and chest when Charles rescued him from the shelter. One day, he hoped Dell would open up to him on his own, but for now he was content knowing Dell was alive and healthy. The rest would follow.

"I appreciate you hearing me out," Charles said. "And you're right. I need to speak with Cristian. Could you do one last favor for me?"

"Of course."

"Could you perhaps locate my phone? I can't recall what I did with it."

Dell chuckled. "It's on your dresser." He fetched the phone. "I'll give you some privacy."

"Thank you. I mean it."

"You're welcome." Dell closed the door on his way out.

Charles stared at his contacts list for far longer than he should have before dialing Cristian's phone. Perhaps he wouldn't answer, and Charles would be given a brief respite from—

"Hey, Chet," Cristian said. "How's the hangover?"

"Tolerable, thank you for asking." He swallowed down a rising lump of fear. "I was hoping to speak with you this afternoon. In person, if possible."

"Sure. I'm my own boss, so I'm pretty sure I can fit you in."

The teasing tone helped ease some of Charles's initial fear over their future conversation. "Then please, thank your boss for me."

"I will. How about a late lunch? That Italian bistro you like over on 3rd? Or would you prefer something lighter on your stomach?"

"Actually, a small bowl of pasta, lightly sauced, may be exactly what my hangover needs." Charles glanced at the alarm clock. After noon already. "How does two-thirty sound?"

"Sounds great. I'll see you there."

"See you there."

After he hung up, Charles stared at his phone's shiny plastic surface for several long minutes. Today's conversation would do one of two things: start something, or end something. And he had no clue which it would be.

Not a single clue.

Jake didn't usually visit Ned on Fridays, but he was so turned around by his conversation with Cris last night that he needed a friendly ear to bend. Oh sure, Richard or Bear would probably hear him out, but he was already sleeping in their guest room and occasionally eating their food. He didn't want to overstep their generosity and make them regret it. Or God forbid, fire him for being a freeloader.

Prairie Hills would never not be a depressing place to walk into, and today was no different. Marla nodded absently at him as he signed in. Ned was awake and watching a soap opera, completely entranced by two characters who were ranting on about mobsters and kids getting killed. Jake had no idea how people kept up with a program that was on every day for fifty years. He could barely manage a single twelve-episode season of a cable show.

Ned didn't notice him until the soap went to a commercial break. "Jacob, lad, what are you doing here? Did we have an appointment?"

"No, I wanted to say hello."

"Oh, I think it's more than that. You have this look about you." Ned turned the TV off, then stood from his armchair. He sat on the bed. Patted it.

Jake sat next to him, grateful for both Ned's undivided attention and that he seemed to be having a really good day.

"There now," Ned said. "What's troubling you?"

"A boy I like."

Ned glanced around the room. "It's dangerous for a boy to like a boy."

He smiled at the elderly man. "It isn't as dangerous as it used to be."

"Oh, to be a young man today, with so much more freedom to be open about who you love. My Wilson and I never told anyone, not even our dearest relatives. We couldn't."

"I know." Jake picked at the bed cover, unsure how to start. He'd never talked to anyone about relationship issues before, because he'd never bothered dating anyone. Fucking around was one thing, but dating? Whole other issue.

"So what's the problem with this boy you like?"

"I think he likes someone else. And I almost screwed it up before we really started, so who knows if anything will happen now?" Jake gave Ned a detailed account of his past five days, from first noticing Cris on the dance floor, to his idiotic wallet trick, to last night's promise of a date. He definitely came across like a flighty asshole that didn't deserve the second chance Cris had given him, and he still didn't believe Cris had forgiven him. The date was probably to let Jake down easy.

"Well, you certainly know how to snare a young man's attention," Ned said. "Stealing wallets?"

"I didn't steal it, I hid it." He'd never live this down. "And I didn't do it to get his attention, I did it to make him hate me."

"Sounds as if that plan failed, because it isn't truly what you wanted."

"No. It's not. We really connected on Monday, and I feel good when I'm around him, and that terrifies me."

"Why is that?"

"Because people I care about either hurt me, or they die. I don't have the strength to risk trusting someone again."

"You're stronger than you think, young Jacob. You also have a chance to do what I could never do, and that's live as you truly are, and love openly. My beautiful Wilson died in the closet. We were never able to show the world our love. You can."

"But what if Cris is humoring me with this date and he wants someone else?"

"What makes you believe he does?"

"The guy I saw him with last night? They looked super close and they were super hot together. Like, melt-your-face-off scorching sexy hot. And this other guy's older, so he's probably got his shit together and doesn't run around hiding people's wallets under sinks. No one wants a hyperactive, impulsive go-go boy for a boyfriend."

"One of our greatest enemies is our own assumptions," Ned said. "Until this boy you like tells you he doesn't want you, don't assume the worst of him. If I'd done that, I would have missed out on forty-six wonderful years with an amazing man."

Jake couldn't imagine forty-six days with the same guy, much less forty-six years. But the wistfulness and adoration in Ned's voice whenever he talked about his dead lover? Jake wanted that.

Not the dead part, but the love. He wanted it, and he was so fucking scared to try and get it.

"Real love is difficult to find," Ned continued. "So if you do find it, love as hard and as long as you possibly can. Take it from an old man. Don't allow yourself to reach my age and end up regretting guarding your heart so fiercely." His eyes went distant, and Jake braced himself for the shift. Ned's clarity had lasted an incredibly long time already.

"What are you doing here, Jacob?" Ned asked. "Did we have an appointment?"

Jake sighed. "No, we didn't. I stopped by to say hi, but I think your soap is on."

"Oh dear, it is. Are you going to stay and watch?"

"I can't today, but thanks. Actually, I need to make a phone call. Enjoy your show."

"Take care, lad."

Jake had his phone out, but didn't call Cris until he'd exited the nursing home and hit the hot, humid sidewalk. He weaved in and out of the midday foot traffic, and after two rings, the call went to voice mail.

"I can't pick up," Cris's recorded voice said. "You know what to do. Peace."

After the beep, Jake said, "Hey, it's Jake. Listen, I want to follow up with you about the date we have coming up. Maybe make some plans. I'm free today until about eight, so call me whenever. Um, bye."

Lame ending, but whatever. He'd made the call. He'd taken the first step forward, and that was a victory in itself. Now he had to find a way not to go crazy until Cris called him back.

Cris was already seated at a small table and waiting for Chet to arrive when his phone began to ring. He was right on time for the unexpected lunch date, so Chet should be there any moment. Not the time to answer a call, but he fished the phone out of his back pocket and checked anyway.

His heart fluttered at the sight of Jake's name on the screen. In his peripheral vision, a flash of salt-and-pepper hair made him send the call to voice mail. Jake would have to wait an hour or two.

Cris put the phone away, then stood to greet Chet with a friendly hug. Chet looked a bit green around the edges, but he was smiling and seemed himself.

A waiter arrived right away. Cris ordered a Sprite, and Chet ordered ginger ale.

"I was surprised to get your call," Cris said. "I figured you'd be in bed until at least tomorrow."

"This old man can still surprise you." Chet studied the simple, one-sheet menu, as if he didn't know it already by heart. "Anything look good to you?"

Avoidance wasn't a tactic Chet usually used, but Cris decided to play along. This was Chet's meeting, after all. "They had a ricotta and pancetta ravioli on the specials menu up front. I may give that a whirl."

Chet grimaced. "I'll probably stick with simple."

Cris studied Chet, trying to divine some hint as to why they were there. To talk, obviously, but about what specifically? Before or after things got weird between them? Cris hadn't called

Taro yet to pick his brain, because he still didn't want to hear "I told you so" about Jake and his wallet. He needed to focus on his relationship with Chet first. He'd known Chet longer, cared about him longer, and he had to fix this problem between them.

Chet had been the most stable element in his life for eight years. Cris needed that stability back, even if it meant returning to the comfortable friendship they'd maintained since they first met.

Neither of them spoke. Chet pretended to study the menu, while Cris studied him. Their waiter returned with drinks. Neither of them wanted a starter, so they both ordered their entrees. As soon as the waiter left to put in their food order, Chet blurted out, "Were you embarrassed last night when Gabriel saw us together?"

Cris nearly knocked over his Sprite. "Of course not. I was having an incredible time with you, and I was kind of annoyed at the interruption." He'd dreamed about dancing with Chet, their sweaty bodies close together, erections rubbing, hands seeking, and he'd woken up with the mother of all morning wood. "Were you embarrassed? Because you kind of beat it out of there when they left."

"A bit, I suppose. Not at being with you, Cristian. By being out at all, I suppose, and with one of my employees."

"We were just dancing."

Chet frowned, then leaned in. In a lower voice, he said, "It wasn't just dancing. We were both hard, Cristian."

"That happens a lot in that place. Not a single person in the club would have looked at you funny for having an erection. It's simple biology."

"It didn't feel simply like biology."

When Chet didn't expand on that comment, Cris said, "I ended up talking to Gabriel later in the evening."

"Yes, I noticed."

Chet had looked for him? Interesting. "He asked if something was going on between us."

Chet's eyebrows winged up. "What did you tell him?"

"The truth as I knew it. We were having an amazing time dancing together, and we're attracted to each other, but nothing can happen while I work for you."

The wide-eyed shock on Chet's face was incredibly endearing. "You're attracted to me?"

Cris held his gaze for a beat before looking at the single candle burning in the center of their table. The yellow flame flickered gently. "I was attracted to you the first day we met, that first interview. I also knew from speaking with you that you were a man of integrity, and you'd never mix business with pleasure. I needed the money, so I ignored my feelings. I ignored them for so long that I think I tricked myself into forgetting about them entirely."

"And what reminded you?"

"Dell's overdose last year. Seeing you so upset and helpless. You letting me take care of you for a while. You're an amazing uncle to him. Hell, you've been a father to that kid since you brought him to live with you, and I really admire that. You're not greedy at all. Mean Green is all about helping us, not yourself. I think you're pretty amazing. Charles."

Chet closed his eyes, then took several deep breaths. Cris, on the other hand, could barely breathe. He'd put it all out there, and

Here For Us   101

now the proverbial ball was in Chet's court. Cris tried to keep still, but he couldn't stop his feet from softly tapping against the floor while he waited.

"I don't want to hurt you," Chet said as he blinked his eyes open. They were red and damp, and it made Cris want to haul the older man into a hug. "I am attracted to you, Cristian, but my only serious relationship was an utter disaster, and I've allowed it to define my life for decades. I'm too old to change now. You deserve someone younger and less set in his ways."

Someone like Jake, who is as predictable as a squirrel on crank.

Cris's heart sank at the predicament he'd put himself in, stuck between a rock and a free spirit—and uncertain how to choose between them. Jake had probably called earlier to talk about their promised date, and that dropped a big rock of guilt right into Cris's gut. Now that he and Chet were baring their souls, he had to be honest about all of it.

"To be fair to you," Cris said, "there is someone else I'm interested in."

Chet flinched, but he somehow managed a genuine smile when he said, "Tell me about him. Her?"

"Him." He told Chet about Jake, sparing no emotional detail. From the great time they had together to his overwhelming anger after the loss of his wallet. Seeing Jake the next night, having it all tossed in his face. And then Thursday night when Jake admitted the truth, Cris found his wallet, and they agreed on a date. "He called a little while ago, probably to set something up."

"I see."

Their food arrived, and Cris took a few minutes to taste his ravioli and collect his thoughts. Chet was reacting as expected, with grace and acceptance, deferring the actual choice to Cris. Trouble was Cris wasn't exactly sure who he wanted.

Chet had ordered his marinara on the side, and he carefully stirred a bit into his bowl of spaghetti. Playing more than eating, his expression difficult to read. He had an incredible poker face, and that had probably aided him in building Green Enterprises from the ground up. A self-made man with deeply held principles. Kind and generous and handsome.

I'd be so lucky to have him.

"You should definitely take this Jake fellow up on his date offer," Chet said after he'd managed to do little more than move food around on his plate. "Do something fun. See where things go."

"Really?" Cris put his fork down, but Chet didn't look at him.

"Yes, really. Cristian, you and I have been friends for a very long time. Let's keep it that way."

His heart skipped a beat, but Cris wasn't sure if it was from happiness or grief. "Are you sure?"

Chet looked up, a sad determination in his eyes. "Yes. It wasn't fair to spring my feelings on you when you've just begun something with Jake. You've given me so much, and I will always be grateful for last night. It was the best night I've had in very, very long time. Thank you."

"Things aren't going to be weird if I start shooting again?"

Shit, I said if, not when.

If Chet noticed the slip, he didn't let on. "It wasn't weird before, and it won't be weird in the future. I'm fine, Cristian, I promise. And it's good that we've talked this out. Settled things."

But are things really settled? Can we really walk away from our feelings?

Chet wasn't giving him much of a choice. He launched into a detailed chat about the shoot he wanted to set up for the following weekend. Adam Swift, one of the studio's biggest new hits from last year, was eager to shoot again, and Chet wanted to match him up with a good switch. They discussed pairing options while they pretended to eat. Cris barely tasted his food, and after a few bites, he gave up.

The dynamic between him and Chet had shifted back to what it had been twenty-four hours ago, but it still felt off. It didn't fit the same, like a sweater that had shrunk in the wash. They could ignore their feelings all they wanted, but their feelings hadn't gone away.

Cris wasn't entirely sure they ever would—or if he wanted them to.

Chapter Seven

Cris couldn't remember the last time he'd visited Big Dick's three times in one week, and he found himself in the unusual position of doing so on Friday night. He settled himself at the bar a few minutes before ten, more interested in watching the dancers than doing any dancing himself. His side was still kind of sore from last night, so he treated himself to a Cap and Coke.

Mixed, to his surprise, by Gabriel, who was behind the bar with Richard.

"You bartend here?" Cris asked after he ordered.

"Sometimes, when they need extra hands," Gabriel replied while he scooped ice into a glass. "My dads own the place. Felix is sick again, so Pax has to dance in his place. I'm filling in back here."

Cris was still stuck on the "my dads own the place" part. Gabriel looked nothing like Richard, but he could kind of see a resemblance to Bear the Bouncer if he tilted his head at the right angle. He slid a ten-spot across the bar in exchange for the drink. "Keep it."

"Thanks, man."

The music and lights changed slightly, and a cheer went up from the dance floor. Three lean, writhing bodies decked out in g-strings, glitter and not much else emerged on the dancing platforms. Cris's attention went directly to Jake, who'd said he would be decked out in blue again.

Cris's favorite color.

After his somewhat depressing lunch with Chet that afternoon, Cris had gone home before calling Jake back. Jake had answered after two rings with a high-pitched, "Hi, Cris?" that had made Cris smile.

"Yeah, hey," Cris had said. "I'm returning your call from earlier."

"Awesome. I mean, uh, that's cool. I was hoping to nail down our date. If you still want to, I mean."

The stuttering excitement had been adorable and cemented Cris's decision to make this date happen. He wasn't entirely certain that he was making the right decision, but Happy Jake was impossible to resist. "I definitely want to. I'm self-employed, so my schedule is pretty open."

"I dance six nights a week, but I'm off on Sunday nights."

Cris hadn't wanted to wait two more days to see Jake. "How about during the day tomorrow? I'll pick you up and we can do something outdoorsy. City Island, maybe?"

Jake was quiet a beat. "I've never been. I could meet you there."

"Kind of defeats the purpose of a date, doesn't it? Let me pick you up, so you can at least pretend I'm a gentleman." A gentleman who fucked first and went on a date second.

"I'd rather meet you someplace."

"Why? I promise I won't judge you on where you live, Jake."

"It's not that." Jake had let out a deep breath over the line. "I'm kind of between places, so I'm crashing somewhere."

"Okay." A terrible thought had occurred to Cris, and he hadn't stopped himself from blurting out, "You do have a place, though, right? A safe place?"

"Yes, I do. I'm not tricking out, and I'm not on the street. I just…I'm crashing with my bosses, and it's hella embarrassing."

Jake was crashing with Gabriel's dads? Could Cris's life get anymore surreal? "Why's it embarrassing? I think it's awesome that they're helping you out. Not every boss would."

Chet totally would, if any of his models needed a place.

"I guess not. It's just that I'm stuck here because I got pissed at my old roommate, did something impulsively stupid, and I lost my old place two weeks early."

"I'm sensing a pattern of stupid, impulsive actions here." Cris wasn't sure he could handle too much of that right now—not when Chet offered so much needed stability.

"Sorry to say I've always been this way." Jake had grunted. "I go crazy, then get super down on myself, and then do it all over again. Second-guessing that date now?"

"Nope, you're stuck going on at least one date, and I am picking you up. Tomorrow. Ten o'clock sharp. Text me the address, okay?"

"Fine." Instead of grumpy, though, Jake had sounded pleased. Maybe even a little excited. "Ten o'clock in the morning, right? Not tonight when I go on stage?"

"Maybe tonight, too. See you, Jake."

"Yeah, you will."

The flirty way Jake had signed off left Cris in a more positive mood for the rest of the afternoon. He'd texted Chet once, to check on his hangover status, and he'd received a brief "much better, thanks" response. Classic Chet, reverting to employer mode in order to keep a distance between them. As much as Cris understood it, it still stung.

Now, surrounded by the heavy bass of dance music and the heady scents of sweat and alcohol, Cris let that hurt fall away so he could focus on Jake. Jake's lean form writhing to the music, sparkling in various shades of blue as he moved. The effect was almost serpentine. Definitely beautiful.

He sipped his drink and watched, ignoring anyone who drifted too close, or who shouldered their way over to place an order. At some point, Gabriel ended up back at Cris's corner of the bar with a towel in his hand. "So I'm guessing one of our go-go boys won the coin toss?" Gabriel asked.

"It wasn't a coin toss." Cris angled in so he didn't have to shout at the whole bar. "Chet removed himself as an option and wished me well with Jake."

"Jake, huh? That kid's a firecracker. You've got your hands full." Cris must have instinctively leveled the guy with a possessive glare, because Gabriel put both hands in the air. "Peace, dude. I've never slept with him. Only interacted with him here. The kid sometimes goes from zero to sixty in terms of mood swings, that's all I meant."

That definitely tracked with what Cris knew of Jake so far. They hadn't talked much beyond surface things, so he was curious about Jake's story—more so now that he knew where Jake was living temporarily. Tomorrow was Cris's chance to see if they had anything in common beyond sexual chemistry.

"We've all got a partner history," Gabriel said. "But the way you reacted just now? You really like him, don't you?"

"I do." He also really liked Chet, and they had so much history. "I suppose I'm not one hundred percent sure I made the right decision in dating Jake."

Gabriel shrugged as he started putting together a round of drinks. "To that, I'd say the fact that you're here is a good sign you did."

True. Except he wasn't there exclusively to see Jake—a fact he reminded himself of by checking the time. Taro had agreed to meet him there for a drink and he was late—atypical for his organized and punctual best friend. No texts or missed calls, so Cris sent off a "where are you?" text.

"Right behind you," Taro said, startling Cris into sloshing his drink onto the bar top.

"Asshole." Cris grabbed a nearby napkin to wipe his hand. "You're late."

"Sorry, I misplaced my phone." Taro squeezed into a narrow spot between Cris and the guy on the next stool. "You didn't order for me?"

"Wasn't sure what mood you'd be in."

Taro grinned, lighting up his dark eyes. "I finally fixed the goddamn glitch in that program, and it wasn't my fault, thank you very much. The client loved it, and I got paid today."

"So champagne?"

"Fuck you. No." Happy Taro tended to swear more frequently than work-obsessed Taro. He caught Gabriel's eye and shouted, "Margarita, blended, lots of salt."

"Braving tequila?" Cris asked. "You are in a good mood."

"I like the flavors."

"In that case, you should have ordered a Big Dick."

Taro squeaked. "What?"

Cris laughed at the wide-eyed shock on Taro's face. "Not a literal dick, you dork. Their house drink is a Big Dick. Apparently it has a similar flavor profile, plus strawberry."

He eyeballed Cris's drink. "And you'd know that how?"

Here we go. This is why I invited him out, though, right?

"Chet had one here last night," Cris said. "He told me what it tasted like, and I also got a fantastic spit-take out of him."

"I can imagine you did with a name like that." Taro frowned. "Wait, Chet Your Boss Chet? You went out with him? Here?"

Cris explained Dell's concerned phone call, his basic kidnapping of his boss, and lowered his voice for some of the more awkward details. Taro's eyes widened and narrowed at parts as he listened, taking in the story, sipping his drink the whole time while Cris ignored his. Taro cackled with delight when Cris described Jake's apology over the wallet and their impending date.

"Oh shit, which one is he? Wait, no. Let me guess." Taro angled to study the three dancers, assessing and cataloguing details, as was his habit. "What will you give me if I guess right?"

Cris snorted. "A handshake."

"Hah. No. How about that new CAD software I've been eyeballing?"

One in three were good odds that Taro would guess correctly, considering how long and how well he'd known Cris. The software in question wasn't going to break his bank account, but it was the principle of the thing. "What do I get if you guess wrong?"

"A foot massage."

"Two." Taro gave the absolute best foot massages on the planet. Cris was always a puddle of goo when Taro finished.

"Fine, two. Deal?" Taro stuck out a hand.

Cris shook it. "Deal."

"The guy in blue paint."

Cris nearly fell off his stool. "What the hell?"

Taro laughed. "I'm right, aren't I? I knew it. You are so predictable."

"How am I predictable?"

"Two things. You don't like artificial hair colors, so despite loving the color blue, the tall guy in the middle wouldn't do it for you."

He was right about that; Cris had no inclination toward Pax. "And the other guy?"

"Wrong vibe."

"You're getting a vibe from the way he's dancing."

"Sure." Taro winked at him. "Plus, the kid in blue keeps looking this way. I think he might be jealous."

Cris's attention snapped toward the platforms. Sure enough, Jake seemed to be focused on their corner of the bar, while his body never stopped moving. And the look wasn't entirely friendly.

I've never mentioned Taro to Jake. Jake doesn't like me talking to another guy.

Huh.

"Do I need to give him a best friend speech?" Taro asked. "Hurt him and I hurt you, blah, blah?"

"No, you don't. It's a date, not an engagement party, Jesus."

Taro shrugged, then downed the rest of his margarita. "You dancing with me tonight?"

"No. I hurt my side last night, so I'm sitting this one out."

"Hurt it how?" Taro plucked at Cris's shirt, as if examining the scar would help somehow. He went into mother-hen mode whenever Cris's missing kidney became an issue. In the vast majority of voluntary donations, the donor had no major side effects. He took blood pressure medication daily, and certain health problems could become issues down the road as he aged, so Cris was careful of his diet and liquid intake.

Cris also hated that he was one of the rare few who continued to experience nerve pain months after the fact—pain that could be managed, but might never fully go away.

"It's a muscle strain, stop fussing," Cris said, smacking gently at Taro's hands. "Go dance."

"Hell, no, without you I need at least one more margarita." He ordered the second drink, and then downed it fast enough to give Cris brain freeze by proxy.

Cris sipped at his melted, watered-down Cap and Coke while Taro slipped into the dancing throng. He tracked his best friend for a while, until Taro got swallowed up by moving bodies and flashing lights. Time melted away under the constant drone of music. Cris alternated between staring at Jake, watching for Taro, and playing on his phone.

Around eleven-thirty, his phone buzzed with a text.

Jake: **New friend?**

Cris glanced at Jake's empty platform, then snickered. Probably on his break. **Old friend. BFF for a long time. Jealous?**

Nope. **Making sure tomorrow isn't a waste of time.**

Challenge accepted. **Oh, I won't waste any time, I promise.**

Jake didn't respond to the flirty text, but when he retook his platform, the looks he tossed at Cris were lighter, less accusing and a lot more open. Cris started yawning around midnight. Not a surprise, given how late he'd been out the night before. Clubbing twice in a row wasn't something he'd done in years, and his body wasn't the same as it was a few months ago.

He sent a "see you in the morning" text to Jake, who wouldn't see it for a while. But the gesture should ring loud and clear. It took a while to find Taro in the throng. He was dancing with a bare-chested guy who looked intent on getting laid tonight, and it made Cris's skin prickle. Taro had another drink in his hand, too.

"Hey, you need a ride home?" Cris asked, nearly shouting into Taro's ear to be heard. "I'm heading out."

"Nah, I'm done after this." Taro tilted his half-empty cup at him. "I'll burn it off before they close down."

"You sure?" Cris glanced at Taro's dance partner, who didn't seem happy about the interruption.

"Yes, Dad, I'm a big boy."

Cris bit back a crude joke. "Text me when you leave, okay?"

Taro rolled his eyes. "Okay, fine." Then he kissed Cris on the cheek. "Enjoy your date tomorrow."

"Oh, I will."

Cris squared his shoulders and leveled a hard stare at Taro's dance partner, using his bulk to make a point. A "you fuck him over, I'll take you apart" kind of point. The guy seemed to get it, so Cris wove his way off the dance floor.

Taro knew how to handle himself, and he'd been clubbing without Cris as a chaperone for years. But so much bad shit had happened to people Cris knew in the last year, and it had increased his protectiveness for the few real friends he had. If anyone hurt Taro, he'd find a way to end them.

At home, it took a while to doze off. It wasn't until a "home safe and alone, Dad" text came through from Taro that he relaxed. He started thinking about his plans for tomorrow and finally fell asleep to the mental image of a blue-painted Jake up on that stage, dancing naked just for him.

Chapter Eight

Jake was a twitchy, nervous wreck, and it wasn't even ten o'clock yet. After his shift last night, he'd been too wound up to sleep, so he'd basically paced downstairs for hours until exhausting himself. Those few hours of rest hadn't helped much, because when his phone alarm rang at nine, he'd been jolted out of amorphous dreams of him royally fucking up this date.

A hot shower and quick breakfast of waffles didn't do much to relax him. Richard tried to offer him advice when Jake finally admitted to the reason for his unsettled state, but nothing was going to help. It was simply part of who Jake was and always had been: winding himself up tight, always expecting the worst case scenario.

He let himself out of the house at five minutes to ten, mostly so he didn't have to go through the incredibly embarrassing motions of introducing Cris to his temporary landlords. The trip to the sidewalk did nothing to calm him down. A blue sedan rolled up to the curb. Jake ducked to peek in the passenger window, and his heart nearly stopped at the happy grin on Cris's face.

Jake yanked open the door and slid inside. The car was older, but clean, and it had an apple-shaped air freshener hanging from the rearview mirror. He inhaled the cinnamon fragrance. "Morning."

"Morning yourself." Cris leaned toward him, then stopped, as if he'd planned to try for a kiss and changed his mind. "Sleep okay?"

"Nope. You?"

Cris chuckled. "Some."

"Because you're nervous about our date?"

"Maybe a little. You?"

"Terrified, actually." Jake wanted to be as truthful with Cris as possible, give the guy everything he needed to either turn him down or take a chance. "Not of you. More of me doing or saying something really fucking stupid and chasing you off."

Cris tilted his head, his lips twitching. "Well, as long as you refrain from wallet thievery today, we should be all right."

"I promise not to touch your wallet without permission." He put enough innuendo into that statement to make Cris's nostrils flare.

"Oh, it's not my wallet you have to worry about touching later."

Jake leaned in and flashed a saucy smile. "In that case, I'm not worried at all." He had half-a-mind to haul Cris in for a kiss, but he wasn't sure if he could stop at just a kiss. Their first kiss on Monday had obliterated all of Jake's higher thought functions, and he'd let Cris do whatever the hell he wanted to his body. When they started making out again, it needed to be in private, not in a car parked on a public street.

"So are you ready to attack City Island?" Cris asked.

"Like I said, never been."

"As long as you aren't allergic to sports, it's a lot of fun."

"I did track and field in high school. Does that earn me any sports points?"

Cris laughed. "Depends on your events."

"Hurdles and pole vaulting. I got second place in state finals for vaulting my junior year." One of Jake's proudest moments. Despite the spectacular way his parents' marriage was imploding, his mom had been there for the meet. She'd seen Jake set a personal record. And maybe Jake hadn't won first place, but he'd never forgotten the pride on his mom's face that day.

Meanwhile, his father had been too busy fucking his assistant to bother.

"Jake?" Cris gently touched his shoulder. "You okay?"

"Yeah, sorry." Jake straightened, pulling out of the memory and away from Cris's touch. "One of those bittersweet memories."

"I can respect that." Cris got them on the road. "So I'm going out on a limb and guessing you didn't go to college."

"I managed two years, actually, but life got in the way. Never finished." Jake wasn't sure he wanted to go there quite yet, so he left the details alone. "How about you?"

"I've taken some night school classes to shore up my skills, but no official degree. I'm a self-taught program designer. Starting designing a bit in high school, and I've been developing ever since. I'm not an incredibly social person, so it's nice working for myself."

"And doing porn on the side?" He hadn't wanted to bring that up today, but Jake's brain-to-mouth filter had never been installed correctly.

Cris shrugged as he navigated a left turn. "Porn was more about getting outside of my shell, showing off a little, embracing that I was bisexual, instead of being ashamed of it or confused by it."

"You're bi?" Jake wasn't sure why that surprised him so much.

"Yeah," Cris snapped. "That bother you?"

"No." The sharp way Cris reacted, though, said that other people in his past had problems with it. "I'm guessing you're used to it bothering people?"

"Yeah, I am."

"That sucks. And since we're clarifying, definitely gay over here."

"Excellent. I'd hate to think Monday night was some fever-induced need for a curious straight boy to walk on the queer side."

"Oh, no. I've loved dick since I hit puberty." The wide-eyed shock on Cris's face made Jake laugh out loud. "Don't worry, I didn't act on it until later. High school was...weird for me. I came out at fifteen but didn't date. You?"

"I dated quite a lot, but it was always girls. At the time, acting on my attraction to men wasn't safe."

Sympathy hit Jake hard. "Family situation?"

"Yes."

Cris's tone suggested he didn't want to talk about family right now, so Jake fumbled for a new subject. "Did *you* play any sports in high school?" he asked as the city whizzed by.

"Not really. Believe it or not, I hated sports and was more into smoking weed and making fun of the nerds and weirdos." Cris flinched. "I was kind of jerk until my junior year."

"What happened then?"

"I switched schools."

Nothing else seemed to be forthcoming, so Jake left it alone. This was the getting-to-know-you part of the date, but Cris seemed unwilling to go very deep on the topic of his past, so Jake searched for something more present. "You told me you took time off from filming scenes for personal reasons. Can I ask about that?"

Cris's jaw clenched and unclenched several times. "It's not, like, a state secret or anything, but my best friend Taro is the only person who really knows."

Taro was the sexy Asian dude Cris had been chatting with last night. The BFF. Jake really, really wanted to know now. "It sounds private, so I'd be really honored to know. And I promise not to tell anyone. I mean, I don't even have my own best friend, so it's not like I have anyone to gossip about you with."

It took several minutes of driving in city traffic for Cris to answer him. "I took time off for a voluntary kidney donation. It saved someone's life."

Jake stared at Cris's profile, stunned stupid. As far as explanations went, he never would have imaged this being the reason for Cris's time off. A memory of their night together flashed into Jake's mind—Cris towering over him, preparing to fuck him through the mattress. The pale line on his left side. He'd noticed the scar, but hadn't given it much thought.

Until now.

"You seriously donated a kidney to someone?" Jake's admiration for the guy swelled. "That's...wow."

"It's not all that wow, and I didn't tell anyone, because it makes me sound way more heroic than I actually am."

"I don't know, giving up a kidney is pretty fucking heroic to me. Was it for someone you knew?"

Cris nodded, still not shifting his gaze off the road. "They don't know who gave up the kidney. I did it anonymously, and I don't plan on telling them it was me."

"Fuck me, you are a saint." Jake slumped into his seat, as impressed with Cris and his selflessness as he was ashamed of his own selfishness.

"I'm hardly a saint. It was something I needed to do, and I didn't do it for accolades or attention, okay? I saved a life, and I helped a friend."

The whole thing had to be way more complicated than Cris was letting on, but despite his act-first, think-second nature, Jake did know when to back off. Maybe if today went well and they had another date, Jake could press further. He wanted to know more about Cris and why he was so guarded about his past. And he wanted to find out if Cris was someone Jake could be honest with about his own past. Maybe be someone Jake could rely on, and vice versa.

They didn't talk much on the rest of the drive to City Island. The place was busier than Jake expected. It had batting cages, an arcade, a food stand, and even a baseball stadium. There were a lot of families and kids, a few couples, and the weather was hot, but not too humid. Cris took him on a brief tour of the place, before asking what he wanted to do.

"Batting cages," Jake said. He used to play ball in the backyard with his dad on weekends. Jake had never been confident enough to try out for Little League, but he treasured those late afternoons with his dad. They were some of the few truly great memories he had of his father.

"Sounds good."

Cris got quarters at a change machine, and they got in line to wait for an open cage. "I know I'm not that great at his," Jake said. "You any good?"

"Normally I'd make some saucy comment about being very good with any type of balls," Cris said. "But not so much baseballs."

He snickered. "Points for honesty."

Neither of them ended up being very good. Jake managed to hit three; Cris hit two. But they laughed and teased each other over their shared lack of baseball skills, then went to play a few rounds of miniature golf. Jake enjoyed the good views he got of Cris's ass when he hunched over to putt a ball. He even caught Cris ogling him a few times when he thought Jake wasn't watching.

After a late lunch, they took a ride on the City Island Railroad, which became Jake's newest favorite thing ever. The train had a real steam-operated engine, and Jake imagined what it had been like traveling across the country by railroad, watching the American west go by in blurs of brown and tan and green. After a private horse-drawn carriage ride around the island, Jake was smitten. Cris was charming, sweet, with a small hint of danger thanks to his secretive past, but he was also a hell of a lot of fun to hang with.

And the kidney thing.

Who does that?

They were walking together, hands brushing but not quite holding, taking in the sites, when Jake couldn't take it any longer. He leaned up on his tiptoes so he could whisper, "I know it's barely dinner time, but I really, really want you to fuck me."

Cris tripped, then stopped walking. The heat in his eyes took Jake's breath away. A feral smile curled Cris's lips. "Right here?"

"While I have no qualms about scaring the straights, I'm not looking to get arrested for public indecency. That would be a sucky way to end our first date."

"Sucky, huh?"

"The bad kind of sucky. Not my preferred kind."

"I could get on board with your preferred kind of sucky." Cris leaned down. "One condition, though. If you stay over, I want you still in my bed in the morning. No sneaking out in the middle of the night, and no hiding my personal belongings."

"Deal." Jake didn't have to think. He wanted this, and even though the idea of opening up to Cris terrified him on a cellular level, he truly believed Cris wasn't out to hurt him, or to screw him over. He'd donated a kidney, for fuck's sake. There was no reason to push Cris away.

Yet.

Cris waited until they were back in his car, heading off the island, before asking, "How much do you like to play?"

"Play?" Jake kind of understood the question, but he wanted to make sure what Cris was asking.

"In bed. You seem to enjoy having your ass played with. You ever go further than three fingers?"

"No." Allowing Cris to do that to him had been pretty out of character. Jake was cool with a finger or two as prep, but he'd never had a guy take him apart like that. The trust he'd instinctively shown to Cris had scared him, probably spurring his stupid-ass decision to hide Cris's wallet.

"Would you want to go further?"

"Maybe." Jake loved getting fucked. He loved a guy licking his ass, playing a bit, but he'd never thought about doing anything too extreme. A certain level of trust was required for that, and trust rarely came with a one night stand. He'd never even played with toys before. And from his porn videos, Jake knew that Cris was a switch, so… "What about you?"

Cris tossed a heated look his way. "Never been with anyone who wanted to try and do more than just fuck me. Why? You want a go at my ass?"

Need blasted through Jake like a fireball, and he had to swallow several times to find his voice. "Maybe. You'd really let me top you?"

"Not tonight, but yes. If this goes anywhere."

Jesus Christ.

Cris was taller than him, broader than him, with muscles that Jake wanted to lick all over. And while he'd seen Cris take it in his videos, it was usually from guys with a similar build, like Tony Ryder. Never someone smaller like Jake. Someone Cris could bend in half and fuck blind without much effort.

Jake pressed a palm over his thickening cock. "About going further. You're not talking BDSM stuff, are you?"

"Not if that kind of thing turns you off. I mean, I'm into light spanking and ass play, but I don't use belts or intend to bruise. That's not my kink."

"What is your kink?"

Cris was silent for several minutes. "Basically what we did on Monday. Taking my partner apart with my hands, and then my dick. Hearing them beg, scream for release. Male or female, it's a huge turn-on to know I've brought someone that much pleasure."

"And you're very good at it," Jake said.

"Oh? Tell me more."

"And inflate your ego? No, thanks."

"Dirty talk might help inflate other parts of me."

Jake eyed Cris's lap, overcome by the memory of holding tight to his very big dick during the drive from Big Dick's to Cris's apartment. Cris wasn't the only one good at using his hands, and if it hadn't still been broad daylight out, Jake might have reminded Cris of that. Still, negotiating things now was better than trying to do it once they were alone, because after that Jake would be putty in his arms.

"Three fingers was intense, in a really good way," Jake said, redirecting the conversation. "Have you ever gone further than that?"

"Once." Cris turned onto a familiar street; they were close to his place. "I don't hook up much outside of doing scenes, but sometimes I want to get off without being filmed, you know? I can go without remembering house style, or where the camera is. A year or so ago, I picked up a guy who seemed pretty vanilla at first. Once we get back to his place, though, he pulls out a rubber sheet, gloves and lube, and he says he wants me to fist him."

Jake's stomach wobbled. While he was cool with a few fingers, the idea of an entire hand up his ass was a little terrifying.

He'd never imagine trusting a guy enough to do that to him. "Did you?" he asked on a breathy whisper.

"I tried. Got to four fingers, but I'd never done it before, and I didn't know him well enough to really read his signals. I was too scared of hurting him, so I stopped."

He fell for Cris a little bit more, hearing how attentive he'd been to his partner's needs. In the underground lot, Cris found a spot and parked. Instead of getting out, he turned to look Jake in the eye, his expression wary but intent. "I need to know that if we start to play and I do something that hurts, you'll tell me. Sex is about fun and feeling good, and I'm all for trying new things, but I don't ever want to hurt anyone. Okay?"

"I promise." Jake tucked a curl of dark hair behind Cris's ear. "I'm not into pain as a general rule, so no worries there."

"Good." He made no move to get out of the car, something in his eyes still uncertain.

"What's wrong?"

Cris chewed on his upper lip, a move so adorable that Jake wanted to lean over and lick the worry away. "When I confronted you about my wallet on Tuesday, you threw the fact that I filmed porn back in my face."

Jake's pulse jumped; he very much remembered flinging that final acid barb. One last attempt to get Cris to leave him alone, when that was truly the last thing he wanted. "I am so sorry about that. I honestly do not judge you for doing porn, and it was a mean thing to say."

"Did you know who I was when you first saw me in Big Dick's?"

"Not right away, but I did after we started talking." Jake had been thrilled to realize the guy he'd snared in the crowd was a porn star. "And okay, maybe a little part of me was turned on by the idea of fucking Dane, but I was mostly interested in fucking Cris. You. The things I felt were real. They weren't part of the porn illusion, I swear."

"I want to believe you, but words still hurt, Jake."

"I know." He flopped against the passenger seat, his hard-on dying a slow death. "I really am sorry that I hurt you. God, I'm such an asshole."

"A little bit, yeah, but I understand where it comes from." The small smile quirking Cris's lips kept the comment light, almost flirty. "But I got burned pretty badly once by a partner who couldn't handle me doing porn, so I need to know you're really, truly fine with it before I do this with you."

Jake turned those words over in his mind. On the surface, it was hella fucking hot that Cris did porn, and he had the body of a Roman god. And all they were doing right now was playing around. But would it feel the same if this thing between them went deeper than playing? Cris wasn't actively filming, but when he started again, would Jake get jealous?

"I don't know what kind of promise I can make here," Jake said. "I've never been in any sort of relationship, never made a commitment to a guy, so I have no idea how I'll feel down the road if this turns into more than fucking. And if I'm bleeding truth all over you, the idea of this being more than fucking terrifies the living shit out of me, and it was exactly the reason I pretended to steal your wallet, so maybe we could take this one day at a time?"

Cris studied him a moment before nodding. "That's fair. I'm glad we both know where we're coming from."

"Me too." He let his lower lip droop into a flirty pout that always worked on the go-go stage. "So, we fucking here or can we go upstairs to your apartment?"

Cris's nostrils flared.

The trip to the apartment was full of random touching and coy glances, because someone else was always on the elevator with them. Being the middle of the day on a weekend, it wasn't as surprising as it was annoying. Jake didn't hide who he was, but he'd been harassed enough over the years to know when to tone it down in mixed company. The instant Cris snapped the deadbolt shut with them both inside his apartment, Jake yanked him down for a kiss, because for some reason he hadn't done that yet today.

It was everything he remembered. Hot, hard, and toe-curling. Cris was very, very good at kissing, and he swept his tongue into Jake's mouth, while one hand tugged at Jake's fly. Jake did one better and used both his hands on Cris's belt, then zipper, moving fabric far enough to get inside and clasp Cris's thickening cock. Cris bit his lower lip, his other hand curling behind Jake's neck. Strong enough to hold him still without trapping him.

"Gonna make you come so hard," Cris whispered. "You want that?"

"Fuck yes."

"Bed. Naked. Now."

Jake's entire being snapped to attention under that order. He yanked his hand out of Cris's shorts, then strode across the apartment to the bedroom, shedding his shirt and shoes as he went. Shorts came down in the doorway, and his underwear landed somewhere on the floor. He stroked his erection as he settled on his knees in the center of the bed, heart racing, blood pulsing. Eager and intent, and still a little bit wary.

Cris's broad frame filled the doorway. He'd lost his shoes, and his fly was still undone, but he was fully clothed, studying Jake with so much fire in his eyes that Jake's belly wobbled under the intensity. No one had ever looked at him like that before—as if Jake was the center of the universe and everything revolved around getting him off.

He didn't know what to do with all of the strange new feelings bubbling up inside, so Jake did what he knew best—seduction. He leaned back on one hand and used the other to make a circle of fingers around his cock. Thrust his hips lazily a few times, pumping himself. Mimicking fucking.

Cris's eyes narrowed. "Keep doing that."

Jake did, using a bit of precome to smooth the way, applying the perfect amount of pressure. He liked being on display, being watched, but this kind of private show was a step beyond his usual comfort zone. "You're still wearing a lot of clothes."

"Yup." Cris stalked to the bed, his erection poking up beyond the waist of his open fly. "Lay back, but keep fucking your fist."

This was going someplace interesting. Jake complied, planting his feet flat to the bed, knees spread wide to give Cris a nice view. Cris fetched lube and a few condoms, dumping them on the bed by Jake's head. Jake's hips stuttered once. His hole clenched.

Three condoms. Dude's got stamina.

Cris crawled onto the bed, knocked Jake's hand away, and sucked Jake's dick into his mouth. Jake gasped at the familiar tight heat. The expert way Cris dragged his tongue, scraped with his teeth, nibbled the crown. Licked into his slit. He worked Jake higher and higher with only his mouth, no other body part touching him.

Jake's restraint shattered, and he yanked at Cris's shoulders and hair, urging him to climb Jake's body for another kiss.

A long, sensual kiss that broke everything Jake thought he knew about kissing. A cloth covered cock rutted against his, driving him higher. Jake thrust his tongue into Cris's mouth, tasting himself along with Cris's unique flavor. A sharp sweetness he couldn't get enough of. He shoved his hands beneath the waistband of Cris's boxer-briefs to squeeze his ass cheeks. Firm, chiseled cheeks Jake could barely imagine parting to finger, much less to fuck.

The needy groan that escaped Jake's throat made Cris chuckle. Cris licked a stripe from Jake's chin to his ear, then said, "Feel something you like?"

"Maybe." Jake nipped Cris's cheek.

"Tell me what you want, Jake."

"Want you to rim me again."

"And?"

Christ, he was going to make Jake say it all out loud. He was used to going with the flow, letting the other guy take control of sex, so long as Jake got off too. Saying the words was embarrassing and insanely arousing. A hot flush crept over his skin. "Want you to put your fingers in me."

Cris's smile went feral. "In you where, exactly?"

Fuck. "In my ass, you jerk."

He chuckled, the sound reverberating right into Jake's own chest. "How many fingers?"

"As many as you want."

"Hmm…anything else?"

Jake pinched the top of Cris's ass, delighting in the way he startled, hips thrusting against Jake. "Then I want you to put your dick in my ass. Do a good enough job making me come, and I might let you fuck me again later."

Cris's wide-eyed surprise melted into laughter. "Oh, I think we both know I'll do a good job making you come."

His ego bounced off of Jake's natural distrust, and Jake snapped off, "Prove it, big boy. How do I know Monday wasn't a fluke? It's not like you'd had much sex leading up to it."

"Prove it, huh?" Cris puffed up, reacting perfectly to Jake's taunts. "Roll over."

"Make me."

Taunting Cris proved to be more fun that Jake expected. Cris's attempts to get him onto his stomach turned into a wrestling match full of pokes, pinches, and a lot of gentle biting. By leaving his clothes on, Cris gave Jake plenty of places to grab and hold on tight, while all Cris had was skin. Jake very proudly ended up pinning the bigger man face-first to the bed, his legs locked around Cris's waist. The position also allowed Jake's cock to rub along the crease of Cris's ass.

"Say uncle," Jake said.

"You're a wily little thing, aren't you?"

Jake thrust hard against Cris's ass, thrilling at being the dominant one for a change. Might even be fun to eventually fuck Cris. He nipped at Cris's earlobe. "I don't hear uncle."

"I don't give up easily." Cris struggled, but Jake held tight. Sometimes it wasn't about muscling through. "You sure you weren't a wrestler?"

"Self-defense class."

"For fun?"

"School bullies. Stopped giving me shit the first time I dropped one."

"Nice."

"Say uncle."

Cris bucked.

Jake bit his earlobe again. "Uncle or you don't get anywhere near my ass tonight."

That threat bled all resistance out of Cris. He went limp beneath him, but Jake didn't loosen his hold. It was an empty threat, yeah, but Cris didn't know that, and Jake wasn't giving him any room to gain the upper hand. He liked being the one with all the power for once.

Cris growled, low and deep, and Jake felt that in his balls. "Uncle. You little shit."

Never had a crude name sounded so much like a heartfelt endearment. Jake laughed, then let go and rolled away, coming up in a kneeling position at the corner of the bed. Cris sat up, his glare softened by the respect shining in his eyes. "I like that you keep me on my toes," Cris said.

"Happy to do it. And as the winner of that little wrestling match, I think you need to strip."

"You do, do you?"

"Definitely."

While Jake meant strip in the "get naked fast" definition, Cris upped the sexy by standing on the bed and, very literally, stripping. With slow gyrations of his hips, Cris lifted his t-shirt, revealing his tight six-pack. The muscles bunched and jumped as he moved, trailing his fingers across his abs, up to his chest. He reached behind his neck to tug the shirt off, then hooked it around one finger. Twirled it like a lasso.

Jake squeezed his dick at the base, because holy damn. Cris was sexy as all hell, and he'd make the entire crowd cream their shorts if he ever danced on the platforms at Big Dick's.

The movements had Cris's shorts slipping dangerously low on his hips. He let them slide down his legs to puddle at his feet. The tip of his straining dick poked out of the top of his boxer-briefs. Jake licked his lips, remembering how amazing that dick felt in his mouth. How much he'd loved sucking Cris.

Cris didn't stop his visual foreplay, either. He danced a slow, sensual circle, hips rolling, fingers skating across tan skin. Teasing at his own nipples. Skimming down the front of his briefs without touching his dick. Jake desperately wished the guy had a stripper pole in his bedroom, because hot fucking damn!

Jake could barely breathe by the time Cris hooked his thumbs in the waistband of his underwear and began to slowly, so slowly, drag them down. Revealing his cock centimeters at a time—until the bastard turned and dropped them, then bent at the waist, flashing a wink of his hole. Jake gasped, mouth falling open at what was both a tease and a silent invitation.

Then Cris drew up again, kicked his clothing off the bed, and turned. His cock seemed to point right at Jake, and Jake didn't think. He crawled across the coverlet and sucked Cris into his mouth. The flavor explosion made him a little dizzy, so he grabbed Cris's ass for balance. And so he could massage those cheeks while he worked Cris's length into his throat.

Cris's gasps and pants made Jake's blood hum with need. Fingers tangled in his hair drove him faster, deeper. He licked Cris's nuts and got more of those sounds, so he figured why the hell not? Jake rubbed a finger across his taint. The grip on Jake's hair tightened. He slid that finger farther back until he found Cris's hole. Hot. Tight. Never stopping his attack on Cris's cock.

"Fuck," Cris said. Clenched his hole. "Put it in."

Jake's heart flipped. He used a little spit because dry wasn't fun, then found that crinkled spot again. Pushed. The tip of his finger popped through, and Cris groaned. Pushed down. Jake took Cris to the back of his throat, nudged his finger in further, and then swallowed. Cris jerked, thrusting deeper. Jake gagged but didn't relent his onslaught. He loved having Cris caught between his mouth and his hand.

"Shit!"

Cris's shout didn't prepare Jake for the release. He struggled to swallow Cris's load, but lost most of it to his chin and chest. But holy damn, the struggle was worth the way Cris collapsed to his knees, red-cheeked, panting, eyes nearly glazed over. Pride washed over Jake in that moment. This time, he'd taken Cris apart.

"Christ, that was good," Cris said. He wiped his hand over Jake's chin. "You look good covered in my come."

Jake chuckled. "Yeah, well, you didn't give me much warning."

"Fuck." His smile vanished. "I'm sorry, I shouldn't have done that. But we're all tested regularly, and it's too late now, but I don't have anything."

"I figured, but thank you." He tweaked Cris's nipple. "It's fine. Same here."

"I also didn't mean to come first."

Jake made a show of licking his lips. "How are you gonna make it up to me?"

Cris narrowed his eyes, and then he pounced.

Chapter Nine

Cris had truly not intended to blast off in Jake's mouth, but Jake didn't seem to care. He actually seemed pretty damn proud of himself, so Cris let it go and made it his mission to turn Jake into a writhing, boneless mess as payment. Jake put up little resistance to Cris flattening him onto the bed, the hard line of Jake's cock riding his lower belly.

Since Jake was still a bit sticky, Cris took his time cleaning him up, licking at Jake's pecs and throat, watching the skin pink up under his tongue. Jake writhed beneath him, panting out soft, content breaths. Cris continued to lick down his chest to his abs, hard from long nights dancing, to a smooth-shaved lower belly. Jake tasted amazing, like sweat and musk and a long, fun day spent in the sunshine.

He nibbled around the root of Jake's cock, spurred on by the restless way Jake's thighs quivered and his fingers plucked at Cris's shoulders, urging without demanding. Needing release and trusting Cris to get him there. That same trust and need shined in Jake's eyes, keeping Cris half-hard while he played.

Accidentally coming during a porn shoot wasn't unusual, and over the years Cris had developed a pretty good refraction time— which was great for Jake, because he wasn't getting out of Cris's bed until Cris got into him.

Speaking of getting into him—he rose up to flip Jake onto his stomach. The bed bounced lightly, and Jake snorted. Took a moment to adjust himself. Cris settled between Jake's spread legs, then gripped his cheeks. Squeezed and rolled the muscles, because hot damn, he loved Jake's perfectly rounded backside. That bubble butt got him tips on stage, and it got Cris super hot playing with it.

His ass would look so good pinked up a bit.

Jake hadn't reacted much to Cris's earlier comment about spanking, so he left it alone for now. He still didn't really know Jake's story, and a few hard swats could turn him on as much it could send him running from the bed in terror.

He pulled Jake's cheeks apart, revealing the crinkled knot he'd been waiting to feast on again for almost a week. To fuck over and over.

Mine.

The first lick from his taint to the top of his ass exploded Jake's unique taste all over Cris's senses. Jake's gasp only fueled Cris's arousal and his attack. He worked Jake loose with his fingers and tongue, stroking, stabbing, rubbing at his entrance. Working him up until Jake was trying to rut against the bed, so Cris used his forearms to keep Jake still. Didn't stop Jake from struggling, though, and that only heated Cris's desire more. Knowing that Jake could give in when necessary, but that he was nobody's pushover, not even when he was so drunk on pleasure that couldn't stop keening. Pleading.

"Fuck me, fuck!" Jake said.

Cris pressed one last, firm kiss to his entrance, then snagged the lube. Drizzled it directly onto Jake's hole, which got him a sharp squeak from the chill. He didn't give the lube time to escape. He pressed two fingers into Jake with little resistance. Jake's groan rolled down his spine.

So good.

Cris fucked him with those two fingers while his cock got back into the game, gentle at first, and then harder, his knuckles slapping against the firm flesh of Jake's taut ass.

"Christ, I love this," Cris said. "Watching you writhe around on my fingers."

"Love this, too. More."

He pulled his fingers free, added more lube, then carefully pressed three inside. Jake reached around to pull his own cheeks apart, giving Cris more access, and Cris nearly combusted at the sight. He worked his fingers in to the second knuckle, watching Jake carefully for signs of distress or discomfort. Jake reacted to his hesitation by humping his hand, urging Cris deeper.

"Oh fuck, shit," Jake said. "Oh."

Cris let Jake do this. Let Jake push down until there was nothing left to take. Pull up and fuck back down. Cris held his hand steady, heart hammering, blood rushing in his ears, while Jake fucked himself on those three fingers. So open. So wanton. So fucking gorgeous with part of Cris inside of him.

"Tell me what you need, Jake. Another finger? My dick?"

Jake whined, and it made Cris even gladder that they'd had the conversation about playing earlier. Caught up in the heat of the moment and the sensations battering his body, Jake didn't seem like he knew what he wanted, which prompted Cris to back off. He started to pull out; Jake grabbed his wrist tight.

"Another," Jake said.

"Are you sure?"

"Yes." Jake angled his head to look Cris in the eye. Wild but determined. "Four."

Christ, he's going to kill me.

More lube and a small, silent pep talk later, Cris nudged his pinkie in with his other three fingers. Millimeters at a time, he pushed, dividing his attention equally between his task and Jake's profile. Determined to stop the moment he saw a flinch or frown.

"God, it's so intense," Jake gasped. "So good."

"The instant it's not good anymore—"

"Promise."

Trusting Jake to be honest about his limits, Cris pressed deeper, mesmerized by the stretch of tender flesh around his fingers, closing in on the second knuckle. Curious, he leaned in and licked at Jake's stretched rim. Jake's response was less than a scream, but way more than a gasp, so Cris did it again. And again, until Jake's entire body went tight, bucked. The force of his orgasm pushed Cris back out of his body. Jake shoved a hand beneath himself, stroking his dick to wring out the last of his release.

Cris gently pushed him onto his back so he could see Jake's blissed-out face. The way his body shook with faint aftershocks. The smears of come on his belly and cock and balls.

Jake's head rolled lazily toward him. "You killed me."

Pride puffed Cris's chest. "I'll take that as the highest compliment ever."

"That was...wow."

"You were wow. That was amazing." Cris stretched out next to Jake, then tucked the boneless man against him. Jake nestled in, exactly as he'd done the first time, fitting in Cris's arms as though made to be there.

Fingers skated down Cris's chest to tease his erection. "That was quick for an old man."

Cris laughed, then pinched Jake's ass just to feel him squirm. "Don't make me spank you."

"Hmm." Jake stroked him harder, which made bantering difficult. "Old man, old man, old man, old—"

He silenced Jake with a firm kiss. "Shut up. I'm not that much older than you." He hoped.

"So how old are you? Thirty-five?"

"Brat. Twenty-eight. My birthday is in a few weeks, though."

"Ooh, almost thirty." He nipped Cris's chin. "I'm twenty-three."

Cris laughed. "Damn, I've robbed the cradle."

"No, I think the other night it was grandpa trying to rob the cradle."

The off-hand comment about Chet caught Cris by surprise. He angled up so he could look Jake in the eyes. "Chet and I aren't together. I'm seeing you."

"I know, sorry." He didn't look sorry, or totally convinced.

Confused and a little annoyed, Cris sat up completely, then tugged at Jake until he did the same. They were both naked and streaked with Jake's come, but Cris needed this to be settled before anything else happened. "Tell me what you're thinking, Jake, right now."

Jake shrugged one shoulder. "You two *were* into each other that night, Cris, I'm not blind or stupid. And you were humping each other right in front of me."

"Were you jealous? Is that why you finally apologized for hiding my wallet?"

"Yes, okay? I was jealous. I mean, you two looked so hot together, the chemistry was obvious to anyone who saw you, and this guy is older so he's probably got, like, a great job. A stable life. I'm a homeless go-go boy whose entire life fits into a duffel bag." The shameless, wanton Jake from five minutes ago was gone, replaced by a frowny, unhappy Jake that Cris didn't like. "Why do you want me and not him?"

I want you both but that's impossible.

"Look, it's complicated with Chet," Cris said. "I've known him for a long time, and he's my boss. A boss who never mixes business with pleasure."

"Your boss?" Jake blinked hard several times. "Your porn boss?"

"Yes." Time to lob a couple of truth bombs and deal with the fallout. "I first got hired by Chet about eight years ago, and there was an attraction between us from the start. But Mean Green was a start up, and I needed the job, so neither one of us ever acted on our feelings. Time went by. When I took a two-year break from filming, I cut off everyone except Taro. It's only been this last year that those feelings have come up again, but I still work for Chet, so it can't happen."

"You can't date your boss, so you're dating me." Jake's mouth flattened. "So what am I? The consolation prize?"

"No." Fuck, all that came out wrong. He had to salvage this before Jake wrote him off as the biggest douchebag ever. "None of the feelings Chet and I have for each other even came up until after you and I slept together. He's been lonely and depressed for months, and Thursday was my attempt to take him out and cheer him up. Neither one of us expected to feel the way we did, and I had no reason to think you still wanted me."

"So being your second choice is my fault." Instead of angry, Jake wilted into something like resignation. "Of course, it's my fault. I'm the stupid jackass who hid your wallet and pushed you away. Right at the guy you've wanted for almost a decade."

"Jake—"

"No, it's fine. I'm a big boy, I can own this." Jake slid off the bed and crossed his arms, defensive but so fucking vulnerable it hurt. "Let me ask you something, though, and be honest with me."

Cris's heart ached. "Okay."

"If you didn't work for Chet and were free to be with him, which one of us would you really be with right now?"

Desperation to make this better had the word "you" bubbling up in Cris's throat, but the word couldn't get past his lips. Because he wasn't one hundred percent sure it was the truth, and he didn't want to lie to Jake.

His hesitation was enough. Jake strode to the door.

"Jake, wait."

"I need a shower," Jake snapped over his shoulder. "Please, wait your turn."

Fuck, fuck, fuck, fuck, fuck.

The bathroom door slammed.

Cris got up and paced his room, frustrated both by his own inability to articulate the complicated situation of his love life, and by Jake's reaction. Fleeing the conversation instead of picking it apart, facing their feelings. Cris's own feelings were as complicated as a Rubix cube, and he had no idea how to get everything sorted. Lying about those feelings might have prevented Jake from storming out today, but what about down the road? What if it had come up a month later? A year?

He wanted to call Taro for advice, but Taro always visited his parents on Saturday. He wanted to call Chet for advice, too, but that was an epically bad idea for obvious reasons. Cris was friendly with some of the other models, enough so that they got together socially once in a while, but there wasn't anyone he trusted enough to unload this on.

Gabriel. He knows the details and he seemed honest enough.

No way was he calling anyone while Jake was still in his apartment. Cris used his discarded shirt to clean himself up a bit, then slipped into a pair of workout shorts. He rescued Jake's clothes and took them to the bathroom door. Knocked.

"Brought your clothes," he said.

No response. He went into a cloud of steam long enough to leave the clothes on the sink, then backed out, giving Jake the space he'd asked for when all he wanted to do was climb into the tub and try to make this better. To find a way to show Jake he wasn't Cris's second choice. He'd have been his first choice if Jake hadn't pulled that stupid fucking wallet stunt on Monday. Sure, Jake had done it out of fear but it *had* begun the rollercoaster week that Cris was desperately trying to ride out. Cris was smack in the middle of all this fuckery. His feelings were involved, too, damn it.

Irritated with the entire convoluted situation, Cris got a bottle of water from the fridge and gulped down half of it in one go. The water in the bathroom shut off. There was no real separation between the kitchen and living room, so Cris hung out near the sofa, keeping a respectable distance between himself and the bathroom.

The door swung open, but Jake didn't emerge right away. When he did, it was a few tentative steps forward that stopped the instant he spotted Cris. Skin still pink from the shower, Jake flushed a darker red from his forehead to his neck.

"I'm sorry," Cris said. "I'm sorry that I can't seem to say the right thing here, and I hate that you're upset with me."

"I'm not upset with you." Jake shoved his hands into his pockets. "I'm pissed at myself. We were having such a great day, and I fucked it up by bringing Chet into the conversation."

"It would have come up at some point. Maybe sooner was better than later."

"So you can end things with me before they get too serious?"

"No." Cris took two steps forward, stopping when Jake took a step backward. "I don't want to end this. I can't change that I have feelings for Chet, but I have feelings for you too, Jake. That's what this whole day has been about. You and me. Seeing how we fit. And yes, the sex was amazing again, but we had fun at the island. I like spending time with you."

"Me too. And as much as I'd hoped to stay the whole night this time, I need to go."

Cris's heart dropped to his feet. "What?"

"I need space to think."

"You mean you need space to convince yourself that it'll be easier to find a way to turn me down, keep me at a distance, because you're too scared of being hurt to try."

Jake seemed to shrink a bit more, but he didn't deny anything. And as much as Cris wanted to hug him until he saw reason, he couldn't keep Jake trapped if he didn't want to stay.

"I get that this is confusing for you," Cris said. "It's confusing as hell for me, too. And I can't promise you that we'll work out, or that we're destined to be an old married couple with five dogs, but I do think there's potential here, so this is what I can promise you. I promise I'm not going to run off to be with Chet, in order to give you a convenient excuse."

Surprise flashed across Jake's face.

"I know your type, Jake. You rabbit, instead of toughing it out, but sooner or later you have to learn to trust. You have to learn to *stay*. Or you'll be me. A guy who's pushing thirty and who's never maintained a relationship longer than six months. A guy who still isn't sure what he wants in life, but who knows he wants to share his life with someone else."

Jake stared at him a few seconds before asking, "What were you running from that kept you from trusting?"

"Sorry, man." Cris shook his head. "That's a story I might tell a boyfriend, but not a guy I fucked twice. But so we're both clear? I'm not walking away from a potentially really good us. I'm here for it. But I can't force you to stay if what you actually want to do is run. I want a willing partner, not an emotional hostage."

"I'm not running, but I can't think with you standing there. I need space."

Cris didn't agree that Jake needed space, but it wasn't his call to make. And he was too tired to keep arguing in circles. As much as he wanted to drag Jake back into his bed and remind him of why staying was a very, very good idea...no. Jake had pushed him away once, and then came back because of his feelings. Cris had to trust that if Jake really needed space to think, he'd come back of his own free will.

"Then go," Cris said softly. "I'm here for us. Call me when you make a decision about where you want to be."

"I'm sorry, Cris."

Responding would hurt too much, so Cris simply nodded. Jake stayed put for another few beats, then collected his shoes. Checked for his phone and wallet. And then he left.

Cris stared at his front door, too numb to react. Sure, Jake could call him in an hour and say he was all in to try. Jake could also never speak to him again and let his silence be the answer. For now, Cris would respect Jake's wishes and give him time.

No matter how much it hurt to do so.

Chapter Ten

"Um, Uncle Charles?"

Dell's uncertain voice drew Charles's attention away from the scene he was reviewing for the umpteenth time. Charles plucked his earbuds out, not bothering to pause the scene. He edited each one himself so he knew them all frame-by-frame. He was searching for information among his active models, reviewing on-screen chemistry, and planning new shoots. He had a business to run, after all, and moping wasn't helping the young men who counted on his company's paychecks.

"Yes, son, what is it?" Charles asked. He was working at his office desk, and it wasn't like Dell to hover at the door. "Come in, please."

"I was going through the Contact Us form responses and there's something you should see." Dell held out a sheet of printer paper.

He and Dell took turns checking the Mean Green website's contact email account. Usually, they received simple things, such as subscription questions or comments about the videos/models. Sometimes they got nasty messages from bigoted trolls who had nothing better to do.

Only on the rare occasion did they receive anything that would make Dell look this uncertain. Last year, the account had received a frantic message from Isaac Gregory after being unable to reach his boyfriend, former model Jon Buchanan, for several days after the death of Jon's best friend and mentor. Dell had brought him a printed sheet of paper in almost the exact same manner that day.

Charles took the printout and read the brief message: *This is Jake Bowden. We need to talk about Cris Sable. He told me who you are, and I need know if I have a chance with Cris.* Followed by a telephone number.

"Hell," Charles said after reading the note twice.

"I guess things are more complicated with Cristian than I thought?" Dell said.

"Dramatically so. There's a third boy involved who's also snared Cristian's attention. They were supposed to have gone on a date today." He glanced at the clock. A few minutes after five. "Apparently things ended early and this Jake fellow requires some manner of explanation."

"Are you going to call him?"

Charles wanted to stay far away from Cristian's current love life, but Jake was taking a huge leap in contacting Charles directly—most likely without Cristian's knowledge or consent. But if Jake wanted answers from Charles—answers he clearly hadn't gotten from Cristian—then he would entertain the boy's curiosity.

"I believe I am going to call," Charles said. "He made an effort. I can return the courtesy and hear him out."

"Is that really a good idea?"

"I'll tell you afterward." He winked at Dell. "Thank you for bringing this to my attention."

"Of course. Good luck." Dell shut the office door when he left.

Charles gazed around the familiar office space, taking comfort in being surrounded by his accomplishments. A few awards for the company, a framed spread from a digital magazine's feature on Mean Green Boys. DVD releases on one bookshelf. A lot of the furniture was new, purchased two years ago, after he'd gotten a redecorating bug in his bonnet. But not his desk.

His old, walnut desk had been with him for twenty-eight years, all the way from Los Angeles and his first vice-president position. While the office chairs and computers had changed, the desk remained a constant.

Even with the one goddamn drawer at the bottom that continued to stick no matter how much he oiled it.

He wasn't nervous about calling Jake. Not exactly. After thirty years building his own business empire, few people intimidated him, especially over the phone. But this was about Cristian, and Cristian was a sensitive topic, as well as a very personal one. Whatever young Jake had to ask, Charles would do his best to provide information.

The number rang three times before the line picked up with a breathy voice saying, "This is Jake."

"Hello, Jake. This is Chet Green."

"Dude, that was fast. I only sent the email, like, thirty minutes ago."

Charles smiled at his desk blotter. "Your timing happened to coincide with an employee checking that account. Your note mentioned a mutual friend of ours."

Jake didn't respond right away.

"Cristian told me you two had a date today," Charles said, hoping to prompt the young man into speaking his mind. "Can I assume my name came up in conversation?"

"Yeah. I actually brought you up."

"I see. What prompted this?"

"Uh, we were joking around about our age difference, which isn't really that big, but I said something about how much older you were, and it all kind of went from there."

Charles did not need anyone reminding him of his age. And Jake didn't add any further comment, which was incredibly frustrating, considering Jake had initiated contact. "I have an idea. You seem to have things you need to say to me, and I am happy to speak with you in order to assuage any fears you may have over my friendship with Cristian. Why don't you come over tomorrow for Sunday brunch?"

Jake made a soft, squeaking noise. "Brunch?"

"Yes, my nephew Dell and I usually cook up a nice brunch on Sundays. We can share a meal, and then you and I can talk at length. How does that sound?"

"You want me to come to your house?"

Charles sighed at Jake's open suspicion. "I promise you that while I may be a pornographer, I am not a sleazy old man who comes on to his guests. And my nephew will be here the entire time."

"Okay, fine."

"Excellent." He gave Jake the address. "White house with blue trim. You'll see a black Explorer in the driveway. Eleven o'clock sharp."

"I'll be there. Uh, thank you?"

"You're welcome. See you in the morning, Jake." Charles hung up, then spent a moment staring at his phone.

After spending most of his Saturday morning cleaning, the house was ready to accept visitors. The only minor fudge in his invitation to Jake was the brunch every Sunday. Charles had severely slacked on that in the last few weeks, mostly due to his overwhelming depression, and he knew for a fact the pantry held few reasonable brunch items.

He found Dell working on his tablet in the den. "I'm going grocery shopping," Charles said. "We're going to have a guest for brunch tomorrow."

Dell blinked at him. "We are?"

"Yes. Is there anything you'd like from the store?"

"Why don't I go with you?" Dell put the tablet down, then stood. "Jake's coming over?"

"He is."

"Is that a good idea?"

Charles sighed. "That, my boy, remains to be seen."

Jake hated shelling out for a Uber to get to Camp Hill, but no way was he asking for a ride from Richard or Bear. And borrowing a car? No fucking way. He'd made some great tips last night, so it wouldn't break him or his small stash of savings. Grumpiness over the paid car ride kept him from stewing in his anxiety over this morning's brunch. He was walking into the house of a stranger, to eat with two strangers, all so he could figure out his riotous thoughts about Cris and Chet and himself.

This was either going to be a really great conversation or a total disaster.

The driver found the house, white with blue trim, exactly as Chet described. Jake fiddled with his wallet longer than necessary, taking his time to pay. He took the brief walk to the front steps as slowly as possible. His stomach was tied up in knots, his palms sweaty, and he probably had pit stains already. Running down the street seemed like a better alternative to pushing the doorbell. He could run and avoid everything: Chet, Cris, his own mixed feelings and personal baggage. Go back to a week ago when he didn't know either of them.

A week ago when I still had an apartment and a small sense of balance.

Right now, his entire life was off-kilter and it was driving him nuts.

He pressed the bell. It gonged faintly inside the house. A lock snapped, and then the ornate wood door swung inward. A guy his age with light brown hair smiled shyly at Jake.

"You must be Jake," he said. "I'm Dell Greenwood, Char—er, Chet's nephew."

Chet isn't his real name. Huh. Wonder if Cris knows what it is.

"Yeah, Jake Bowden." He shook the hand Dell offered, a little surprised by the strong grip.

"Nice to meet you. Please, come inside. Chet would have answered the door, but he had raw egg all over his hands."

Jake stepped into a nice entry with simple décor. The house was less pretentious than he expected, considering the owner probably made good money off his porn. He followed Dell down a short hall to a large eat-in kitchen and attached den. More simple fixtures and furniture. Chet was standing at a wide kitchen island chopping vegetables, and now that they were up close, Jake took a second to cruise the guy.

Definitely old, but not so old that Jake couldn't appreciate the man's hot factor. Slim, tight linen trousers and a white button-down showcasing the entire package nicely. His dark hair had just enough gray to be noticeable, but not overwhelming. Very few actual wrinkles, too. For someone over forty, he was…kind of appealing.

"Good morning," Chet said. His bright smile made Jake's belly flip in an unexpected way. The grin lit up Chet's eyes and made him look ten years younger. And he seemed genuinely happy to see Jake. Chet's gaze lingered on him another beat before he said, "I hope you like omelets."

"Sure." Jake usually ate his eggs scrambled, but he was game for something fancier.

Chet wiped his hands on a towel, then circled the island. "It's a pleasure to meet you, Jake."

"Likewise." He shook Chet's hand, surprised that he meant it. There was something about Chet that instantly put him at ease. "I, uh, like your house."

"Thank you. Can I offer you something to drink? We have coffee, tea, orange juice and milk. I'd offer a Bloody Mary, but I'm not sure you're legal."

Jake laughed. "I am, I promise. I'm twenty-three."

"So young and so much potential left in you yet. Just like Dell over there. So, to drink?"

He nearly asked for a Bloody Mary to help steady his nerves. "Orange juice is fine, thank you."

Chet poured him a glass of juice, while Dell pulled a glass baking dish out of the oven and transferred it to a cooling rack. They moved around the kitchen so easily, a practiced manner that made Jake think of his mom. Grief punched him in the gut, and he nearly fumbled the glass Chet gave him.

"Are you all right?" Chet asked.

"Yeah, sorry." Jake tried to smile. "I got lost in my own head for a second."

"It happens to all of us. Now, what would like in your omelet?" He waved his hand at a lineup of small dishes, each one filled with different vegetables.

Jake had no idea what would taste good with eggs. "Um, surprise me?"

"That I can do. Please, have a seat."

Dell moved the cooling rack and pan to the center of the rectangular kitchen table. Three places had been set. Jake chose the seat against the wall, so he could face the rest of the room.

"What's that?" he asked, pointing at the browned thing in the glass dish.

"It's a hash brown bake," Dell replied. "It has potatoes, bacon, chives, and lots of cheese. You can eat all of that stuff, right? I didn't even think about food allergies."

"It's all good. I actually kind of love cheese and salty, bad-for-you food."

Dell chuckled. "So does my uncle."

"I heard that," Chet said from the stove. Something was sizzling away in a pan.

"Well, good, because it's true." Dell stuck a serving spoon into the baked hash. "Meanwhile, I'm lactose intolerant."

Jake tilted his head. "Then why'd you make something full of cheese?"

"Because Uncle Chet loves it. I arranged it so there's a corner with no cheese for me."

The thoughtfulness of something as simple as a breakfast bake made Jake ache for that sort of connection. A relationship full of give and take with someone who knew him inside and out. And Jake didn't know what to say that didn't sound…well, cheesy, so he left it alone.

Dell put a healthy scoop of the bake onto Jake's plate, then a smaller portion from another corner into his own. A moment later, Chet swooped in and slid a half-moon of eggs and various other things onto Jake's plate next to the cheesy potatoes. His proximity made Jake's skin prickle in an unexpected way.

Jake lifted one corner of the omelet with his fork, curious about the red, green, and bits of orange cheese.

"Uncle Chet makes fantastic omelets," Dell said as he squeezed ketchup over his hash browns.

"And please, eat while it's hot," Chet said, already back at the stove cooking another.

Jake did, surprised by how much he loved the mixture of tomatoes, spinach and cheddar with the fluffy eggs. The hash brown thing was good, too. Nice and salty, with lots of bacon. He ate slowly, taking careful bites so he didn't finish before Chet even started. Chet delivered a similar omelet to Dell, but it seemed stuffed with more vegetables than Jake's. When Chet finally sat down with his own food, Jake was more than halfway finished eating.

"So, do you live in the city, Jake?" Chet asked.

"I did." He had no reason to give Chet personal details, but he did anyway. "Um, I'm kind of between places right now. Staying with friends until I can find someone looking for a roommate."

Chet nodded as he cut into his eggs. "Rent is difficult to make on a single salary these days, especially for people your age."

That was definitely part of his problem, but Chet didn't need details on what a loser Jake really was. "Plus not a lot of straight guys are gonna be comfortable living with a gay go-go boy. I lucked out with my last roommate."

"And that situation has recently ended?"

"Yeah." Chet didn't seem to be putting him on at all. He really didn't know who Jake was. "You actually knew my roommate. Jon Buchanan."

Chet froze with a forkful of hash browns halfway to his mouth, his slim eyebrows arching. "Really? What a small world we live in. Jon has recently moved on from the company, but I hear he's doing very well for himself."

"Yeah, sure. His perfect relationship means I no longer have a place to live." Jake hadn't meant for that to come out as grumpy as it did. He hadn't come over to grouse about his own life. He wanted to talk about Cris.

"Isn't Benny looking for a roommate?" Dell asked.

"He is," Chet replied. He kept staring at Jake in a way that made Jake squirm. His gaze seemed to take Jake in, all of him, and no fucking way had Chet just cruised him! "Benny recently broke up with his girlfriend, and he's been having trouble covering the rent since she moved out."

"Girlfriend?" Jake didn't do straight roommates. No way. Too dangerous. Even if the guy was gay-friendly, there was no guarantee his friends were.

"Young Benny has recently accepted that he's bisexual. He's a very energetic young man, and also quite loyal. Someone you can trust." Chet slammed the hammer down on Jake's biggest issue with people: trust.

"Would Cris vouch for him?" Jake asked.

"He would, yes." Chet smiled, warm and kind, and Jake's stomach did that weird flip again. "Cristian's opinion is important to you, isn't it?"

"I guess so." Jake poked at the remnants of his omelet. "It's weird to think that a week ago, I only knew him as a porn star, and now we're...something." This was the reason he'd come here, so why was he having so much trouble finding the words?

"Uncle Chet, do you mind if I finish eating in my room?" Dell asked.

"Of course not," Chet replied. Jake didn't miss the grateful look that passed between them. Dell seemed like a nice guy, but he wasn't part of this conversation.

After Dell left the table, Jake poked at his food a few times before asking, "Have you talked to Cris this weekend?"

"We haven't spoken since Friday afternoon."

"Is that when you dumped him?"

Chet's fork scraped across his plate. He held Jake's gaze, his pale eyes kind of sad. "Cristian and I were never together, so it's unfair to phrase it as dumping him. I merely removed myself from the situation so that he could pursue you with a clear conscience. For him and for myself."

Jake tried to gather his thoughts together. Thoughts that were a swirling tempest in his head, taunting him to find one and focus on it. "Cris said you guys were attracted to each other from the day you met."

"That's true. Neither one of us admitted it or acted on those feelings until this past week."

"Acted on them?" Shit, he hated when his voice squeaked. He sounded like a jealous tool.

"The dancing, Jake. Cristian and I have never been intimate."

Jake grunted. "You've filmed him having sex. That seems pretty fucking intimate."

"It's also business. I have never touched Cristian in a sexual manner. I would never do that to one of my employees."

Hearing that from Cris was one thing. Hearing it directly from Chet, who'd pinned him with a very serious look, drove the point home. Jake believed him.

"Tell me what's really troubling you about my relationship with Cristian," Chet said. "We're friends, yes, and he helped me through a very tough time this past year. We're also employer and employee, and if he chooses to return to the studio, I will be filming him as per usual. But we are not in a romantic relationship. He's dating you, not me."

"You wanted him to pick you, though, right?"

Chet released a long, slow breath. "I want Cristian to pick whoever he truly believes will make him happy."

Jake crossed his arms and glared. "Except by removing yourself as a choice, didn't you kind of make that decision for him? You pushed him at me, knowing maybe he wanted you more."

"I…" Chet frowned, his attention dropping to the table.

Scored one, you bastard.

"You didn't let Cris choose to quit porn and be with you," Jake snapped. "You made me the default choice, and that hurts. And it makes it hard for me to trust that Cris really wants me." In that moment, all of Jakes uncertainty over his relationship with Cris came crashing into full-color focus. It was exactly why he'd needed distance to think, because he hadn't been sure what was holding him back.

Until now.

Chet closed his eyes and pinched the bridge of his nose. When he opened his eyes again, they were glimmering. Damp. "I owe you an apology, then," he said. "When I made my decision on Friday, I didn't factor in how you might react to it, or how it might affect you. I know it doesn't change what's happened, but I'm genuinely sorry."

Jake blinked, stunned by the apology. "Thanks." He admired Chet for being so honest and for owning the hurt he'd caused. He also kind of hated him for how selfless he was. Every time he said Cris's name, Chet's feelings were clear, coating every letter. And he'd given Cris up because he believed Jake was the better choice. Chet had set someone he clearly loved free to pursue another man.

I don't think I could ever do that. Chet is definitely the better man here.

Except… "I asked Cris a version of this question yesterday," Jake said, his stomach already in knots over what he suspected Chet's answer would be. "But let me ask you this: if I hadn't met

Cris first, if I didn't know him at all, would you have turned him down on Friday?"

"I don't know." Chet seemed sincere, and he scored even more points by answering, instead of avoiding the question. "In my life, I've learned not to spend too much time agonizing over the past. I make a choice and I live with it. Hypothetical situations solve nothing. What's done is done."

"Seriously? So you're, what? Sixty, and you have zero regrets?"

Chet laughed without humor. "Forty-eight, and I do have regrets. I simply don't dwell on them. I no longer allow my regrets or mistakes to control my actions or my emotions."

"Must be nice."

"You're far, far away from where I am now, Jake. You're at exactly the right age to make mistakes and still be able to learn from them. You have so much living left to do."

Jake snorted. "Jesus, dude, you sound like you're giving your retirement speech."

"I like to think of it as my motivational speech. It goes over well with most of my models."

"Yeah, well, I'm not a model."

"You could be." Chet's eyes widened. "Forgive me, that was rude."

Jake shrugged, surprised by the statement—except the guy had cruised him, hadn't he? "I'll take it as a compliment, but I've got enough on my plate right now."

"I can't imagine Cristian would see it as a compliment. I would never presume to interfere. But you're very handsome, and you have an energy around you that is quite infectious. I can see why he's so drawn to you."

"I can see why he's drawn to you, too." Shit, he hadn't meant to say that out loud.

Chet shook his head, then pushed his plate away. "What a unique pair we are. Each trying to convince ourself that Cristian is better off with the other man, while still hoping he chooses us."

"I'm a flighty, impulsive, homeless go-go dancer with no higher education and no real ambition. You're a rich, successful businessman with a house and a car, and I honestly don't see why he'd rather have me." Jake sank into his chair. Now that he'd met Chet and seen what Cris had turned down, he was more confused than ever.

"You also seem to be a very selfless, compassionate soul," Chet said. "Cristian is a gorgeous man, on that we can both agree. He built his own business from the ground up. He loves what he does and he's loyal. He's also caught between two different desires, and a lesser man would take him and run with no second thoughts."

He was giving Jake too much credit. "A stronger man wouldn't be terrified to accept that Cris's feelings are genuine. A stronger man wouldn't be constantly waiting for the people in his life to leave or disappoint him. I'm trying to protect myself, not Cris."

"Consciously, perhaps, but the subconscious is a tricky thing. You've been hurt in the past by people you trusted, that much is quite clear. And I'm not asking you to tell your tale, but perhaps hear me out for a few minutes?"

Jake nodded. Chet has an alluring voice, the kind he'd gladly listen to read the phone book for hours. And he seemed full of insight and advice, so why not?

"I grew up in the south, in a very conservative, very Catholic household," Chet said. "The middle son, with two older and two younger siblings. We five were taught that sex before marriage was a sin, and that homosexuals would burn in hell. I realized during puberty that I was attracted to other boys, but I was so scared of going to hell that I convinced myself I was wrong. During my junior year of high school, I briefly dated a very nice girl. We went to a spring dance together and afterward, we parked in her father's car, drank cheap wine, and got drunk enough to have sex."

Jake had kind of guess where the girl date was going, and he suppressed a shudder. His parents had accepted him when he came out, and he couldn't imagine having sex with a chick, drunk or not.

"Needless to say, we didn't use protection," Chet continued. "When she became pregnant, both of our families insisted we get married. I refused. I knew in my heart that I didn't love her and I never would. I told my parents I was a homosexual, that I didn't want to marry a woman. It wasn't the first time my father raised his belt to me, but it was the last. When I refused to repent, I was put on a bus to Philadelphia with fifty dollars in cash and told not to return until I'd gotten right with the Lord."

"Jesus Christ," Jake said. "Wait, you've got a kid?"

"No, I don't." Grief pinched the corners of Chet's eyes. "She miscarried a few weeks after I was sent away. I found out years later, after I'd begun to establish myself in California. I went home to visit, but none of my accomplishments were enough. Not my money, my million-dollar home, or my businesses. I was still gay and unwelcome in their homes. I did maintain contact with my youngest brother, so I knew when a new niece or nephew was born. I knew when my father had his first heart attack, and when my sister-in-law developed cervical cancer.

"The point of this story, Jake, is that I can empathize with the cage you've locked around your trust. It took me many years to open my own heart, and when I did, my trust was broken all over again. It's why I've been a single man ever since. Dell coming to live with me last year was both a blessing and a damning reminder of how much loss can hurt."

"How's that?"

Chet glanced at the ceiling. "Without revealing too much of my nephew's private history, he had a medical emergency that required a kidney transplant this past spring."

Jake's skin prickled.

Cris just donated a kidney. No fucking way.

"Dell received an anonymous donor kidney back in March, but his health was quite precarious in the months leading up to it. I don't know what I would have done if I'd lost him."

"I didn't do it for accolades or attention, okay? I saved a life and I helped a friend."

Cris gave Dell an anonymous kidney to save his life, because he loved Chet that much and didn't want to see Chet devastated by Dell's death. Cris was the best person Jake had ever met, and Jake was a stupid little shit who didn't deserve him.

Fuck my life.

The change in Jake's demeanor was so sudden that Charles momentarily forgot what he'd just said. Jake wilted in his chair, clearly unhappy, and Charles wasn't certain why. Yes, Dell had nearly died, but he was thriving now, thanks to some generous soul. Jake seemed to be taking the whole thing personally, which was quite strange.

"Dell is doing very well now," Charles said, hoping to lift Jake's spirits. He liked the young man more than he'd expected to, with his blunt nature and shining inner strength. A strength Jake probably didn't see in himself, but Charles had interacted with enough young men over his lifetime to see the truly strong ones. And Jake was beautiful in his own way, with a lean dancer's body and strikingly thick eyelashes. Flawless skin and dark hair. So very close to Charles's own type, and so very, very forbidden.

"He, uh, seems to be doing great," Jake said. "Dell's lucky to have you."

"I can make an educated guess that you don't have a strong support system in your life right now."

"I don't know. The people I work with at Big Dick's are pretty cool. I'd have been sleeping on the street, probably, if my boss hadn't insisted I use his guest room."

"What about your parents? Other family?"

Jake's expression soured. "No. None who gives a shit about me."

"I'm sorry." Charles had heard the story a thousand times over, but it never stopped tearing at his heart. "May I ask what happened?"

"Probably not what you think." Jake's attention skipped all around the room, focusing on anything except Charles. "My parents were actually pretty great for most of my life. Didn't make a fuss when I came out to them at fifteen. I was bullied some at school, but nothing I couldn't handle. Everything was good, until my senior year. My dad decided he didn't want the burden of a wife and kid anymore, so he filed for divorce to be with his younger, hot assistant."

Charles's heart ached for misery in Jake's voice. He wanted to comfort the young man, but wasn't certain his touch would be well received, so he stayed still.

"It was bad for a few months," Jake continued. "I was eighteen so Mom couldn't get any child support. She'd been a stay-at-home mom my whole life, so she had to start working again. The job offer in Harrisburg was a shock and a blessing. We moved, made a fresh start. I even started college. Got through two years with good grades. We were happy."

Jake's eyes filled, and it took everything in Charles to remain seated when all he wanted to do was hug Jake. "A few days before junior year classes started, Mom collapsed at work from a massive heart attack. She was forty-two when she died. She didn't have a life insurance policy, and her savings had been wiped out in the divorce. We hadn't closed on the condo she wanted to buy, so there wasn't anything left. I was broke and alone."

"I'm so sorry, Jake. Truly."

He swiped at his eyes. "My father sent a condolence card, but that was it. Not that I'd have accepted any help from him, even if he'd offered. I got multiple part-time jobs, but even working sometimes around the clock, I couldn't afford to keep the apartment my mom had leased. I couch surfed for a while, with help from college acquaintances, until a lucky encounter with Jon. He needed a roommate, and I needed a home."

Something inside of Charles relaxed a bit as Jake concluded this part of his narrative. He'd known too many men in the same situation who'd lost parts of themselves because of homelessness. Men who'd turned to prostitution and drug dealing in order to make ends meet. Jake had been incredibly lucky.

"I'm grateful you were able to land on your feet," Charles said. "Not everyone does."

"I know. I was also lucky to get the job dancing at Big Dick's, considering I was only twenty. Richard made all the underage dancers wear green bracelets so everyone, especially the bartenders, would know not to serve us."

"This boss of yours sounds like a wonderful man who takes care of his employees."

"He's pretty cool." Jake sipped his orange juice, less visibly upset than a few minutes ago.

Charles still wanted to hug him, though, if only to show he cared. And he did care, despite having only known Jake for half an hour. Charles was drawn to the man in an unexpected way that he needed to tuck away and ignore. This was about Jake and Cristian, and it was becoming more and more obvious why Cristian liked Jake. They both had darkness in their pasts and a tendency to close themselves off from genuine affection. As did Charles.

We're all three peas in a pod, aren't we?

Three peas in a pod meant only for two, and that was exactly the reason for Jake's visit today. "So has our conversation made your decision any more clear?" Charles asked. "Or have I only muddied the waters further?"

"No, I think everything is pretty clear right now." Jake's voice was firm, but his expression seemed less certain.

Charles wasn't sure he believed him. "Then why don't you let me get you in touch with Benny about that room to rent? You'll help complete my good deed quota for the week."

"Yeah, sure. At this point, what have I got to lose?"

Much less than Charles had to lose at this point, but that was all right. Over the weekend, he'd come to terms with the idea that he might never find someone to grow old with. Bachelorhood was his future, and that was all right, as long as helping young men be happy and succeed was his legacy.

He could live with that.

Chapter Eleven

By the time Cris's Tuesday dinner with Taro rolled around, he was so distracted that he showed up ten minutes late without even realizing it. His first clue was Taro's usual steak salad already in front of him, along with his drink. Cris's stomach pitted. Even Gina made a joke about his tardiness, and that only made him feel worse.

"You're some kind of mess right now," Taro said after Cris ordered a beer. "Talk."

"Same shit, different day." Cris stole a crouton off Taro's plate. All of the varied food smells of the diner had clued him into the fact that he hadn't eaten since breakfast.

"Still torn between Jake and Chet?"

"No, I very definitely chose Jake. Now I'm waiting for him to fucking choose me."

Taro fumbled his fork. "How's that?"

Cris summarized Saturday's date with Jake, bypassing the scandalous details and focusing on the emotions. Particularly, Jake's doubts about Cris's choice and Jake's sudden need for space. Jake had sent him a handful of texts since Saturday afternoon, mostly "thank you for being you" and "thinking of you," but never the one text Cris wanted to see most: Let's do this.

Or some variation on that, Cris wasn't too picky.

"This is exactly why I avoid relationships," Taro said. "You're life has become more complicated than a daytime soap opera love triangle."

"No shit." He gulped at the beer that appeared in front of him. "I mean, he hasn't outright dumped me yet, so that's a good sign, right?"

"A good sign of what? That he's afraid to hurt you by dumping you?"

Cris rolled his eyes. "Thanks for the positive attitude, dude, really."

"I'm going to put my best friend hat on for a minute here, Cris. You are an amazing guy, and anyone would be lucky to call you their boyfriend. If Jake hasn't realized that by now, if he's too scared of his own shadow to realize what a prize he's got, he doesn't deserve you. And you, my friend, deserve better. Someone who knows you and knows what a great person you are."

"Someone like Chet, you mean?"

Taro shrugged. "You said it, not me."

Cris sagged against the back of the booth. "How come I can go years at a time with no real interest in dating anyone, and then suddenly I've got two guys who want me? What is that?"

"Bad luck, especially when the one you chose can't seem to commit."

"And Chet told me to go for it with Jake. What kind of asshole will I be if I have to admit it didn't work out? I can't start something with Chet, because then he'll think he's my second choice."

Taro popped a cherry tomato into his mouth. "Isn't he?"

"If Chet had told me about his feelings before I met Jake, then..." The words tangled up, and he couldn't figure out what he'd been about to say. "Fuck if I know. I can't change how all of this shook out, so what's the point in second guessing it?"

"All you can do is move forward."

"Exactly." Cris frowned at his quickly delivered dinner, not liking the implication of Taro's comment. "How am I supposed to dismiss the fact that I have feelings for two different men? Why does my life have to be so complicated?"

"Better you than me."

"Thank you, that's very helpful."

"Seriously, though." Taro leaned forward. "I love you for your loyalty, and because you value my advice on these matters, but maybe you should be talking to someone with a little actual experience with this kind of attraction. I do my best, but at the end of the day, I'm mostly guessing."

Cris studied his best friend, grateful for his bluntness. Taro always heard him out and tried to help, but he was right. This wasn't a topic with which Taro had experience. Cris hadn't reached out to Gabriel yet. Maybe this was the push he needed to bend his quasi-new-friend's ear.

His phone chimed with a text. He checked it out of curiosity, not too surprised to see it was from Jake.

I can't do this, Cris. I'm sorry. Friends?

Cris's hand trembled; he nearly dropped his phone. Blood rushed in his ears, blocking out everything except his pounding heart. Jake had dumped him. Via fucking text.

"Cris?"

He ignored Taro, and with a shaking finger, stabbed out a response: **No. Do this to my face. I'll be at the club before you dance.**

"Cris, what's wrong?" Taro pried his phone away and read the screen. He blanched. "Fuck, that's harsh. Dumping you with a text?"

"No." Cris yanked the phone back, then slammed it onto the table. "No, if he wants to dump me, he's doing it to my face."

"Are you sure you want to put yourself through that?"

"Yes." He swallowed hard against the weird lump in his throat. "There was something there, between me and him. It was real, and I know he felt it too. Fuck."

"I'm sorry. You need backup tonight?"

"You'd really miss *Agents of S.H.I.E.L.D.* for me?"

Taro shrugged, smiling in a way that was supportive without being pitying. "That's why they made DVR's."

The offer was generous for more than simply missing a television show. Taro had built his life around routines: daily work routines, evening and weekend routines. They kept him focused, gave him a sense of control in his life. "I'd love it if you came with me tonight," Cris said. "But I'm giving you an out. If you don't show up, I won't be mad."

"You won't be mad at *me*. You already look like you just chewed on glass, so I can't imagine your mood will improve after you speak to Jake."

"You're right." Cris picked at his dinner, no longer in the mood for his regular gyro and fries. As much as he didn't want this thing with Jake to end, he couldn't force Jake to date him if he wasn't into it. There was no point. Jake would be unhappy, and that would make Cris unhappy, and they'd only waste time and energy.

It would hurt. He'd opened himself up to Jake in ways he rarely did, telling him things only Taro and Chet knew. He'd dared to hope he'd found someone who accepted not only that he was bi, but also that he shot gay porn—and he had hoped, only to be dumped after a week of incredible ups and disastrous downs.

Maybe Taro's onto something and single is better.

Cris pulled a twenty out of his wallet and slapped it onto the table, more than enough to cover his food and drink. "I'm sorry, pal, but I'm not feeling it tonight."

"It's all right, I understand. Call me later if you need to talk, okay?"

"Yeah, thanks."

Taro stood for a brief hug, then returned to his meal. Cris shuffled out of the diner, not looking forward to the rest of his evening—and also eager as hell to get it over and done with.

Jake rode into the city early with Richard and Bear, all of his stuff neatly packed away in his duffel bag. After working his shift tonight, Jake would move into his new digs.

He'd met Benny earlier in the day and checked out the apartment. Benny—whose real name was Michael Sanders, but it was easier to just go with the porn name, since that was what everyone else called him—was, as promised, a super chill guy, and the bedroom was a decent size. The building was only a seven block walk to Big Dick's, which worked out perfectly for Jake. He could walk again, instead of relying on rides, taxis or Uber to get around. He loved being back in the heart of the city he'd learned to traverse on foot after moving there with his mom.

He also rode with his stomach in knots, one foot constantly tapping against the floorboard. Texting Cris had been cowardly, and Cris's demand to hear it in person at the club hadn't surprised him. It only added to the storm of emotions that had consumed him since his brunch with Chet. More than once, Jake had almost asked Richard for advice. Once, he'd even considered reaching out to Jon, but they weren't friends. Never really had been. More like acquaintances moving past each other on their way elsewhere.

No, Jake had made the decision on his own, and he'd stand by it, even though it hurt like hell.

He helped with initial setup behind the bar, then hid in the dressing room until a little after nine. Greeted his fellow dancers when they came in to change. Jake's silver g-string and leather harness were hiding under his shorts and t-shirt, because no way was he talking to Cris mostly naked. No fucking way.

Pax stuck his head into the dressing room. "Hey, bub, that guy you like's asking for you at the bar."

Fucking fantastic. Now Pax gets to see what an incredible screw up I am.

"Yeah, thanks," Jake said. "Be out in a sec."

"Don't take long. Tall, dark and handsome looks wound up tight. He might not wait."

Cris would wait all night if Jake blew him off now, and that would only make it worse. Might as well rip off the bandage. Dancing later would help him deal with some of the inevitable pain.

He followed Pax out to the main club. As promised, Cris was standing near the bar with a dark drink in his hand. The instant he spotted Jake, his expression shifted from annoyed to excited, then into a coldness that made Jake's insides twist up tight. Jake tilted his head; Cris stalked toward him. He led Cris through the employee door and into the break room, then shut the door. Wandered to the middle of the room, unable to look Cris in the eye.

"I spent the last few hours trying to figure out what to say to you," Cris said. His voice was strained, unhappy, and it scraped down Jake's spine like ice. "Right now, I can't think of a single thing, because all I want to do is kiss you."

Jake turned slowly, desperate to keep his breathing even. To maintain his planned course of action, despite the very real need to drop to his knees and beg for forgiveness. "I'm sorry," was all he could get past the lump in his throat.

"For what?" Cris planted both hands on his hips, somehow both angrily defensive and so fucking vulnerable that Jake couldn't stand it.

"For the text."

"Which text? I mean, we haven't really sent that many, but I figured I should clarify."

"Tonight's text. Dumping you."

Cris's frown deepened. "And you're sorry for which part, exactly? Dumping me over text? Or deciding to dump me at all?"

Both. Neither. Kiss me.

"I really don't understand you," Cris said. "The push and pull all week. The real connection that you refuse to acknowledge we have. And it isn't just great sex, Jake. Maybe we haven't talked about all the deepest, darkest parts of ourselves yet, but I think we have a lot more in common than surface stuff."

"I'm sorry," was all Jake could manage. His chest hurt and he couldn't breathe.

"Yeah, you said that already." Cris spread his arms out to his sides, his expression so pained that Jake wanted to sob. "So that's really it. We're done?"

I can do this, I can do this, I can do this.

"We're done." The words were acid on Jake's tongue. "I'm not the one, Cris. Not for you."

"I think you're wrong." Cris strode toward him, not stopping until Jake's back was against the snack machine. He didn't touch, though, just used his height and bulk to pin Jake in place. "I think you're letting fear get in the way, and that really fucking sucks for both of us. Fear doesn't lead to a happy life."

Jake pulled back hard on his instinctive need to touch Cris— to hug him, kiss him, let Cris hold him tight. To push away all of Jake's fears and doubts. To be his knight in shining armor and slay all of his dragons.

Except real life didn't work like that. "Please go," Jake said.

For one brief moment, Cris seemed poised to argue. Or maybe lean in and kiss him. Instead, his expression hardened into stone, a scary face that made Jake's insides quake. Cris pivoted neatly, then stormed out of the break room, taking that cloud of anger with him. Shaking from head to toe, Jake slid down the front of the snack machine until his ass hit the floor.

He'd done it. He'd given up the best thing he'd ever had in his life. He'd set Cris free to pursue the man he truly wanted. A man deserving of Cris's love and attention. The most selfless thing Jake had ever done in his entire life.

But if he'd done the right thing, why did it feel like he was dying a little bit inside?

The combination of strange sounds and the sharp scent of coffee jerked Cris awake. He was on his stomach, in a bed that smelled like lavender, and the blue flannel sheets beneath him were definitely not his own. Only one person he knew slept on flannel sheets in the summertime.

"Cris? You awake now?" Taro asked. A blue mug appeared in Cris's line of sight, followed by his best friend's frowning face. "Good morning."

"Guh."

"Hello to you, too. Although I should expect as much. You drank yourself stupid last night."

"Sorry." Shame rolled over him and did nothing to ease his sloshy stomach. "Wait, when did I call you?"

"You didn't. A very nice bartender cut you off, and then asked if he could call someone. Naturally, you gave him my name and he woke me from a sound sleep."

"I'm so sorry."

Taro put the coffee mug on the side table. "Don't be. I wish you'd called after Jake dumped you, instead of going out alone."

"Was already out alone." A bit of his night came back to him. "You found me at Dominion, didn't you?"

"I did."

After getting formally dumped by Jake—a move Cris still didn't believe had been what Jake truly wanted—Cris had left Big Dick's to find a different place to tie one on. He'd wanted to get numb, to forget his pain, and no way could he do that with Jake shaking his ass thirty feet away. Dominion was a popular bar for people in his age group, and he'd tossed back three tequila shots before a hot redhead slid into the stool beside him to buy his fourth. They danced, laughed, drank more. Eventually, she left with her friends.

Everything else? Blur.

"Listen," Taro said, "if you need to shower the hangover away, please go do it, because my work schedule begins in twenty minutes." Taro was a thousand times more dedicated to his work-from-home schedule that Cris was, and Cris respected his friend too much to disrupt his schedule more than he already had.

"No, I'll wait and shower at home. The coffee is good, though, thanks."

"You're welcome."

Cris rolled over so he could sit up properly, only to realize he was rubbing mostly bare skin on Taro's sheets. He only wore his underwear. His gut churned. He never drank himself stupid, because he needed to know his partner was totally into whatever they were doing, and he and Taro had fooled around in the past.

Fuck, what did I do?

"Your clothes are in a bag in the kitchen," Taro said. "You vomited on yourself during the walk from my car to the house, and I didn't want your upchuck smeared on my sheets. You can borrow something of mine to wear home."

Thank fuck.

He'd much rather suffer the embarrassment of having barfed on himself than knowing he'd done something with Taro he couldn't remember. "It'll have to be the biggest sweats you own."

Taro chuckled. "I've already pulled a set. They're on the dresser. And in case you were wondering, we didn't do anything. You were wasted, and I know how you feel about consent."

That final band of worry that had held tight to Cris's heart loosened, then fell away. "Thank you."

"Anytime. Drink your coffee and get dressed. I have work to do."

Taro left. Cris took a moment to thank his lucky stars that Taro had been the one to take him home and care for him during one of the shittiest nights in recent memory. Getting dumped by Jake had hurt, and Taro was right. Cris should have called him before he got so drunk he didn't remember part of his night.

Never again.

The bathroom was attached, so he pissed a hell of a lot of liquid, then splashed some water on his face. He looked rough, but not terrible, and the sweats weren't too tight. He sipped the coffee on his way out of the bedroom. Taro's place was one half a two-story duplex, so he descended the stairs, then walked straight ahead to the kitchen.

The stark white walls were bare, the appliances shiny chrome. He'd always liked the tidy, orderly place, so different from the organized chaos of Cris's apartment. Taro leaned against the counter, drinking coffee while looking at something on a tablet. Cris's wallet, car keys and phone were in a neat pile next to a tied plastic grocery bag.

The sight of those keys made his stomach pitch. "Shit, my car. It's in the public lot downtown."

"I figured as much," Taro said. "Grab your shit. I'll drive you over there."

"I'm so sorry." Taro's house was closer to the lot than to Cris's apartment, but it would still disrupt Taro's routines. He lived for his routines.

"You're lucky I love you, or I'd make you pay for a Uber."

"I love you too, brother." Cris pulled Taro into one-armed hug. "Seriously, thank you."

"Make it up to me sometime. Come on." Taro put his mug in the sink.

Cris added his own mug, then collected his things from the counter.

Taro's silver Ford Focus was parked on the street. The interior smelled like cinnamon, and it wasn't until he started the car that Cris caught the time. Only seven-fifty. No wonder he wanted to crawl back into bed and sleep for a few more hours. Working from home, especially after staying out so late, meant sleeping in when he wanted to. Taro kept his schedules, though, and started his workdays at eight a.m. sharp.

They didn't speak for the short drive, letting a rock station fill the silence in the car, and soon Taro was navigating the parking garage, searching for the level and spot Cris remembered.

"There it is," Cris said, pointing.

Taro idled behind Cris's car, then unlocked the doors.

Cris grabbed the handle. "I know I keep saying it, but thank you. For everything."

"No problem. And I'm very sorry about Jake."

"Yeah, see you later."

He waited to unlock his own car until after Taro had driven away. The past few days had well and truly sucked. Jake had dumped him. Chet had turned him down flat. He had the hangover from hell and wanted to sleep for a week. Maybe a forever guy wasn't in the cards. Maybe it never had been. Maybe another night out, stone cold sober and on the prowl for a willing ass, was exactly what he needed.

Maybe.

Chapter Twelve

Charles didn't make a habit out of throwing birthday parties for every single model who'd ever worked for him. If he did, he'd be having one every weekend. Some models worked for one video, others for many long, productive years. He celebrated every young man he was able to boost up, but he reserved his rare parties for the boys who were the foundation of his studio—and always with their permission.

He was a bit nervous calling Cristian to ask about a small party to celebrate his upcoming twenty-ninth birthday, despite having never been nervous to call him before. Perhaps he was nervous because it had been two weeks since they'd last spoken; perhaps because he was afraid of disturbing whatever it was that Cristian and Jake were creating together. He would never presume to interfere in that relationship again.

But Cristian's birthday was the following Friday, so he couldn't put it off any longer. A week was still fairly last minute for many people, Charles included.

Cristian answered on the second ring. "Hey, Chet, how's it hanging?"

Charles laughed. "Low and to the left these days. How are you?"

"Not too bad, I guess. I see the site's been updating regularly again."

"Yes, life seems to be back on schedule now, thanks to you." Charles winced. He hadn't intended to bring up Cristian's attempt to provide Charles with a social life.

"You just needed a kick in the ass," Cristian said with a chuckle. "Is that why you're calling? Scenes?"

"No, actually, I was hoping you'd allow me the honor of hosting a birthday party for you next Friday. Small attendance, of course, but consider it my thank you for all of your support these past eight months."

"You've thanked me plenty. But a small party might be nice. Taro's been picking at me for not being very social lately."

"Ah, honeymoon phase, I take it?"

Cristian's silence unnerved him. "If you're talking about Jake, no, we never got any further than that first date."

Charles's hand jerked, and he nearly dropped his phone. "You didn't?"

"No. Jake called it off a few days later, and I really don't want to talk about it."

"I understand." Charles didn't understand it one bit, but he wanted to respect Cristian's feelings. However, it did hurt a bit that Cristian hadn't reached out in friendship afterward. "I'm sorry. Truly."

Cristian made a soft sound, not a laugh and not quite a grunt. "Thanks. So next Friday?"

"Yes, seven sharp. And bring your friend Taro along. I'd like to meet him."

"I'll see if he wants to come. Thanks, Chet."

"You're welcome."

With Dell's help, planning the party didn't take long, and by that Friday evening the house was decorated in tasteful pink, lavender and blue streamers and matching balloons—their nod to the bisexual flag. Charles ordered a small ice cream cake—chocolate cake, mint chocolate chip ice cream, Cristian's favorite combination—and they set up snacks on the kitchen island.

He'd asked the other guests to arrive around six-thirty, so Cristian could receive a much-deserved greeting from his friends. Besides himself and Dell, his home was also hosting two former models and their significant others—Jon and Isaac, Gabriel and Tristan—as well as three current models friendly with Cristian—Shiloh, Adam and Benny. He'd have invited any friends of Cristian who weren't connected to Mean Green, except he didn't know of any besides Taro.

The consummate host, Charles did his best to make all of his guests feel welcome in the house, particularly Tristan and Isaac. Tristan bounced on his tiptoes for the first few minutes after his arrival, excited to be in the Mean Green home where his boyfriend used to shoot porn. His enthusiasm for the business was very refreshing for Charles. So many people looked down at porn —gay or straight—with upturned noses, while Tristan seemed to think it was the coolest job ever.

Even if Gabriel had retired over a year ago.

Isaac seemed to be the most shy among the group, more so than Dell, and that surprised Charles a bit. Isaac's partner Jon was a boisterous young man, and they seemed quite the opposite pairing. But when they smiled at each other, their love was clear, and it made Charles ache a little bit more.

Charles kept himself busy offering snacks and drinks, until the doorbell rang promptly at seven. Dell went to let the birthday boy in. Cheers went up from the attendees when Cristian entered the kitchen. He was dressed in hip-hugging slacks and a black button-down shirt that did funny things to Charles's insides. Behind Cristian was a young Asian man who looked about as comfortable being there as a cat in a dog pound.

Cristian went through a long round of hugs and best wishes, taking time to introduce Taro to his other friends and former coworkers, before they finally made it to Charles's position behind the island. He hadn't seen Cristian in person in three weeks, and despite a lingering sense of sadness, he looked well.

"Happy birthday, love," Charles said. The hug was kind of awkward and far too brief.

"Thanks," Cristian said. "Chet, this is Taro Ichikawa. Taro, Chet Green."

"It's a pleasure to meet you, Taro. I've heard only excellent things about you."

"Uh, same here," Taro said.

Charles smiled. "You look like you could use a drink. Wine or the hard stuff?"

"A glass of wine would be great, thank you."

"Excellent. Red or white?"

"Surprise me."

"Cristian?"

"Sprite, actually, if you have it," Cristian said. "Or ginger ale."

"Something pale and non-caffeinated?"

"Yeah, thanks."

They moved away to mingle while Charles poured a glass of shiraz and a cup of Sprite over ice. He'd purchases a variety of two-liter soft drinks for the party, somewhat embarrassed that he wasn't certain of the drinking habits of any of his guests, except himself and Dell. He kept bottled water downstairs for his models during shoots, but he was rarely this social with any of them.

It was truly a bizarre experience to have so many of his models in one room and know no one was taking their clothes off.

Unless someone got intoxicated enough to lose all inhibitions.

Music began playing on the surround sound system in the den, loud enough to feel like a true party without angering his neighbors.

"...never spent an entire week at the beach before," Jon was saying. He and Isaac were standing nearby, chatting around the bowls of chips and salsa with Adam and Shiloh.

The friendly conversation surprised Charles a bit. When he'd hired Rick Fowler into the company last fall under the name Adam Swift, Rick/Adam had informed him of a shared history with Jon. Charles had meant to have a sit-down conversation with Jon and break the news of Rick/Adam's hiring gently, but they'd run into each other by accident before Charles could do that. Jon had been unusually furious, and while Charles respected the younger man's feelings, Jon didn't know Adam's full history. Charles would never schedule them together, but he wasn't firing a new model over a he said/he said personal history.

The pair had found a way to coexist last December, after an unhinged fan of Jon's porn persona stalked him, attacked him, and nearly killed Adam. Charles had been horrified when he got the full story. He always thought he'd been careful to protect his models' personal information, and he'd taken it personally. He'd nearly shuttered the studio altogether. But Charles had stopped living his life in fear when he was sixteen. He wouldn't start again at forty-eight.

Jon's own heartfelt "it's not your fault some crazy-ass douchebag decided my character was real and wanted to terrorize me and my boyfriend" had certainly helped his decision. Adam took a three-month hiatus to recover and get back into shape before returning to the Mean Green fold. Adam Swift had quickly become one of his most popular current models.

"A week at the beach?" Charles asked, inserting himself into the conversation with his own glass of wine in hand. "Summer vacation?"

"Yup," Jon said, beaming a smile at Isaac. "We've been planning it months. A timeshare at a beach house in North Carolina, private beach so it doesn't stress Isaac out too much. I just hate leaving Bear behind."

"She'll be fine," Isaac said. He patted Jon's forearm. "She's going to love spending time with other cats." To Charles, he said, "Tristan and Gabe are going to cat-sit so we don't have to subject Bear to a kennel while we're gone."

"That's very kind of them," Charles said. He hadn't realized any of them had adopted pets. And cats of all creatures.

"Hey, how come you don't have any pets, Chet?" Adam asked. "Dog? Cat? Goldfish?"

"I never gave pets much thought, I suppose. My life has always been work focused." To Jon he said, "May I ask where in North Carolina?"

"Ocracoke Island." Grief pinched the corners of Jon's eyes. "It was one of Henry's favorite places. I like the idea of scattering his ashes there."

"I think that's a beautiful idea."

Charles had never met Jon's best friend and mentor Henry Pearson, who'd been a huge part of Jon's adult life. Henry had passed away from cancer last year, two days after Thanksgiving, and it had devastated Jon. Charles was glad that Jon not only had Isaac, but also the support of Gabe and Tristan, throughout that ordeal. Spreading Henry's ashes in a favorite place was a lovely way to honor Jon's late friend.

"We want to drive cross-country, too, one day," Jon said. "That was one of Henry's bucket list things he never got to do, so me and Isaac will. When Isaac is ready."

Isaac blushed and ducked his head. Jon looped an arm around his waist and tugged him into a sideways hug. Charles's understanding of Isaac's history was severe agoraphobia brought on by a series of past traumas. But Isaac had seen the beauty in Jon's soul, allowed him into his home and heart, and the two couldn't be more in love.

So beautiful, young love.

He glanced toward the den. Cristian stood in a small huddle with Gabriel, Tristan, and Benny. Tristan was doing most of the talking, engaging the attention of the other three men. Cristian seemed a bit detached from the conversation, a melancholy hanging over him like a heavy blanket. Something deep inside of Charles reared up, demanding his fix it, make Cristian smile again —only Charles had no idea how, especially when Cristian was keeping his distance.

"Chet? Hello?" Adam tapped the rim of his own wine glass against Charles's.

"Yes, sorry." Charles blinked at him, aware that he'd missed a question. "Forgive me, my mind wandered."

"I could tell. Jon was talking about driving cross-country, and I mentioned you once lived on the west coast."

"Yes, I did. Many years ago, during another life."

"Did you ever see Washington state?" Isaac asked. He'd raised his head, attentive to Charles's answer. "I've heard it's beautiful, and I've seen so many pictures online."

He enjoyed the innocent excitement of Isaac's comments; the boy still had so much living left to do. "I was based in Los Angeles, but I traveled quite often for business. I visited Seattle many times. The scenery is more beautiful than any photograph could capture. If you boys have the chance to visit, I highly recommend going."

"We may have to write that into our trip itinerary now," Jon said, giving Isaac an indulgent smile.

Adam caught Charles's gaze and rolled his eyes at the pair. He was smiling, though, and Charles had gotten to know Adam well enough this past year to see the teasing in the gesture. And the longing. Adam had made some serious mistakes, battled with his own demons, and Charles believed that he'd changed. And he seemed to be as lonely as Charles, perhaps thinking himself unworthy of love due to his past.

Charles quite understood that feeling.

The music changed, going from pop to something more techno. Dance music. Benny started it. A high-energy flirt and exhibitionist, he began to shake his hips and sway in small circles, dancing as heartily as if in the middle of a nightclub. Tristan joined in a few moments later, and the pair found an easy rhythm.

Jon wolf whistled. "Come on, Gabe, you donna let another dude grind on your guy like that? You got moves, bro!"

Gabriel gave Jon the finger without taking his eyes off of Tristan, who made quite the sensual dance partner for Benny. Shiloh joined them not long after, and that seemed to jolt Gabriel into claiming his partner. The four of them together became so entrancing that Charles barely noticed when Adam and Jon entered the mix. Isaac hung back, watching with a shy smile. Dell and Taro had their heads together on the far side of the kitchen, paying no mind to the heathen display in the den.

It took several minutes for Charles to realize that someone was missing. Cristian had disappeared from his own birthday party. Curious and a bit nervous, Charles drained his wine glass, and then went in search of his friend. The ground floor bathroom was empty, and he couldn't imagine Cristian invading their privacy by going upstairs, or poking around in Charles's office.

More curious than worried, Charles opened the door to the basement. A set of sturdy carpeted stairs led down to the permanent studio he'd created for Mean Green Boys almost six years ago to the day.

The main lights were off, but a dim glow made its way up the stairs. All of the filming equipment and lights were packed away while not in use, and one corner of the spacious room held a variety of set pieces and furniture collected over the years. Straight ahead was the spot where most of the scenes were filmed, a rectangle of space that became whatever he needed for the shoot: living room, bedroom, office area. Their last scene had been a living room fuck, so the sofa was still in place, with a painting on the wall above. Fake potted plant, throw rug, a few scattered pillows.

Cristian sat on the floor, his back against the sofa, drink in his hand. The set's table lamp was on, giving the studio its only illumination. He didn't seem surprised to see Charles. The ghost of unhappiness that had shadowed Cristian all evening was still there, a stronger presence now that he wasn't the center of attention.

"You've disappeared from your own party," Charles said. "Was Benny's dancing really so terrible."

The tiny smile playing on Cristian's lips was a small victory. "I've seen worse. It wasn't Benny."

"Then what was it?" He took a few steps forward, remaining on the edge of the set until invited closer.

"The happy couples, I guess. Jon and Isaac planning a trip. Gabe and Tristan going on about their cats and Gabe's new job." He raised his head, so much confusion and pain in his eyes. "I feel so stuck."

Screw an invitation, he's hurting.

Charles sat next to Cristian on the rug, aching for this man he cared for so much. "Tell me why you feel stuck."

"Because even when I commit to a relationship, the other person blows me off. Because I've done porn off and on for eight years, and even though I'm not sure I want to come back, I can't seem to quit. Everyone else is moving forward, while I'm standing still."

Despite having suspected it, hearing from Cristian's own lips that he wasn't certain he'd return to the Mean Green fold hurt.

But it hurt less than he expected, because this was what he'd wanted for Cristian ever since he returned to Mean Green as Dane. Charles wanted all of his models to find their passion, to find a life that made them happy. Being around two men who'd done exactly that seemed to have finally shaken Cristian up enough to admit he needed to move on.

"You are spectacular at what you do onscreen, Cristian, you always have been. It's why you have such a dedicated following. But what's onscreen is an illusion. It isn't real life, and Dane isn't you. Wanting something else, especially now, is a good thing."

Cristian shrugged, so Charles attempted a new approach. "Tell me what happened with you and Jake."

"I'm not even sure, to be honest. We had a great time on Saturday. We went to City Island, played around. I mean, we didn't really talk about anything all that in-depth, but we joked and laughed a lot. Went back to my place and had mind-blowing sex."

Jealousy wormed its way into Charles's gut, followed, to his surprise, by a small tingle of arousal. He'd seen Cristian have sex, and while he'd only met Jake once, he could easily imagine the intensity of their pairing. But Charles wanted Cristian for himself, so why did the idea of Cristian and Jake together appeal to him so strongly?

Focus.

"What changed?" Charles asked.

"Jake brought you up, and then he got incredibly insecure. He said I only chose him because you removed yourself as a choice. He said I didn't actually make the choice between you and him." Cristian looked up, a new, simmering anger in his dark eyes. "And he's right. The choice was made for me, Jake decided he didn't like being second best, and he dumped me. Tried to do it over text, the little shit, but I made him say it to my face."

"I'm so sorry. Truly. Your affection for him is still very clear, and I'm sorry you were hurt. This entire production feels as if it's my fault."

"It's not your fault Jake dumped me."

Charles wasn't entirely certain of that. "When you last spoke with Jake, did he happen to mention our conversation?"

Cristian blinked hard. "No. When did you talk to Jake?"

"Saturday evening, after your date concluded. Jake sought contact with me via the Mean Green site. We spoke briefly on the phone, and rather than try to discuss the situation that way, I invited him over for Sunday brunch."

"Jake was here?" Cristian looked more perplexed than angry. "You two talked about me behind my back?"

"I suppose we did, if you need to phrase it that way."

"What were you doing? Dividing me up like a prize?"

"Of course not. Since I was the cornerstone of Jake's hesitation to date you, I thought it only fair that we meet to discuss it. He is quite the handsome, charming young man. I can see why you're taken with him."

"He's also a huge pain in the ass, and for some reason, I like that about him."

"He challenges you."

"Yeah, he does. Did. So what exactly did you guys talk about?"

"We discussed my relationship with you, which I assured him was completely platonic. He also said the same thing as you a few moments ago, which was that I didn't allow you to make up your own mind. We also spoke a bit about our pasts. I told him about my own struggles as a teenager and the mistakes I've made. I may have also spoken quite highly of you and your capacity for kindness."

"You did?"

"I told Jake how you held me together when Dell overdosed, and how supportive you've been since. He reacted a bit strangely when I told him about Dell's kidney transplant, but that's not something you learn about a person every day. Especially one who answers the door when you ring the bell."

Cristian stared at him, his expression indecipherable. "Jake knows about Dell's kidney?"

"Yes." Charles could make no sense of Cristian's face or reaction. "Is there any reason I shouldn't have told him?"

"Of course not, sorry. I mean, you said you told Jake personal stuff to build a rapport but that seems…really personal."

"It was, but Jake was personal with me, in return. I can understand now why the boy is so guarded, and why he expects you to hurt him."

Cristian startled. "Seriously? He told you stuff about his past he hasn't bothered telling me?"

"Really?" Charles studied his friend's face, only to find genuine surprise. "He didn't tell you about his parents?"

"No. He vaguely mentioned he doesn't see them anymore. Why?"

"It's not really my place."

"Charles, please." Cristian squeezed his wrist. "Please."

Maybe it was the second please, but Chet visibly acquiesced. His entire body relaxed, shedding the rigid posture and boss persona he'd descended the stairs with. Cris had come down to the studio to think, perhaps even make a decision about quitting for good. Chet showing up hadn't shocked him, but to hear that Chet had spoken with Jake about personal shit Cris didn't know?

That hurt.

"When Jake was a teenager, his father left him and his mother for another woman," Chet said. "It hurt him deeply. He and his mother moved here to start over, but when his mother died unexpectedly, Jake was left to fend for himself. He landed on his feet, according to his own words, but I believe his sense of being left behind and/or abandoned by those closest to him was exacerbated by the recent situation with his former roommate. It left him in an emotional space that limited his ability to trust you."

Christ, he could have been a shrink.

Cris turned the words over in his mind, horrified by what Jake had lost, and still worried about what he'd done in order to "land on his feet." Cris had been in a similar position at a similar age: alone, with no family to help him, desperate to scratch out a life in a very cruel world that did its best to punch down on anything it saw as "other".

"His hesitation makes more sense," Cris said. "But to flat out dump me and not even explain himself? All I got was 'I'm not the one for you.' No actual reason for that, by the way. And I get fear, believe me, but...fuck if I know but what anymore." He slumped against the couch, sad and angry and confused—the same state he'd been in for weeks.

The best answer Cris had come up with was that for some reason, Jake had decided Cris was better off either 1) alone and single, or 2) with Chet. And since Chet had made his feelings perfectly clear on the matter, option one was all that was left.

"Jake did say a few things to me," Chet said slowly, "that intimated he may have thought you were better off with me."

Even in the dim light, Chet visibly blushed. He also tensed, retreating into a less intimate, more official persona.

"What did he say?" Cris asked.

"That you deserved someone solid and settled. He thinks very poorly of his own impulsive nature. In fact, he seems to think poorly of himself in general, which is disheartening in someone with so much potential."

"This is all such a mess. I feel like all I've done this month is hurt two people I really care about." He twisted his wrist so he could squeeze the palm of Chet's hand. "I've been super unfair to you in all this, and I'm sorry."

"You've done nothing to apologize for, but if it helps to hear it, you're forgiven. We're both grown men. We know how to own our choices." Chet winked. "Speaking of choices, may I assume you came down here to ponder another that you've yet to make?"

Cris didn't insult Chet by playing dumb. "Yes. I have so many memories of this room and this house. It's scary to think of leaving it behind."

"You'd still be my friend, Cristian, even if you were no longer my employee. I hope that, even if you quit, we'd remain good friends."

"How can you still want to be my friend when I chose Jake over you?"

"Because I can rest with the knowledge that you did not, in fact, make that choice on your own, as we've already discussed. And I own my part in that. Perhaps we should all learn how best to move forward from here."

Chet had a great point. Dwelling on the past, on the might-haves and should-have-dones wasn't going to help any of them. And he respected the hell out of Chet for saying so. "Then yes, I absolutely want to stay friends. Eight years is too long to throw away."

"Excellent."

They sat in silence for a few minutes, hands still clasped in a comfortable, supportive way. So much could be said in the quiet moments, so much encouragement given without doing anything bigger than existing together. Chet had always been good at that, propping someone up from the shadows. Nudging you forward without pushing too hard. Being there for the exact right pep talk.

Plus he's a hell of a sexy dancer.

Memories from that fateful Thursday night flooded Cris's mind, everything from the motions of their bodies, to the scents of the club, to the exact songs they'd danced to. So much fun. So much chemistry. They fit in so many ways, but their timing was off. And nothing could happen until Cris made a damned decision about leaving or staying with the studio.

He enjoyed porn. He had a good time with his partners, despite always playing the serious badass character of Dane. But coming back to film was bigger than his dislike of change. He had no way to hide his surgical scar. It was thin and somewhat hidden by the lines of his abdominals, but Chet would still see it. The camera would see it. He would ask, and Cris would have to tell him something, because he hadn't had the scar before his hiatus.

Before Dell's anonymous transplant.

Chet would put it together as quickly as Jake apparently had at their brunch. A brunch meeting that Chet said seemed to help Jake make his choice. But why would Jake dump Cris over a kidney donation? It made no fucking sense...unless Jake took it as a sign of Cris's feelings for Chet. Feelings that were very real and hadn't gone away, but goddamn it, he'd wanted to try with Jake.

He wanted to try with Chet, too.

And what kind of selfish, arrogant asshole did that make him? To want two guys? Probably why he didn't have either of them.

"What are you thinking about so hard?" Chet asked. "I can see the smoke pouring from your ears."

Cris laughed with no real humor. "Thinking how ironic it is to have been single for so long, and now I've got two great men in my life, but I don't really have either one of them."

Chet's breath hitched. He angled toward Cris. "You'll always have me, Cristian."

"I don't mean as my friend." Cris squeezed Chet's hand tighter, needing that connection. Needing something he'd never been able to ask for. He never wanted to be the reason Chet crossed a professional line. But the heat of the man beside him, the familiar scent of his cologne, the sharp planes of his face... everything about Chet called to him on a cellular level.

"You know why that can't happen," Chet said, so softly the words were nearly lost to the thundering of blood in Cris's temples.

Cris leaned in, his shoulder pressing against Chet's. "Are you asking me to quit?"

"All I want is for you to be happy. It's all I've ever wanted, since the day we met."

"I'm not sure I know how to be happy."

Chet's gaze flittered from his eyes to his mouth, then back again, glimmering with something so profound it took Cris's breath away. "Are you so sure about that?" Chet whispered.

He won't make the first move. He won't.

So Cris did, easing gently into Chet's personal space, tilting his head to the side. Warm breath gusted across his lips moments before he crossed that final line and kissed Chet. Sober and in perfect control of his actions, Cris pressed his mouth to Chet's, surprised by the instant arousal that jolted through him. Chet made a soft, desperate sound deep in his throat, and then Cris was lost.

Hands and lips and tongues became his world. The wonderful taste of Chet's mouth, the way his hands tugged at Cris's hair, the body heat all around him. And then on top of him, holding him down in the most wonderful way, as Chet's entire being engulfed Cris in a whirlwind of passion and joy. The kiss was harsh and soft, powerful and gentle, and Cris could live in it forever.

He spread his legs, allowing Chet to settle there, his slim body cradled between Cris's thighs. Their erections pressed together as they were always meant to, and Cris pushed up, needing friction. Chet only attacked his mouth harder, his tongue sweeping inside to lay claim to Cris's mouth, and holy hell, this forceful, possessive side of Chet was hot. Cris gave in to it, needing to hand over control to someone else for a while, confident in Chet's ability to take care of him.

Cris tugged Chet's shirt out of his slacks, then slid his fingers beneath the cotton fabric to scrape across smooth skin. Chet moaned softly, then broke the kiss, rising up on his elbows to look down at Cris. His lips were damp, his eyes bright, and everything in his expression silently asked if Cris was okay.

This wasn't the time for words. Cris didn't have any. His only answer to the unasked question was to grab Chet's ass and pull him tighter, thrust their dicks together. Chet gasped, then threaded his fingers into Cris's hair. Held his head still.

"I need you to say yes," Chet said. "Even if it's only this one time, I need to hear it."

"Yes." *Fuck yes to anything and everything you want from me right now.* "Please, Charles."

The use of his given name cracked the last of Chet's hesitation. He raised his hips and reached between them. Thumbed open Cris's fly. Tugged the zipper. Cris's blood buzzed with adrenaline and arousal, and he had no idea what Chet wanted but he'd go with it, as long as it ended with them both coming.

Fingers brushed his cockhead, and Cris shivered. Then gasped out loud when Chet pulled his boxer-briefs down far enough to release his dick. He stroked him a few times, too damned softly for Cris's liking, before letting go. Cris growled, needing that touch again. Chet smiled at him, then shut him up with a fierce kiss that went on and on, until Chet settled down, hip to hip, his own naked cock riding Cris's.

Fuck yes.

Skin on skin in the place that counted most, Chet set a gentle rhythm that increased with each thrust. He fucked Cris's mouth with his tongue. Cris pushed their shirts up, out of the way, needing more skin contact. Loving the way their bare bellies rubbed together. He shoved his hands beneath Chet's pants, fingers digging into bare skin and twitching muscle. His entire world telescoped into the man embracing him, driving him to orgasm, holding him like nothing else in the world mattered except this moment.

Chet came first, and Cris swallowed the desperate sounds he made. Held on tight as his hips stuttered, interrupting Cris's own cresting climax. Chet shivered once, then broke from the kiss to stare down at Cris with so much affection it nearly undid him. Chet reached between them and clasped his come-slicked dick. Without once breaking eye contact, he jacked Cris to completion, not letting go until Cris panted for him to stop.

He tugged Chet down for a soft kiss, surprised when Chet pulled back almost right away. "What's wrong?"

"I didn't expect this to happen," Chet said. Tenderly, almost heartbreakingly so. "Please tell me you don't regret it."

"Of course I don't regret this." Cris reached down to tug on Chet's softening dick, because so far Chet had done all the touching. Chet's eyes got adorably wide at the contact. "I loved this, I promise. No regrets."

"We crossed a line. *I* crossed a line."

"Hey." Cris kissed Chet's forehead, then both cheeks. "A line is only there if you decide to put it there. I haven't been your employee for months, and nothing we did today is wrong. In fact, it felt pretty damned right."

"It did." Chet's smile punched Cris right in the heart. "You've given me a tremendous gift."

"An orgasm is a gift?"

"In its own way. I loved hearing the real you, especially when you climaxed. It was beautiful."

Cris traced a finger down the line of Chet's jaw, entranced by the comment and understanding it immediately. Chet had filmed him coming dozens of times, probably had his O-face memorized by now. But that was Dane's money shot. Not Cristian Sable's. "When you put it like that, you're welcome. We both got to see and hear something for the first time."

"Yes we did. And you're certain you don't regret it?"

Cris poked him in the ribs. "Ask me that again and I'll tickle you to death, old man."

Chet sat up, making a cross sign with his fingers. "Stay back." He hated few physical touches more than he hated tickling, according to that one drunken night they spent together. Cris loved using it against him.

The sitting position gave Chet a good view of Cris's naked torso—a realization that went from super-sexy to oh-shit in a heartbeat. Cris tugged his shirt down to cover his abs, right over smears of come that immediately stained the fabric. "Shit."

"Give me a moment." Chet crossed the room to a storage locker. He returned with baby wipes.

Cris cleaned himself up, then tucked back in, grateful the stained part of his shirt was hidden inside of his jeans. Chet's shirt hadn't fared as well, so he traded it for one of identical color from the wardrobe rack. It didn't fit right, but it was unlikely anyone would notice. He still seemed uncertain about what they'd done, and Cris couldn't have that.

He looped his arms around Chet's waist and pulled him into a hug. Chin resting on Chet's shoulder, he said, "This is whatever we want it to be, okay? Something or nothing. A one-off or just the beginning. But it's ours alone, until we choose to tell others about it."

Chet relaxed in his arms. "Thank you, Cristian."

The upstairs studio door swung open, allowing in a shaft of light. "Yo, kids!" Shiloh shouted down. "Quit filming your private porn and get up here. The stripper arrived!"

Chet jerked, but Cris stilled him with a kiss on the mouth. "No one heard us, it's just Shiloh being Shiloh," Cris said. "And even if he did hear us, this is nothing to be ashamed of. Consensual sex between adults never is. Isn't that what you've always told us?"

"It is. You're right." Chet's smile, so loving and compassionate, made Cris's heart soar. "And we don't have to discuss this or define it tonight. I didn't hire a stripper, but it sounds as though your birthday party is continuing without your presence."

Cris chuckled. "Yeah, I'm a little scared to go upstairs and see what the guys have cooked up."

"Then it's a good thing you have me by your side."

"Yeah, it is."

They didn't hold hands as they went upstairs, but they were still connected. And any anxiety Chet might have had about anyone hearing them having sex was quickly quelled. The "stripper" turned out to be a very drunk Benny, dancing on the coffee table in only his boxer briefs. Tristan was in the midst of tucking a dollar bill into his underwear, while Adam took pictures.

No one asked where they'd been, or why they were gone for so long. The party continued, his guests completely unaware that the world has shifted for Cris tonight. Or that he'd finally, in his heart, made his decision about his future in porn.

Chapter Thirteen

Living with Benny for the last two weeks was way less stressful than Jake had initially anticipated, mostly because of how high-energy Benny was the first time they met. Jake did better with laid back people who came and went with little fanfare, like Jon had. But exuberant or not, Benny was also pretty chill regarding pretty much everything in the apartment, from the food in the fridge to the shelves of Xbox games near the giant flat screen TV.

Besides doing porn, Benny was also an assistant sales manager for a home goods store, so he always had funny customer stories to share with Jake whenever their paths crossed—which wasn't frequently, because he mostly worked days while Jake worked nights. Benny also wasn't shy in asking questions pertaining to the finer details of his newfound attraction to men. Things that you couldn't answer on a porn set, but maybe could with a gay guy who'd embraced his sexuality since he was fifteen.

So yeah, living sitch was cool. The rent was reasonable, the room was already furnished, and he had free run of Benny's Xbox during most weekdays. The only time they tended to see more of each other was on weekends.

Like today. They were both on the living room floor playing Fallout 4. Benny was going on and on about how fun the birthday party was last night, while Jake silently planned how to shut him up with the Xbox controller. It hurt to hear about how great Cris's birthday had been—Jake had no idea it was his birthday!—and that Jake hadn't been there, but Chet had hosted the whole thing, and boy it was a blast, and blah, blah.

Benny had no reason to know that Jake and Cris had almost been a thing, or that Cris had a thing for Chet, so he couldn't really tell Benny to shut it, he wasn't in the mood. Mostly, Jake tried to play and half-listen so he wasn't being completely rude.

"...totally inspiring to see Boomer and Tony there with their boyfriends, you know? Like, it's super possible to leave porn behind and have a real relationship. I mean, it'd be totally cool to find someone who didn't mind if I stayed in porn, because I really like it, but not forever. No one can do that shit forever, right? It goes to show you there's life after porn. Or even life during porn, I guess, since Tony was totally still filming while dating Tristan, so..."

It didn't stop for a full ten minutes, during which Jake managed to advance his player, while Benny got himself killed. That turned Benny's voice off for a few minutes while he got his character back into the game. It also gave Jake a chance to realize something about the bulk of Benny's chatter: he'd barely mentioned Cris/Dane at all. At his own birthday party.

"So did the birthday boy have fun?" Jake asked.

"I think so. He seemed a little withdrawn, but he's always like that on set, and I don't know him well in real life. Actually, he disappeared for a while, maybe a half hour or so. Shiloh found him and Chet downstairs in the studio, so they were probably talking about Dane going back to work soon."

Something dark wormed its way through Jake's gut. Cris and Chet had been alone. In the studio where they filmed gay sex. And why not? Jake had dumped Cris, because he knew Cris wanted Chet more, deserved Chet more. Of course they were together. Didn't seem like they were showing it off yet, but how much longer before Benny came home from a shoot, hooting about the boss fucking a model?

Of course he was withdrawn. He probably couldn't stop thinking about fucking Chet, so he had to keep his distance. Play it cool in front of the others.

Unless Cris was withdrawn because he'd tried with Chet, but Chet turned him down, because of the boss/employee thing? The whole mess made Jake's head want to explode. He hadn't spoken to Cris since dumping him—the single hardest thing Jake had done in his life, and his heart was still a little bit bruised by the self-inflicted wound—so it wasn't as if he could call Cris up and ask if he'd fucked his boss.

Cris could be over the moon in love. He could also be totally miserable because neither Jake nor Chet wanted him. Jake thought he'd done the right thing in setting Cris free to pursue Chet, but what if Chet hadn't liked being second choice either, and now Cris was heartbroken twice, and it was all Jake's fault?

An odd melancholy spread over him, settling into his bones like a heavy wet blanket. He ended up letting his character die so he could curl up on the couch and watch Benny play. When Benny made burgers for dinner, Jake manage to get half of one down before his stomach hurt too much. Weird, because he loved food, but whatever.

Saturday night at Big Dick's meant better tips, and Jake tried. He really did. The music couldn't seem to get into his body like it used to, held back by the bone-deep weariness from that afternoon. Xander mentioned his lack of energy during a break, and Jake brushed it off as a cold or something. Could be true, even though his throat didn't hurt and his nose wasn't stuffed. The flu made your bones hurt, though, didn't it?

The deeper into the night he danced, though, the worse Jake felt. His joints ached, his head was too heavy to keep upright, and his focus was slipping away. At some point during a techno remix of "Dark Horse," Richard waved Jake offstage.

He followed Richard into the dressing room, too tired to worry about whatever his boss wanted. Except Richard didn't look angry or upset.

"You don't look very good, kiddo," Richard said. "You're lethargic and out of rhythm. You getting sick?"

"I think so." Jake hadn't been sick in so long that he hated the idea of catching anything, but more and more, he was starting to feel like he'd been hit by a truck. "I'm so sorry."

"Hey, you can't help it if you catch a virus, none of us can. But you can help not spread it around. Why don't you cut out early and get some sleep? I'll still pay for the whole night."

"You don't have to do that."

Richard smiled. "I know, but I will. Go home. Lots of fluids. Tylenol if you spike a fever."

"Thanks. Really."

He left, and Jake got dressed. Since he hadn't bothered with makeup, there was nothing to wash off, and it was easier to get through the thick Saturday night crowd to the front door. Bear was looking at something on his phone when Jake exited—probably a text from Richard, because Bear looked up and said, "Feel better, son."

"Thanks, Bear."

The walk home took forever, plus change, and by the time Jake crawled into his bed, he never wanted to get out of it again. The next time he opened his eyes, the sun was up. Finding his phone to check the time was out of the question. Whatever. He closed his eyes, and woke up again with someone shaking his shoulder.

"Dude, you sick?" Benny asked. "You've slept all day." Jake grunted, but didn't move when Benny actually put the back of his hand on his forehead. "Don't feel like you've got a fever."

"Go away," Jake said. Even that hurt. "Wanna sleep."

"Do you work tonight?"

"No." Jake pulled the sheet up over his head.

"Yeah, okay. You need anything, yell for me, okay, pal?"

He grunted again, then blocked out the world for a while longer. Everything was just too damned much right now.

Too damned much.

"The poor kid was so nervous, we had to stop for twenty minutes so he could watch porn and get it up again," Chet said. His warm, comforting voice seemed to be in the same room with Cris, despite them only chatting via Facetime.

Phone calls during Cris's allotted lunch break hour had become a regular thing since the birthday party. Time where they talked about everything and nothing. A chance to connect in some way, since they hadn't seen each other in person since Friday night. Cris wasn't avoiding Chet, as much as he was avoiding a conversation he didn't want to have about the scar on his abdomen. And Chet didn't seem to mind the slow progression of their relationship. Every day they spoke, Chet seemed happier, more relaxed. Less the grumpy, depressed man from nearly a month ago.

And apparently, Chet was having issues with a new model on his first day. "So was he nervous about the camera? Or about taking it from Perry?" Cris asked.

"Hard to tell. Perry is nowhere near as big or intimidating as you were, and I thought I'd paired them well. Perhaps I'm losing my touch." Chet added that final comment with a wink.

"Or maybe the new model is more camera shy than he wanted to let on."

"Perhaps so. Even you were a bit camera shy once."

Cris laughed. He'd been a big ball of bravado the day he interviewed to be a web cam model for Mean Green, desperate to prove himself. To be seen and to know his new face was more than just a disguise. That he was actually Cristian Sable and no longer Vincent Maroni. "I take it you finally got your scene?"

"We did, yes, and it won't be a scorcher, but there is some good chemistry. It's a shame you never got to shoot with Perry. I think that would have been a lovely scene."

Even though Cris hadn't told Chet about his decision to leave porn, Chet spoke in a way that said he knew. Somehow, instinctively, he knew, despite not having received a resignation letter from Cris. He kind of loved how well Chet knew him. Perry had joined the company back in January, and while he and

Cris had met—tall, freckled and ginger had been a bit of a turn on at the time—Cris had taken his hiatus before they could be scheduled together.

"So do you have any exciting plans for the evening?" Chet asked. "I'll be spending mine editing yesterday's shoot."

"It's Wednesday, so about as exciting as an overnight volunteer shift at the hospital can be." Cris didn't have a set schedule for his volunteer work, allowing the staff to slot him in when they needed additional hands.

"It could very well be exciting if you work in the ER again."

"True." ER shifts tended to end with at least one amusing story.

Their chatting came to a slightly awkward halt. They'd been beating around the bush on this for the last five days, and Cris needed to get it out of the way. "So, you want to do something this weekend?"

Chet's eyebrows jumped. "I'd love to. Do you have anything particular in mind?"

"Um, no." His favorite place was City Island, but that wasn't quite Chet's thing. Chet liked museums and the theater. And Cris wasn't sure he could take him there and not spend the day thinking about Jake.

"The weather's been lovely this week. What about a beach weekend? I have a friend who owns a summer apartment in Rehoboth Beach. I could call and see if it's available."

Cris's pulse raced at the idea of a weekend away with Chet, nervous and excited all at once. "Uh…."

"We could invite Dell along, as well, if you'd like," Chet said, picking up on Cris's hesitation. "It doesn't have to be an excuse for a weekend orgy, simply a chance to get away from the city for a while. Relax in the sun, ogle some fit beach bodies."

The invitation was incredibly sweet. Cris knew Chet was offering in all innocence, not as an excuse to demand sexual favors in return for a beach weekend, but the backpedaling to add in Dell was adorable. He was being so careful not to screw things up, and Cris fell for him a little bit more.

"I think that sounds really nice," Cris said. "You don't have any shoots scheduled, do you?"

"Friday evening, so we could either leave late that night, or early Saturday. I'm game for either. I'll call and make sure the apartment is available before we cement our plans."

"Okay." Another call came through on Cris's phone. Gabriel. Curious, but not willing to end his chat with Chet yet, Cris let the call go to voice mail. "Let me know when you find out."

"Absolutely. And if those plans fall through, I'm sure we can come up with something local. Perhaps something as boring as dinner and a movie."

"Doesn't sound boring at all." It had been a long time since Cris had been on a dinner-and-movie kind of date. Almost sounded better than the beach.

Almost.

Dinner and a movie doesn't require you to remove your shirt. The beach does.

A flash of anxiety sent his pulse racing again. He must have kept his thoughts off his face, though, because Chet's indulgent smile never wavered. "I love the sound of dinner and a movie," Cris said.

"We'll have to work that in no matter what, then."

"Awesome." An update on his computer chimed. "I should get back to work. And you need to get into the editing booth."

"So to speak." Chet edited in his home office. "Take care, Cristian."

"You too." Cris ended the Facetime, then checked the voice mail Gabriel left.

"Hey, man, it's Gabe. Listen, maybe I shouldn't be calling you about this, but I thought you probably should know what's going on." The tension in Gabriel's voice put Cris on high alert. "Jake's missed work at the club the last two nights, no call outs, he flat out didn't show up. He isn't answering his phone at all, so I called Benny, who's his roommate now, and Benny says he hasn't gotten out of bed since Saturday night. He just... lays there. Sleeps. Doesn't eat. He's really worried, and now I kind of am, too, because it sounds a lot like when my mother got depressed. Anyway...I don't know. I just wanted to tell you what's going on."

The voice mail ended there. Cris stared at his phone, unease slithering through his gut like hot tar. Something was very, very wrong if Jake had been in bed for the better part of four days, and the side of Cris that still cared about him roared to life. He couldn't sit by and let Jake suffer, no matter what was going on, so he called Gabriel back.

"Hey, man," Gabriel said on the first ring.

"Dude, what's Jake's new address?" Cris asked, already shoving his feet into a pair of shoes. Gabriel gave it to him. "I'll meet you there."

The apartment building was, much to Cris's surprise, only about five blocks from his own. Getting to his car and navigating midday traffic would take too long, so he sprinted. In early June heat, he dogged foot traffic, jaywalked through cars, and ignored crossing signals so he could get to Jake and find out what was wrong. He needed to be there.

He arrived a sweaty, panting mess, and his left side ached like hell but he took the stairs anyway, instead of waiting on the elevator. The fourth floor didn't come fast enough, and then he was finally knocking on 4J. Benny yanked open the door, unsurprised to see him.

The apartment was an older style, with a tiny entry and a compact living room. The kitchen was separated by a wall that was part of the hallway. Gabriel exited a room at the end of the hall, his face pensive. Uncertain. Even Benny, who cracked jokes to make everyone else smile, looked upset.

"What's going on?" Cris asked.

"I don't know," Benny said. "He was kinda quiet on Saturday, not really talking much. Didn't do much. Then he got sent home early from Big Dick's and slept the night away. I tried to get him up Sunday, but he wouldn't move. Said he felt bad, but he didn't have a fever. I didn't think anything much, until he didn't go to work Monday. Last night either. Gabe called me earlier and said he wasn't answering calls from the club, so could I check on him? The dude's still in bed. The only time I've seen him move is to take a piss."

"Has he eaten anything?"

"Not much. I've left bottles of water and crackers and stuff by his bed. Some of it disappears but not a lot. I mean, should we call a doctor or something?"

"I talked to my dads about Jake," Gabriel said. "They told me he's never once missed a shift since he started, much less pull two no-call, no-shows in a row. They're worried, too."

"And it, like, came out of nowhere," Benny added. "Saturday morning he was fine. We played video games, and I told him about your birthday party. Then he just…I don't know. Shut down?"

Cris turned to Gabriel. "Your voice mail said something about depression?" It sounded like depression, but the super-serious kind that made people do scary things.

"Yeah." Gabriel flinched. "My mom is a recovering alcoholic, and she's suffered from manic depression most of my life. Instead of medication, she chose to treat it with wine and Chinese food binges. She'd have episodes where she was upbeat, even promised to quit drinking. But when she was down, she'd lay on the couch and not move for days unless I moved her."

Manic depression. Christ, that's scary.

"You think that could be what's wrong with Jake?" Cris asked.

"I don't know man, I honestly don't know Jake or his behavioral patterns well enough to guess. I'm not a psychiatrist, I've just seen symptoms like this before, you know?"

"Okay." Cris looked down the hallway, his heart seizing with trepidation and fear. He had no idea what he'd find when he walked into Jake's room, but he knew whatever it was, it would break his heart.

"So wait a sec," Benny said to Gabriel. "Why did you call Dane again?"

"My first name is Cris, so you can call me that instead of Dane," Cris said. "And Gabriel called me because Jake and I dated briefly. He dumped me, even though we really connected, and I still give a damn about him."

"Dude. Okay."

Cris strode down the hall, putting more confidence into his steps than he had in his ability to improve Jake's situation. He peeked through the half-open door. Beige room, no real decoration. Blue blanket on the bed covering a Jake-sized, unmoving lump. The room had a stale smell but was otherwise clean.

"Jake?"

No reaction from the lump.

He circled to the side of the bed to get a better look at Jake's face, and he kind of wanted to cry. Jake was paler than humanly possible, his cheekbones too sharp. His eyes were open, but had a dull glaze to them. Jake didn't seem alive, except for the gentle flare of his nostrils as he breathed.

"Jake? It's Cris." He squatted to eye level, trying to put himself into Jake's line of sight. Jake's only reaction was a slow, half-blink that didn't quite leave his eyes shut. Cris's throat squeezed tight. "I'm worried about you, babe. Are you sick?"

Nothing.

"You know, I've missed you these last few weeks. I hate how we left things. I should have reached out to talk sooner, and I'm sorry about that. Sorry I haven't been there, even as a friend, because I still care about you."

Jake's eyes flickered, then dimmed again.

Cris swallowed hard against the lump in his throat and glanced at the bedroom door. No one seemed to be lingering outside, but he lowered his voice anyway. "Chet told me about the brunch you guys had. You figured out I donated my kidney to Dell, didn't you? Is that why you broke up with me?"

Another flicker. Jake was listening, at least.

"What I did doesn't mean I care about Chet more than I care about you. All it means is I saw a friend hurting, and I did what I could to help him. Trust me, big noble gestures aren't usually my thing. I'm actually a pretty selfish guy. I'd tell you to ask my sister, but she's dead."

Grief seized Cris's lungs, making it hard to breathe for several seconds. He never talked about his late sister, not even to Chet. But he needed Jake to know that Cris wasn't some noble, awesome guy who'd do anything for his fellow man. Cris was deeply flawed, and he still had so much to pay for.

"She died while I wasn't paying attention. I couldn't let another person die when I could save their life. Dell and I have the same rare blood type. I saved his life because I couldn't save Grace's. And I don't know what's going on here, but I won't let you quit on me."

Cris swiped at the tear that had trickled down his cheek. "I still need you in my life, and I'm so sorry you're hurting."

Jake turned his face into the pillow, his entire body shuddering. Heart aching and eyes still leaking, Cris toed off his shoes. Climbed into the bed and slid under the stale sheets. He curled up against Jake's back, then pulled the smaller man in close. Tucked Jake's head beneath his chin. Jake didn't fight, didn't offer any protest. His breathing quickened slightly, but he remained relaxed.

They existed like that for a while, Cris holding him, willing life back into the guy he'd come to care about very quickly and should never have let walk away without a fight. Jake fit so perfectly in his arms, as if made to be there.

Except Chet. What about how he makes me feel?

Not the time to think about Chet. Cris needed to put all his energy into getting Jake through whatever hell he was living in. To find the flirty, smiling Jake who'd seduced him from a nightclub platform with a single roll of his hips.

In the pleasant warmth of Jake's bed, with Jake in his arms, Cris dozed, until a knock on the door made him raise his head. Benny peeked inside. "Hey, if you guys are hungry, we've got Chinese food."

"Thanks, man," Cris said.

"Sure thing." Benny ducked out.

Cris smoothed one hand up the length of Jake's right arm. "What do you say? A little fried rice and noodles? Or are you more of a spicy beef kind of guy?"

Jake's right shoulder moved in what he assumed was a shrug— and the biggest physical reaction he'd gotten out of Jake so far.

"Come on, babe, sit up for me."

With a little effort, Cris got Jake upright, legs dangling off the side of the bed. His shoulders remained hunched, his head down, but it was progress. He wore boxers and a t-shirt, all acceptable for a trip to the living room. The walk down the short hallway took forever, Jake moving with all of the speed of a hundred year-old man.

Food cartons were spread across the living room's coffee table. Tristan had joined them at some point, and he clung to Gabriel's side, watching Jake and Cris with a pensive look. When Cris caught his eye, Tristan tried on a smile that Cris almost believed. Cris eased Jake onto one end of the couch, then sat next to him. Benny tried to make the entire situation somewhat normal by chattering on about a movie he'd watched on Netflix that had zombie vampires in it.

Forgoing the challenge of chopsticks, Cris used a spoon to feed Jake some pork fried rice. He ate the same way he walked—slow, careful, as if doing it at all caused him physical pain. Cris didn't know for sure when he'd last eaten, so he didn't force too much down. He picked some veggies out of a carton Benny promised wasn't spicy, and Jake ate those too. Drank some water. He still hadn't said a word, but that was okay. Baby steps.

Tristan engaged Benny in a discussion of vampire versus zombie movies, and that droned on in the background. The pair had apparently bonded after the birthday party, because they talked to each other like they'd been friends for years, hurling friendly insults and making jokes at the other's expense. Gabriel, at least, seemed amused by the chatter.

Even Jake glanced their way a few times, his expression clearing a bit more with each passing minute. He was nowhere near his old self, but he was up and eating. Cris absently snacked on some sesame chicken, not very hungry himself, but doing it out of solidarity.

"You feel like a shower now?" Cris asked. "Try to wash some of that funk off?"

Jake shrugged, but something in the way his face changed suggested he approved of the idea more than his body allowed him to express. Cris helped him stand, and they began the long shuffle back down the hall. The bathroom was tiny, packed tight with a small tub, a sink and toilet, and barely enough room for two adults to fit together.

Cris turned on the water, then helped Jake undress. Okay, so mostly it was Cris undressing Jake, and it was a lot like undressing a giant doll for all the help Jake gave him. But he got Jake into the tub. Cris watched until Jake reached for the bar soap, then shut the curtain. He wanted to wait until Jake was done, but he also needed to speak to the guys about this. Get their take on it. Try to form a plan to support Jake through whatever the hell this was.

Their merry band of support had grown by another member. Jon was there, visibly up, and talking to Gabriel near the front door. He spotted Cris and charged across the room. Cris braced for a fight, but Jon surprised him by throwing his arms around Cris's shoulders and hugging him. Cris awkwardly patted Jon's back, uncertain what the hell the hug was for.

"Thank you." Jon pulled back far enough to look Cris in the eye. "Thank you for taking care of him."

"Uh, you're welcome. I didn't think you guys were close."

"We aren't, and I've been kicking myself about it ever since Gabe called me. I mean, I lived with the guy for three years, but I never really tried to make friends with him. When he snapped at me, I gave in, instead of working harder, and I didn't make anything better when I told him about losing the apartment. I'm such an asshole."

"You're not an asshole. You're human, you were busy living your own life, and hindsight is twenty-twenty. We all could have maybe done something differently to prevent this, I don't know. Right now, we need to work on helping Jake through this, not wallowing in what we didn't do."

"You're right." Jon stepped back, then scrubbed both hands over his face, leaving the skin red. "Gabe said he ate and now he's showering?"

"Yeah, he's finally out of bed and moving around, but I don't know how long that's going to last. I've never known anyone who fell into this kind of depression."

"I've had my own issues with it in the past, but not the kind where you stay in bed for four days straight," Jon admitted.

"Oh no?" Gabriel said. "I seem to remember you spending the weekend in bed after Henry died."

"That was grief, though. Wait, does Jake know someone who died?"

Cris shook his head. "I doubt it. His mother is dead, his father doesn't give a damn, and he never mentioned other family. He doesn't seem to have any really close friends, either, but I've only gotten to know him recently, so…"

"Well, you know more about his family than I ever did," Jon said, sounding a little hurt. Cris didn't take it personally though. Jon had had three years to learn shit about Jake; Cris had only had a week.

"So what do we do next?" Gabriel asked. "From my brief interactions with him, I'll be the first to admit that Jake is a prickly little bastard, but he's clearly suffering."

Cris couldn't deny that Jake was prickly, but beneath the tough exterior, he was as lost and confused and lonely as anyone else, and Cris hadn't helped at all—first by seducing him, then falling for him, and finally by nudging Jake into breaking both of their hearts. Cris wasn't self-absorbed enough to think all of this was over him, but he *had* contributed to it. And the four men standing in support of Jake deserved to know the details.

He told them a condensed version of the truth: long-time feelings for Chet that they never acted on, meeting Jake, his night out with Chet, and all of the confessions and decisions that had been made by both Chet and Jake—decisions that had left all three of them alone. He did not tell them about the night of his birthday party, or the kidney transplant. Those details were not necessary at the moment. Gabriel was the only one who didn't look surprised, because he'd heard a lot of this already. And the fact that Tristan looked shocked as hell said a lot for Gabriel's capacity for discretion.

"This clearly isn't all about me and Jake," Cris said, "because that ended weeks ago. But I have a feeling that it's part of whatever this is. I figured you guys should know. You're obviously here because you care about Jake, and so do I. So much."

"Holy crap," Tristan said. "This is like a real life *General Hospital* love triangle situation, except you've all got penises."

"Didn't they actually do a gay love triangle on that show?" Benny asked.

Tristan's already wide eyes went wider. "Seriously? Is it on YouTube?"

"Guys, focus," Gabriel said, giving Tristan a gentle poke in the ribs. "This is about Jake, not a soap opera."

"It's about Cris and Chet too, don't you think?" Tristan asked. "One person doesn't make a threesome."

"There is no threesome," Cris said. "There isn't even a twosome. But depression is serious. I think we can all agree on that, and I think we can also all agree that for now, someone needs to be here with Jake at all times."

"Do you think Jake would hurt himself?" Jon asked.

"I honestly don't know, and I'd rather not chance it."

"Agreed."

Everyone else chimed in with their support. Jon even volunteered Isaac's help, if they needed extra bodies once everyone's work schedule was figured out. Lucky for Cris, he could take his laptop anywhere to work. And Taro would lend a hand, if necessary, so they had volunteers covered.

But staying close to Jake was a patch, not a solution. If they were going to help Jake, they needed to know exactly what they were dealing with, and that meant getting Jake to talk. Cris might have let his sister down many years ago, but he wouldn't let Jake down. They'd get through this together.

Nothing else was acceptable.

Chapter Fourteen

Charles hadn't heard from Cristian about their weekend plans when he called him Thursday. He'd texted Cristian last night, informing him that the beach apartment was theirs if they wanted it, and the lack of response was more disappointing than alarming. Cristian had seemed excited about the idea at first, and then less so by the end of the conversation. Charles had chalked it up to nerves over what might be expect from him.

He hoped to reassure Cristian that he expected nothing more than the pleasure of Cristian's company at the beach for two days.

Cristian's phone rang and rang, long enough that Charles braced for voice mail.

"Hey, give me a sec to move rooms," Cristian said, somewhat breathlessly.

"Of course."

Rustling came over the line, and then, "Sorry about that."

"Moving rooms? Shouldn't you be working, young man?" He kept his tone light, but something in Cristian's voice sounded off.

"I am, but not from home. I needed a private minute, anyway."

Alarms developed by years of life experience began going off in Charles's head. "What's wrong? You sound stressed."

"Where to start?" He made a soft, almost choking sound that raised hairs on the back of Charles's neck. "I fucked something up, and I don't know how to make it right."

"Where are you? Are you alone?"

"Not alone. I'm at Jake and Benny's place." He made that noise again, and Charles swore Cristian was doing his best not to cry.

That was unacceptable. He didn't know why Cristian was at Jake's, or what had gone wrong, but Cristian obviously needed support.

Charles used his employee files to double check Benny's address, then stood from his office chair and strode toward the door, his fingers going painfully tight around his phone. "I'm on my way. Keep talking to me."

"You don't have to come over."

"The fact that you sound as if you're one wrong word away from losing it completely is reason enough for me to come over." Down the hall, pausing to grab his keys off the hook by the door. "I'm coming no matter what."

"'Kay."

That single, broken word nearly undid Charles. He flung himself into his car, switched the call over to Bluetooth so he could drive, then jammed the key into the ignition. On Cristian's end, a steady but soft series of harsh inhalations sounded suspiciously like sobs. "I'll be there soon, I promise," Charles said around a lump in his own throat. Whatever this was about, it was bad, and it also involved Jake.

His mind spun out with dozens of scenarios during the drive into the city, his only soundtrack the hum of the car engine and

Cristian's steady crying. It hurt that Charles wasn't there to comfort Cristian when he clearly needed it.

Soon, soon, soon, I'll be there soon.

He needed navigation to find the exact building, as well as nearby parking. "I'm almost there, Cristian. See you soon."

"'Kay."

Chest tight and palms sweaty, Charles hung up. He finally found a parking spot. Stuffed the keys and his phone into his slacks pockets. By the time he reached the apartment door, he'd worked off enough nervous energy to pull himself together. To be strong for Cristian and anyone else who was hurting. Charles took a few deep, cleansing breaths before knocking.

A few seconds later, Adam opened the door. His wide-eyed surprise probably mirrored Charles's own. "Hey, Chet, what are you doing here?"

"I called Cristian earlier, but he became quite upset on the phone. I'm here to see him."

"Uh, okay. Come in."

The apartment was littered in what Charles could only describe at "frat boy chic." Takeout boxes and cartons, decks of cards, video game paraphernalia scattered about. Someone's closed laptop was on the sofa. The place had an old Chinese food odor to it. Adam was the only person in sight.

"Forgive me if this sounds rude, but why are you here?" Charles asked.

"Babysitting duty with Cris," Adam replied as he settled back in front of the TV and his paused game. "Cris went down the hall. Benny's room, I think. First door on the right."

"Thank you."

His mind spun out again with what this was all about. The indicated door was closed, so he knocked gently before opening it. "Cristian?"

"Yeah."

He slipped inside. The room was a chaotic mess of strewn clothes and piles of comic books, with a bed dead center. Cristian sat on the floor against the far wall, knees drawn up, cheeks still streaked with drying tears. His dark eyes swam with utter misery and nearly undid Charles's composure.

"Oh, love." Charles walked over and pulled Cristian into his arms, heart racing at the way Cristian shivered, then started to cry again. "I've got you. You're safe."

"Not me," Cristian choked out. "Jake. God."

Charles heart broke a little bit more. He held Cristian tight, giving him all of the support he could. Stroked his back and hair. Whispered soft words of encouragement. Existed with Cristian while he exorcised whatever was tearing him up inside. The only thing Charles knew for certain was that something was wrong with Jake—wrong enough that two people were in an apartment they didn't live in so they could keep an eye on him.

Cristian began to settle, his sobs turning into soft hiccups, then gentle sighs. Instead of allowing Charles to simply hold him, Cristian looped his arms around Charles's waist and held him back. Tightly. The hug gave Charles hope that they could talk soon, so he could figure out how to help.

"Tell me what's going on, love," Charles whispered.

"It's Jake. He's been having some sort of serious depressive episode since Saturday night. Until yesterday, Benny said he hadn't gotten out of bed. Was barely eating or drinking. Now he's at least eating and drinking, but it's tough to get him up."

The described behavior had all the hallmarks of severe depression. "What changed yesterday?"

"Me." Cristian lifted his head. His eyes were red and puffy, a study in misery and grief. "Gabriel called. I came over. Got Jake to get up, eat, and shower. He doesn't really respond to anyone else."

"Then I'm grateful that young man had you here to help him."

"You aren't upset?"

"Why would I be upset?" Charles wasn't thrilled that Jake still had such deep feelings for Cristian, but he couldn't change it. He needed to fix this before he sorted out his own emotions. "He still has feelings for you, that much is clear. I'm glad you could be there for him when he needed you."

"I just want to see him smile, you know? He's got a great smile."

"I understand." He was a bit jealous, as well, but Charles did understand. "Can you walk me through exactly what's happened?"

Cristian described what he knew from both Benny's stories and his own experiences with Jake, as well as the support system that was rallying around the clock for Jake, taking turns staying close by, because no one knew what he'd do.

"You're afraid he may attempt self-harm?" Charles asked.

"I don't know. That's why someone is always here with him. I can't fail him, too. I can't." His voice broke again.

Charles tucked him in close, concerned by the qualifier. "Who else have you failed?"

"My sister. Graziella, but we called her Grace. She was sixteen by two days when she died, and it was my fault."

"Surely that's not possible." Charles had never heard of Cristian's sister before today, much less that she died so young. "Will you tell me about her?"

"She had Type 1 diabetes." Cristian turned so his cheek rested on Charles's shoulder, warm breath fanning over Charles' neck. "It was hell for her, managing that her whole life, but it got worse in high school. Some shit went down with our dad, so we had to move in with our aunt. Going from Long Island to western Maryland was a big change. A culture shock. Kids were faster to bully. I did my best to protect her, but I was a seething ball of rage over my dad, and all I wanted was to get away. Our aunt complained how expensive we were, with food and Grace's medications and care. It really sucked.

"After I turned eighteen, my aunt made me move out, so I got a shitty apartment, two jobs, and I started doing web design work. It was also when I was really getting a handle on being bi, even though I didn't tell anyone. Not even Grace. She loved that I had a place, and I used to let her and her friends hang at my pad, instead of going out and getting into trouble, you know? I tried so hard to keep her safe."

Charles traced soft circles on Cristian's back, aching for this beautiful man's pain. "What happened to her?"

Cristian shivered. "I wanted to hit up a gay bar one Friday, so Grace and her friends went to a house party. A few hours later, I got a call from the emergency room. They said my sister had been admitted and she was in a diabetic coma. Her friends thought someone had spiked Grace's drinks, because she knew better than to mess with alcohol, and she collapsed at the party. Started seizing. By the time I got to the hospital, her kidneys had shut down completely. She died the next day."

"Goddamn it, Cristian." Charles wanted to weep for the heartbreak in Cristian's voice. For the depth of guilt he'd been carrying for nearly a decade over his sister's accidental death. "That was hardly your fault."

"They wouldn't have gone to the party if I'd stayed home."

"Doesn't matter. If there is anyone to blame, it's whoever spiked her drinks. Did the police investigate?"

"Yeah. No one admitted to anything. Big fucking surprise. I blamed me. My aunt blamed me. So after the funeral, I packed up my car with what little I had and decided to drive until I ran out of gas. I ended up on empty just outside the Sheetz on Paxton Street."

"That's how you ended up moving to Harrisburg?"

"Yeah. In my head, I think I wanted to go farther, but I didn't realize how little gas I had in the car." Cristian wheezed something close to laughter. "The web design business came with me, so I wasn't totally broke. I worked at a car wash while I kept growing and evolving the business. Took some night school classes on programming. Then I met you."

"And two lives were forever changed."

"In ten years, you're the first person I've ever told about Grace. I never even told Taro how she died."

"I'm honored that you trust me with such a weighty secret. Truly." Genuine affection for Cristian burned in his blood, followed by something much stronger. Cristian fit in his arms, felt amazing against his body, and he'd accepted the comfort Charles offered. His level of trust and compassion was amazing for someone who'd lost so much, so young. "What happened to Grace isn't your fault, and what's happening to Jake now isn't your fault, either. Many people took actions in both cases, so instead of blaming yourself, let's try to fix it, all right?"

"Okay. Thank you."

"Anything for you. Now, when was the last time you were home?"

"Not since right after we spoke yesterday."

"Hmm. Shower?"

"Yesterday morning."

"I suspected as much. Why don't you go do that now? I'll have a quick look in on Jake."

Cristian lifted his head, still sad but also curious. "Why?"

"Because you're important to me, and he's obviously still important to you, which makes him important to me. Trust me?"

"With my life, Chet. You know that."

"I do. Come on. Up you go." He stood first, then helped Cristian to his unsteady feet. Cristian wobbled a bit, but he made it across the hall to the bathroom and shut the door.

Charles made an educated guess that the only other unopened door was to Jake's room and knocked. He expected no response and received none. Instead of a human lump hiding beneath covers, Jake was sitting up in bed, a pillow hugged to his chest, staring at the sheets pooled around him.

"Jake? We meet again, young man."

Jake's head tilted slightly. Hearing about the depths of one's depressive episode was a far cry from seeing it in the flesh. Jake's empty, unresponsive nature was scary from someone Charles recalled as being full of energy and quick to bite back. He could see why this had frightened Cristian so deeply. It frightened Charles, too.

"For a self-declared loner, you have quite the support system rallying around you right now. Perhaps you're a more lovable person than you give yourself credit for."

That earned him a full shrug, but Jake tilted his head more. "Cris needs you," Jake said. The words were so soft they barely carried across the small room.

"Yes, he does." Charles eased onto the corner of the bed, keeping his body open and angled toward Jake. "And so do you. How do you feel right now?"

"Tired. There's no point. It's too much. All too much."

"It does feel that way, doesn't it? It's all so overwhelming to the point where even thinking of getting out of bed wears you out." Charles scooted closer. "I haven't walked in your shoes, Jake, and I can't pretend to know exactly how you're feeling, but I once trod a similar path, so I think I can relate. Perhaps better than some of the young men in your life."

The shift in Jake's expression silently asked him to continue. Jake was listening, and that was a big step.

"Ten years ago, I reached the lowest point of my life. I'd fallen into a deep cycle of depression after a falling out with one of my business partners. In much the same way I allowed Stefan to openly cheat on me for years, I looked the other way while Arnold made....questionable choices with an investment. It was making us money, so why question the methods, right? And then I was faced with the human consequences of those choices. We hurt hundreds of people in the name of the almighty dollar, and I regret that to this day.

"I told myself I was unworthy. I was a terrible person, a horrid person. I drank a lot, rarely left my home, cut out all of my friends. Life became a dark, empty space, devoid of light or joy. Can you see light right now, Jake? Or joy?"

"Cris," Jake said. "He's light. Joy. But it's too late. He needs better."

"I know you believe Cristian deserves better than you, but I think it's rather clear to us both that he wants you, despite your flaws. Or perhaps because of them. He isn't perfect, either, and he carries his own pain."

Jake flinched, then rolled onto his side, facing away from Charles. Undaunted, Charles moved to the other side of the bed so he could still see Jake's face. A constant reminder to Jake that he wasn't alone, despite the overwhelming darkness keeping Jake isolated in his own mind. "Now, now, I haven't finished my story," Charles said. "And trust me, it has a happy ending. Although at the time, I very much believed I'd reached the end.

"I became so isolated, so entrenched in my darkness that I wanted it all to be over. I wanted to die, but I was too much of a coward to swallow the pills or buy the gun. So I left my house in Venice and began walking. I figured I'd walk until I collapsed, or a car hit me, or maybe I'd walk into the ocean and disappear. I didn't much care. Somehow, I ended up all the way in Culver City, on a corner near some working boys. One of them approached me and asked if I was looking for a date.

"I wasn't, of course, but this boy was beautiful. Something made me pay attention to him, to this beautiful boy who sold his body in order to survive. He reminded me how lucky I'd been after my own family turned their backs on me. I hesitate to call that conversation an epiphany, but I didn't walk into the ocean that night. I gave that boy every dollar I had in my wallet, then used my credit card to buy him and his friends a motel room for a week. It wasn't nearly enough, but I went home alive. And I felt a little less worthless. I saw a bit more light through the darkness.

"This stranger who approached me was the seed for what eventually became Mean Green Boys. I didn't snap out of my depression overnight, and no one here expects that from you, Jake. This is a journey and a battle, and you have so many people here to fight with you, including myself. Lean on us until the light comes back."

Jake blinked hard several times, not seeming to notice the tears trickling down his cheeks. Those tears fueled something new in Charles—an intense desire not only to help Jake, but to make sure he stayed safe, no matter what. Safe, protected, and happy. He wouldn't let Jake walk into the ocean. Not ever.

Charles eased closer, watching Jake's physical cues and seeing no fear or repulsion. Only a silent need for love and support, and Charles had more than enough to share. He slid behind Jake and tucked him against his chest, thrilled when the boy relaxed. His hands rose to clasp Charles's tight over Jake's abdomen. Jake's head listed back to rest on Charles's shoulder. Charles soaked in his body heat, amazed at how lovely Jake felt in his arms. How much he liked having him there.

A shadow by the door caught Charles's attention. Cristian stood halfway inside, his hair still damp from the shower, watching them both with a strange smile. More than gratitude, the smile contained hints of something else. Something that reflected Charles's own feelings about holding Jake close. Cristian didn't show an ounce of jealousy, either, which urged Charles to smile back.

Jake extended one hand to Cristian. He didn't pull away from Charles. He was reaching out. For support.

Cristian's entire body relaxed as he shut the door, and then walked to the bed and climbed on, dressed in too-tight sweatpants and a t-shirt—probably borrowed from Benny's room. Together, they eased onto the bed, Jake still the little spoon to Charles, facing Cristian. Jake grabbed one of Cristian's hands and brought to himself, tucking it under his chin.

They lay there for a long time, no one speaking, existing in a formation that shouldn't have worked, but did. A trio of support and caring with Jake at its center. Charles didn't try to define it or quantify what it meant. It didn't matter. The emotions stirring in his chest were real. Powerful.

And a little bit terrifying for what they might mean.

Today wasn't the day to understand it. Today was about helping Jake through this, getting him out the other side in one piece. Until that happened, the rest had to wait.

Chapter Fifteen

Cris hadn't expected to return from his shower to find Chet in Jake's room, holding Jake in his arms like he'd already done it a hundred times. The way Jake had clung to Chet, absorbing the support, had also done a funny thing to Cris's heart. A funny thing that continued to turn over and over while the three of them relaxed in bed. Existing in a comfortable silence born of solidarity and strength. And for the first time since he got Gabriel's voice mail yesterday, Cris had hope that they'd get past this.

Jake would be okay; Cris and Chet would make sure of it.

Both Jake and Chet were facing him, so Cris saw when they each dozed off. Jake went under first, his breathing smoothing out, the crinkles at the corners of his eyes disappearing as he relaxed. Chet took longer, until his hold on Jake loosened, taut muscles going soft. Asleep, Chet took on an innocence that Cris had never seen in the man before. And the sight of Chet and Jake sleeping in each other's arms?

Arresting.

Astonishing.

Beautiful.

The two men Cris wanted most had found each other in their own way, and it made Cris want. It made him want something he'd never imagined possible. Never dreamed of, not even in his wildest imaginations. And now he didn't have to dream, because he was looking right at it.

Beyond the bedroom, a door opened and shut loudly enough for the sound to carry. Probably the front door, someone else arriving to the apartment. Maybe Benny home from work, maybe one of the other guys here to relieve Adam.

Cris's heart flipped. Adam had let Chet inside the apartment, and he had to be wondering what was going on. He hadn't been there yesterday when Cris laid out everything that was going on between him, Jake and Chet, and Cris didn't know what Adam had or hadn't been told. And now the three of them were cuddling in bed together.

Shit was not supposed to be this complicated.

He eased out of bed, careful not to jostle or wake his bedmates. Jake snuffled once; Chet didn't move at all. Cris sneaked out of the bedroom, opening and closing the door as silently as possible. Followed muffled voices to the enclosed kitchen. Adam and Benny were inside, backs to him, fussing over some bags of groceries on the counter.

"…for a few hours," Adam said. "Any idea what that's about?"

"Some, yeah," Benny replied. "Cris said some stuff yesterday, but I'm not sure how much he wants us gossiping about right now. Maybe you should ask Cris?"

"Ask Cris what?" Cris said.

Both men jumped, then turned. Adam looked kind of guilty, but Benny only glared at him once, before turning back to what looked—and smelled—like a rotisserie chicken.

"What's up with you and Chet?" Adam asked.

"Long story that can wait." Cris's stomach rumbled from the scent of the chicken that Benny was carving up. "You sharing, or do I have to beg?"

Benny snickered. "While I'd love to hear you beg, honey, yes, it's to share. I've got potato salad and a mixed fruit bowl. Deli stuff was easier than coming home to cook for you hungry invaders."

"Excellent." Cris reached past Benny to snag a piece of white meat. Hot and juicy, and holy crap, he was hungry. Had he even eaten today?

He tried to get another piece, but Benny smacked his fingers. "You can wait five minutes for me to get this shit onto the dining table. Geez."

"You think Jake is gonna join us?" Adam asked.

"Yes." Jake's voice from outside the kitchen startled all three of them.

Cris turned, surprise and joy jolting through him at the sight of Jake and Chet standing together near the dining table. Jake still seemed listless and tired, but also more aware than a few hours ago. Chet had his business face on full-force, but one of his hands was resting on the small of Jake's back.

"The zombie rises," Benny said with a cheeky grin. "You want white or dark meat, dude?"

Adam snickered at the unintended innuendo.

"Not picky," Jake said. Chet led him to one of the table's four small chairs, then pulled it out for him to sit. Cris smiled at the attentive, gentlemanly action.

"You know what, guys?" Adam said. "I'm gonna bounce. I've got stuff to get done, so...Chet, Friday at six o'clock, yeah?"

"Friday at six," Chet replied with a nod.

The scene Chet mentioned. Shit, we were planning to go away this weekend.

He met Chet's steady gaze. Chet shook his head in a barely perceptible way that eased Cris's anxiety. In his own silent, wonderfully supportive way, Chet was telling him it was okay to change their plans. Jake needed them more.

After Adam left, Cris helped Benny put food, drinks, and paper plates on the table. Chet took point and created a small plate for Jake, mostly slices of chicken, a small scoop of potato salad, and a healthy portion of the fruit. Jake thanked him, then began to eat with the same slow, steady precision Cris was growing accustomed to seeing while he was low. So different from the way he'd scarfed down hot dogs at City Island.

The meal was mostly silent, with Benny offering a few brief stories from his job, mostly about a new, somewhat clumsy employee. Great with customers, terrible at handling fragile things.

At the end of the meal, Jake surprised them all by rising from his chair and collecting their empty plates. He silently helped Benny put the leftovers away and clean up. Cris watched it all with hope in his heart, certain that Jake had made a turn. Beneath the table, Chet squeezed his knee. Cris saw the same hope in Chet's eyes, as well as another emotion Cris couldn't identify. A positive one, for sure, but also a complicated one.

Instead of returning to his room, Jake settled on one end of the couch, facing the dark TV. Benny looked at the three of them and wisely chose retreat. "I'll be in my room, uh, reading or something," he said, then disappeared down the hallway.

"Are you feeling more settled?" Chet asked softly.

Cris nodded. "Much more settled, thanks." He'd been a hot mess when Chet first arrived, and for an instant, he'd been ashamed of himself for sobbing all over the man. But Chet had stood strong, supporting him through it, letting Cris deal with the emotions he'd bottled up for more than twenty-four hours.

Opening up about Grace and his lingering guilt over her death had been another gut-punch, but also strangely therapeutic. The rational side of his brain knew her death wasn't his fault, but the grieving big brother couldn't accept that. Not until Chet said it. Chet almost made Cris believe it, almost made him want to let go of the guilt.

Almost.

"It doesn't seem quite as dark anymore," Jake said, apropos of nothing. More to himself than to them.

Cris glanced around, not sure what he meant. The lighting in the apartment was the same as yesterday.

"That's wonderful to hear," Chet said. He approached the couch. Instead of sitting next to Jake, he perched on the coffee table opposite him. "More of the light is showing."

Oh, this is a metaphor.

He had no idea what Chet had said to Jake while Cris showered, but when Jake raised his head and his lips quirked into something very close to a smile, Cris nearly cried. Chet had reached Jake, helped him turn some kind of corner with this deep depression, and he wanted to kiss Chet for it. He also wanted to kiss Jake for how far he'd come since yesterday.

I want to kiss them both. Hold them both tight and never let anything bad happen to them.

"Jake, this is somewhat personal," Chet said, "but have you ever had a depressive episode like this before? Where you've been so tired, so full of darkness, that you couldn't move for days?"

Jake shook his head slowly, a steady back and forth. "No. I've never felt like this before."

"How about the opposite? I've heard you're an energetic young man, but have you ever felt like your mind was in overdrive? Like you had to achieve goals and be the best at what you're doing? Driven to relentlessly pursue?"

He took longer answering that one. "Not really. Sometimes I have a hard time sleeping because my brain won't quit. Dancing helps. I can channel it, you know?"

"All right. Thank you for answering my questions."

Cris tried to catch Chet's attention, but he and Jake were ten feet away, angled toward each other. The precise questioning hinted that Chet knew what they were dealing with, but Cris hesitated to interrupt. Watching Chet and Jake interact—something he'd never seen before—was entrancing. Chet might have been twice Jake's age, but nothing about his reactions to the younger man were paternal. They were laser-focused and personal—not unlike the reactions of a concerned lover.

Holy shit.

Chet had known Jake for a total combination of maybe six hours, but there was definitely some kind of attraction there.

"This gets better, right?" Jake asked. "I can't...I hate this. Feeling like this."

"I know." Chet reached out and gathered both of Jake's hands in his. "And it does get better. From what I've been told about your decline this past week, I'd say you're already improving. Quite a lot, actually, by sitting here talking to us."

Jake tilted his head in question, then looked over at Cris. Offered that same not-quite smile. Cris's insides melted, and he grinned back. "You changed clothes," Jake said.

The random comment made Cris laugh. "Yeah, I borrowed some from Benny. Chet there seemed to think I smelled enough to send me off to the shower."

"I didn't say you smelled," Chet said. "I merely suggested you might benefit from the relief of a hot shower." He paused, quirked an eyebrow. "You smelling better was merely a side benefit."

Jake made a funny noise, not quite laughter, but close enough for Cris to cheer inside. "Can, uh, you guys stay for a while?" Jake asked.

"Absolutely," Cris replied. He migrated to the couch, giving Jake a comfortable cushion of space between them.

Chet switched to a side chair, to which Jake squawked an objection. The three of them rearranged themselves on the couch so that Jake was in the center, loosely sandwiched by Cris and Chet. The positions felt strangely perfect. They found a comedy to stream and settled in to watch it. Everything was so comfortable, so easy, this could have been the thousandth time they'd done this, instead of the first.

Cris wasn't entirely sure how it happened, or which part of Jake moved first. Only that by the end of the movie, Jake's head was resting on Cris's lap, while his feet were in Chet's. As the credits rolled, Cris brushed a lock of hair from Jake's temple, happy to see he was still wide awake. Jake hadn't laughed during the movie, but he'd paid attention, and he seemed...brighter.

"I have a proposition for you boys," Chet said.

"You want me to put out, you have to buy me dinner first," Jake said.

Cris busted out laughing, as amused by the deadpan comment as he was delighted by the fact that Jake had told a joke.

Even Chet chuckled. "It's nothing like that, I promise, and I'm asking this in all innocence. I have two more guest rooms that are sitting empty right now. Granted, they're both quite small, but they are usable. I'd like to offer them to you two."

"To both of us?" Cris asked, stunned by the offer.

"Yes. Right now, Jake needs a continued support system, and he'll more easily get that around myself, Dell and you, Cristian, than by a rotating ring of visitors. The other boys have been lovely to come by and keep you company, but they have their own lives to attend to. Jake, I know it's much farther from your job, but—"

"Shit." Jake sat up too fast and had to grab the back of the couch to steady himself. "Fuck, Richard and Bear probably fired me." He teared up, his lips pressed tight.

Cris didn't think before putting his arm around Jake's waist. "They didn't fire you. Gabriel's been in contact with everyone on both sides. They're worried about you, but your job is safe, I promise."

Jake looked at him, his brown eyes brimming with tears. "Promise?"

Fuck, he's going to be the death of me.

"I promise. Take the time you need to get well, before you think about going back to the club, okay? You make me that promise."

"Okay."

Cris tutted. "Not good enough."

Jake lips twisted, showing off a hint of that old snarky personality. "I promise."

"Thank you."

"My God, you two are adorable," Chet said.

Cris jerked in surprise, and even Jake seemed startled. Chet was watching them with that same indecipherable expression. A mixture of amusement and adoration, without a single hint of jealousy, but also tinged with something Cris still couldn't put a finger on.

"So the, uh, housing offer," Cris said, hoping to redirect. "What's the timeline?"

"The offer is open-ended, for however long Jake feels he needs the additional support," Chet replied. "We both want him well, and I think Jake will agree he wants the same thing."

Jake nodded. "Okay."

"Excellent. Cristian?"

"I'm on board," Cris replied. Moving into Chet's house temporarily hadn't been on today's To Do list, but it made sense. They still didn't know what had caused Jake's episode, or if it would happen again, so keeping him surrounded by people who cared about him was their best option.

"I'm happy to hear it." Chet stood. "It's too late to do much more tonight, so I'll leave you both to yourselves."

"You don't have to leave."

He smiled fondly at both of them. "I have two guest rooms to air out and additional groceries to purchase. I'll see you both in the morning. Cristian, I expect you'll bring Jake with you?"

Cris searched Chet's face, worried that Chet was starting to pull away from them both, trying to take the high road now that Jake was improving. All he saw was kindness and anticipation. Maybe a little fatigue. Chet seemed to expect Cris to stay the night with Jake, and he also seemed totally okay with it.

Could he be more amazing?

"I can definitely do that," Cris replied.

"Excellent. Be well, and I'll see you both tomorrow."

Chet let himself out without any further commentary or actions, not even hugs, which didn't surprise Cris. Chet didn't help for accolades or thanks. He helped because he had the energy, time, and resources, and because he genuinely gave a damn. He gave a damn when so few did, and he fought hard for the people he cared about.

"You want to watch another movie?" Jake asked.

"Definitely."

Jake settled into his previous position, with his legs up and his head on Cris's lap, while Cris surfed for another film. Everything about it was domestic and wonderful. But as he chose a movie and the opening titles played, he couldn't help the keen sense that the two of them were incomplete.

That sense remained long after the second movie ended. After he and Jake went to bed, curling up wonderfully close beneath the covers. And as Cris finally began to drift off into sleep, Chet's ghost leaned in and whispered that he missed them, too.

Chapter Sixteen

Packing for his temporary move to Chet's house didn't take Jake very long. In the few weeks since moving in with Benny, he hadn't accumulated much more than he'd brought there, so his life went into the duffel bag once more. He did leave a single pair of boxers behind, though, as a kind of stake on the place. Benny knew the relocation was temporary, but still.

His room, and he was coming back to it.

Eventually.

The packing didn't take long, but it left Jake exhausted anyway. Everything was exhausting, even thinking about the next step—which Cris told him about before he left to pack his own stuff. Jake couldn't remember what it was, other than he was supposed to hang here for now. He was perfectly fine laying on the couch with morning TV droning in the background. Preparing for the eventual task of getting up. Walking downstairs. Climbing into Cris's car. So many things to do yet, and all he really wanted was to crawl back into bed.

Except his bed was empty. He hadn't realized how much he craved human contact until Cris crawled into bed with him...two days ago? Something like that. Being held had made him want to cry for how great it felt—the first thing he'd really felt in forever. Cris made it better. He brought light.

So did Chet.

More and more, he understood why Cris was drawn to the man. Chet was solid, strong, oozed empathy from every pore, and he was…kind. Treating Jake like he mattered when Chet didn't know him. Had no reason to care about him. Comfort him. Hold him so he could fall apart.

And now he was going to Chet's house, so Chet could keep looking after him.

The mental gymnastics necessary to unpack that weighed Jake down and kept him flat on the sofa. No sorting it out now. Simply accept the offer. Take the help.

Anything to make Cris smile again.

The TV droned on. Time moved like honey, thick and oozy. The front door opened and shut, and then Cris loomed over him. Not quite smiling, but he looked a lot happier than yesterday.

"From the bed to the couch," Cris said. "That's progress."

Jake mentally flipped him off; raising his hand would take too much of his limited energy. "Packed?"

"Yup, I have my stuff in the car. You ready to go?"

"Guess so." He kind of hated how long it took him to sit up, and that Cris was carrying his duffel bag for him. Every step felt like dragging his feet through knee-high mud, taking six times as much effort, leaving him completely spent by the time he finally sank into the passenger seat of Cris's car.

The morning sunlight hurt his eyes, so he closed them and rested his cheek against the window. Heat soaked into his skin for the first time in forever. He couldn't remember the last time he'd been outside. Wasn't sure it mattered. He was out now. With

Cris. Moving in with a porn producer, because Jake had terrified a lot of people.

"Something's wrong with me," Jake said, mostly to himself.

"We're going to figure it out, okay?" Cris replied, his strong voice its own kind of sunlight. Pushing away more and more of the darkness. "Whatever help you need, we'll get it for you."

We.

He still didn't understand the "we" but he'd go with it for now. Going with it was easier.

Eventually, Cris turned onto a street Jake had visited once before. Weeks ago. Brunch. Chet. Kidney transplant.

Jake raised his head with effort, blinking Cris into focus. "Does Chet know?"

Cris stared back at him, confused. "About what?"

"The kidney."

His eyes went briefly wide, then shuttered. "No. It was anonymous, and I don't want him to know."

"But your scar." Jake had noticed it the two times they'd had sex. It was impossible to miss when Cris's shirt was off. Sooner or later, Cris would return to porn and Chet would know.

"Chet hasn't seen the scar yet," Cris said. "Please, Jake, I know you're having a really tough time right now, but don't tell Chet I donated my kidney to Dell. Please."

The desperation in Cris's voice and expression punched Jake in the heart. This wasn't his secret to tell. "Promise."

"Thank you. I know I need to tell him myself, before he finds out another way, but not yet. Let's get you better first, okay?"

"Okay."

The trip from the car to the front door left Jake's limbs full of sludge, his joints aching. Chet greeted them with huge smiles and hugs. He even did that whole French thing where he air-kissed both sides of their faces. It was kind of cute in its own way. Chet took Jake's bag from Cris, because he was carrying both of their stuff. Jake followed them both upstairs, using the banister to get himself to the next step.

His room was painted pale blue, with white furniture and a kind of seaside theme to the decorations and bedspread. Chet was talking about something Jake didn't really hear, beyond "settle in" and "your room for as long as you need it." He vaguely thanked Chet, then sat on the bed, ready for a break. Going back downstairs at some point was really going to suck.

Chet and Cris left, his door wide open, probably to show Cris to his room. The whole production still didn't seem real, like some kind of daydream he couldn't shake himself out of. Or maybe he was still back in his bed at the apartment, huddled under the covers, imagining a better life than his never-ending, exhausting existence. Maybe he'd never really left that room.

Except the bedspread beneath his hand was soft and silky. The room smelled like cinnamon. Real live voices were rumbling in from the hallway. He still remembered the way Cris had held him. The way Chet had held him.

Chet's words about walking into the ocean had struck a real chord in Jake, clearing enough of the fog from his brain for him to realize how fucking scared Chet was. Chet had once been suicidal, and he'd been afraid that Jake was suicidal too. Jake wasn't sure if he was, or if he had been before Cris found him in the dark. Doing anything except sleeping took too much energy. Killing himself? Way too much work.

Maybe….

Chet brought me here so I don't slip that far away. He won't let me walk into the ocean.

Jake didn't want to die. He didn't know what else he wanted, other than to soak in the comfort of the two men quietly passing by his bedroom door. They didn't glance in, giving him privacy in their own way, heading back downstairs. Stairs that were going to take a hell of an effort to descend, but Jake didn't want to be alone. Not anymore. Not when he could be with them.

Chet and Cris were gone by the time Jake shuffled to the hallway. He took in the dark wood and thick carpet, the scattering of framed artwork on the walls. Mostly abstract stuff Jake didn't understand. The door across from his seemed to be the bathroom, which was good to know.

He stood at the top of the stairs for a while, unsure how to navigate them when he was still so fucking tired. Growing up, he vaguely remembered moving from a single story to a two-story house sometime during his toddler years. Going down the steps had terrified him for a long time, so he'd sit at the top, then lower his butt to the next step. It took longer, and his mom used to tease him about polishing the wood steps with his butt. The method seemed his best current option to get his ass downstairs.

It worked. Eventually, his feet landed on the foyer hardwood. He used the banister to stand, then took a moment to breathe. The scent of vanilla, familiar from that Sunday brunch, permeated the entire house. Past the formal living room were two more doors. One marked Studio, the other either a closet or bathroom.

Into the more familiar eat-in kitchen and attached den. Chet and Cris stood at the island, chatting over drinks.

Cris noticed him first, his entire face lighting up with his smile. "Hey, you came down."

Chet turned, his own smile warm and inviting, and their combined attention drew Jake across the room to them. "It was lonely upstairs," Jake said.

"We weren't sure if you wanted to rest or not."

"I've been sleeping for a week. I'm tired but...tired of being tired, you know?"

"Very understandable," Chet said. "Please, have a seat." He pulled out a stool, which Jake sank into. "Cristian and I were discussing lunch options."

"Are you two going out?"

"No, no, options here at home. The refrigerator is stocked full of food, including a variety of lunchmeats and cheese. I also have whole wheat and rye bread, as well as various condiments. Occasionally during filming, the boys need to take a break and have a snack. I hope there's something in there you like."

Jake tried to smile for him. "I'm all for processed, high-salt stuff. Used to drive Jon crazy."

"I bet it did," Cris said. "Benny showed me your half of the freezer."

"Those Hot Pockets were his."

Cris winked.

"Jake, I'd like to ask a favor of you," Chet said, suddenly all kinds of serious.

As if Jake would say no to anything Chet asked. Chet was letting him live in his house and was already offering him food. "Okay."

"I'd like you to speak with a good friend of mine. She's a psychiatrist who specializes in mood disorders, and she'd very well-regarded in her field."

"Mood disorders?" Cris said. "You think you know what's wrong with Jake?"

"As I've said, I have a suspicion, but as I'm not a professional in any field of medicine, I hesitate to put a label on it myself. That's for Nancy to do."

"Okay," Jake said. Maybe if this Nancy lady knew what was going on with him, she'd also know how to fix it. He hated feeling this way, so heavy and bogged down by the world and everything in it. He wanted his life back.

"Excellent. Thank you. I'll call her this afternoon and set up a time for her to come by the house to meet you."

"Why are you being so nice to me?"

Chet put his drink down and turned to face Jake full-on, that gentle, compassionate expression a bright light in the ever-present dark. He pressed two fingers beneath Jake's chin, a feather-light touch that made Jake's insides squirm. "You need help, and I'm in the position to offer it freely, with no strings attached. And I'll say this as many times as you need to hear it: you're important to Cristian, which makes you important to me."

In that moment, something shifted in a way Jake couldn't describe or completely understand. Not only a change between Jake and Cris, but between Jake and Chet, and maybe even Cris and Chet, even though they weren't looking at each other. Chet's pale eyes never wavered from Jake's, a silent promise in them that removed a little bit more of that darkness. Jake had no idea what was actually happening, so he held tight to the knowledge that he was safe, protected, and everything was going to get better.

He pulled Chet's fingers away from his chin, twisting his wrist so their hands were clasped together. "Thank you."

"Thank me by getting better. That's all I ask in return."

"I will." Jake squeezed his hand tighter.

Chet returned the firm hold, then gently pulled away, retreating to the other side of the counter. "Now, about those sandwiches."

Jake caught Cris's gaze. His dark eyes were hooded, his smile such a beautiful thing. Jake wasn't sure why he was smiling like that, but it fueled Jake's desire to get better. Not only for Chet, but also for Cris. Somehow Jake had become part of a dynamic that required all three of them in order to function properly—a notion as exciting as it was terrifying. His entire world had taken a dramatic shift in a new direction. Time would tell how it all turned out.

After a few minutes of picking through the contents of the fridge, they all three settled at the dining table with sandwiches and sourdough pretzels. Jake asked for a simple combination of turkey and mustard on rye. Cris put together several layers of meat and cheese on rye, while Chet created something with sliced tomatoes, mayo and roast beef on wheat.

Halfway through his sandwich, Jake realized someone was missing. "Where's Dell?"

"Out, surprisingly," Chet replied. "He mentioned meeting a friend for lunch."

"Adam?" Cris asked.

"I'm not certain. As far as I'm aware, Dell and Adam haven't socialized in months. But the fact that the boy is going out again, attempting a social life, is miracle enough. I don't want to pry. As long he's back to help me prep for the shoot, he can do what he likes."

Jake started to ask why Dell didn't go out much, but a quick glance at Cris reminded him. The overdose and the transplant. Words dangled on the tip of his tongue, but he'd promised Cris to let him bring it up.

Not my secret.

"I suppose it's a bit late to ask you this, Jake," Chet said, "but does it bother you that we'll be filming a scene tonight? The studio is in the basement, and the boys will be coming over around six."

Jake blinked hard at Chet, thrown by the question. He was living in Chet's house, eating his food, drinking his soda, but he wanted to know if Jake was uncomfortable with how Chet made money? "Doesn't bother me at all. It's what you guys do."

Cris frowned.

Okay, so maybe Cris doesn't do it right now, but he also hasn't said he's quit.

"I appreciate that," Chet said. "Not everyone is as accepting of our profession."

Jake shrugged. "I'm a go-go boy. I'd be a hypocrite if it bothered me."

"Not necessarily. While some people throw all manner of sex work under the same umbrella, there are folks who would do your job, while sneering down their nose at mine."

"Not me." He didn't care. "Hell, if all of your Mean Green dudes fuck like Cris, anyone would be lucky to date them."

Cris inhaled his soda and started coughing. Chet chuckled as he smacked Cris on the back, helping him clear his airway. "He's feisty, isn't he?" Chet said. "I like it."

A strange sound burbled up from deep in Jake's chest, and it felt a lot like laughter.

Once he got Cris sorted, Chet turned his attention back to Jake. "May I ask, then, if you're a fan of the site?"

"I guess," Jake replied. "Never could afford to subscribe, but I've seen stills and watched the previews online. Sometimes your stuff pops up on free sites."

"After you've finished eating, would you like a tour of the studio?"

"Sure." He'd never been on any sort of film or TV set before, and a porn set in a basement wasn't super glamorous, but it would be cool to see the place Cris worked. Used to work. Whatever.

Cris volunteered to clean the table and put stuff away, so Jake followed Chet into the foyer to the door marked Studio. Down a set of carpeted steps into a much larger space than Jake had expected. One area was full of pieces of furniture and various accessories, including fake plants and artwork. A smaller corner had a shelving unit full of cameras and things Jake didn't have names for, since the most complicated piece of technology in his life was his cell phone.

The centerpiece of the studio, though, was the area where they clearly did the shooting. A bedroom set was up, complete with lamps and fluffy pillows. Jake tried to imagine Cris on that bed, naked, having sex with someone.

Having sex with me. Fuck, but it was so good with us.

Stop it. He wants Chet.

Except…even through the fog still swirling around his brain, Jake got the impression Cris still wanted *him*, too.

"Is it weird for you?" Jake asked. "Having feelings for Cris, and then filming him having sex with other guys?"

"It isn't weird for me, no." Chet brushed his hand over the bed's coverlet. "This is a job for both of us. I can compartmentalize the sex that happens in this room as part of the job. Business as usual. It makes it easier to separate myself as a man from myself as a producer. As a producer, Cristian is my employee and nothing else."

"As a man?"

Chet sat on the corner of the bed, hands loose in his lap, his expression strangely serene. "As a man, I had feelings and nowhere to put them."

"Why not? I broke up with Cris weeks ago." Jake had set Cris free to be with the man who deserved him, but the two stubborn jerks still weren't together.

"Which I only learned about recently. Cris didn't come to me for support when you two broke up. Perhaps he was afraid of hurting my feelings, making me out to be his second choice. He kept his pain to himself, and we only talked about it at his birthday party last weekend."

A party Benny hadn't been able to shut up about. "Benny said you and Cris were down here for a while that night."

Chet broke eye contact. "We were."

Something happened. Something happened between them, but they aren't dating, and what the ever loving fuck has my life turned into?

"So all this time you thought me and Cris were together," Jake said, "and I thought you and Cris were together, but really we've all been apart. That sucks."

Chet chuckled. "I suppose it does suck. We're all ships passing in the night, unable to truly connect with each other."

Jake disagreed, but couldn't find the words to express it the right way. He'd connected with Cris like crazy. Chet and Cris had connected a long time ago and strongly enough for Cris to give up an internal organ. And somehow Jake and Chet had connected through their connections to Cris. Chet had given Jake a safe place to fix himself, to figure out what went wrong.

We are connected. So what do we do now?

Tired of standing, Jake sat next to Chet, their thighs close enough to touch. He caught a waft of Chet's cologne, something heavy and wonderful that tickled his nose. The same scent that had wrapped him in warmth and safety yesterday, when Chet brought him back with kind words and an open heart.

"So…ah, what do you do besides dance?" Chet asked.

Diversion tactic achieved.

"Not much. Mostly play video games, screw around on my phone."

"Any thoughts as to a career beyond the stage?"

"Not really." Jake hated thinking about the future. One day at a time was about his fucking limit. "What do you do when you aren't shooting porn?"

"I have a fondness for antiquing. I don't buy often, but I do love the thrill of the hunt, and our great state had many wonderful places to do that. I also love to cook. Exploring cultures through cuisine. Creating new flavors to tantalize the senses."

Jake loved how Chet made cooking sound so sexy. "I can't cook, but I can microwave a mean frozen lasagna."

"So I've heard. You really should look into improving your overall diet and health. The food we put into our bodies feeds our emotional and spiritual growth as much as it feeds our muscles."

"I've gotten that speech before, but nuking a box takes a lot less effort."

Chet bumped his knee. "Then what if I teach you to cook? We'll start with the basics and work our way up. One day there may be someone special in your life that you'd like to woo with food."

"Dude, you just said the word woo."

"Yes, I did. We're of two very different generations, Jake. I hope you don't hold my elderly word choices against me." Chet's lips twitched, cluing Jake into the teasing. Which was awesome, because Jake didn't know Chet well enough to pick up on his more subtle humor. Jake much preferred flaming sarcasm.

"As long as you don't hold my young, hip word choices against me," Jake said.

"Deal."

Jake couldn't explain his impulse to hug Chet, so he went with it. Slung his arm across Chet's chest in slightly awkward sideways hug—awkward until Chet twisted his body toward him and hauled him in, chest to chest. Strong arms around Jake's waist, promising something Jake couldn't think about right now. Jake melted into the embrace, content in its safety.

Complete.

Chapter Seventeen

Teaching Jake how to butcher a whole chicken turned into the most fun Charles had had in months. Somehow, the young man had managed to get to twenty-three without ever handling raw chicken, so he protested that right away. Charles reassured him over and over that yes, washing his hands with soap and water would be enough. One didn't get salmonella by osmosis.

Jake had also never held a large, sharp kitchen knife before. Charles decided to use his height to his advantage and stand directly behind Jake, his own hand directing Jake's hand. In the end, the breasts were a bit ragged and he missed part of one thigh, but they had eight pieces and a carcass Charles planned to freeze and use later for chicken stock.

"Now what?" Jake asked, while scrubbing his soapy hands under steaming water.

"Now we bread it and fry it." Charles loved few things more than homemade fried chicken—something he'd learned to do at a young age from his grandmother Dottie, God rest her soul.

"I am definitely down with fried food."

Charles began assembling their breading station. "Three bowls, three different contents, and the secret? Season everything." He added salt and pepper to the plain flour bowl, as well as to the beaten eggs. The third bowl got flour, corn meal, and a mix of seasonings he'd tweaked to his own liking over the years. "A few dashes of chili powder makes the chicken sing."

"Chili powder in fried chicken?" Jake eyeballed the mixture. "Isn't that for, you know, chili?"

His suspicion made Charles laugh out loud. While Jake was nowhere near the bright, bull-headed boy he'd first met nearly a month ago, he was leaps and bounds better than even yesterday. Getting him up, into a new environment, and engaging in activities was slowly breaking him out of the cocoon of severe depression he'd slid into. And Charles very much enjoyed engaging with Jake.

"The uses for chili powder may surprise you," Charles said.

"Uh oh," Cristian said as he walked into the kitchen. He'd asked to use Charles's office for a little while to make some business calls. "You guys already getting into kinky shit?"

"We haven't even begun. There are thighs yet to be fondled and legs to be caressed."

Cristian stared at him a beat, then spotted the chicken parts resting on a sheet tray. He almost looked disappointed that Charles hadn't been speaking of human legs and thighs.

"Is fondling it necessary?" Jake asked. "I don't even want to touch it, much less get up close and personal with it."

"Fondling tenderizes the meat," Charles said. His perfectly deadpan delivery made Jake laugh. Truly laugh for the first time, with a wide smile and a bit of a sparkle in his eyes. "Watch and learn, young man. Watch and learn."

He showed Jake how to coat the chicken pieces in flour, then dip them in beaten egg, before rolling them in the corn meal mixture. The cast iron skillet was already on the stove, oil heated to the correct temperature for them to ease the chicken into it. "Slowly and away from you, or you'll splash oil and burn yourself."

Jake took to the process quickly, and he seemed to enjoy the task very much. "Cooking isn't so bad, I guess," he said. "With the right teacher."

Charles didn't try to squelch the pride that comment bloomed deep in his chest. Cristian, naturally, stepped in with a snappy, "Chet is definitely an expert at fondling meat."

"Certainly you aren't proposing I, as the expert, give young Jake a demonstration of said expertise?" Charles asked.

"Wait a second," Jake said. "Are we still talking about chicken?"

"Perhaps we should be talking about what Cristian intends to offer to the meal," Charles said, taking a fast conversational re-route.

"Um..." Cristian crossed to the refrigerator and opened the door. "A salad, maybe?"

"A salad with fried chicken," Jake said. "Sounds balanced."

They each moved around the kitchen with ease and grace, like three men who'd spent years cooking together. Charles helped Jake oversee the chicken, while Cristian put together a chopped salad full of goodies from the crisper bins. The domesticity, the sheer delight of it all, made Charles want to protect this with his life—even though he had no idea what *this* actually was.

Dell came home in time to eat with them, and their quartet settled at the table with a platter of steaming, golden fried chicken and a big bowl of salad. Jake took his first bite of a chicken leg with an audible crunch. His eyes went wide, and he moaned. Chewed. Licked his greasy lips in a way that made Charles's dick twitch.

"Holy fuck, that's amazing," Jake said.

"Told you so." Charles could watch him eat fried chicken all night, and then die a happy man. And then Cristian tried a thigh, reacted almost the exact same way, and Charles started toying with the idea of adding fried chicken to his next shoot. The noises Jake and Cristian made were practically orgasmic, and Charles had to bite the inside of his cheek to stave off an erection.

He spent more time pretending not to watch Cristian and Jake eat than he did on his own plate. At twenty minutes to six, Dell excused himself to start setting up downstairs. Charles promise to join him shortly, then shoveled a few forkfuls of salad into his mouth.

"Jake and I can handle cleanup, if you need to help Dell," Cristian said. "Consider it a thank you for that amazing chicken."

"I appreciate it," Charles replied. "And as you said, I am an expert with meat."

Jake sputtered his soda.

Charles washed his hands thoroughly, so he didn't get any grease on his equipment. Adam arrived at the same moment Charles headed for the studio. They exchanged greetings, then went downstairs together.

Adam had been with the company for less than a year, looking for a confidence booster after having survived a few painful years of addiction and torment, and he'd been a terrific addition. Focused and energetic every time he filmed. Even being shot last fall and nearly dying hadn't broken his enthusiasm for each new day. He had a small scar on his chest, but a little makeup and careful camera angles made it difficult to see on the finished product.

"You're Avery's second scene partner," Charles explained on the descent. "He was incredibly nervous his first time, but I think you'll do well with him. You have a very charming personality that should set him at ease."

"I appreciate the compliment," Adam said. "I've come a long way from being told my personality causes people to self-harm."

Charles stopped and put a hand on Adam's arm to stay him, concerned by the comment about Rick Fowler's checkered past. "I thought you and Jon had reached a level of peaceful coexistence over your shared past?"

"We have. Sometimes I start thinking about how fucked up our relationship was and how much that was on me, and it gets me down."

"You're not that person anymore. People can change. You wouldn't be here if I thought otherwise."

"Thanks, boss. I appreciate it."

"You're welcome."

The doorbell rang. Charles chuckled. Most of them still rang when they were new, instead of barging inside like the old hat did. Dell dashed upstairs to let Avery in, and they waited for the pair to come into the studio.

Like most of his models, Avery was in his early twenties and absolutely stunning. Piercing eyes, flawless dark skin, and carefully tended dreads he kept back with a thick blue tie. He was shorter than Adam, but more muscular. Avery had been expressive and eager in his interview, so the shyness during his first shoot had surprised Charles. But the way Avery's eyes lit up when he met Adam? The smooth way Adam shook his hand?

Chemistry for days.

Oh yes, it was definitely going to be a good shoot.

Cris didn't mind that he ended up doing more of the actual cleanup than Jake. He had energy to spare, while Jake leaned awkwardly against the island, probably needing it to remain upright and somewhat at attention. Chet had a system of cleaning as he cooked, so a lot of their prep tools were already in the dishwasher. Mostly Cris scraped plates clean, added those to the wracks, plus some silverware, and then turned on the wash cycle. The only thing that needed a little extra attention was the cast iron skillet.

Watching Jake and Chet cook together had delighted Cris to no end. He loved seeing the pair interact. They had a connection they probably didn't even see, but Cris did. In the small smiles, the gentle touches, the way Chet managed to get Jake laughing again. Nudging him further out of his depression, closer to the fun-loving guy Cris had fallen for. Hopefully this shrink friend of Chet's would make a difference.

Once the kitchen was back in order, he led Jake into the den and plunked him down on the couch. "How about a movie?" Cris said.

"Sure."

"In the mood for anything?"

"You pick." Jake never seemed to have an opinion on what they watched, so Cris found a comedy that looked interesting. Kept the mood light and all.

He sat next to Jake, who immediately scooted up to him. Gave him a questioning look Cris couldn't resist. He raised his left arm, allowing Jake to settle against his chest, half-leaning into the crook of his shoulder.

"I'm sorry," Jake said to the TV.

"For what?"

"I hurt you. I really did think you'd be better off with Chet. He has more to offer you."

Cris sighed, then rubbed his palm up and down Jake's arm. "I know you think that, but maybe I disagreed."

"Thought you'd go to Chet, but you didn't."

"No, I didn't. My heart was too bruised to risk giving it away again. I really liked you Jake."

"Me too. Sorry." Jake sagged harder against Cris. "Fuck."

"Stop apologizing, okay? I forgive you." He didn't hold it against Jake anymore. Three people had been involved in this romantic mess, so three people had made choices and mistakes. Jake didn't have to bear the brunt of it all. "And if we're being truthful, I still have feelings for you."

Jake finally twisted his head to look at Cris, his eyes wide. "You do?"

"Yeah, I do." God, Jake's pretty pink mouth was so close to his, those lips slightly parted. Ready to be kis—nope. "But right now, you need to concentrate on getting better. Work with Nancy tomorrow. Everything else can wait."

"I will. Work with her. I hate how I feel right now."

"Good." He kissed Jake's temple. "Good."

They settled in to watch the movie, but Cris remained distracted by the man pressed against him. By the lean shape of the body stretched out on the couch. The way that body had responded so beautifully to Cris's touches—not going there. Not when remembering those two nights in his bed would end with a hard-on that he'd have a difficult time hiding from Jake.

Especially not when he hadn't told Jake about his birthday. About first kissing, and then rubbing off with Chet in the studio, and how amazing it had been. They hadn't been physical since, hadn't even kissed on the mouth, and it had been difficult to keep his hands to himself several times today. But every time he looked at Jake, he kept his distance from Chet.

This is all so fucking confusing.

By the end of the first movie, Jake had slid down the couch until his head was resting on a pillow, which was propped on Cris's lap, and he'd fallen asleep. Unwilling to interrupt the lovely, domestic moment, Cris turned down the TV's volume and played another movie. Mostly, though, he watched Jake sleep.

Voices rumbled from the foyer area. A door shut, and moments later the water in the first floor bathroom rushed to life. The shoot was finished. Eventually, the water shut off. More voices. Footsteps. The front door opened and shut twice.

More footsteps. Chet appeared in the den's archway, his face lighting up with a grin when he saw them. The fondness in his eyes shifted from Cris to Jake, then back again. Cris held his gaze, sending those same feelings right back. Feelings that were about more than sex. They went far beyond anything Cris could describe to himself or anyone else.

It wasn't normal, it wasn't socially acceptable, but the three of them together simply felt *right*.

Enough room existed at the far end of the couch for Chet to ease down, then put Jake's feet in his lap. Such a familiar position. So homey. They watched the rest of the film, then a bit of late night news before silently agreeing it was time for bed. Instead of waking him, Cris hefted Jake into his arms. Jake snuffled once, then settled.

Chet followed him upstairs to Jake's room. Pulled the covers down so Cris could deposit the man in his arms onto the bed. Jake blinked his eyes open, as if awoken by the sudden loss of contact. He snagged Cris's wrist. "Stay."

Sweet Jesus, I can't say no when he asks like that.

Cris nodded yes.

Chet started for the door.

"Wait," Jake said. "Both of you. Stay."

Chet turned, eyebrows arched in surprise. "You want me to stay?"

"Please?"

"The bed is quite small." He eyeballed the full-sized mattress, which would barely hold all three of them comfortably. "Mine is a king."

Jake's relieved smile made Cris's heart turn over. "Okay."

After some changing of clothes and bathroom negotiations, the three of them piled into Chet's large bed. Jake rolled around on the sateen sheets like a dog in grass, before settling on his right side in the center. Without over-thinking it, Cris slid up behind him, close without crowding. Chet turned off the room's lights, then lay on the other side, facing Jake.

"Thank you," Jake said in the darkness.

"Anything you need," Cris whispered.

Chet's echo of "Anything," stuck close to Cris's heart. He fell asleep certain that this unknown thing building between them all had just shifted in a new direction—and Cris couldn't wait to see where it led.

Chapter Eighteen

Jake wasn't used to waking up on super-silky sheets with two human blankets smothering him into the mattress. Not that he was going to complain, because other than being a little hot, he was perfectly content to soak in the overwhelming sense of safety from being surrounded by both Cris and Chet.

He remembered falling sleep facing Chet, but he must have turned over in the night. His head was now tucked under Cris's chin, one of his arms draped over Cris's waist. The warm body draped across Jake from behind was Chet, leaner and less muscled, but no less welcome. His forehead pressed between Jake's shoulder blades, warm breath tickling his skin. Jake wanted to stay like that forever, cocooned in support and comfort.

Too bad his bladder had other ideas. He shifted, trying to ease up without waking the others. His thigh nudged Cris's morning wood. He had half-a-mind to reach down and give Cris a hand, but Cris had made it clear they weren't pursuing anything right now. Sexual or otherwise. So groping him without permission? Probably a bad idea.

He wiggled some more, which dislodged Chet from his back, giving Jake enough room to sit up. It woke Cris, too, who blinked at him with adorably sleepy eyes. Jake couldn't help himself. He kissed Cris's forehead, then whispered, "Gotta whiz. Be right back."

After escaping the bed, Jake did his business in the master bathroom, which was as tasteful and unpretentious as the rest of Chet's house. It had a double-sink counter and simple white and brown accents. Instead of a bathtub, there was a huge glass-door shower with both sideways and overhead shower faucets, which looked insanely cool

I wonder if he'll let me shower in here. That'll be cool.

Chet himself was pretty fucking cool. The guy had money, but he didn't live like he had money—something Jake found insanely appealing.

Cris had fallen back asleep. Jake took a minute to study the way he and Chet had moved closer together, one facing the other. As a pair, they were stupidly sexy, and watching them sleep? Like the opening scene of a porno, and he half-hoped they'd blindly grope for each other, start making out, shed some clothes…fuck, but that'd be hot. The mental images did nothing for Jake's dick, though, which hadn't been interested in anything for a while.

They'd both been hovering around Jake for so long, they needed a break from him. Jake went into his room for some things, then used the other bathroom to shower and dress. Dell was eating a bowl of cereal at the kitchen counter. Jake had never been alone with the guy, and he honestly had no clue what Chet had told his nephew about why Jake was there.

"There's a couple different cereals in the cupboard," Dell said after they exchanged boring good morning's. "Or oatmeal. Or eggs. Help yourself."

Jake usually slept his mornings away, because of his vampire hours job, so breakfast wasn't a typical thing for him. He ate a banana instead, not really hungry. More for something to do besides stare at the walls.

Chet came downstairs first, dressed, hair neatly combed. Jake had yet to see the man disheveled or otherwise not-perfect, even on a Saturday morning. His sunny smile warmed Jake in the same place that had enjoyed Chet teaching him to cook. Standing close, directing his hand, praising him when Jake succeeded. He *liked* pleasing Chet, and that scared him a little.

Coffee finished brewing by the time Cris joined them. Chet made omelets with mushroom and spinach for him and Cris. They looked nice, but smelled funny. Jake had never been a fan of mushrooms.

Chet and Dell kept up most of the conversation, including Cris in it once in a while. No one tried to make Jake talk, which was awesome. He'd be talking enough later when he met with Nancy Englade, the shrink friend who could hopefully fix whatever was wrong with him. The more aware Jake became of exactly how disconnected and morose he felt, the scarier it all seemed. And the more grateful he was to everyone who'd helped him. Not only Cris, Chet, and Benny, but all the other guys who'd assembled, because they gave an actual damn about a guy they didn't know.

The rest of the morning passed slowly, time inching closer to his eleven o'clock appointment. Chet answered the door when the bell rang, then brought her to the den where Jake and Cris were watching TV.

Lady didn't look like a doctor, or a therapist. She was short, plump, with shiny black hair and thickly lashed eyes. Her dress looked like something out of the forties, and she wore really tall heels. But she also smiled at him like he was an old friend, and something about Dr. Nancy Englade put Jake instantly at ease.

He followed her to Chet's office, which was, like the rest of the place, all dark woods and affordable décor. The only thing that seemed out of place was the massive desk that looked like it had seen better days. Two high-back brown chairs faced the desk, and they each sat in one.

"It's nice to meet you, Jake," she said. "I'm Dr. Nancy Englade."

"Jake Bowden."

"How about I start off by telling you a bit about myself? I have a Master's degree in counseling, as well as my doctorate in clinical psychology. I specialize in mood disorders, which is why, I suspect, Chet called me to speak with you. I've been practicing for eight years here in the Commonwealth of Pennsylvania, and in my free time I like to knit."

He had no idea why it was important he know she liked to knit, but whatever. "I'm a go-go dancer."

Not even a twitch. "And do you like your job as a go-go dancer?"

"Sure. I dance for a living, get to stare at a sea of hot guys six nights a week."

"Do you have any plans for after you're finished go-go dancing?"

"No."

She tilted her head a bit. "Do you plan on dancing forever?"

"Dancing is what I do now. Thinking about the future is too much."

"I understand. Tell me more about your last couple of weeks. Your activities, your general mood."

Jake steeled himself for how exhausting this was going to be and told Nancy about his past month, everything from meeting Cris, to hearing about the party from Benny. His descent into darkness. Chet shining some light in. Moving into Chet's house.

"In reference to hiding Cris's wallet," she said, "you mentioned a pattern of impulsive, occasionally erratic behavior. Can you tell me more about that? Perhaps another instance besides the wallet?"

"And moving out of my apartment two weeks too soon?"

She nodded.

Okay then.

He pushed against the fog in his mind to find something else. "Um, my hair used to be a lot longer, like super-shaggy, and I really liked it. Like, really liked it. But then I'm out grocery shopping, and this asshole tells me I look like a faggot. I was pissed, and he was bigger than me, so I dropped my basket in the middle of the store, went home, and shaved my head." Jake tried to remember how he'd felt that day. Angry, sure, but not at the asshole. "Other people had made fun of my hair, but that day I let it get to me. I didn't even think, I just did it, and I regretted doing it right after."

"Why do you think you shaved your head, despite liking the long hair?"

"I don't know. I was mad."

"Mad at whom?"

"Myself."

"Why were you mad at yourself, Jake?"

"I don't know!" He took a deep breath, annoyed that he'd shouted. "I'm sorry. Aren't you supposed to be telling me why I'm doing this crazy shit?"

"It isn't crazy to do impulsive things that, when you look back, don't make any sense to you, especially when you have a chemical imbalance in your brain."

"A what?"

"Jake, a lot of the actions you've described from before this week-long depressive episode is behavior that can be classed as hypomanic. I believe that you have type 2 bipolar disease."

Bipolar. Holy shit.

He vaguely knew what that was from TV, but he didn't know anyone who was bipolar. "But...you can tell that from me getting depressed for a week?"

"You weren't simply depressed. You were in such a state that you didn't get out of bed. You didn't go to work, you cut yourself off. Your mind kept you prisoner, unable to see the world for the wonderful place it is."

No, this wasn't right. "It was just one time, though."

"One depressive episode is often enough. You're twenty-three, correct? That's within the age bracket for when symptoms of bipolar first begin to appear in young adults."

No, no, no, I'm not crazy. This isn't what it is.

"Being bipolar is nothing to be ashamed of," she said. "And the good news is that the symptoms are manageable through a combination of medications. They'll keep your good days more even, and they'll help prevent depression such as you've experienced recently."

"What was that other word you said before?" Jake asked, still not ready to believe this crap. "Hypermanic?"

"Hypomanic. There are two types of bipolar disease. Hypomanic is common in type 2. In type 2, you exhibit symptoms similar to manic states experienced in type 1, but they're far less severe. Many people function just fine in a hypomanic state, such as yourself, and they don't realize there's anything different about them until the depression hits. The highs seem normal, and then you're stuck in such a low that you can't function anymore."

"Sounds familiar." Jake sank deeper into his chair. "Pills will fix me?"

"Medication will help, but it's not a cure. If I'm going to treat you, it will be officially, as your clinical psychologist. I'll want to meet with you twice a week for the foreseeable future to talk about your moods, your thoughts, and to monitor your medication. See what combination works best for you."

"What if I say no?"

She blinked. "That is absolutely your right, Jake. I can't force treatment on you. But you also can't ignore this until it goes away, because it won't go away. It's part of you. You can either choose to manage it, or you can allow it to continue managing you."

Jake despised the idea of anything except himself managing his life, but it seemed ridiculous that his own brain was now his enemy. He didn't want to feel this bad ever again. More than that, he didn't want to let Cris and Chet down. They wanted him better, too.

"I won't demand a commitment from you right now," she said. "I'll leave you my card, and you can call me on Monday with your answer. If you wish to work with me, I'll get you in same day so we can get the right prescriptions set up. How's that sound?"

"Okay." He kind of wanted to say yes and get it over with, but he had to think. Do his own research. She had no reason to lie about what she thought was wrong with him—clearly something was fucking wrong—but even shrinks got it wrong sometimes, right?

She left the office.

It didn't take long for Chet and Cris to come looking for him.

"You want to talk about it?" Cris asked. He squatted in front of Jake, so damned concerned it make Jake want to cry.

I don't deserve him.

"She didn't tell you?" Jake asked.

"Of course not. Confidentiality and all that."

He studied the earnest way Cris was looking at him, terrified that would change into revulsion when Jake told him. Even Chet's patient smile, cast from his post by his desk, could evaporate once they knew.

"We're here for you, babe," Cris said, then put a hand on his knee. Squeezed. "No matter what, I promise."

Swallowing down a rush of acid, Jake said, "She thinks I'm bipolar." He hated the way his voice cracked on the final word.

Instead of freaking out or leaving the room, Cris put a hand on his other knee. "Do you think she's right?"

"I don't know. I told her a lot of stuff, and the shit she said made sense." He looked at Chet, who didn't seem surprised at all. "Is that what you thought was wrong with me?"

"I suspected that was the underlying cause of your actions, yes," Chet replied. "I've known two other people who live with bipolar. The good news is that it's manageable, Jake."

"That's what Dr. Englade said. There're medicines."

"How do you feel about treating this with medication?"

Jake was getting really fucking sick of people asking him how he felt about shit. "I hate taking pills, but I also hate feeling like this. I want to be normal again. Or at least not"—he gestured at himself—"like this anymore."

"The medications are to help manage your mood and your manic episodes."

"Yeah, well, she said I was, uh, hypomanic? Apparently that's the less crazy kind."

"Hey, stop using that word," Cris said with a fierceness that surprised Jake. "You aren't crazy. You have a manageable illness, okay? And you have two people in front of you who are ready and willing to help you manage it."

Jake's heart fluttered at both the words and the sincerity in Cris's eyes. "I'm scared of what this means."

"It's okay to be scared of the unknown. But you aren't facing it alone."

"You mean it?"

"Absolutely." Cris pulled him forward into a tight hug, and Jake melted. So much stress from his meeting with Dr. Englade faded away, leaving him boneless and exhausted. He soaked in Cris's heat and strength, so grateful to have him.

A shadow moved as if to pass by his chair. Jake reached out and snared Chet's hand. He unearthed himself from the weight of Cris's embrace to look up. "Why are you leaving?" Jake asked, terrified of the answer. If Chet couldn't handle this, too....

"You two appeared as though you needed a private moment," Chet said. He gently stroked Jake's hair. "But I'm all in, as well, helping you get better. I promise."

The words broke loose another big chunk of apprehension, freeing more of Jake's optimism. He had two strong, intelligent, sexy men in his life willing to help him put his fractured mind back together again. It was a hell of a lot more than he deserved, but he wasn't taking anything for granted. Ever again. He couldn't do this by himself.

"Good," Jake said.

"The three musketeers," Cris said.

Jake made a face. "Can't we be something less old. Like Harry, Ron and Hermione?"

"Do I even want to ask who among us is Hermione?"

"The super smart one? Definitely not me."

"Don't count yourself out, love," Chet said. "You're smarter than you think, and you have an incredible strength of spirit."

I will not cry, I will not cry, I will not cry.

"I don't feel strong right now," Jake said, throat tight. Voice hoarse.

Chet squatted so he was level with Cris, side by side, a wall of support Jake never expected. "Then let us be strong for you," Chet said.

Jake did cry then, unable to stop the sob or the flood of tears. He was tired and scared and overwhelmed, and it all came out in a rush of emotion. Cris gathered him up, pulling him down to the floor and surrounding him with his bigger body. Chet was there, too, somewhere, his cologne mixing with Cris's into something beautiful and comforting. Jake let go, mourning an existence where he simply made rash decisions, while trying to accept one where he had a mental illness. He let go of his loneliness, because the two men holding him made him not feel so alone anymore. He let go of anger and frustration and fatigue, and he cried until he had nothing left except hiccups and gasps.

Chet and Cris never left, holding him together while he fell apart and staying close to help him put it all back together again.

Eventually, they moved the whole production to a leather sofa he'd never noticed, Jake still sandwiched between them. The soft couch felt way better on his ass than the hardwood floor. Tissues appeared, and Jake took a few. Blew his nose and wiped his face, a little embarrassed by how badly he'd lost it, but also positive they'd never hold it against him.

"I need to call Richard," Jake said. His throat felt raw and speaking hurt, but whatever. "Let him know what all's going on. I gotta go back to work. It's been a week."

"You won't lose your job," Cris said. "You know that. But yeah, I'm sure he'd be glad to hear from you directly, rather than through me or Gabriel."

Chet gestured at his massive desk. "You can use my office phone, if you wish."

"Yeah, right." Jake snorted, but that hurt his nose. "Like I have anyone's number memorized."

"Your generation will never understand the pain in the ass that was screwing up a number on a rotary phone."

"Good." Phones without a backspace key. Ugh. "My phone's in my room. I think. Need to lay down for a bit, anyway."

"Of course."

Jake hated to break the moment, but he was bone tired and teetering on emotionally exhausted. Time to make a call, and then take a nap. "Thank you, guys." He hugged Chet first, then Cris. They stayed behind while he began the long journey upstairs to his room. His entire body felt like jelly when he finally stretched out on his bed, phone in hand.

I don't want this. I don't want to be bipolar.

Calling Richard, telling someone else outside of this tiny inner circle, made it real. Maybe he should get a second opinion? Talk to another doctor? Google it? Anything except blindly accept the words of one woman he'd known for an hour.

Chet suspected the same thing. I trust him.

Didn't mean he had to accept what they were saying. Not yet. He could call Richard and explain without really explaining. And if Jake did start meds on Monday, maybe he'd be focused enough to go back to work by the middle of next week. The idea of climbing onto that small platform and shaking his ass in a thong didn't hold a lot of appeal anymore, but that was probably the depression. The low, or whatever the shrink had called it.

Dr. Englade had asked what he wanted to do when he was done dancing, and Jake still didn't have the mental energy to think about it. But maybe this was the time to work up to it. To alter his course toward something new.

Tomorrow. Not today.

He called Richard's cell.

"Jake, my boy!" Richard's perky voice made him flinch. "It's lovely to hear from you. I've been so worried."

"I'm sorry I worried you."

"Pish, posh, don't apologize. Gabriel mentioned you've been having a tough time, but you had some good friends rallying to help you."

Jake closed his eyes and imagined Chet and Cris, both smiling at him with so much devotion. "I do. They've been amazing, and I'm, uh, starting to get better."

"Excellent. You don't rush it, though, okay? Your job is here when you're ready."

Grateful tears stung his eyes. Hearing it directly from his boss, rather than other people, made all the difference. "Thank you. Maybe I'll be able to come back sometime next week."

"You take care of you. The rest will work itself out."

"Yeah. Thanks again."

"Talk to you soon, son."

He hung up, throat tight, eyes stinging. He'd worked for Richard for three years, and he'd lived with the man for a week, but for the first time "son" felt less like a general means of address for Richard's younger employees. It felt personal, affectionate. The way his mom used to say it.

I'm not as alone as I thought. Maybe I never was.

The happy thought stayed with him as he drifted off to sleep, phone still clutched to his chest.

Charles and Cristian remained on the leather couch after Jake went upstairs to nap. Cristian had settled his broad back against

Charles's chest, a warm weight who seemed content to stay put. They existed in silence for a while, finding peace and companionship in each other's presence and in their loose embrace.

He'd suspected the bipolar diagnosis before Jake said it. His own experience with the disease, as well as some additional research last night, had given him the answer that Nancy confirmed. Jake seemed stuck in a place between being relieved to know what was wrong, and scared to face the future with such a diagnosis around his neck. He'd certainly looked as if he expected Charles and Cristian to walk away the moment he said the words.

Cristian had been amazing with him. So amazing Charles had wanted to give them privacy—only Jake had asked him to stay. In less than two days, Jake had come to rely on both of them for emotional and physical support, and Charles was happy to offer whatever Jake needed. He only prayed that the need wouldn't end once Jake got his disease under control.

Charles enjoyed having Jake in his home and in his life, and Jake seemed at ease there. Cristian, as well. The three of them fit together in an unexpectedly amazing way that made Charles dream of a future where three men could be happy in their own unique ways. More than anything, he wanted Jake and Cristian to be happy—with or without him.

"You were remarkable with him today," Charles said, breaking the spell of silence.

"You were pretty great, too." Cristian squeezed his knee. "And if I'm being totally honest, I'm a little surprised at how fast he's bonded with you."

"I'm surprised, as well. I felt a kinship with him the day we met for brunch, but these past two days have been...different. Emotionally intimate."

"Physically intimate, too."

"In a way, yes." Charles adored the way Jake tucked in nicely against his own body. "It's a blessing that he allows me to show him physical comfort, and I'm happy to give it to him."

"Are you attracted to him?"

Charles startled at the question, his heart skipping a beat. Cristian sat up and turned, his expression open, un-accusing, giving no hint as to what answer he hoped for. He didn't ever want to lie to Cristian, not ever, and Charles had spent enough time running from what he wanted. "I am, yes," he replied. "Unexpectedly so, but he's incredibly vulnerable right now, and I would never dare come between you two."

"There isn't exactly an 'us two' to come between."

"There could be. It's clear how much he still cares for you, Cristian."

Cristian frowned. "But what about us? You and me and last Friday night?"

Charles hadn't walked into that basement intending to seduce Cristian last weekend, but he had no regrets over what they'd done. It was one of his most cherished memories. "We still haven't defined what Friday night was, other than two consenting adults having sex."

"We were supposed to be at the beach right now. You and me and a weekend away."

"And the longer we discussed it, the more uneasy you became." Cristian flinched, and Charles reached out. Cupped

Cristian's jaw in his palm. "It's all right, it was probably too much, too soon. Going away together. I will never pressure you, Cristian, I promise."

"I know." Cristian scooted out of reach, his mouth drooping. His need for distance stung. "I'm so confused right now, and I'm scared of hurting you guys, but what if I'm not the one for either of you. What if you and Jake were waiting for each other?"

Charles's heart fluttered. He reached for a possibility so outrageous that he could barely form the words. But what if...? "What if the reason you and I haven't acted on our feelings for all of these years is because *we* were both waiting for *him*?"

Something like hope lit up Cristian's eyes, then dimmed as quickly. "I can't make a relationship work with one person. How the hell would I manage two?"

"I could say the same thing, love, but perhaps one isn't enough. Perhaps it takes the love of two men to make our hearts truly sing."

"What are you saying? You want to date both me and Jake?"

Charles took Cristian's nearest hand and squeezed. "I'm saying that we've found ourselves in a very unique situation, and perhaps traditional rules do not apply. I'm saying we don't have to define anything right now. We take this one day at a time. There is chemistry here, between all three of us, and that's too precious to lose because of society's hetero-normative views on what relationships should look like."

"What if a three-way isn't what Jake wants?"

"Then that's his decision to make and ours to respect. But it's too soon for Jake to think about a relationship with anyone, much less two men at once. He has other work to do first, and we need to support him while he does it."

Cristian didn't look happy with that answer. "What about you and me, though? I haven't told him about last Friday. Us rubbing off together."

Charles turned that one over for a moment, trying to see the best way to proceed that would spare the most feelings. "I don't think it would be fair to Jake for us to pursue a sexual relationship while he's here, unless he's included in it. And especially not before we tell him what we've spoken of right now."

"Okay, so no sex."

"That doesn't mean we three can't find a way to explore a romantic relationship with each other. You and Jake have already done that, and you and I have tiptoed our way around it. In some ways, we three have been developing a relationship since the moment you two arrived on my doorstep yesterday, and I'd like to see that continue. I enjoy having you both here so much."

Cristian seemed accepting of that idea, until his half-smile turned into a full-on frown again. "What about Dell?"

"What about him? He's discreet and open-minded, and it's not as if I plan on mauling either one of you in front of him."

"Bummer." Cristian winked. "So when should we bring this up with Jake?"

"I think it's best that we give him a few more days. I suspect he'll call Nancy on Monday, so he'll can begin medication. It's not an instant fix by any means, and he may still have episodes for the first few months as he adjusts to the meds."

"You want to wait months?"

"No, love." He squeezed Cristian's hand. "Days. Jake is a very independent young man who's been managing his own life for several years now. We need to support him through this without smothering him. Let him adjust to the idea that not only one, but two men want him in their lives as an equal, rather than as someone they need to take care of."

"I do want to take care of him, though."

"As do I. But I've known men like Jake. If he starts to believe our feelings are based on being his emotional support system, rather than true attraction and desire, he won't trust it. He won't trust us."

"That makes sense." Cristian let out a long, frustrated breath. Then he pinned Charles with a flirty smirk. "How did you get to be so amazingly insightful and smart?"

"Years lived, love. Many, many years lived."

Chapter Nineteen

Despite Jake's meltdown after his Saturday morning session with Dr. Englade, Cris couldn't remember a more relaxing weekend. It wasn't a getaway to the beach, but he kind of loved Chet's house. The den had a huge TV, complete with all kinds of cable and streaming options. No game system, but Cris wasn't a huge gamer anyway, so he didn't mind. Jake came down from his nap in time to help Chet cook dinner, and that was quickly becoming one of Cris's new favorite things.

After a few more hours cuddled together on the couch in much the same way as the previous night, Jake went to up bed first. Cris and Chet relaxed a while longer, before deciding to turn in—except Jake wasn't sleeping in his own room. He'd fallen asleep in the center of Chet's bed. Chet's tender smile made Cris's heart sing with so many feelings. They joined Jake beneath the covers, bookending him like before, close without touching.

Cris woke Sunday with Jake plastered across his back, and Chet already awake and watching them sleep. The three of them cooked brunch as a group, and Dell ate with them as if nothing was unusual about the situation. They lazed around the house the rest of the day, watching a baseball game for a few hours, sometimes reading from the vast library of books in Chet's office. Their conversations were light and easy.

For Cris, the best part of the weekend was the natural way the three of them touched as they went about their day. Small pats on the back, squeezes to hands or shoulders. Leaning close together on the couch. Brushing past in the kitchen. Not only Cris and Jake, or Cris and Chet, but also Jake and Chet. Their touches weren't necessarily those of lovers, but of two people completely at ease with each other. Small points of contact that, added up, meant so much more.

On Monday, Cris and Chet both volunteered to drive Jake to see Dr. Englade. He turned them down, asking instead to borrow Cris's car to go alone. Cris stood at the front door and watched Jake climb into the driver's seat, then pull away from the curb. Disappear down the tree-lined street.

Chet came up behind him and slid both arms around his waist. "He'll come back."

Cris relaxed into Chet's embrace. "I know. I've been in his orbit almost constantly for the last five days, so seeing him drive away...."

"I understand. But this is also him acting as an independent adult. He has to do this for himself."

"By himself."

"Precisely."

Chet's cologne wrapped around Cris's senses, reminding him how very much he liked it when Chet held him. Comforted him. He let his head fall back to rest on Chet's shoulder. Not super comfortable, since he was taller than Chet, but it put Chet's jaw in kissing range. Memories of how amazing it felt to kiss Chet flooded his mind and stirred arousal in his belly. He nuzzled the smoothly shaven skin on Chet's neck, so fucking tempted....

The hands loosely clasped over Cris's belly slid backward to squeeze his hips. Cris inhaled sharply. He wouldn't have argued against a reach-around if that's what—

Chet pushed him gently away.

Disappointed, Cris straightened and turned. Sadness and regret reflected back in Chet's eyes. "You have no idea how badly I want to go to my knees right here in the foyer," Chet said.

So not helping.

"I know why we can't," Cris said. "Jake leaving the house can't be an excuse for us to fool around."

"Exactly. He doesn't need to see himself as somehow standing between the two of us."

Cris licked his lips. "Between us is exactly where I want him."

Heat flared in Chet's eyes, and he swallowed hard. "But he has to want that too. And to come to us willingly."

"For him to do that, we kind of need him to know we want him to come. Uh, to us. Come to us."

"Soon, Cristian. We can keep our hands to ourselves for a few more days."

"Easier said than done."

Chet's laughter echoed in the foyer. "Don't I know it. But after eight years, a few more days is nothing."

"Why are you so optimistic?" A unexpected sense of dread slithered through Cris's gut. "What if this doesn't work out like we think it will? What if we tell Jake we both want him, and he runs away screaming? What if we lose him?"

"And what if he says yes?" Chet cupped his cheeks in both palms, a steady presence that pushed Cris's dread away. "It may scare him in the beginning, but do you truly see him running?"

"I don't know." Cris had too much personal experience with being pushed away by Jake to blindly trust in a future with him.

"He's hurt you, Cristian, and that makes it difficult to trust in him."

Cris blinked hard. "Are you psychic or something? It's scary the way you read my mind."

"I know you. And I know your history with Jake. But I also know some of Jake's personal history, and he's an incredibly lonely young man with an incredible capacity for love. He simply needs to find a stable, steady place from which to share that love. You and I are helping give him that."

"I know, you're right."

"Of course I am."

Cris snorted. "And so modest."

"Always." Chet patted his cheek, then dropped his hands. "First step? Trust him to come home."

Home. This feels like home.

"He'll come home," Cris said.

He shared another warm smile with Chet, then wandered into the den to work for a while, trusting in his heart that Jake would return to them—not because all of his stuff was here, but because he truly wanted to be there with Cris and Chet.

Something that got harder to believe in after two hours had gone by with no word from Jake.

Cris didn't want to smother him. He really, really didn't, which was why he didn't text Jake after he'd been gone for three hours. Therapy appointments didn't take that long, not even with city traffic, but Jake was an adult. Free to go shopping, or visit a museum, or whatever the hell else he was doing right now. Jake had been cooped up for more than a week, first in his own apartment, and then at Chet's house. With his energy returning, he probably wanted fresh air.

At hour four, Cris snagged a beer out of the fridge, because he was getting the urge to pace. He took his first pull from the longneck when Chet wandered in, rubbing the back of his neck.

"Sometimes I get so lost in my work, I lose track of time," Chet said with a smile. He glanced first at the beer, then the den. His smile dimmed. "Jake isn't home yet?"

"No." Cris glared across the kitchen to where his phone sat on the couch. "I have refrained from texting or calling, but now I'm wondering if that was a bad idea. What if he thinks the reason why we haven't contacted him yet is because we don't care? What if that's why he hasn't come back?"

Chet closed the gap between then and slid a hand around to grasp the back of Cris's neck. "Breathe, love. Breathe."

Cris grunted, his hand tight around the beer bottle. "I'm not freaking out, thank you very much. I'm just…over-thinking it, I guess."

"A little bit." He glanced at the microwave clock. "I'll text him and inquire if he'll be home to help me cook supper. How's that?"

"That's good." Non-invasive and non-judgmental. Leave it to Chet to know what to do.

Cris nursed his beer, while Chet sent the text. He hadn't eaten much at lunch, so the warmth spreading to his veins helped immensely. Chet opened the fridge to root around for dinner possibilities, and his phone pinged less than a minute later.

Chet read the text and grinned. "He'll be home in twenty minutes."

"That's it?"

"That's it. And be gentle when you grill him about where he's been all afternoon."

"I'm not going to grill him." Cris glared at his bottle. "Much."

Chet tutted. "Don't meet him at the door, either. Relax, Cristian. He's been gone less than half a day."

"I know." He leaned against the counter. "It's hard to forget how lifeless he was when I found him on Wednesday, you know? At least if he's here, I can keep an eye on him and his mood. Perk him up if he gets down."

"It's an admirable desire, but that's not how bipolar works. The lows are caused by a chemical imbalance, not by being upset because your favorite ball team lost a big game. Life stress can trigger them, yes, but keeping him cheerful won't prevent them. That's why he'll need to take medication."

Cris nodded, then drank the last of the yeasty beer. He'd done research of his own since Saturday, but reading about something and living with it were two different things.

By the time the front door opened, Chet had shrimp defrosting in the sink, and he'd finished chopping up a variety of vegetables. Jake wandered in wearing a shy smile and carrying a pharmacy bag in one hand. He was home and safe. Tension unfurled from where it had knotted behind Cris's breastbone.

"Excellent timing," Chet said. "I was about to get the wok heated up. Tonight is shrimp stir fry."

"Sounds good." Jake put the bag on the counter. "Got my meds. Mood stabilizer and an antidepressant."

Cris bit the inside of his cheek to keep from demanding Jake explain why picking up two prescriptions had taken four and a half hours. Jake was there now, showing fewer signs of stress and exhaustion than yesterday, and Cris needed to trust him, damn it.

"I'm glad to hear it," Chet said. "Now wash your hands, we have cooking to do."

Jake chuckled, then did as told. Cris watched silently while Chet showed Jake how to cook the broccoli first, then add the red peppers and onions. Jake allowed Chet to direct his hand, as usual, pushing the veggies around in the screaming hot wok. Then the shrimp, which sent up a mighty sizzle.

"You cook in stages so everything is done at the same time," Chet explained. "Shrimp this size only take a few minutes. Now add those last few vegetables."

In the end, they had three bowls of rice covered in the hot stir fry.

"Dell isn't eating with us?" Cris asked, once they'd settled down at the kitchen table with drinks.

"He's out with a friend," Chet replied. "Said he'd be home around eight."

"Is he on a date?"

"I didn't get that impression, no. He's not been on a date since he came to live here. At least, none he's told me about."

"Maybe he is dating," Jake said, "and doesn't want his nosy uncle to know about it?" The teasing tone of his voice steadied any harshness in his words.

Chet laughed. "Perhaps. Oh, I forgot to mention, there's a shoot tomorrow night. Six, as usual."

"Cool." Jake shrugged, then shoved a shrimp in his mouth.

"I won't be home," Cris said. "I have a weekly dinner date with Taro on Tuesdays. Been doing it for years."

"That's a wonderful tradition," Chet said. "He seems like quite a put-together young man."

"When did you meet Taro?" Jake asked.

"Cristian brought him to his birthday party the other weekend."

"Oh."

Cris glanced at Chet, who was trying to play it way too innocently.

Jake didn't seem to notice, though, too focused on stabbing a snow pea. "You guys don't have to keep pretending, you know," he snapped.

Cris nearly flung a piece of broccoli across the table. He stared at Jake, confused.

Chet put his chopsticks down. "Pretending what?"

"That you two aren't a couple," Jake said. "Christ, I'm not stupid. I see the goo-goo eyes you make with each other when you think I'm not looking. I see the way you touch each other. I'm sick, but I still see things."

"Cristian and I are not a couple. We've never been on a date."

"You want to. You want *him*. Don't tell me you don't."

Cris's heart started beating double-time. He looked at Chet, but Chet hadn't stopped staring at Jake with a calm patience Cris would love to feel himself. His own nerves were strung tight now that Jake had begun the conversation Cris was dreading.

"I won't lie to you," Chet said. "Of course I want him. I have for many years. And if you want complete honesty, Jake, I want you, as well."

Jake's fork clattered to the table. He gaped at Chet, eyebrows arched. He looked as if he'd been told unicorns actually were real —which was better than looking like he'd been kicked in the balls. Or worse. Cris braced for some sort of explosion, though. He'd seen Jake's temper.

"Why?" was all Jake croaked out.

Chet smiled so sweetly, like Jake was everything right in the world. "Why is any man attracted to another? Your exuberance. Your joy. Your vulnerability. You're also beautiful, probably in ways you don't even see. You reached for me, when you already had Cristian to help you. You keep reaching for me, and I don't know why. We've known each other for a matter of days, and yet I can no longer imagine my life without you in it. Those are some of the reasons why."

Jake kept staring at Chet, owl-eyed and silent, and Chet's calm fractured. "I hope I haven't overstepped or offended you," Chet added. "And please believe me when I say that your invitation to stay will not be revoked if you tell me to go to hell."

"No." Jake squeaked the word. He blinked hard, his gaze sliding to Cris briefly, then back down to his bowl of stir fry. "But you like Cris," he told his shrimp.

"It's less common, but it isn't impossible to have feelings for two people at the same time."

"I know, but…" He looked at Cris, so sad and confused that Cris had to grab the sides of his chair to stay put. "You were supposed to choose him."

"But I didn't," Cris said, hating how strangled his own voice was. "I chose you. We both do."

Jake's dinner sat heavily in his rioting stomach, threatening to revisit him sooner than later. His hands were cold, his face hot, and he couldn't make sense of anything they were telling him. Cris wanted him, he knew that. Fine. But Chet? This amazing, put-together, successful man who'd pined after Cris for eight fucking years wanted Jake, too? It made no sense. None.

Except...maybe? The way Chet held Jake in his arms. Those soft smiles. The gentle pressure of his hands as he guided Jake's across the cutting board. Praise and encouragement and laughter. Chet made him feel safe in ways no one else had in a long, long time. Jake wasn't sure if he had sexual feelings for the man, but he had *feelings*. He couldn't deny that without lying to them and himself.

Cris had chosen him. Apparently Chet had chosen him, too. But Cris and Chet were so amazing together! They were perfect for each other. None of this made any sense.

"I don't understand," Jake said.

"Have you heard of polyamory?" Chet asked.

"Yeah." Duh, he was on the internet like everyone else.

"All right. Do you truly understand what it means?"

Jake shook his head no.

"Polyamorous relationships are exactly how it sounds: multiple relationships at one time, and those relationships can vary greatly depending on the people involved. I knew a married couple in California, a man and woman. Cat was polyamorous, while her husband Victor was not. Now, Cat and Victor were very much in love and committed, but she also had a boyfriend she loved very much."

"But that's cheating." People didn't get married and keep boyfriends on the side.

"On the contrary. Victor was well aware of her other relationship. They had rules in place, and he knew she was poly very early in their dating, long before they married. Victor has never had another relationship outside of the marriage, but he understands that Cat does. And he understands why."

"Well I don't." Jake couldn't even make it work with one person, never mind handling two at once. "Wait, are you polyamorous?"

Chet's warm, comforting smile was back. "Not to my knowledge. My example was to help you see that relationships don't have to be defined in the traditional one-to-one ratio. In some cultures, it's still common to have multiple spouses."

His chest got hot. "Spouses?"

"Relax, Jake, I'm not proposing." Chet reached across the table and curled his warm hand around Jake's wrist. "Breathe, please. You're starting to worry me."

"I'm just…overwhelmed."

"I understand. To be honest, Cristian and I had planned to wait a few more days before having this particular conversation. To give you time to get your feet more firmly beneath you."

He bristled and yanked his hand away. "You mean, so I'm a little less crazy."

Chet's smile disappeared. "You aren't crazy. Please stop using that word. You are leaps and bounds better today than you were even two days ago, and your prescriptions—"

"Will help stabilize my mood while also fighting my depression, yeah," Jake snarled. "I got that from Dr. Englade, thanks." He stared at Chet, who was watching him with a great poker face. Cris, on the other hand, looked like he was one wrong word away from a full-on panic attack.

Which was totally weird, because he'd seen Cris aroused, angry, and concerned, but never scared. What was he so scared of?

Why do I care so much?

Jake pushed away from the table but didn't stand. Cris's feelings made more sense than Chet's. Cris and Jake had a history, however brief, and they had chemistry for days. But Chet's feelings made no sense. At all. Maybe his supposed feelings were simply a reaction to Cris's feelings, and Chet was pretending to like Jake to get closer to Cris. That made a hell of a lot more sense than a top-notch guy like Chet falling for a zero like Jake.

"You don't want me," Jake said to Chet. "Maybe you feel sorry for me, and you want to fix me, but that's not wanting me. You want Cris. You'll say and do whatever you need to so you can have him."

Instead of getting mad, like Jake expected, Chet's entire face fell. His pale eyes started to glisten, and holy fuck, the guy looked like he was going to burst into tears. That punched Jake in the gut, but he didn't take back his accusations.

Cris shot to his feet so fast his chair nearly fell over, and Jake shrank under his angry glare. "Let's be clear about one thing, okay?" Cris snapped. "I know what my feelings are. I know how I feel about both of you, and no one. I repeat. No one manipulates my feelings. Not Chet, not you. No one. But I won't keep chasing you if all you're going to do is shit on those feelings, Jake. I can't."

He stormed away from the table. Jake couldn't move to stop him, too stunned by the words Cris had thrown at him. Stinging barbs that hurt because they were true. Jake was scared, so he was pushing back. Pushing Cris and Chet away as hard as he could in order to protect himself.

Cris was rightly pissed and he'd walked away. Jake couldn't bring himself to look at Chet, too scared to see what damage he'd done. "I'll pack my stuff and call a Uber," Jake said to the table.

"You certainly will not."

Jake snapped his head up, surprise jolting through him. Chet's poker face was back.

"You'll finish your meal," Chet said, "and then we'll go about our evening. As I said, you staying here is not dependent on your acceptance of our feelings. I won't make you leave, and to be honest, with everyone's emotions running so high right now, I'd feel better if you stayed."

"Won't me staying be weird?"

"No more weird than it would have been ten minutes ago. In fact, I feel much better now that we've all been honest with each other." Chet tilted his head. "Well, most of us have."

"You don't think I'm being honest?"

"I think you're scared and confused. I think your experience is telling you to run before it gets any more complicated than it already is. I also think your feelings for Cristian are unlike anything you've felt before, and that terrifies you. Because having someone to love means potentially losing them. Like you lost your mother."

Pressure in Jake's throat made it difficult to swallow or get any air to speak. Every time Chet deconstructed him, Jake wanted to throttle the man almost as much as he wanted to hug him. Jake *was* scared, damn it. So fucking scared he couldn't see straight sometimes. Being with Cris made him feel safe. Strong. Like maybe there were great things in the world, things worth working for. Toss Chet into the mix? Both of them kept Jake together when all he wanted to do was break apart and float away.

"I'm sorry," was all Jake could manage.

"Apology accepted." Chet rose, then walked to Jake's side of the table. Squatted to put himself at eye level. "My feelings for you are vastly different than my feelings for Cristian, but they are still mine, and they're still valid feelings. It hurts that you don't believe me."

"I do believe you. I think that's why I said what I said." Jake reached out, then pulled his hand back. Chet watched him with a patient, tender smile that seemed to give him permission, so Jake tried again. He brushed his knuckles across the sharp plane of Chet's left cheek, barely-there whiskers rasping against his skin. "You know you're old enough to be my dad."

Chet burst out laughing. "That thought has occurred to me, yes. But age often doesn't matter when two souls connect in a genuine way. Whatever we become is up to us."

"I'm here for us."

"All three of us," Jake said. Hope flared deep inside of him, chasing away more of the darkness he'd been battling for so long. He didn't have to be alone. He didn't have to fight the darkness alone anymore. All he had to do was embrace this. "Fuck, I need to apologize to Cris."

"Then go." Chet rose.

Jake stood and leaned up to kiss Chet's cheek. He bolted for the stairs. Cris's room was at the end of the hall. The door was open, but Jake didn't go in. He peeked inside first. Small, like his, decorated in soft greens and blues. Cris stood near the only window, arms crossed, staring out. His profile was stony, but still so beautiful.

He wants me. I don't know why, but he does.

"Cris?"

His shoulders tightened but he didn't turn away from the window.

Jake tried to get a handle on his racing heartbeat, but the anxiety spread to his limbs, making his fingers tremble. He could fuck this up in so many ways. Maybe he didn't deserve Cris's forgiveness. He'd finally gone too far, and there was no coming back from what he'd said at dinner.

Cris turned, arms still tight across his chest, an immovable object whose face gave away nothing. Jake swallowed his pride, his fear, and his guilt, and he dropped to his knees right there in the doorway. Cris's eyebrows went up, but he still said nothing.

"I am so fucking sorry, Cris," Jake said, unable to keep soft tremors out of his voice. Nothing had ever felt as important than this apology. "I'm sorry for all of it. For your wallet, and the things I said to push you away, and for dumping you when I really wanted to keep you for myself, and for everything I've ever said or done to hurt you. I can't promise I'll never do stupid, impulsive shit again, because apparently my brain is broken but I promise to try. I promise to do my very best to be someone who deserves you, because I still don't think I do."

Cris stared down at him, his face still unreadable, but his arms fell to his sides. "That really hurt, Jake. What you said at dinner."

"I know." His whole body sagged, butt resting on his heels. He'd fucked it all up.

"This is hard for me, too, you know. I put myself out there for you. More than once. I don't know if I can do that again. Once bitten, twice shy."

Twice bitten is what? No more second chances?

"Okay." Jake used the door jamb to stand, his legs rubbery. His insides ached in a new, strange way. Too late and not enough. Story of his fucked up life. He'd done this to himself, and no matter what Chet said, it was better if Jake left. Then Cris and Chet could be together like they wanted.

"You little shit." Cris engulfed him before Jake processed the statement. Heat and muscle and the deep, masculine scent he loved so much surrounded him. He clung to Cris's waist, terrified this was the last time they'd hug. The last time he'd ever feel the thundering of Cris's heart against his chest. The strength of those arms holding him close.

And then Cris plundered his mouth, and hope sprang anew, beating back fear and dread, and Jake gave him everything. He let Cris take his mouth, tongue sliding against his, fingers gripping his hair. Keeping him still. It was messy and needy and everything Jake loved about kissing, and he didn't register moving until his feet weren't on the floor anymore. They were spinning. Falling. His back hit something soft—the mattress. Cris never broke the kiss, even as his bigger body pressed Jake into the bed, a perfect human blanket that covered him completely. Jake's heart soared, and he let go, totally on board for whatever Cris wanted.

He was panting and half-hard by the time Cris released his mouth. Cris braced himself on his elbows, his lips wet and eyes blazing with desire, and Jake's stomach tightened. He knew what Cris could do to his body.

"My brain keeps telling me this is a bad idea," Cris said. "But fuck if I can resist you, especially when you're on your knees."

"Don't resist me." Jake hitched his legs up and wrapped his ankles around Cris's thighs. The position shift put Cris's erection directly over Jake's semi, and holy shit, that felt good. "Take me, if you still want me."

Cris growled softly, then licked a damp stripe from Jake's throat to his ear. "I want to, but I don't have anything here."

"What about—?" Jake stopped himself before he brought Chet into the bed with them by asking about the supplies down in the studio.

Except Cris seemed to be on the same wavelength, because he settled on top of Jake, head resting on Jake's shoulder. Neither of them moved for a while. Jake soaked in the comforting warmth, until it started getting hard to breathe. And while Jake couldn't seem to get past a semi, Cris was still rock hard above him.

"Roll over," Jake said, giving his ass a swat.

Cris growled softly and did as told, allowing Jake to sit up. He straddled Cris's knees, then attacked his belt and fly. Got everything down and out of the way so he could free Cris's erection. Jacked him a few times in a loose hold.

"Wanna suck you off," Jake said. "Please?"

"Fuck yes."

Jake held him steady at the root, then licked around the head, soaking in the soft sounds Cris made with every touch. Every slide of his tongue up and down the shaft, putting the flavor of Cris's dick back in his mouth before taking him in. Rubbing with his tongue, tickling with his teeth. Getting him as deep as he could. Swallowing around Cris's length.

Cris curled fingers in Jake's hair but didn't pull or direct him. He held on, thighs trembling, making so many wonderful, needy noises that spurred Jake on. Jake played with Cris's nuts, rolling them, massaging just behind. He wet his finger, then rubbed against Cris's hole. Pushed inside.

Cris muffled a shout with one hand, while the other tightened in Jake's hair. Jake fucked him with a single finger, while redoubling his efforts to suck Cris's brains out through his dick. To make Cris forget the stupid shit Jake had done. To show him Jake would take this new chance and cherish it.

"Two," Cris said.

Jake nearly asked what he meant, then realized Cris was asking for two fingers. He pulled off Cris's dick long enough to thoroughly wet two fingers with spit—not the best lube, but all they had—then he sucked Cris back in. Two didn't go in as easily as one had, and Cris clamped down hard once Jake's fingers popped through to the first knuckle.

"Fuck, so close." Cris pumped his hips and Jake held still, letting Cris fuck into his mouth while he fucked himself on Jake's fingers. It was desperate and unsteady, kind of messy, and everything Jake loved about sex.

Jake pushed his fingers deeper, thumb pressing Cris's taint, and the first hot burst of come hit the back of his mouth. Jake braced his free arm across Cris's lower belly to hold him still, so he could suck him through it. Not miss a single drop of his release. He waited until Cris settled to ease his fingers out, then pressed a firm kiss to the head of Cris's softening dick.

Cris tugged on his shoulders. Jake climbed his body and kissed him hard. Cris rolled them so he was on top again, then fucked his tongue into Jake's mouth, until Jake was breathless. He groped at Jake's dick, which liked the attention but still wasn't cooperating. Jake pulled his hand away, then kissed the knuckles.

"It's okay," Jake said. "Haven't gotten it all the way up in a while."

"Hmmm." Cris nuzzled his cheek. "I'd be insulted if I didn't understand your recent history."

"Gee, thanks. Actually, yes. Thank you. That means a lot."

"Good, because you mean a lot. To me. And so does this. Us."

Far away, something in the house creaked.

Jake groaned. "Fuck, I can't believe I just blew you in Chet's house."

For some reason, that made Cris chuckle. "This house has seen its fair share of raunchy sex. I don't think he'll be scandalized over a blow job."

He pinched Cris's hip. "I know that. I didn't mean…fuck. I didn't come looking for you to do this. The apology and groveling, yes, but not the sex."

"Chet isn't going to be mad, believe me. Maybe a little jealous he didn't get to watch."

Instead of embarrassing him, the idea of Chet watching him and Cris have sex kind of turned Jake on a little bit. He loved dancing and showing skin at the club, writhing around in nothing but a thong for two hundred people, but he'd never imagined having sex for an audience. Not even an audience of one man who'd expressed clear, non-platonic interest in Jake.

"Would you want that?" Jake asked. "Chet watching us have sex?"

"Sure." Cris's eyes flashed with want. "Hell, I'd like him to participate. I—shit." Cris sat up so fast that Jake looked around the room, expecting to see someone watching them.

They were alone, but Cris still scooted away and started tucking himself back in.

"What's wrong?" Jake asked, not liking the sudden distance.

"Nothing's wrong, exactly." Cris wouldn't hold eye contact, which made him look all kinds of guilty.

They'd been talking about Chet. Jake had accused them earlier of pretending not to be a couple for his benefit, because every single way they interacted screamed "we're together," but Chet argued they weren't. So why—oh. "You and Chet had sex," Jake said.

Cris nodded, then raised his head. He seemed so uncertain, like he'd done something wrong. Jake turned the confession over in his mind, but he wasn't upset. Maybe a little annoyed that it had taken this long for someone to say so, but not upset. "When?"

"My birthday party. We didn't plan it, it just…I was still down over you dumping me, and he tried to be a good friend and listen, and it happened. I mean, we didn't fuck. We rubbed off together on the floor."

The mental image of Cris and Chet rutting around on the floor together made his belly tighten. "You liked it."

"I loved it." Cris flinched. "But it didn't change the fact that I was still hurting over you, or that Chet was still, technically, my boss. We haven't been together since."

"But you wanted to be."

"Part of me did. Part of me also still wanted you, and having you both never seemed possible until now."

Jake frowned. "This whole poly thing is weird."

"It is non-traditional, but look at us. A pornographer, a porn star, and a go-go boy. We're not exactly traditional people, are we?"

"No." And speaking of porn… "Are you going to keep doing it?"

Cris shook his head. "Porn? No. I made the decision a while ago. I'm not sure why I haven't officially resigned yet."

"Maybe subconsciously you were putting it off, because no longer having the boss excuse meant you were free to pursue Chet."

"Maybe. Maybe I kept that barrier intact because I still hoped you'd come around."

Jake grunted. "Took me long enough. You know, my shrink said most first major depressive episodes occur because of some kind of big emotional trauma, and I remember wondering why my mom's death didn't trigger it."

"What did your shrink think?" Cris blanched. "Shit, can I ask that? Was that rude?"

He snared one of Cris's hands and squeezed. "I brought it up, it's fine. We talked about it, and while I was grieving and worried, back then I was still optimistic. Like, even though everything was in the shitter, I still had hope that things would turn around. Get better. This time, I was torn up by you and my feelings, and the stress of losing my apartment with Jon, and then last week was my mom's birthday. She would have been forty-six."

"Hell, Jake, I'm sorry."

"It's okay. Even though I hate knowing what this is, it helps knowing I can control it. I never want to go back to that place again. When it was too dark to see, and everything hurt too much to move. It was really scary for. Until you and Chet came and brought in the light." He squeezed Cris's hand. "I'm sorry I keep doubting you."

Cris scooted closer and tucked Jake against his chest in a sideways hug. "I get it. Florence Nightingale syndrome. You think we care about you because we took care of you, but those feelings were in place long before that. Even Chet's, in his own way."

"Even Chet's own what?" said the man himself, standing outside the open bedroom door.

Oops.

Chapter Twenty

Charles wasn't entirely confident in his decision to send Jake upstairs after Cristian. Yes, Jake had needed to make a sincere apology to Cristian and waiting would only make it worse. But some of Jake's statements still stung, including the one about Charles being old enough to be Jake's father. He'd said it in jest, but…it was painfully true. Two beautiful young men with barely a gap in their ages wanted each other, and Charles couldn't help but feel as if he was standing in their way.

So he stayed downstairs, puttering around in the kitchen, cleaning up their barely eaten meal, while gods knew what happened upstairs. He hoped they came together emotionally, even if not physically. So much passion sparked between them, even when they were arguing at a distance, that it was impossible not to see their potential as lovers.

Lovers who didn't need an old fart in their way.

An old fart too stubborn and far too lonely to let them go. He wouldn't stop them if they chose each other and left, but Charles wanted them to stay. No matter what their unusual combination turned into, his life was better with both men in it.

The front door opened and shut far sooner than he'd anticipated. Dell wandered into the kitchen moments later with a strange look on his face.

"You're home early," Charles said. "Something wrong?"

"No, the friend I was meeting for dinner cancelled." Dell glanced into the den. "Um, are Jake and Cris upstairs?"

"Yes, why?"

"No reason." His cheeks pinked. "Um, it's just that I heard, uh, noises from the foyer."

Charles didn't need any further explanation. "Cristian and Jake had an argument earlier, and they're probably making amends."

"Amends, right." Dell poked around in the fridge, mumbling something.

If Cristian and Jake were making amends in a way that embarrassed Dell, then it had to be sex of some kind. Charles was happy for them. Truly happy, considering how far apart they'd been for so long.

"There's shrimp stir fry in the blue container," Charles said.

"Thanks."

He waited until Dell had heated up a bowl of stir fry in the microwave before saying, "You know I don't like to be the nosy, overprotective uncle."

"But who was I having dinner with?" Dell took his bowl to the counter and sat. "Taro."

Charles blinked. "Cristian's friend?"

"Yup. My friend, too, now."

He rather liked the protective way Dell said that. "I saw you two chatting at the party last weekend. I take it you hit it off?"

"We did. He's a cool guy, and he's easy to talk to. He gets stuff not everyone else does."

"That's wonderful. I'm so happy to see you making more friends your age." Charles truly was happy for him. Now that Dell's drug use and kidney transplant were behind them, Dell could blossom into the young man he was always meant to be.

"Speaking of friends your own age." Dell blew on a steaming piece of shrimp. "Are you really okay with Cris and Jake fucking in one of your guest rooms?"

Charles leaned one elbow on the counter. "Would you prefer they fuck in the den?"

Instead of being embarrassed, Dell narrowed his eyes. "Would *you*?"

"If they were to have an audience, the studio would be a much more appropriate place, don't you think?"

The sideways answer didn't deter his nephew. "Something tells me I wouldn't be filming that particular scene, because it would be a private set. You can tell me to fuck off, Uncle Charles, but what's going on between you three? Because something clearly is."

"My feelings for Cristian haven't been a secret since the night we went out together." Charles straightened, then pretended to tidy up the counter.

"No, they haven't. You've been less clear about your feelings for Jake, though. You've been acting different ever since Thursday."

Of course Dell would notice. He sat quietly in the background and observed, studying human nature through the lenses of his cameras. "It's complicated."

"Because Jake likes Cris, and Cris likes Jake, but Cris also likes you, and you like him back."

"Dizzying but true."

"Do you like Jake too?"

Charles rubbed at a small imperfection in the marble countertop. "My feelings for Jake are different than my feelings for Cristian."

"Well, duh. You've had feelings for Cris for eight years. Naturally they run deeper." Dell frowned. "Aren't you jealous that they're upstairs fooling around?"

"Not at all." He briefly described their discussion over dinner. "Jake is extremely slow to trust, and he hurt Cristian's feelings terribly. They need this time alone to reconnect. Define what they are to each other."

"What about what they are to you?"

"I suppose that's step two."

"Well, you aren't going to figure it out sitting down here talking to me." Dell pointed his fork at the kitchen entry. "Go talk to them."

Charles would prefer they come to him, but he would never admit that out loud. So he steeled his spine and did as ordered.

"Maybe listen in the hall for sex noises before you knock on the door," Dell shouted after him.

Resisting the urge to flip his nephew off, Charles crossed the foyer and ascended the stairs. The hall was mostly quiet. Definitely no sex noises. The closer he got to Cristian's open bedroom door, the louder the two muffled voices became, until entire words began to form.

"—before that," Cristian said. "Even Chet's, in his own way."

"Even Chet's own what?" Charles asked, boldly stepping into the doorway. Thankfully, both men were dressed. They sat close together on Cristian's bed. He'd interrupted a moment, but not an intimate one.

"Your feelings for Jake," Cristian replied. "I was telling him that you'd felt something for him since your first brunch together, because he doesn't quite trust that your feelings aren't coming from Florence Nightingale syndrome."

"Ah." Charles came farther into the room and stopped by the edge of the bed. Studied them both. Cristian's cheeks glowed with the light of someone very satisfied, and Jake's lips had a suspiciously puffy look to them. The idea of Jake going down on Cristian as a form of apology delighted him. "It's true, Jake. You made a lasting impression on me that morning. Your courage in facing someone you'd identified as an obstacle in your relationship with Cristian. I saw so much strength and heart in you that day, and I saw sadness, as well. It seemed inappropriate to acknowledge my attraction to you at the time, and in a way, it still feels inappropriate."

Jake's eyes widened. "I'm so sorry about the father crack earlier. I mean, for being almost fifty, you're super-hot, and you don't even look it. Fifty, I mean. Fuck." He covered his face with both hands.

"Don't hide from us, please." Charles slid onto the bed, close enough to tug Jake's hands away from his face. "With three sets of feelings involved, it's incredibly important that we're all honest with each other. If we're upset, we say so. If we have questions or concerns, we address them. Agreed?"

"Agreed," Cristian said.

"Okay," Jake said. "Sorry."

"Jake, does it bother you that I'm so much older, and yet attracted to you?" Charles asked. His heart pounded. This was the million dollar question.

Jake shrugged. "Not really. I mean, it would make me a hypocrite, right? Since I think I'm attracted to you."

"You think?"

"It's not the same as with Cris. With him, at first, it all about lust and sex, but I really felt something during the sex. Things I've never felt with anyone else, and it scared me. With you...I mean, I haven't even kissed you, but I feel a connection anyway."

"Attraction is more complicated that just sex," Charles said. "It's about emotional connections. A sense of knowing someone your whole life when you've only just met them. That's how I felt with you that first day, and how I still feel. And while I hope one day those feelings will develop into a physical relationship between us, I won't push you. I would never try to manipulate you into something you aren't ready for."

Jake visibly relaxed, as if he'd been worried that admitting his feelings would require immediate sexual gratification, and Charles was glad to give him that relief. He wanted their relationship to develop organically, so it could grow to its fullest, best potential.

"So you're not mad that I just gave Cris a blow job," Jake said, "but I'm not ready to give you one?"

"Of course not." He glanced at Cristian, who was smiling so indulgently at Jake that it made Charles's heart turn over. "When you're ready, though, I would like to kiss you."

Jake blinked several times, then smiled. "I like your house."

Interesting segue. "Thank you. I'm quite fond of it myself."

"You have money, but you don't act like it. You run around saving crazy—sorry, Cris doesn't like that word. You run around saving messed up people you barely know, and then you invite them to live in your house. It's bizarre and weird but also hella hot, because who does that? You're, like, a superhero for gay boys."

"I'm no superhero." Charles brushed a lock of hair from Jake's forehead, grateful Jake didn't pull away from the touch. "I help because I can. No more young men are going to walk into the ocean if I can help it."

"What about the ocean?" Cristian asked.

"A metaphor for depression and suicide. I'll tell you the story another time." Charles didn't want to make this moment about him. He needed to keep it centered on Jake and getting him comfortable with this new situation in which they found themselves. To Jake, he said, "You didn't eat much before our dinner was disrupted. Are you still hungry?"

"A little bit," Jake said. He gave Cristian a sly looked. "The protein shake helped."

Cristian flushed as pink as his complexion allowed.

"Come on, then, let's go downstairs," Charles said. "The shrimp gets a tad rubbery when it's reheated, but it's better than going hungry."

Jake snared his wrist, preventing him from sliding off the bed. "Can I ask a question first?"

"Certainly."

"Are you really okay with it if Cris and I fool around behind your back?"

"Well, no." Before Jake could get upset, Charles continued. "I would hope you wouldn't be doing anything behind my back. You don't have to inform me of all the details, of course, but please don't feel as if you need to hide your physical relationship."

"Oh. Okay." Jake sucked on his bottom lip in an adorable way. "You should know that Cris told me about you guys fooling around on his birthday, and I'm cool with it."

A bit of weight lifted off Charles's shoulders now that their secret was in the open. "Jake, how would you feel if Cristian and I pursued a physical relationship, while you and Cristian explore yours?"

"I think it's kind of hot." Jake shrugged. "Besides, it's not like any of us are exclusive couples or anything, so…you know, if Cris wants us both…." Another shrug. "As long as we're all safe and stuff."

"I'd like to throw something onto the table," Cristian said. "If this exploratory three-way is going to happen, can we at least declare that we three are exclusive to each other? No dating anyone else?"

"Of course," Charles said.

Jake chuckled, a raspy sound that tickled across Charles's skin. "I don't know how I'll manage dating both of you, much less a third person."

"Dating both of you."

He wanted to date Charles as well, not simply live in his home and be his companion. The thought made Charles's dick perk up, so he bit the inside of his cheek. Now was not the time for improper erections. "That's settled, then," Charles said. "We're dating on our own terms."

"Dell isn't going to think this is weird?" Jake asked.

"He'll be fine. He came home a bit ago and heard you two up here, and he knows my feelings for both of you. He won't blab our private business to the other models or anyone else."

Cristian made a sound that was half-grunt, half-sigh. "I guess this as good a time as any to do it." He took Charles's free hand and squeezed. "I'm officially resigning as a model for Mean Green Boys."

The words made Charles's heart ache with the loss, as much as it soared for what Cristian was gaining. He was finally leaving his comfort zone and taking a chance on something new.

"You've given me so much, Charles," Cristian said. "Both as a boss, and as a friend. I can never thank you enough for Mean Green, and for what it means to me. But it's time to move on."

Charles swallowed against the emotion clogging his throat. "It is with a heavy, yet joyful heart that I accept your resignation. I do hope you'll shoot a final goodbye video for your fans."

"Definitely." He rubbed at his eyes with his free hand. "That was harder to say than I thought. But it feels good."

"Change can be difficult, especially after so many years. Some days I think I should hand the reins of Mean Green over to someone else. Allow them to run the business so I can do something new. But then I have a Willie Wonka moment and wonder if a new producer will run the business as I have, with the same standards for safety and consent, and with the models' welfare the highest priority, or will they change it for the worst?"

Cristian's grip on his hand tightened. "You'd really turn the studio over to someone else?"

"I think I would, if the right person came along. Someone I trusted implicitly. Dell's far too young and inexperienced, but perhaps in a few years." Eight years was a long time to run the same business, and Charles occasionally got itchy feet. But Mean Green was about more than porn, and Charles wouldn't risk giving the studio to the wrong person. He'd never betray his models like that.

They returned to the kitchen as a group to reheat the stir fry. Dell was in the den watching television. Charles couldn't help but wonder if Cristian knew Dell and Taro were seeing each other socially. It also wasn't his place to bring it up.

"You know, I'm surprised," Jake said once they'd resettled at the table with food.

"Surprised by what?" Charles asked.

"Neither one of you has asked me where I was all afternoon."

He glanced across the table and caught Cristian's eyes. They didn't want to be nosy or overly protective of Jake. He was a grown man, after all. But Charles couldn't help a keen curiosity over Jake's afternoon.

"We figured you'd tell us if you wanted us to know," Cristian said. "I mean, we aren't going to police your every move, but we do want you to be careful. Especially while you're adjusting to your meds."

"It wasn't anything crazy or impulsive." Jake poked at a shrimp, then chuckled. "Okay, maybe it started out as a crazy, impulsive thing, but it's not anymore. Now I like going to see him."

Charles's skin prickled. "Him?"

"Ned. He's this really old guy who lives in a nursing home in the city. He's got dementia and no family, so I'm the only person who ever visits him."

Well…that wasn't what Charles expected Jake to say, and it increased Charles's fondness for him. Jake visited a friendless old man in a nursing home—a man who wasn't even family. "How did you meet Ned?"

"By accident. After my mom died and I lost the apartment, I struggled for a while. I used to sneak into the nursing home to steal food from the residents' trays, and I know how awful that sounds. Believe me, I do. Ned caught me, but he thought I was someone else, and we got talking. I told the nurses I was his great-grandson, so they let me keep visiting him without having to sneak in."

"That's remarkable," Charles said. One simple, selfless act probably made all the difference for a lonely man—not only Ned, but also for Jake.

Jake turned to Cristian. "That's why I had that bruise on my face the night we met. Sometimes Ned gets violent, and he doesn't mean to. It's the dementia. He's protecting himself, because he thinks he's in danger. He's accidentally hit me a few times, but he never means to."

Charles hated the idea of Jake being hit, accident or not, and the anger on Cristian's face clearly said the same. "Did you report it to the nursing staff?" Cristian asked.

"I did the first time. They told me the warning signs to look out for in dementia patients. He's really a sweet guy, Cris. He spent his whole life in the closet with his lover, and he regrets that so much. Sometimes he even thinks I'm his dead lover, which is both sweet and creepy."

"It sounds as though you both benefit from the relationship," Charles said.

"I guess." Jake grinned at him. "I didn't know my real grandparents. They all died either before I was born, or not long after, so it's like having an actual grandfather for the first time. Or great-grandfather. Or even great-great-grandfather. He's ninety-six."

Cristian nearly choked on his food. "Holy shit, that's old."

"He's practically the same age as the three of us combined." Jake shot Charles a wide-eyed look. "Sorry."

Charles laughed. "It's quite true, if somewhat disconcerting that the two of you together are nearly the same age as I am."

"See! You admit it bothers you."

"Finding a fact disconcerting isn't the same as it bothering me. And it certainly will not hinder my pursuit of the both of you."

Jake crossed his eyes. "Man, the word pursuit makes it sound like you're gonna start chasing us around the house, or something."

"Don't tempt me."

"I'll tempt you," Cristian said. His sultry smile made Charles's belly wobble in the best possible way.

Charles put his fork down. Jake looked back and forth, probably uncertain if they were teasing or serious. Charles, for his part, was perfectly serious. He'd never in his life made a game of chasing another man around his house, but something in the way

Cristian was watching him from across the kitchen table made Charles believe the pursuit would be worth it if he won his prize.

"You two are crazy," Jake said.

"Probably," Charles replied without breaking eye contact with Cristian. The stare-down was heating his blood, but Charles refused to move in order to adjust himself. He barely breathed.

Cristian bolted from the table. Charles stood, giving Cristian a few seconds head start before chasing him toward the foyer. Up the stairs to the second floor. The house really wasn't large enough for a proper chase, but the rush of movement had blood pumping, adrenaline surging. His cock thickening. Cristian raced straight to the end of the hall, which stopped at a large picture window with a view of the backyard. He turned and stooped down, like a football player anticipating a tackle.

Charles stopped a few feet from him, his breaths shorter, loving this spirited side of Cristian he never saw on set and rarely saw off. This was the boy who liked to forget his woes and simply play.

"Come on, grandpa," Cristian said, wagging a finger at him. "Come and get me."

"I don't know, I rather like seeing you backed into a corner."

Cristian growled. Charles's skin prickled, and he braced for Cristian to tackle *him*. And Cristian did surge forward, only to duck at the last moment and slip right past Charles. Charles nearly lost his balance turning, grasping at air because Cristian was already disappearing into Charles's bedroom.

Interesting.

He followed, only to find his bedroom empty. The only blind spot was the far side of the king bed, and the bathroom door was open. Charles eased toward the bed first. He realized his mistake as the first rush of air hit his back—behind the door, he'd hidden behind the door—and then Charles was face down on the bed with Cristian's larger, broader body holding him.

"So the predator becomes the prey," Cristian whispered, his mouth close to Charles's left ear.

"So it seems." He bucked, simply to test Cristian's hold. Cristian tightened his grip, knees caging Charles's legs in. The grip was firm, but tender, and the submissive position made Charles want to fight. But he also trusted Cristian implicitly. "What do you plan on doing to your prey?"

"Not sure. Maybe nibble on it a bit." He licked the shell of Charles's ear.

Charles gasped. "Nibble which parts?"

"Don't you want to know?" Cristian rose up enough to try and manhandle Charles onto his back. Charles used the looser grip to surge toward the headboard, only to be tackled again. He wiggled and twisted, and their chase became a wrestling match of sorts. Cristian played dirty by tickling him until Charles cried uncle.

"You've got me, I'm yours," Charles said through his laughter. His eyes were damp from it, his dick even harder from the constant friction.

"Good." Cristian reached between them and squeezed Charles's erection. "Hmmm."

Charles humped against his hand, desperate for Cristian to really touch him. "Please."

Cristian nuzzled his cheek, dropping butterfly kisses against his skin. "What was that?"

"Please, Cristian."

"I like when you beg. It's sexy as fuck." He worked at the belt buckle, managing it and the fly of Charles's trousers with one hand. Slid right beneath the band of Charles's briefs to clasp his dick. Charles gasped. "This all for me?"

"God yes." The light touch on his cock was driving Charles crazy. He needed more. Anything Cristian wanted to give him. "Please, love."

Cristian licked at the side of his neck, then began to suck on that spot, right over Charles's pulse point. His hand slowly jacked Charles, a tease of pressure and motion, and light years away from actually making him come. Charles slid his hands beneath Cristian's shirt, raking his fingers down the man's back, needing the contact. It got him another of those wonderful growls, and then Cristian tried to swallow him whole.

The kiss was possessive and needy, and the deeper it went, the harder Cristian worked his cock. Charles didn't particularly wish to come in his pants, but if that was as far as Cristian wanted to go, he'd count his blessings and eat the dry cleaning bill. He slipped one hand into Cristian's jeans to squeeze the top of his ass. Cristian had a perfect ass, chiseled and tan, with the right amount of muscle—whether tightening with each stroke as he fucked another guy, or spreading so beautifully to be fucked.

A mental image he'd never allowed himself to explore flashed into the forefront of his mind. Cristian on his back beneath him, legs spread wide, accepting Charles's cock into his body. Pounding against that perfect ass. Driving them both to completion. Coming deep inside of Cristian's body with no barrier between them.

Cristian bit sharply on Charles's lower lip, then crawled down his body. Shoved his shirt up and pants down, and Charles barely had time to savor the image of Cristian hunched over his straining erection, before Cristian closed his lips around the head of his dick. He wanted to watch, but goddamn, Cristian was too good. Charles threw his head back and moaned, clutching at Cristian's hair and shoulders, needing more. Needing everything. The hot pressure on his cock was like nothing he'd ever felt, and he soared on the sensation. He'd known on some level that being with Cristian would be amazing, but this was more. This was intimacy and emotion on a level he'd never reached before.

This was sex with someone he loved. Really, truly loved.

Cristian rolled his balls while he sucked and licked. It was messy and unscripted and perfect. Charles wanted it to last forever, but his body was betraying him. Tightening. Sending him hurtling toward the edge.

"Fuck," Charles gasped. "Coming."

Cristian pulled off his cock without stopping his strokes. Charles slammed his eyelids shut as wave after wave rolled down his spine. No tell-tale wetness struck his belly or exposed abdomen, and as his release settled, the bed shifted. He blinked his eyes open. Cristian loomed over him, his cheek, chin, and neck spotted with Charles's semen. The sight of Cristian marked like that cemented what Charles already knew to be true: he loved Cristian.

And Cristian was his.

He drew Cristian down, then took his time licking every last drop from Cristian's skin, leaving his face damp and red. Cristian kissed him, tongue thrusting into his mouth, staking his claim in his own way. Charles groped Cristian, hoping for a chance to return to the favor, only to find a semi.

"Sorry," Cristian said. "Need a little more recovery time."

"Don't apologize. This was amazing. Thank you."

"You are very welcome." Cristian settled next to him, half draped over his body, head propped on his hand. "That was a hell of a money shot."

Charles chuckled. "I'll take your word for it."

"That was a hell of a money shot," Jake said, startling them both into sitting straight up on the bed. Jake stood barely inside the door frame, both hands deep inside the pockets of his shorts. His cheeks were red, eyes sparkling with desire, but he made no move toward them. Nor did Charles spot a tell-tale tent at his crotch.

"You watched us?" Cristian asked, the question coated in curiosity, rather than anger.

Jake shrugged. "Most of it. Didn't see who won the chase."

"I did." He preened. "Then I took advantage of my prey."

Charles poked him in the side, then began the business of tucking himself away. He wasn't embarrassed for Jake to see him, but he was a little self-conscious at being the only one with his junk hanging out. "And your prey very much appreciated being taken advantage of."

"I could tell," Jake said. "Um, am I intruding?"

"Of course not. Come in, please."

"I mean, I didn't mean to perv on you guys." Jake took a few steps inside the room, still tentative in his posture and tone. "I was curious what was happening, and then you guys were so wrapped up in each other. I've never seen that kind of real chemistry before."

Charles held out his left hand; Jake hesitated, then crossed the room to clasp it tight in his right. "I see that kind of real chemistry whenever I look at you and Cristian together. You both light up in a way I can't begin to describe. I think that's why it's so easy to share him with you without being jealous."

Jake grinned. "I guess that's why I'm not jealous either."

"Good. But if you ever do get jealous for any reason—and this goes for you, as well, Cristian—we need to talk about it. Hiding our feelings will only make things worse, not better."

"Right."

"Totally on board with that," Cristian said. "Also? Not jealous of you two liking each other, either."

Jake shot him an assessing look. "Do you think you'd get jealous if things between me and Chet got physical?"

"I'd like to think no, but I can't make a promise based on a what-if."

"Hmm." Jake freed his hand, then slid it behind Charles's neck, the unexpected touch lighting his skin on fire. Charles barely had a moment to understand Jake's intent before Jake pressed cool lips to his. The kiss was soft, a pleasant pressure on his mouth, and Charles wasn't sure what to do.

He wanted to kiss Jake the same way he'd kissed Cristian, but it was too soon for that. This dance was far more delicate and refined. So he parted his lips a fraction and allowed Jake to take what he wanted. Jake explored a bit more. The tip of his tongue darted out to tease at the edges of Charles's lips without stealing inside. The sweetest goddamn kiss of Charles's life seemed to last forever, and then it was over too soon.

Jake stood back, his smile so tentative that it bordered on bashful. "Was it okay to do that?"

"It was very much okay," Charles replied. "I quite enjoyed it."

"Me too." He glanced at Cristian, and Charles did as well. Cristian was watching them like he wanted to devour them both. Most definitely not jealous. "Anyway, uh, I'm going to go back downstairs. Maybe see if Dell will give up the TV for a Christmas movie marathon."

"It's June," Cristian said.

"I know, but Christmas movies always cheer me up. Can't let the meds do all the work, right?"

Charles found the idea of a Christmas movie marathon in June incredibly charming. "Would you mind if I joined you? I make a very tasty bowl of Old Bay popcorn."

Jake's eyes lit up. "Definitely. Cris?"

"I'm in." Cristian slid across the bed, then tugged Jake down and planted a firm kiss on his mouth. "I love this plan."

Their threesome went downstairs and easily won television control. Jake surfed Netflix for a good first movie choice, while Charles prepared two batches of popcorn for the four of them to share. Dell curled up in a side chair, while Jake seemed content to sit on the couch, firmly sandwiched between Charles and Cristian, their bowl of popcorn in his lap. Charles couldn't recall a more perfect evening in his life.

And he'd fight tooth and nail to have this again, and again.

Forever.

Chapter Twenty-one

Cris loved everything about waking up in Chet's big bed with Jake in the middle and Chet on the far side. It was comfortable and comforting and simply felt right. He didn't mind that Jake snored, or that Chet stole the covers and left Cris without much on his side. No one had outright said they should share one bed last night; they'd all simply gravitated to Chet's room once the movie marathon was over.

He hated getting up and leaving his two men in bed without him, but he had a volunteer shift at the hospital that started at eight. He showered and dressed, then went downstairs. Dell surprised him by being awake, still in boxers and undershirt, eating a bowl of cereal at the island.

"Do you ever sleep?" Cris asked. Dell had still been up when the rest of them went to bed.

Dell shrugged. "When I can."

Something about Dell's tone made him stop and pay attention. "Insomnia?"

"I guess. I have weird dreams a lot, and I don't like to take sleeping pills because they make me sleepwalk. Sometimes it's easier not to sleep."

Cris touched his side, right over the scar. "How long has that been happening?"

"A while." Dell stirred his cereal, playing now more than eating. "The dreams started before the overdose last fall, but they got worse, believe it or not, after the transplant. I guess the surgery freaked me out more than I thought it would. I don't know."

He eased onto the stool next to Dell, drawn by an odd responsibility for the kid who had one of his kidneys. "Have you talked to Chet about it?"

"No. He's got enough going on, and he's worried about me too much already."

"You guys are family. I don't think worry has a quota." Might as well go fishing a bit. "Do you have other friends you can talk to? Boomer mentioned that you and Adam were friendly."

"We were last fall, but he had his own stuff to deal with, and after the overdose, he didn't need all my extra drama. We haven't talked in a while."

Ah ha. I get it.

"You don't like leaning on other people, because you're too sensitive to the fact that they've also got drama to deal with, right?" Cris said. "You don't want to add more to their plate, so you deal with it all yourself."

Dell blinked hard several times, then frowned. "How did you do that?"

"I'm an observer of human nature, same as you. But Dell, part of having friends and relationships means trusting them to take care of you when you need help. I can't pretend to know exactly what you're going through, because I don't. But I do understand nightmares and secrets, and if you ever need to talk, I'll listen."

"Thanks, Cris."

"Anytime."

Cris wasn't entirely sure he'd reached Dell, but he had to get to his hospital shift. He grabbed an apple to tide him over until his break, then grabbed his phone and keys.

Volunteering had been his way of dealing with his continued grief and guilt over Grace's death. Cris wasn't a doctor or a nurse, and he had no desire to become one, but this gave him a chance to help. To give back and occasionally make a patient smile. Sometimes it led to surreal moments, like last fall when Boomer and Adam were attacked by a stalker.

With everything else Chet had been dealing with at that time, making that phone call had been painful.

A few hours into his shift, he got a text from Taro begging off tonight's weekly dinner date. Their date had been a tradition for years, and the only reason one of them called out was either a work emergency (Cris did that once) or because one of them was super sick (twice for Taro, once for Cris).

He texted back, asking how sick he was. Taro wrote back that he just wanted to sleep.

Cris spent the rest of his shift in a state of confusion and concern, and once he was finished at the hospital, he swung by his favorite deli for a pint of Matzo ball soup—perfect homemade cure when you felt bad, and this place made the best in the city.

A nice straight couple and their baby lived in the other half the duplex Taro rented. They shared a porch, and the straight side had a toddler's style tricycle and all kinds of scattered toys. Taro's side had a single potted plant that was looking a little extra-droopy.

He rang the bell and knocked, then waited. If Taro was asleep, it would take him time to shuffle downstairs and answer the door. When a second summons when unanswered, Cris called him.

"That better not be you banging on my door," Taro snipped.

Damn, he was grumpy. "I brought you soup."

"I didn't ask you to."

"No, you didn't. It's what friends do, now let me in. It's hot as balls out here."

Taro snorted. "Be right down."

Cris counted to ninety-eight before Taro slid back the deadbolt and opened the door. Cris stepped into air conditioning that instantly cooled his sweaty skin. He enjoyed that sensation for a moment, but didn't miss the way Taro stood angled sideways, his head down. Not like someone who was sick, exactly. More like hiding.

"What's going on?" he asked, the soup in his hand no longer a priority. He put the plastic bag on a nearby table, then gave his friend his full attention.

"I've just been really overwhelmed lately," Taro told the floor. "I don't feel like going out."

"Look at me."

"Why?"

"Because in all the years we've been friends, even when you're overwhelmed or upset, you never have trouble looking me in the eye. Taro?" Real concern tightened his stomach. Cris wanted to reach out and force Taro's head up, but he didn't.

Taro's shoulders sagged, but he did raise his head. Turned to face him.

Blood thundered in Cris's temples, and he curled his hands into tight fists. Taro's left cheekbone was bruised, and a scabbed gash ran at least two inches through the center. The underside of his eye had blackened, too. Dark thoughts raced through Cris's mind—all the various ways how that mark was on his best friend's face, and how Cris would punish them for putting it there.

"Who hit you?" Cris asked.

"This is why I wanted to avoid you tonight. You get all overprotective, and it's not as bad as you're over-thinking it is."

"That didn't answer my question."

Taro slumped onto his sofa, hands loose in his lap. Cris sat next to him, on edge, ready to seek out whomever needed to be punished for this.

"It was an accident, all right?" Taro said.

"Why would hide it from me if it was an accident?"

"Because you have enough going on with Jake and Chet, and I didn't want to heap something else on you."

Christ, but Taro and Dell are peas in a pod.

"I will always have time for you," Cris said. "You know that. Tell me what happened."

"Fine. But allow me to preface this story with no, I wasn't attacked or date raped, so please, get that out of your mind right now."

Thank Christ. I don't have to murder anyone and hide the body.

"I've been thinking about what you said to me a few weeks ago," Taro continued. "That I don't ever go out looking to make friends or people connections. Thinking about it a lot. And then I did make a connection. At your birthday party."

"You did?" Cris didn't recall seeing Taro talking to anyone except—hell. "Did Dell hit you?"

Taro shot him a withering glare. "Of course not. Will you stop guessing and allow me to finish?"

He mimed locking his lips with an invisible key.

"Thank you," Taro said. "Dell and I have become friendly since your party, yes. He's surprisingly easy to talk to. He also doesn't jump to conclusions about things, unlike certain parties present."

Cris actively liked the idea of Taro and Dell becoming friends. They had very similar personalities.

"Anyway, befriending Dell prompted me to go outside of my Saturday routine this past weekend. Instead of going to my gym super-early to avoid people, I went mid-morning. I made eye contact and even spoke to strangers."

The chaotic anger in Cris's brain eased, replaced with pride over Taro's courage. He'd stepped outside of his comfort zone, but that still didn't explain the bruise.

"I ended up having a lengthy conversation with a man my age," Taro continued, "about the importance of representation in modern film blockbusters. The newest *Star Wars* films, in particular, and for a white guy, he was incredibly open to other points of view. We ended up taking our conversation to a nearby coffee shop. He had to work in the afternoon, so we didn't stay long, but we did exchange numbers. We also decided to meet for lunch the next day.

"I was nervous, of course. Even though he'd openly flirted with me the day before, we hadn't established if lunch was a date or not. I also wanted to be up front about myself, so I told him I

Here For Us 339

was demi. He didn't understand. I explained, and he seemed accepting."

Seemed.

Despite Taro's insistence that this wasn't going to become a date rape story, Cris had known too many guys who pretended bad things weren't as awful as they actually were. And Taro had a dangerous habit of downplaying drama.

Taro's lips twitched. "During our lunch conversation, we both revealed that we're obsessive collectors of Funko POP vinyl figures. He even showed me photos of his collection, then invited me to his place to see it. I agreed and followed him to his apartment. He doesn't own as many as I do, and you have no idea how difficult it was for me not to rearrange his collection. They weren't even in order by set, much less by number."

Cris knew how hard that must have set off Taro's OCD. Taro's own collection was in the upstairs guest room, on neatly installed shelves and carefully arranged to his liking. Once, Cris had swapped out two just to see how long it took Taro to notice, and the POP's were back in the correct place within a day.

"Does this guy have a name?" Cris asked.

"Marty. Anyway, we sat on his couch, and he brought us drinks. We talked as friends, but I could see his interest in his body language. He asked more about being demi, and if I was open to kissing him on the first date. I joked about not realizing we were on a date, and he teased back about gathering information for the future."

Taro's expression went distant, almost wistful. "So I told him it depended on the person, and it had been so long since I've been kissed, Cris. I've been so lonely. I didn't realize how much I've missed physical contact until he asked me, so I told him I didn't mind if we kissed right now."

"Did you mind, though?" Cris squeezed Taro's wrist. "Tell me the truth."

Taro shrugged. "I kind of minded, but he was so sweet and attentive, and I should have said no, but I said yes. We started kissing. It started off sweet, gentle." His half-smile turned sour. "Then he started using tongue and his hands began to wander, and I know it was instinctive for him to—"

"Hey, don't do that. Don't make excuses for him pushing your limit. That's on him, babe." Cris turned his wrist so he could hold Taro's hand. "That wasn't your fault."

"Maybe not. But the touching made me panic. I shoved him away, tripped over my own stupid feet, fell off the couch, and hit my head on the coffee table."

Ouch.

"Naturally Marty freaked out," Taro continued. "He got me a towel with ice for my face, which hurt like hell, thank you very much. I was so embarrassed I bolted." He glanced in the direction of the kitchen. "I still have his towel."

"Why did you think you couldn't tell me?" Cris asked. It hurt a little that Taro had kept something like this a secret. "I wish you'd called me on Sunday to talk it out, instead of waiting two days."

"I'm sorry. You have so much—"

"Of my own drama, yeah, I know. But I always have time for you. So talk to me. How do you feel about what happened with Marty?"

"Still embarrassed. A little angry now."

"Angry at who?"

"Myself, mostly, for overreacting to a kiss. At Marty, too, for letting his hands wander. But that's not something most allosexual people think much about, is it? You're attracted to someone, so you react accordingly. I should have been more clear about my limits."

"Has Marty reached out since it happened?"

"He's texted a few times to see if I'm okay."

"And?"

"I haven't responded."

Cris tilted his head. "Why not?"

"Because I wasn't okay. I felt like an idiot. I embarrassed the hell out of myself, and I suppose...I needed to talk to you first."

"And now that you have?"

"I feel better." Taro covered their clasped hands with his free one. "Thank you for being stubborn about this and not letting me blow you off."

"You're welcome. So was cancelling dinner you not wanting to talk about this in public? Or about people seeing your face bruised up?"

"A little of both. Believe me, it was a difficult text to send."

"I bet." Cris hated letting their tradition slide by because Taro had a bad reaction to a guy getting handsy. "How about I call the diner and get our food to go? Bring it back here. We can picnic in the living room."

Taro blinked hard. "You'd do that?"

"Sure. What's a little driving to help out my brother?"

In an unexpected twist, Taro tugged him into a hug. Brief but firm, and it said so many things. *Thank you. I love you.*

Brothers in arms, no matter what. Cris didn't have many friends, but he protected the ones he did. He hated the bruise on Taro's face; he was also glad he didn't have to find this Marty character and deliver a beat-down.

Instead, he could get take out and spend the evening with his best friend, as planned.

Tuesday night, Jake found himself in the unique position of being completely alone in the upstairs of Chet's house. Cris was out with Taro. Chet and Dell were downstairs filming and would be tied up for a few hours. Jake was used to someone else being around, so having the run of the house was weird.

It also didn't leave him many entertainment options, other than playing on his phone, reading or watching TV, but he was too restless to sit still. After days of exhaustion and mental sluggishness, the tide was turning in his favor. Kind of. His next appointment with Dr. Englade was tomorrow, so they could talk about his mood and see how his pills were working.

Jake wanted to believe that his relationships were as important to his mental shift as those fucking pills, but he had a feeling his shrink wouldn't like him jumping into a threesome, while trying to get his head on straight. He could talk about Cris, maybe, but not Chet. Besides, all he and Chet had done was sleep together—totally platonically—and share one kiss.

One hell of a hot, sexy, sweet kiss that Jake wanted to plant on him again.

Maybe tonight after Chet was done shooting. And after Cris came home. Part of what had made that kiss so amazing was knowing Cris was watching. Cris knew what Chet's kisses tasted like, and now Jake sampled them. And he wanted to know more.

Cris got home a little after eight. He walked into the den and swept Jake into a smothering hug that put Jake on instant alert. Not a greeting or a smile, just a hug.

"What's wrong?" Jake wiggled until Cris loosened his embrace.

He tucked Jake's head under his chin and held him there. "Nothing's really wrong. Taro had a bad day, and I'm upset for him. Needed this."

"Oh." Jake didn't totally understand the complex relationship between Cris and Taro, only that they'd been close for years. But Cris had a hyper-sensitive side hiding beneath his macho, alpha exterior. It made sense that he'd be hurting if his best friend was hurting. "Is Taro okay?"

"Yeah. Now."

"I'm glad."

Cris tilted his chin until their eyes met. "I hate it when people I love are in pain and I can't fix it for them."

Jake's heart pounded. No way did he mean what Jake thought he meant. "Sometimes listening is the best fix for a problem."

"If you hadn't noticed, I'm more of a man-of-action guy."

"I'd noticed." He pulled Cris's head down to kiss his mouth. A soft press of lips, nothing more. "You take charge, try to fix things, and I love that about you. It kept you from giving up on my sorry ass."

"Don't insult this ass." Cris squeezed his left cheek. "I like it too much to let you insult it."

"You like my ass, huh. What do you like about it?"

Cris's nostrils flared; heat lit his dark brown eyes. "I like watching it spread for four of my fingers. I love watching it spread for my dick."

The dirty words hit Jake in the balls, and his dick started perking up. It had been weeks since Cris last fucked him senseless. "Pretty sure you had a good time eating my ass, too."

"Fuck yes, I did." Cris's hand slid into Jake's crease. "You know, I still haven't repaid you for yesterday's blow job."

"You don't have to repay that."

"I know I don't *have* to. You wanna fool around?"

Jake bit his bottom lip. "Should we wait for Chet?"

"We could." Cris nuzzled at Jake's cheek before licking a stripe across his skin. "Or we could keep playing until he's finished downstairs and joins us."

Oh God.

"Um, okay."

Cris stepped back, then hauled Jake over his shoulder into a fireman's carry that made Jake squawk in protest. Cris smacked his ass once as he marched toward the stairs. Jake got his revenge by shoving one hand into the back of Cris's jeans and pinching his ass multiple times. Cris carried him to Jake's small room—probably because it was the first open door—and dumped him onto the bed. Jake bounced once before Cris was on top of him, kissing him hard. Thrusting his tongue into Jake's mouth, while thrusting their groins together. Cris's erection rode Jake's thigh, thick and heavy, and Jake's dick tried. Sensations rolled all over his body from every point of contact.

But some combination of depression and his meds kept Jake's dick from perking up completely. Cris reached between them.

Got Jake's jeans open. Kissed his way down Jake's chest, shoving his t-shirt up to lick at his nipples and navel. He yanked Jake's jeans and underwear down, then off completely. Before Jake could tell him he didn't have to, Cris took his half-hard dick into his mouth.

Cris took his time working Jake's dick, licking his balls, eating his ass. He made the most wonderful noises of appreciation and desire, and he never once seemed annoyed at the lack of progress. In the end, Jake pulled him away from his uncooperative junk, annoyed at himself for being unable to get a goddamn erection.

He tried to sit up, to get away from his failure, but Cris held him down. Cris's gentle smile was too much to endure, so Jake shut his eyes.

"Hey." Cris nipped his chin. "Hard or soft, I could spend hours tasting you."

"I hate this. I used to pop wood by looking at a thong, and I can't even do it for you while I'm in your mouth."

"Open your eyes."

Jake squinted at Cris. "Sorry."

"For what? It won't always be like this. Your body will sort itself out." Cris frowned, uncertain for the first time since coming home. "Unless you didn't like it. I can back off."

"No, I liked it." He threaded his fingers through Cris's black hair. "It felt great, all of it. This is me. I'm used to being able to perform. I'm twenty-three, for fuck's sake."

"And dealing with something new that has your body out of whack. Give it time." Cris bent to lick the shell of Jake's ear.

"We'll get back to a place where I can make you come with four of my fingers in your ass."

Jake shivered, then pulled Cris down for another long, intense kiss. Full of lips and tongues and teeth and wandering fingers. He reversed their positions, then blew Cris with most of his clothes still on, swallowing every drop of Cris's release. Jake loved that he could still do this, at least. Show Cris how much he wanted him.

They both fixed their clothes, then curled up side-by-side on the bed, Jake tucked neatly against Cris's broad body. He loved these quiet moments most, when Cris expected nothing more from him than his company. Jake could soak in the heat of his boyfriend's body—and yeah, that word was weird, but that's what they were. Boyfriends.

Boyfriends who couldn't have sex the way they wanted, but whatever.

Jake dozed, startling awake at the sound of Chet's whispers.

"There he is," Chet said. "I wasn't certain if we'd have to carry you to bed or not."

"Nah, I can walk." Jake rolled up to kiss Chet properly in greeting, loving how Chet, again, allowed him to control the kiss. "Hi."

"Hello, yourself."

"How'd the shoot go?" Cris asked as they crossed the hallway to Chet's room.

"It went very well, thanks for asking."

They went about the familiar routine of brushing teeth and changing clothes. Cris deliberately swapped shirts with his back to Chet, vividly reminding Jake of the secret they were both keeping. Jake climbed into bed with that secret weighing heavily in his heart. It kept him awake long after the two men beside him fell asleep. The secret would either bring them all closer together, or tear apart this fragile thing they were creating. And the latter scared Jake more than anything had in his life.

For the first time since his mom died, Jake had something truly precious to lose.

Chapter Twenty-two

By Saturday, Jake was ready to get the fuck out of Chet's house and go back to work. As much as he loved the attention showered upon him by both Cris and Chet, Jake was going stir crazy. He felt less underwater, less foggy. He still couldn't manage a full erection, but Dr. Englade assured him it wasn't permanent; his body would adjust. Cris still lavished attention on his dick and balls, though, and more than once Jake had watched Chet and Cris blow each other.

No one had pushed for more than that yet, even though Cris and Chet both had fully functioning penises. But if they were fucking behind his back—not that he expected them to—Jake couldn't tell.

Richard was ecstatic when Jake called that morning to ask about dancing again. "Of course we have a spot for you, my boy! Shane's been filling in a few extra shifts here and there, and I'm sure he'd be glad to have his time back. I can't wait to see you on stage again."

"I'm excited to be back, thanks," Jake said. And he *was* excited. Nervous, too, since he hadn't danced in two weeks. So much of it was muscle memory. All he needed to do was get there, listen to the music for a while, let it filter into his blood. Wake him up inside and out.

"Usual time. See you tonight, son."

"Thanks, Richard."

Jake had made the call upstairs in "his" room for privacy. He went downstairs where Chet and Dell were playing chess at the kitchen table. Cris was in the den working on his laptop—scratch that. No earbuds, so Cris was probably fooling around online. Jake picked a position halfway between the men, then said, "I'm going back to work tonight."

Chet fumbled a pawn, head snapping up from the board. "You are?"

"Yes. It's time. And Dr. Englade says physical activity is good for my overall mental health. What kind of activity could be better than dancing to techno music?"

He'd been speaking directly to Chet, so Jake didn't notice Cris sneak up behind him until two big arms looped around his waist and lifted him into the air. "I'm so proud of you for trying," Cris said.

"Yeah?" Cris set him down; Jake turned, overjoyed at the pride shining in Cris's eyes. "Really?"

"Definitely. But I need you to promise me something."

"Okay."

"Don't be too hard on yourself your first night back. Ease into it. If you aren't feeling it, take a break."

Jake wanted to pinch him for doubting his first night back would be anything other than a success, but Cris was being realistic. Jake knew he could fall on his face—literally and figuratively—by going back this soon. He wasn't even a week on his meds, but he felt miles better than at the start of this week. He had miles left to go, and that was fine. He wasn't taking this journey alone.

"I'll do my best, I promise," Jake said.

Cris kissed the tip of his nose. "Acceptable."

"Good, because I want you guys to come tonight, too. All of you. Invite Taro, if you want."

"You want all of us there?" Chet asked. His chair scraped.

"Of course." Jake turned his head; Chet was walking toward them. "Having you guys there, cheering me on? It'll help big time."

"I'm up for it," Cris said. "Chet?"

Chet stopped next to them, his eyebrows slanted. "You really want me to be there?"

"Why wouldn't I?" Jake twisted in Cris's arms so he could put his hands on Chet's shoulders. "I want both of my boyfriends there." He hadn't used that word directly to Chet yet to define their relationship, but he'd definitely chosen the right time to say it. Chet's frown melted into the brightest smile.

"Then this boyfriend will happily attend," Chet said. "I may have to borrow the appropriate attire again."

Jake blew a raspberry. "Dress like yourself, dude. You're hot in anything you wear." His cheeks warmed. He still wasn't used to openly complimenting Chet, especially in front of Dell. Or ten feet from Dell. Whatever.

"Taro probably won't be able to come," Cris said. "He spends Saturdays with his parents."

"Cool." Jake looked past Chet. "Dell?"

"No, thank you, though," Dell said. "Not quite ready to face the temptations of a club."

Oh fuck, I'm stupid. The guy isn't even a year sober.

"Sorry, man," Jake said.

"Don't worry about it, it's my deal. Thanks for the invite, though."

"Sure."

"So will this be our first official outing together?" Cris asked. "As a threesome?"

"Sort of, I guess." Jake's stomach tightened. "I have to be there by nine-thirty to get ready, but, I mean, if you guys want to go earlier, we can hang. Have a drink." He flinched. "Well, you guys can have a drink. I can't mix with my meds."

"Then how about a sober night in solidarity? I'm fine with drowning my kidneys in Sprite."

"Kidney." The instant the word slipped out, Jake froze. Cris's arms tightened around his waist. Jake floundered for anything, no matter how stupid. "Kidney drowning in Sprite is, uh, less fun than in rum, but hey. You do what you gotta do." He couldn't make himself look Chet in the eye, and that was a mistake.

"Cristian," Chet said, a funny tremor in his voice. "I can't pretend to know all of Jake's nervous tics quite yet, but I know your tells. Why did he correct you?"

Oh shit, Cris is going to kill me. I totally fucked this up.

Cris released him and took a step back. Jake angled so he was facing everyone, even Dell, who'd paused by the counter to watch them. Chet looked confused. Cris looked like an animal backed into a corner, and it was all Jake's fault. He couldn't keep his stupid mouth shut.

What did I just do?

This was one of those moments when Cris silently cursed how well Chet knew him. He hadn't managed to keep a straight face when Jake blurted out a kidney count correction, and Chet had noticed. If it had been any other organ, no one would have noticed. Kidneys were a trigger word in this house for a very good reason.

Why the fuck didn't I say liver?

Cris could lie. Come up with some convoluted reason why Jake had corrected him. Redirect the conversation so he didn't have to deal with the fallout of keeping this secret for so long.

No. Lying now would make it worse later. Secrets always came out.

With his heart in his throat and his pulse in his temples, Cris said, "Because I only have one kidney."

Chet's eyebrows arched. "Really? You never mentioned that to me before. How did you lose yours? If I may ask?"

Another opportunity to lie, to cheat, to play it off like he'd had an accident years ago—except for the damned scar. Sooner or later, Chet would see the scar and he'd know. "I didn't lose it, so much as give it away."

In the kitchen, Dell's entire body went rigid, but Cris couldn't tear his eyes off Chet. His beautiful, amazing Chet, whose face was twisted up in confusion and the distant dawning of the truth Cris couldn't seem to blurt out. Confusion gave way to shock, and Chet blinked several times, his eyes brighter, wetter with each harsh movement.

Cris nearly reach for Jake's hand, desperate for the grounding touch, but he remained still. He didn't deserve comfort while Chet was floundering.

"Your hiatus," Chet said, rough, strained. "It began a week before Dell's transplant."

"Yes," Cris replied. God, why couldn't he say it and spare Chet the agony of working it out for himself?

"You voluntarily donated a kidney."

"Yes." He owed Chet more than a single, choked answer. "A direct, voluntary, anonymous donation."

Chet's face crumpled; his breaths got shorter. "To Dell."

Cris's chest hurt so badly he thought his heart might shatter. "I couldn't stand seeing you both suffering when I could do something to help."

"Help?" Chet released a strangled breath. "You saved his life. Why didn't you tell me?"

Chet seemed more flabbergasted than furious, which helped Cris find the words to explain. "We were in such a complicated place. Our feelings coming back, but still being boss and employee. Watching you hurt over Dell's illness killed me inside a little more every day. Seeing both of you stressing over finding a donor...so I got tested and I was a match." Tears stung his eyes and nose. "I didn't do it for praise or thanks. I did it because I love you."

The room fell silent, as if someone had hit the mute button. Cris couldn't breathe. He'd said the words he'd felt for a long time, and with that release came a rush of relief. The secret was out. No more hiding. No more hoping he could keep his shirt on, his scar hidden, for one more day. The two people who deserved the truth knew it now, and that's what mattered most.

"I, ah, need a moment, please," Chet said. He turned without further comment and left the den.

Cris wilted. Jake hugged him from behind, and Cris sagged into the embrace, for once the one in desperate need of support.

Dell appeared in front of him, moving like a ghost, his cheeks streaked with tears. "Thank you," he said. "For the kidney, and for loving my uncle."

"He's pretty easy to love," Cris replied.

He didn't anticipate Dell's hug, the force of which knocked him back a step. Only Jake's firm grip kept them all upright. He held Dell while he cried, unable to stop a few tears of his own, overwhelmed by the gratitude of the young man in his arms. Dell had made mistakes, he'd paid dearly with his health, and now he had a second chance. To live, to love, to find his dream.

Cris regretted nothing about his choice to donate his kidney.

Time would tell if he'd regret his decision not to tell Chet.

The afternoon slogged away. Chet stayed holed up in his office for the rest of the day. Dell went inside once, probably to confirm Chet was alive and well, but said Chet needed time. It hurt, but Cris told Dell he understood. So did Jake, who took more responsibility for this mess than was his to carry. This was all on Cris.

They made dinner and left a tray by Chet's door. Eventually, Jake took a shower so he could get ready for the night. He'd let himself go a little wild these last two weeks, Jake had said, and a few spots needed some trimming. Cris worried himself into a stomachache that didn't relent when he changed into club clothes. Didn't ease on the drive into the city with Jake in his passenger seat, sliver thong and mesh shirt on under sweat shorts and a regular t-shirt.

"I'm sorry," Jake blurted out once Cris had parked in the public lot. "I'm so sorry if I fucked this up for you, because I couldn't keep my mouth shut."

"This isn't your fault." Cris shut off the engine. "I shouldn't have kept it a secret for so long. Maybe at all, I don't know. It was stupid to think I could get away with donating a kidney and no one finding out."

"Still, I feel like I outed you or something."

He reached across the console to squeeze Jake's hand. "You didn't out me. You forced an inevitable conversation. I'm not mad at you, I promise. You didn't have to keep my secret, but you did, and I hate thinking Chet could be mad at you because of me."

"Keeping your secret was my choice. If Chet's mad at me, it's on me, not you."

"It's on both of us." He pulled Jake toward him, needing the comfort of a firm, desperate kiss. "You ready?"

"I think so."

"You'll be amazing."

"You're biased."

"Probably. It was your amazing dancing skills, after all, that caught my attention all those weeks ago."

Jake laughed. "And here I thought it was because blue is your favorite color."

"Also true. I love that you were blue. I love how you dance and flirt and eye fuck people in the crowd. I love your strength and snarkiness and your big, big heart that you try very hard to hide." Cris curled his hand around the back of Jake's neck, holding his gaze. "I love you, Jake Bowden."

Jake's eyes went wide, then soft. Almost dreamy. "Really?"

"Yes. I never thought I'd find one person to love again after my last relationship, much less two men who mean so much to me. And I know it's a lot to take in, and you're dealing with so much. I'm not putting pressure on you, I swear. I needed you to know how I feel."

"Thank you. For everything. I never thought I'd be here, either, and I mean that about a lot of things. And no matter what happens with Chet, you've got me, Cris. I promise."

An unexpected weight lifted from Cris's heart. He kissed Jake one more time, sealing that promise, before they left the car. They walked side-by-side to the entrance of the alley, and then hand-in-hand to the industrial door.

Bear stood from his stool and extended a meaty hand to both of them. "Great to see you back at work, Jake. You look good, son."

"Thanks, Bear," Jake said.

The throbbing base of the club beat in Cris's chest the instant they walked inside. Jake had an hour to kill before he was supposed to dance, so they eased their way to the bar. Richard came out from behind it to give Jake a big hug and congratulate him on returning to work, then served them Sprites on the house. They sipped their drinks, while Jake fielded the occasional greeting from a regular who'd missed him. Cris tried not to be too territorial about those compliments. Yes, Jake shook his ass well, but that ass was Cris's now, thank you very much.

The whole time, Cris scanned the crowd, hoping that Chet would surprise them with an appearance. Time passed, and then Jake had to go backstage and prepare. Cris eased his way over to his favorite spot near the elevated platform Jake favored, letting his body sway to the music.

At ten o'clock, the club lights lowered and spotlights lit up the stages. Four dancers came out at the same time, gyrating to a techno cover of "Dark Horse." Jake had added silver glitter to his hair and face paint to his cheeks, and he looked absolutely delicious. Ass perfectly outlined in that silver thong. Mesh shirt sliding over skin Cris knew intimately. Jake's dancing stumbled a bit at the start, his body slightly out of practice. As more endorphins flowed, his movements smoothed out. Became more fluid and seductive.

That's when the dollar bills started pouring in, and Cris pulled back hard on his instinct to snarl at those fingers getting too close to his boyfriend's junk. He stayed by the wall, eating up every minute of Jake's performance, noting each time Jake relaxed a fraction more. As the first hour passed, more of the old Jake peeked out from where it had hidden behind his depression. He came alive in the very best way, and Cris soaked it in like sunshine.

Jake frequently looked his way while he danced, eye-fucking Cris each time, until Cris was hard in his jeans and unable to hide it. Jake's first break was coming up, and Cris hoped they could sneak off someplace to at least make out for five minutes. Cris couldn't wait for the day when Jake's meds and his anatomy played nice again—he'd never had a quickie in the bathroom with favors, and something told him Jake wouldn't turn down the idea

—but for now, Cris savored everything they did to make each other feel good. Jake would blow him if he asked, but that wasn't —

Jake's expression shifted from seductive to surprised, then back again in a blink. Cris tried to track the direction of his gaze, and he found himself watching Chet ease his way through the dancing throng. Toward them.

Toward me. Holy fucking God, he's walking this way.

Chet wore the same casual blue polo and khaki shorts as earlier, and his hair was a bit disheveled, but he walked with a determination that turned Cris on as much as it scared him. He didn't know what to expect after allowing Chet to brood the day away. He absolutely did not expect Chet to crowd him against the wall, then plant the mother of all kisses on him.

Cris had been kissed a lot in his life. Friendly kisses. Determined kisses. Seductive, fuck-me-soon kisses. Even his other kisses with Chet hadn't been this...raw. Hands and mouths and chests and tangled legs. Chet kissed him with a ferocity that bordered on terrifying, eliciting a few hoots from people around them, and then he eased back. Dropped light kisses along Cris's lips and cheeks until Cris was panting.

"Wha?" He didn't even have full words.

Chet cupped his cheeks in sweaty palms, his eyes gleaming with so many things that made Cris's knees shaky. "I'm sorry I shut you out today." Chet practically shouted to be heard over the music and chatter of the club. "I had to think about all of this."

"I get it."

"Jake put it together after our brunch date, didn't he? That you donated your kidney to Dell?"

"Yeah."

"That's why he thought you loved me more than him."

Cris nodded, the new lump in his throat making it impossible to speak.

"You gave us an incredible gift, Cristian. I don't know how to thank you."

"Forgive me. I'm sorry I hid the truth, and I'm sorry I bullied Jake into keeping my secret."

"I think I understand now why you did."

"You do?"

Chet smiled, easing some of the fierceness in his expression. "You've never been an attention seeker. You wanted to do something kind and not make it a big deal, even though it very much is a big deal. And tell me if I'm wrong, but I also believe you didn't want your gift to affect my feelings for you."

"You aren't wrong."

"Your donation *does* change my feelings. It makes them stronger in the very best way. I loved you before I knew you gave my nephew your kidney, and I love you even more for the gift. Few people would have been as selfless if put in your position."

"Maybe that's what wrong with the world. We don't give enough without expecting something in return. I didn't want to trade my kidney for your love."

"You didn't. I loved you before the transplant. I'll love you until the day I die, Cristian Sable."

Cris released a breath that was part sob. "I love you too. I told Jake the same thing. I love you both so much."

"Good." Chet kissed him again, a hard claiming of lips and tongue, and by the time they came up for air, a third presence hovered next to them.

Jake beamed at the pair of them. "You guys made up!" He bounced on his tiptoes. "Fuck yeah!"

"We were never really fighting," Chet said. "But I do understand his motivations, and all is forgiven."

"Good." He leaned in, all sly smiles. "I hate it when Mom and Dad fight."

Cris laughed at the awful line. Chet, on the other hand, slid his arm across Jake's shoulders and pulled him into their circle of confidence. He kissed Jake's temple, then said, "If you ever need someone to call Daddy, please let me know." The sultry tone of voice perked Cris's dick right the hell back up.

A mental image of Chet in leathers, with Jake kneeling at his feet, left Cris a bit lightheaded. "Only if I can watch," Cris said.

Jake rubbed himself through his thong, cheeks red from either exertion or arousal. "Can we, uh, work up to that, maybe? Jesus."

"We'll go at your pace, Jake," Chet said. "I promise. Now that we've found each other, there's no rush. We have time to settle into this new relationship."

"Thank God. So we're all okay, right?"

"Yes, we're all okay."

Cris kissed Jake's temple. "Definitely okay. I love watching you dance, even if it makes me want to snap fingers off for touching you."

Jake laughed, then captured his mouth briefly. "You say the sweetest things." He turned his attention to Chet, kissing him long enough to leave Chet red-cheeked and breathless. "You're pretty amazing, too. Both of you keep me from feeling broken."

"That's because we love you," Cris said. "Now, go shake that ass some more, before you get in trouble with the boss on your first night back."

With a snort and a snapped-off salute, Jake disappeared into the dancing throng.

Cris slipped his arm around Chet's waist. "Feel like dancing, old man?"

Chet tucked his own arm across Cris's shoulders and pulled him in close. Chest to chest, groin to groin, Chet began to sway them both to the music. "Love, I thought you'd never ask."

Chapter Twenty-three

Jake hadn't expected Cris and Chet to hang around Big Dick's the entire night, especially after the hot-and-heavy reunion make-out on the dance floor. They kept giving each other some serious eye-fucking action, which often redirected to Jake as he swung his hips to the club music. And all of the attention was doing wonders for his uncooperative libido.

Maybe it was the direct attention of both men at once. Maybe it was the fact that he was mostly naked, decked out in a silver thong, writhing to techno music on an elevated stage. Maybe it was knowing he had two handsome, amazing guys to go home to after his shift.

Whatever the fuck it was, Jake wanted more. He danced for his boyfriends and, for a while, the rest of the club crowd disappeared. Only the three of them existed: Jake on his stage, Chet and Cris together on the floor. Sometimes they danced; mostly they watched him. No night of work had ever felt more perfect.

They stayed until last call. Jake flew backstage to get dressed, not surprised to find a text from Cris on his phone, promising they were waiting outside. He vaguely said his goodbyes as he hauled ass out of the club faster than he'd ever done in his life. As promised, Cris and Chet were waiting in the alley, arms around each other's waist. Happy.

Jake had worried himself sick over outing Cris's kidney secret and Chet distancing himself from them all day. Seeing them together again, smiling at him, released the last bit of tension around his heart. No more secrets. Only the three of them, ready to keep building this strange three-person relationship that had begun thanks to a random Monday night hookup. Or maybe it had begun eight years ago when Chet and Cris first met. Didn't matter, really. They had each other and that was that.

He bounced over to them and threw his arms around both of their necks, not surprised to find himself engulfed by their bodies. The hug didn't last long, thanks to the sweltering summer night, but it was enough.

"You were magic up there, love," Chet said. "Poetry in motion."

"Thank you." The praise didn't make him feel as self-conscious as it usually did. "You guys didn't have to stay all night."

"Thankfully, we both make our own hours. We can all sleep in tomorrow."

Cris swooped in to kiss Jake's temple. "Sleeping in sounds amazing."

"Yeah it does." Jake wiped a hand across his forehead. "After a shower. I'm a gross, sweaty mess."

"Need someone to scrub your back?" Cris's seductive purr sent shivers down Jake's spine. "Because I volunteer as tribute."

He bit back an automatic "yes" and looked at Chet, who was watching them with an indulgent smile. Chet would let them shower together without a negative word, because that's who he was—unselfish, trusting, and loyal. Jake's belly wobbled, but he said with the words with absolute certainty. "Only if Chet volunteers too."

Chet's eyebrows shot up; his lips parted. "Really?"

"Yes." He's used Chet's master shower. It was definitely big enough to fit the three of them with extra elbow room to spare. And it would be the first time all three of them would be naked together.

"Then I certainly volunteer," Chet said. "Any particular parts you'd like me to scrub?"

"How about we play it by ear?"

The car ride home, sandwiched between Chet and Cris on the front bench seat of Chet's car, was the longest fifteen minutes of Jake's life. They decided to leave Cris's car behind and get it tomorrow, because Jake didn't want to choose who he'd ride home with. Besides, he liked being in between them. In the car, in bed, or on the couch, he never felt safer or more content than when he was bookended by his men.

His two very sexy, very different men who both smelled amazing. The combined scents of sweat and cologne heated Jake's blood in a new, unexpected way. He had no expectations for their combined shower beyond a lot of wet, naked skin and some soap, but his dick was starting to get its own ideas.

Please God, give me a boner tonight.

God must have been listening for a change, because when Chet parked in the driveway at home, Jake was half-hard and resisting the urge to adjust himself. Chet was telling a story about clubbing in his younger years that Jake only half-heard. His brain was stuck on wet, naked skin and that happening very, very soon. Once inside the house, he marched right for the stairs, keenly aware of his men following him.

Jake started shedding clothes the instant he crossed the threshold to Chet's room, tossing his t-shirt to the floor, and then shoving down his shorts. He still wore the silver thong from the club, and he kept it on while he flipped on the bathroom lights. That big, glass-door shower beckoned to him.

Jake fiddled with the water temperature, while clothing rustled behind him, keenly aware of his companions without even looking at them. He bent at the waist the slightest bit, tipping out his ass in a way that always worked well at the club. The soft growl from Cris sent more blood to his dick. Jake rubbed himself through the thong, a flash of performance anxiety clashing with his own desire.

Warm hands circled his waist and pulled his bare cheeks back against lightly furred thighs and a long, hard cock. Cris. They'd only fucked twice, but he knew that cock. And those hands holding him in place.

"Do you have any idea how fuckable you look in that thong?" Cris asked with a seductive purr.

"Yup."

"Brat."

"I know you are—"

Cris put a hand over his mouth, cutting off Jake's silly retort. "Get in the shower, sweaty boy. I have skin to scrub."

Jake licked his palm. Cris let go, and Jake obediently stepped under the cascading spray. Hot water sluiced across his skin and soaked his hair. Cris stayed close, wetting his own body. Just the two of them. Jake blinked through the glass wall, surprised to see Chet still on the other side of it.

Naked. Half-hard. And kind of...shy?

He didn't hide his long study of Chet's body. Chet was close to Cris in height, but leaner. Toned without Cris's defined muscles. A thin mat of gray-brown hair on his chest and more around his navel. So beautiful that Jake ached, because this amazing man wanted him.

He wants us.

Jake reached out. With a bright smile, Chet stepped into the shower and closed the glass door behind him. He took Jake's hand, their palms sliding together, and Jake tugged him under the spray. Chet laughed as the water hit him, a deep sound that bounced off the walls enclosing them. Creating a wonderful bubble of safety and love, and Jake relaxed even more, finally able to truly let go.

Cris wasted no time in fulfilling his promise. Soaping up a sponge and dragging it up and down Jake's back in hypnotic circles, the motions as much a massage as a bath. Jake closed his eyes and soaked in the attention, still holding Chet's hand, needing contact with both of them. He sensed Chet's movement in the way the water spray changed direction, and then a hot mouth pressed against the side of his neck.

Jake gasped, his free hand flailing out, only to be captured by Chet's. Chet carefully pulled his hands together between them in a loose grip, then continued to make a snack out of Jake's neck and throat. The strangely submissive position had Jake panting, his dick rising. Chet switched his grip so he held Jake's wrists in his left hand, freeing his right to trace circles and other shapes on Jake's chest. Studiously avoiding Jake's nipples, the bastard—no.

Not a bastard. Sweet, attentive man waiting for permission.

"More," Jake said. "Chet."

Chet's teasing mouth moved upward while his questing fingers went down. Caressed over his belly and around his navel. That talented mouth finally found Jake's, and Jake surrendered. Cris wasn't washing his back anymore. Jake had fallen against him, needing Cris for support under the onslaught of Chet's kisses. Cascading water forced his eyes shut, and that was okay. All he wanted to do was feel.

Cris's left hand joined the teasing, plucking at Jake's nipples hard enough to send small shocks up his spine, while his left reached around to clasp Jake's cock. Stroked him with long, hard pulls that finally—fucking finally!—had Jake fully hard.

He couldn't speak, because Chet still had sole ownership of his mouth and hands, so Jake used what little mobility he had to hump his ass against Cris's hip. It had been so long since he'd managed to come, and with his first real erection in weeks, Jake was desperate for release. He could free his hands with a simple yank, but being restrained, being used, had him soaring in a way he'd never experienced.

With Cris's hold on him providing balance, Jake nudged around with his right foot until he found Chet's toes. He curled his foot around Chet's ankle, tugging him closer, closer, until Chet's wet skin pressed against his. A hot dick brushed his clasped hands. Chet's dick. Jake shivered, crazy aware of this final boundary being crossed and the sense of relief that came with it.

He broke Chet's hold on his hands, too desperate to keep playing that game. Chet released his mouth in the same moment Jake clasped his erection. The intense fire in Chet's eyes made Jake's knees wobble. Cris's constant stroking of Jake's own cock wasn't helping his rational thought processes, either.

"Tell us what you need, love," Chet said.

"Need to come."

"Of course. What else?"

Jake wasn't sure. He needed a mouth on his dick, but he also needed a mouth on his mouth, and the novelty of having two boyfriends meant that could actually fucking happen. "Want Cris to suck me off."

"I do think I'd love to watch that."

"Uh uh. Need to keep kissing you."

Chet's nostrils flared. Behind Jake, Cris nipped at his neck, then released him so fast Jake nearly fell. He tumbled into Chet's arms, who consumed him again with his lips and tongue. Jake didn't have time to miss the full-bodied way they usually kissed, their torsos barely touching now, because Cris was sucking his cock into his mouth, and Jake was lost. Lost to these two men who'd chosen him, who wanted him, who *loved* him. It was too much and not enough.

Jake flailed with his free hand until he safely found Cris's hair, the other hand still stroking Chet's dick. Getting the other man off, while Cris worked to get him off. Jake wanted to come for himself, but more than that, he wanted to come for *them*. To show them how much he wanted them both.

I'm so close, please!

Chet's fingers brushed his nipple, teasing it before pinching with the exact right pressure to send Jake over. He might have screamed as he came, but Chet swallowed the sound as Jake pulsed into Cris's mouth, his entire body trembling with the force of his release. They carried him through it, before gently pulling away. Chet folded Jake into his arms; Cris pressed into him from behind, a solid wall of support that Jake took absolute advantage of.

As reality pushed through the haze of contentment that made Jake want to roll over and sleep, he realized only one erection was still poking him. Cris was soft behind him. Jake pressed backward, unable to find the words to ask.

Cris nuzzled his ear. "Came right after you did. That was all so fucking hot, babe."

Jake nodded his agreement, then raised his head. Chet's laser focus made Jake's heart turn over hard. He took Chet's erection in hand, unsurprised when Cris's larger hand joined him. Together, they stroked Chet to his own orgasm, and Jake loved watching him spill over his and Cris's skin.

The rest of their time in the shower was a blur for Jake, as he submitted to the care of his boyfriends. Eventually, they finished washing and dried off with lots of joint touching and teasing. By silent agreement, they tumbled into the big king bed naked. Safely tucked in the middle, with Cris and Chet on either side of him and darkness surrounding them, Jake reached out and found their hands.

"Thank you," he said.

No one asked why he was thanking them. No one needed to.

"I love you," Cris said. "Both of you."

"I love you both, as well," Chet replied.

"Me too," Jake said.

Jake never imagined he'd fall in love at the age of twenty-three, and especially not with two men at once. Their triad wasn't perfect, and they still had hard work to do, but they also had a foundation firmly in place. All they had to do was work together and keep building upward, strengthening as they went. Jake had found something precious and amazing with Cris and Chet, and he'd do whatever he had to do to keep it. To keep them.

To keep us, for as long as they let me have them.

Jake, Cris and Chet's journey continues in *Sound of Us*, coming soon!

About The Author

A.M. Arthur was born and raised in the same kind of small town that she likes to write about, a stone's throw from both beach resorts and generational farmland. She's been creating stories in her head since she was a child and scribbling them down nearly as long, in a losing battle to make the fictional voices stop. She credits an early fascination with male friendships (bromance hadn't been coined yet back then) with her later discovery of and subsequent love affair with m/m romance stories. A.M. Arthur's work is available from Carina Press, Dreamspinner Press, SMP Swerve, and Briggs-King Books.

When not exorcising the voices in her head, she toils away in a retail job that tests her patience and gives her lots of story fodder. She can also be found in her kitchen, pretending she's an amateur chef and trying to not poison herself or others with her cuisine experiments.

Contact her at am_arthur@yahoo.com with your cooking tips (or book comments). You can also find her online (http://amarthur.blogspot.com/), as well as on
Twitter (http://twitter.com/am_arthur),
Tumblr (http://www.tumblr.com/blog/am-arthur), and
Facebook (https://www.facebook.com/A.M.Arthur.M.A).

Also by A.M. Arthur